Compass

Jeanne McDonald

PUBLICATIONS

First Edition: November 2015

Edited by: Amy Gamache of Rose David Editing

Cover Design by: Jada D'Lee Designs

Interior Formatting by: Lindsey Gray Formatting Services

Cover images by: Felix Pergande, Sergey Yarochkin , and ratkom

Dedication

For Katy

Thank you for all the late night Monopoly games and drunken IHOP runs, but most of all, thank you for believing in me when I didn't even believe in myself..

"We shall not cease from exploration, and the end of all our exploring will be to arrive where we started and know the place the first time." ~ *T.S. Elliot*

Table of Contents

Prologue

The hideous stench of blood, smoke, and burnt flesh siphoned all of the fresh air from the lower half of the hospital. Gurneys were pushed in by the droves. The halls were lined with injured and mangled bodies perched on bleached cotton linens, screaming in agony and despair. The pale stains of tears mixed with blood splattered the usually white walls of the facility.

Total chaos erupted in the emergency room. Orders were shouted from every direction but they were mere noise in a sea of panic.

Being the closest hospital to the wreckage site, Agape Medical Center was the first location to receive survivors. All available staff members —no matter their specialty— were summoned to assist with the overflow.

There was no way anyone could be prepared for a disaster of this magnitude. Sure, every healthcare professional trains to be prepared, but being faced with the actual carnage of a plane crash wasn't something that anyone could truly be ready for.

Fear gripped Doctor Alexis York as she entered the ER and observed the carnage. Her heart weighed heavy in her chest and the threat of tears burned the back of her eyes. The moment she heard the news, she could only think of one thing. *Him.*

Every step she took carried *his* name. Each breath expelled from her lungs ached as a reminder of *him.* Face after face passed by her in a blur, but none were that of the face she longed to see. She searched through a field of bodies aching to know *he* was all right. The smell of death was all around her, and yet there was only one thing on her mind.

Finding *him.*

A twinge of terror physically struck the young doctor to her core while she slinked through the crowd. The rhythm of her heart slowed down, as the world seemed to drift around her. No words could be heard, even though her mind registered the shouts of those in her vicinity. Dizziness set in as she tried to comprehend her surroundings. *He* had to be there. Somewhere.

It was her job, her duty to find *him.*

The image of his face and smile was at the forefront of her mind. All she could hear was the sound of his voice breathing her name. His memory lingered in the very depths of her soul, and though her mind tickled with dread, her heart refused to believe the worst. Giving up wasn't an option. Not this time. Too much was at stake, and her heart couldn't take losing *him.* Not again.

She gritted her teeth, sucked in a breath so deep it stretched her ribs, and forced her body into action. No matter what, she'd find *him.* Even if it was the very last thing she did.

A tall, lanky boy, practically a man, meandered across the street.
From behind dark sunglasses, the bathing beauty honed in on his
unique swagger. She fought the urge to smirk when, in his usual
thoughtless habit, he lifted the faded ball cap that perched on his
head to swipe his dark colored hair away from his brow. A smile
teased the corner of his lips sending her heart into spasms.

Her long, lean legs bounced anxiously, as they always did,
against the peeling white paint of the rickety porch swing. Her long
brown hair fluttered softly in the gentle breeze. She rocked back
and forth, her feet planted on the wood slats of the stoop.

"Sunbathing, York?"

Alexis York's eyes focused on the lean figure shadowed over

her. She pushed her sunglasses down her nose and glared up at him. The sunlight shined around his body, making him look as if he were on fire.

Fitting, she thought, *he's practically a heavenly being after all.*

"Yeah, I am. And you're a great sunblock. So, get your scrawny ass out of my sunlight."

Ryan Fisher gasped in mock offense. He turned to look at his backside, much like a cat would when chasing its own tail. "How dare you call this fine ass scrawny? I'll have you know, I work impeccably hard to keep this ass in shape."

She impatiently waved him away. "I hardly call sitting in front of the T.V. playing video games hard work. Now move it."

Ryan and Alexis were the best of friends. They had basically known each other since birth. Their parents lived across the street from each other for as long as they could both remember. But things change. Life has a way of transforming and ripping people apart, and now, after sixteen years of watching the boy next door, she would be alone.

Only two years earlier she was happy, carefree, with the world at her feet. Now, she watched as movers carried boxes out of the only home she'd ever known, preparing her and her mother to move to a huge city, hundreds of miles away from everything that mattered to her, including Ryan.

Ryan laughed as he plopped down beside her. "Man, you're grouchy when you don't get your way."

Alexis slightly turned her head to see the handsome young man gazing back at her. She loved and hated the smile he had on his face. It burned a hole into her memory, leaving an ache in her soul. She longed to tell her best friend that she harbored feelings for him, that she loved him beyond their cherished friendship, but she couldn't bring herself to utter the words.

Things were different now. She was moving to New York. He was staying in Edenton. Even if she thought there was a chance he felt the same for her, which she knew he didn't, she couldn't bring herself to tell him. It was too late.

4

"I'm sleep deprived. Someone was throwing rocks at my window at two in the morning. Can you believe some psycho wanted me to get out of my warm, comfy bed to watch a moon turn red?"

Alexis stretched her legs to their full length. She linked her fingers behind her neck and cut her eyes at Ryan. Heat flooded his cheeks, turning them almost as red as that damned moon she sat on the roof of her house to look at with him hours earlier.

Ryan shrugged a shoulder. Alexis could hear him swallow and she reveled the way he squirmed under her scrutinous stare. "You didn't have to watch with me."

She reached out and smacked his knee. "You know better. Besides, it's probably the last time we'll ever get to do that." Sorrow filled her tone.

Ryan lifted his sea green eyes, his bushy black brows pulled together. "Lex—"

A large man, carrying a television out of the house passed by, right as Alexis kicked her foot out toward Ryan, stopping him from saying anything that might break her heart. She and Ryan had already promised no goodbyes, and she could see the words forming behind those magnificent eyes.

"Ow!" Ryan reached down and rubbed his ankle. "What was that for?"

Alexis nodded toward the sweaty man, removing her belongings from her house. "That was my nice way of saying, 'Shut your pie hole, Fisher!' I don't need someone tattling to my mom about us sneaking out of the house this morning. Geez!"

"You didn't have to kick me!" he mewled.

"Oh, suck it up."

An evil glint sparkled in his eyes. He pulled off his ball cap and tossed it to the porch. "You'll pay for that one, York!"

Ryan shifted forward, ready to pounce his friend when the same mover returned to the porch. The sweaty man chuckled and muttered something about "young love".

The two teenagers pulled apart from one another. Ryan

crossed his arms over his chest and Alexis felt her heart thundering in hers. She tried to play off her feelings by producing the most childish of grimaces and then stuck out her tongue at the stranger. Ryan immediately laughed at her response.

The glorious chime of his laughter filled her soul to the brim and ripped her heart to shreds. She'd miss that laugh. She'd miss this boy. The strange yet intuitive moving guy had nailed her feelings and that bothered her. Not that she was ashamed of her feelings. Had she thought he felt the same, she would've...well, she wasn't sure what she would've done. Alexis and Ryan were from different circles in school, and yet because of their relationship, those circles always seemed to mix well. Alexis was popular, a cheerleader, and Ryan was the sort of nerdy boy who loved to read, enjoyed science, but most of all lived for the world in the skies. He had an unusual obsession with planes, one that both excited and scared Alexis. The thought of flying terrified her. Not that she'd ever admit that to him. Never in a million years would she tell him her greatest fear was his greatest passion. It was a moot point, anyway, because Ryan's fascination instilled a love for planes in her that confused her logical nature.

Alexis blamed her love of music for her fear. Musicians and planes didn't mix well. Until recently, it had been her dream to become a famous singer. She loved the stage, she loved to sing, and she loved to dance. But that dream shattered the day her baby sister, Cora, passed away. It was that day she decided to become a doctor instead of pursuing her dream in the arts. It was that day where her family fell apart and set the events she now faced into motion.

Alexis dared a glance at Ryan. Long days at the beach together had left its golden evidence on his darkened skin. Thick black eyebrows shadowed the most glorious green eyes. He was kind of scrawny, slender, and boney, unlike the usual guys who attempted to date her, but she liked that about him. His long, thin frame was simply who he was. Evidence of potential muscle could be seen in his arms and legs, but then again, he was so skinny that any muscle mass would be visible under his skin. Her lips twitched at the thought of this limbs wrapped around her, cuddled against her best friend. That, above all else, she would miss.

"So, are you ready for tomorrow?" Ryan asked, producing a box of Cracker Jack out of thin air. He ripped the box top open and offered her a piece. Alexis willingly accepted, extracting several kernels of popcorn from inside the box. She tossed a piece in her mouth, savoring the flavor of the caramel goodness.

Cracker Jack was their snack of choice. Ryan had a sweet tooth that would drive any dentist insane. How he had that perfect beautiful smile was a miracle to say the least. He always had some sort of candy at hand, and a box of Cracker Jack always made his day.

He had the quirkiest ritual about the toy in the box, one to which Alexis abided by religiously. The box had to be empty before they would reveal the toy. He always said it was bad luck to see the toy beforehand.

Alexis released a heavy sigh.

"I'm packed." She jerked her head toward the movers escorting boxes out the door. "I guess you could call that ready." She popped another piece of popcorn in her mouth.

Ryan dug around inside the box searching for a peanut. His tongue pushed out of his mouth, angled toward his nose, as if he were deep in concentration. His eyes lit up when he found the nutty treat he had been craving.

"You know, you could stay for one more year. I bet your dad wouldn't mind." Ryan nibbled on the peanut, savoring it.

Alexis felt her stomach sour at the thought. Staying with her dad wasn't an option. It was his fault this was happening to her. Had he not cheated on her mom then she wouldn't be forced to make a choice between them. No, New York was her future and Edenton was her past. A past that she wanted to cling to simply because it held Ryan. Moving to New York meant she would be alone, and being without Ryan scared her more than anything.

"You know I can't do that," she admitted.

"Yeah," he mumbled. "It was just a thought."

Alexis dusted the remainder of sugar off her hands. "Can I tell you a secret?"

Ryan popped another kernel in his mouth. "You know you can tell me anything." His tongue darted out over his smooth lips. Alexis removed her sunglasses needing to see him clearly. A small breath stopped in her chest when their eyes met. Sincerity. Safety. Love. She could see it all in his gaze.

Locked in his patient stare, she swallowed. Nothing was said, which was Ryan's way. He never pushed her. He was always willing to wait for her to come around in her own time. She took in a deep breath, sucked in her bottom lip, and then exhaled. "I won't know anyone there."

Ryan put the box down on the porch at his feet, took her by the shoulders, and turned her to face him.

"Listen, Lex, you're smart, you're funny, and you're beautiful. You'll make more friends than you'll know what to do with. And Edenton, along with everything in it," the sound of his voice dropped to a mere whisper, sorrow filling his tone, "will become nothing more than a dream of the past." Her heart pounded in her chest at his mere touch. The smell of his skin was intoxicating, infiltrating her mind. Where his fingers held her shoulders, she burned with the most beautiful ache. She'd lose this. She'd lose him, and the thought of losing him to someone new ripped her insides to shreds.

Alexis swallowed back the pain of losing him and rested her mind on the present. Ryan had called her beautiful. She stared into his deep green eyes and felt the heat rise up her face. His eyes were gentle and his expression sincere. Alexis tilted her head as his hand slowly pushed her hair back from her eyes.

"You think I'm beautiful?" she whispered.

His hand drifted down her cheek, cradling her face. The soft glow of the sun bounced off of his deep chocolate locks, reflecting beautiful shades of black, mahogany, and a hint of blue. The smell of his skin tickled her senses the closer they drew to each other.

"Of course I do. I've always thought you were beautiful."

The world seemed to be moving in slow motion. With each tender caress of his thumb over her cheek, her pulse skyrocketed. It felt so good to have him touch her with such intimacy. Alexis wanted to pinch herself because she knew she had to be dreaming.

Alexis bit her lip, nervous tension dampening her palms. Their eyes locked together, neither blinking as their faces inched closer. His thumb tugged her lip from between her teeth and she let out a deep breath.

After all these years of thinking that her feelings of love weren't reciprocated, of thinking they would never be more than best friends, to suddenly find herself with him, in an intimate moment such as this, was surreal. Alexis closed her eyes in anticipation of his smooth lips finally touching hers. She waited and waited, but the kiss never came. She opened her eyes to find him staring at her. His lips flattened in a straight line. His face twitched, and his eyes closed for a fraction of a second. Alexis knew that everything she thought was about to happen had been her imagination.

Unrequited love would remain as such.

Ryan pressed his lips against Alexis' forehead. In an instant, her heart sank in her chest. She heard him let out a deep breath as he released her face. She bit her lip again, but this time it was to keep it from trembling. She pulled away, unable to meet his gaze. How silly she'd been to think Ryan would see her as more than his best friend. He'd never showed interest in her that way. He'd always treated her more like a sister ·than anything else. He protected her honor. When the boys in school flocked to her, he came to her rescue, slaying the rumor mills that often occured with pretty girls in small towns.

Alexis swallowed down the ache that tightened her throat and leaned against the back of the swing. She looked up into the sky, letting the sun hide the tears that were threatening to escape.

"Lex," he rasped.

She shook her head slightly, determined not to show him that she was hurt by his blatant rejection. She hated herself for getting lost in the moment. She had always known he didn't see her as anything more than a friend and this only proved her hypothesis.

"You're probably right," she croaked. "It's New York City. That place is crawling with people. I'll make new friends in no time."

Ryan tilted his ball cap forward, crossing his arms over his chest as he kicked the swing into action. "No doubt about it."

Yeah, she meant that to sting a little. And from his reaction it bit him hard.

They lapsed into a lingering silence, neither daring to speak.

Out of nowhere, Alexis kicked out her leg, driving it into Ryan's ankle. He popped his cap back, glaring at her. "What was that for!" he screeched.

"Does everything I do have to have a motive?"

Ryan twisted his mouth, analyzing her. "You forget I know you. I know you better than *you* know yourself." He grabbed her by the neck and mussed her hair.

"You don't know crap!" she screamed, smacking his hands away.

He released her from his grasp and picked up the box of Cracker Jack pouring some into his hand.

"Believe what you want. But I know you, Alexis York. No matter how far away you are, no matter what you do, I'll always know you." He popped the handful of caramel corn into his mouth and nodded proudly.

"Stalker much?"

Alexis struggled to hide her smile from him because she didn't want to confirm his accusations, even though they were true. He did know her better than anyone. He'd been there for every major event in her life. From the day the doctor confirmed that Cora had Leukemia, to the day they put her tiny lifeless body in the ground, to the day she walked in on her father kissing Cora's nurse and unveiled the lying, cheating bastard that had helped give her life. Ryan had been there, seen the pain, and never let her go, no matter how much she begged to be left alone. Ryan knew her and she knew him. And now, that would be gone.

"I can *stalk* you as much as I want once I become a pilot."

The mention of his obsession made her smile. For as long as Alexis could remember, Ryan had wanted to be a pilot. His passion for flying was immeasurable. He could tell you every make, model, and statistic on every plane ever made.

After Cora passed away, Ryan spent many nights holed up in Alexis' bedroom with her, putting together model airplanes. With each piece, he would explain the importance of flying and how it was man's way of defying the laws of nature. It consumed him.

Ryan cupped his hands around his mouth, muffling his voice to sound like he was on a radio. "Pssh, Pilot to co-pilot. Come in, co-pilot."

Alexis laughed, imitating his actions. "Pssh. Co-pilot here."

"Our flight pattern is set. Are we ready to embark on our new adventure?"

Alexis looked over at him and smiled. His eyes bright with excitement and humor. "Oh, no, captain. There's something wrong with my readings. We're going to crash and burn." She whistled loudly, dropping her hands from her mouth, then made a massive explosion sound while extending her fingers wide.

Ryan dropped his hands, suddenly very serious. "No, we're not. We're going to have everything we've ever dreamed of and more. Just you wait and see."

She breathed in deep through her nose. "I'm glad you think so."

Ryan shook the box of Cracker Jack at Alexis. She opened her hand to which he poured the remainder of the box in her palm. Along with the popcorn, the red and white package that held the toy tumbled into her hand. He extracted the package from the sticky popcorn mix. Alexis poured the handful of caramel corn and peanuts into her mouth. Ryan watched as she chewed the last bite. Once she had swallowed, he ripped open the package and pulled out a tiny red object. It was small and circular. Alexis assumed it was a game of some sort.

"I know so," he proclaimed.

Ryan turned to Alexis and studied her for an impregnated moment. The way he looked at her left Alexis feeling warm all over. She tried to remind herself that he'd rejected her only moments earlier, but that didn't matter. This tall, skinny boy, strange and yet wonderful, captured her heart and held on tight.

"Lex, promise me that we won't lose touch. Promise me that you won't forget about me."

Alexis reached for his hand, ignoring the tingle in her body as their skin touched. "Of course, I promise. How could I ever forget you? You're my best friend in the whole world."

Ryan smiled and turned her hand over in his placing the red toy in her palm. "It's a compass. Keep it with you always. In those moments when you feel lost, alone, or confused, pull it out and let yourself remember. Let this compass lead you back home. Let it lead you back to me. Forever and always, okay?"

His eyes burned into hers as he closed her hand around the piece of plastic.

"Forever *and…*"

Alexis woke with a jolt. Her brown eyes opened wide as she took in her surroundings. For the most part, all of her belongings were boxed up and ready for the movers the next morning. Fifteen years had passed and once again, she found herself leaving her home to embark on her next adventure.

She sighed realizing her moment with Ryan had all been a dream, a memory. She lifted her head. A page from the book she had been laying on followed her. She stripped it away from her left cheek, wiping her hand over her face. The glossy page reflected the soft glow of the lamp that hung over the desk.

There before her was her old high school yearbook. She had dozed off while looking over the tattered pages. Her left hand pressed down on the sheet, smoothing it out while her right clutched tight. She smiled when she noticed the handsome face shining back at her. There was a picture of her and Ryan at a Pep

Rally. She was wearing her cheerleader uniform and he was dressed in a pullover sweater, baggy jeans, and aviator sunglasses. Under his picture was a note he had written before she left for New York.

Lex, you're my best friend in the whole world. Just remember, every time you feel off course, follow your heart. It's your compass. It will always lead you to where you belong.

Flying high, Ryan

Alexis opened her right hand, and there rested the faded red compass. The once clear plastic face was now clouded with age. The red encasement scratched and marked with time, but the navigational piece withstood anything that came against it. The compass may have been devoid of actual feelings, but for Alexis, that compass felt every bump, every scratch, every inkling of the time it wore.

All those years it had rested in a box with the reminders of her once best friend. Only then had she pulled out that box because Ryan had recently accepted her friend request on Facebook. The moment she saw that smiling face in his profile picture, she felt her heart pump again. It was a strange feeling that drove her to look through the old box of memories.

She rubbed her thumb over the tiny compass surprised that it still worked. With her eyes closed, she let the memories wash over her. She would never forget the look on Ryan's face the day she left for New York. It was one of the few times she had ever seen him cry.

"Call me every day," he pleaded in her ear, as he hugged her close. The smell of his skin still lingered in the recesses of her memory.

"You, too. I mean it. I expect to hear about all of your adventures."

"You will. You're my best girl. I could never go without hearing your voice."

Alexis closed her eyes tighter, feeling the sob strangled in her throat. They had both broken their promise. Time passed, life took over, and she and Ryan lost touch over the years. From what she could tell, after looking through his Facebook page, Ryan had accomplished everything he wished for and more. He'd grown up. Made a life for himself. Something about that made her feel happy and lonely at the same time.

A light thud reverberated as she closed the yearbook. The faded burgundy cover was worn and tired having been a lifeline of memories. Alexis gently dropped the tattered book back into the box on her desk and closed the lid. One last time she rubbed her finger over the soft plastic of the toy compass. It too had been a reminder of all she lost but that home was always just within reach.

She placed the compass in her wallet for safe keeping followed by a flick of the switch, exterminating the single light illuminating her tiny, rent-controlled apartment before resting into bed. There she lay in the darkness for the last time in her little New York hovel, wondering where Ryan was and what adventure he was embarking on at that moment.

Alexis sat in the front seat of her mother's sedan staring down at the picture on her phone. Ryan's Facebook page was vague. There was very little indicated about his personal life, but there were ample amounts of pictures of him — tall, lean muscled, rich jet-black hair, and a smile that haunted her dreams. The boy she knew was gone, leaving in his place a man.

Photo after photo revealed a very full and happy life. There was one that made her heart flutter that she rationalized saving it on her phone. It was a picture of Ryan with another pilot in the cockpit of a plane. They were both leaning in, wide smiles, and twinkling eyes. She told herself that she saved it because it was a reminder that Ryan had accomplished his dreams. He was in fact a pilot. It didn't hurt that he looked amazing in his uniform, either.

She scanned each picture but she stopped when she came across a photo of Ryan standing in front of an IronMan pavilion. He held up a medal, pointing at it with pride. She thought back to the boy who was sort of clumsy and a bit nerdy, which caused a chuckle to bubble in her throat. If only she could tell her seventeen year old self about thirty-two year old Ryan. Neither of them would ever believe that scrawny, adorkable Ryan would turn out to be an athletic stud.

"Are you even listening to me?" came her mother's voice with a hint of annoyance. "Earth to Alexis!"

Alexis jumped, almost dropping her phone but recovered it before it hit the floor. "What?" She snapped her head in her mother's direction, catching a glimpse of what she would look like in twenty years. Melanie York's chocolate brown hair was cut into a long pixie cut, with her bangs hanging over her brow. Streaks of silver highlighted her dark locks and eyes, a lighter brown than Alexis', sparkled in the afternoon sunlight.

"You haven't heard a single word I've said, have you? What's got you so enamored over there?" Melanie dropped her gaze down to the phone in Alexis' hand before returning it to the congested freeway. "Who's that?"

"Ryan Fisher," Alexis responded, using her index finger and thumb to zoom in on his face. That sweet smile of his hadn't changed. His eyes showed age, a life well lived, but his smile carried the same boyish charm she'd loved so much as a young girl.

"Wow. He's *grown* up. He was always a cute kid, but damn."

"Ew. Mom!"

"All I'm saying is he turned into a good looking man. I'm not blind, you know. Geez."

"This coming from the woman who hasn't had a date in fifteen years," Alexis droned. She clicked her phone off and dropped it into her messenger bag that sat at her feet.

"You're wrong."

Alexis jerked her head in her mother's direction. "How so?"

A smirk twisted Melanie's lips. "I guess you should've been listening to me."

"Fine. I'm listening now."

Melanie tapped her thumbs against the steering wheel. "I *said* I've met someone."

Alexis' mouth popped open in shock. This news came as a complete surprise. After leaving her father, Miles, in Edenton, her mother seemed to ward off men. Not that Alexis blamed her. Between her adulterous father, the string of unfaithful boyfriends her best friend Doctor Jenna Harmon dealt with, and her no-good bastard of a former boss, Alexis had witnessed enough cheating men to know she never wanted to commit to one. She'd taken a vow of commitment celibacy. Alexis liked men and she enjoyed sex but she didn't trust the male gender what-so-ever.

Alexis rolled her shoulders. "You're choosing now to tell me this? When I'm about to move fifteen hundred miles away! What do you know about this guy? Where did you meet? What does he do? How do you know you can trust him?" Alexis spouted off.

"His name's Dan Stevens and I met him at my book club. He's a retired firefighter and a widower. He has a son about your age who lives in California with his wife and two children. He asked me out for coffee and we sort of hit it off."

"Hit it off? Is that old person code for *gettin' bizzy*?" Alexis teased.

"Alexis!" Melanie's face turned a bright shade of fuchsia.

"Mom!" Alexis pressed her fingers against her eyebrow. "Does this have anything to do with the fact that I'm moving near Dad?"

From the corner of her eye, Alexis could see her mother slump her shoulders. Melanie shook her head, her smile disappearing. "No, and speaking of your father, you really need to ease up on him. It's time to forgive him. I have."

Alexis shrugged. "There's nothing for me to forgive, Mom. He moved on. I get it. But at least he could've waited until Cora was cold in her grave before banging her nurse."

"Stop it!" Melanie slammed her hands against the steering wheel. The vein in her forehead popped and pulsed against her creamy, smooth skin. "If you can't show some respect for your father, then show it toward your sister. You understand me?"

A lump formed in Alexis' throat at her mother's outrage. They didn't argue often, even when she was a teenager. Alexis never wanted to put her mother through anymore stress than she'd already endured with the loss of Cora and then her father's infidelity. So when they did have a row, it left Alexis feeling guilty and ashamed. "I'm sorry." The words sounded hollow coming from her lips, but there was nothing more that she could say. She never meant to slander Cora. Not a day went by she didn't think of her. Each patient she handled, every case, reminded her of her sister.

"I know, honey," Melanie whispered. "I'm sorry, too."

They sat in silence for a moment. Alexis twisted the hem of her black *I Heart New York* t-shirt around her index finger. The shirt did not lie. From the moment she arrived in New York City, she couldn't imagine living anywhere else. She loved the sights and smells of the city. Day or night, there was always something to do, some place to go, and interesting people to meet. The only thing missing was Ryan.

To say she would miss New York was an understatement. With a heavy heart, she was leaving it all behind to embark on yet another adventure in her life. Alexis was moving to Texas where she'd accepted a fellowship in the oncology department at Agape Medical Center in Grapevine, a suburb of Dallas. This was an amazing opportunity for her, but there was one major drawback as her mother pointed out — she would be much closer to Miles and Kellie.

Four months after Alexis and her mother left Edenton, Miles married Kellie, Cora's former in-home nurse, and moved to Texas. Alexis always hated the humid state because she'd been forced to visit her dad and his new wife there. She'd vowed to stop visiting Miles on her eighteenth birthday, but her plan was thwarted when

Kellie got pregnant. Alexis wanted to hate her half brother, Henry, for existing, but her heart wouldn't allow it. That innocent little boy had nothing to do with her father's betrayal, but it still stung that Miles started a whole new family after abandoning hers.

When she received the fellowship offer, she almost turned it down for the simple fact she hated the idea of living in Texas. It didn't matter that she would enter at a PGY-5 salary, which was unheard of for a fellow, or that she was promised an actual position at the hospital once her fellowship contract was complete. As much as she hated the thought of being any closer to her dad than necessary, this was an opportunity of a lifetime and allowing the past to negate her future was out of the question. Granted, it still took her mom and Jenna talking her through the decision for her to see what she'd be giving up if she didn't take the position.

Alexis rested her head back against the headrest, as Melanie maneuvered slowly through traffic. Her mind drifted to Ryan and what adventure he might embarking on. Her fingers twitched to grab her phone and check out his profile again. What were the odds of finding him on the eve of her move?

Just one more peek. He did accept my friend request, after all. That gives me the right to look, right?

She leaned forward; ready to snatch the phone from the bag when she realized what she was doing.

A small laugh bounced in her chest at the realization that she was behaving the same way Jenna did when she discovered a new suitor online. Jenna would spend days stalking their Facebook page, learning every minute detail about the guy, which was one reason why Alexis had refused to create a Facebook account before now. Alexis sat back up, leaving her phone in the bag. Facebook stalking a guy was not a healthy pastime, and she wouldn't fall into that trap. Just because she wanted to know more about Ryan didn't give her the liberty to invade his life.

I'll just private message him when I land. Yeah. That sounds good. Not nearly as stalkerish, she convinced herself.

"Remind me." Melanie scratched her nose.

"Hmm?" Alexis perked up. "About?"

"When do you start again?"

"Monday."

Melanie let out a heavy breath, blowing her bangs upward in the process. "What were you thinking? The truck doesn't arrive in Dallas until Sunday. That won't give you any time to unpack. Can't you take a week off to settle in?"

"I could've, but I don't want to. That's why I paid extra for a furnished apartment and all I need to last me for the next week is packed in here," she patted her leather messenger bag, "and in those two suitcases in the trunk." She hooked a thumb behind her toward the back end of the vehicle.

Melanie shook her head. "You'll never change, will you, my darling girl?"

"What do you mean?"

"Do you remember the time you talked Ryan into jumping off the house with you?"

"Yeah," Alexis snorted, "he broke his leg."

"Remember why you wanted to jump off the house?"

Alexis clicked her tongue, trying to recall why her eight-year-old self wanted to jump off a house. She remembered the pink tutu she wore and the amount of trouble she got into after Ryan was rushed to the hospital, but for the life of her she couldn't recollect what led her to suggest such a reckless activity. "Not off hand," she admitted.

Melanie laughed. "Ryan wanted to fly so bad he could hardly see straight. It was your belief that if you jumped off the roof, the two of you would be able to fly."

"Oh, yeah. I remember now." Alexis let out a soft laugh. Neither her mother nor Ryan realized that she orchestrated that stunt, not for Ryan to fly, but for her to not be afraid of flying. Needless to say, it didn't help. "But what does this have to do with me starting my new job on Monday?"

Melanie flipped on the blinker and switched lanes. "You always jump into things head first, never considering the consequences of your actions until it's too late. You're going to regret not giving yourself time to settle."

If only that were true. Where Ryan was concerned she always considered the consequences of her actions. It was that reason alone she never told him how she truly felt. Time had passed, but seeing his face again reminded her of the feelings that lost little girl once felt.

"I gave myself the weekend, Mom. What more do you want?" What she didn't want to explain to her mother was she knew if she'd given herself a week to move in, then she'd be forced to spend some of that time with Miles and Kellie. It was bad enough that her father was picking her up from the airport. She had no desire to see him beyond that or to endure a big "family" dinner. Not yet, anyway.

"Absolutely nothing," Melanie relented. It was a moot point anyway. She reached out and turned the dial to increase the radio volume, filling the void with pop music.

Alexis flopped her head back against the headrest again and continued to observe the sights as they exited the interstate, forking into JFK International Airport. Planes were flying low to the ground, both taking off and landing. She watched as one eased up into the sky, heading west from the airport and wondered where it was traveling.

As they approached the departures gate entrance, anticipation mounted inside Alexis. Her fear of flying never subsided and she now had a four-hour flight ahead of her. Dramamine was packed in her trusty messenger bag, just in case, and she'd booked her flight with the assurance of a window seat.

Melanie parked the car behind a row of cabs and helped Alexis unload her luggage. After checking in her two bags, she stood on the sidewalk with her mom, shuffling her feet. The weight of the moment bore down on Alexis. She was leaving her life behind, her friends, the city she loved, but most of all her mother. The last time she made a move like this she lost Ryan, but at least her mother was there to help her adapt. Now, as a grown woman, she was facing the world alone.

Alexis wrapped the leather strap of her messenger bag across her chest. Melanie gripped her daughter's shoulders, forcing Alexis to look her in the eye. "I'm going to be fine, as will you. This is merely a new experience. One you deserve. Don't second guess this, Lexi. Embrace it."

"I know," Alexis whispered.

"Miles is still picking you up, right?"

Alexis nodded, swallowing down the lump in her throat. Tears burned behind her eyes. This was goodbye. Not forever, but fifteen hundred miles was no laughing matter. She couldn't simply pop into a cab and go see her mother anymore. They'd promised to Skype and email, text and call, but it wasn't the same.

"Good, good. Well, I guess this it then."

Alexis wrapped her arms around Melanie's neck. The two women, locked in a warm embrace, cared nothing about the on goings around them. They rocked back and forth, holding tight to one another, saying goodbye to the girl and welcoming the woman that was Doctor Alexis York.

Sometime later, Alexis found herself standing in line at airport security, humming her favorite tune. She slipped off her sneakers and pulled her bag over her head, resting them both in the plastic bins provided. A man behind her leaned forward, grabbing a bin for his articles. "How's it going?" he asked, his voice rough and sensual.

Alexis stopped humming. She cocked her head to the side, catching a glimpse of the man. He was tall, with wild dark hair and a winning smile. His suit suggested he was a businessman and Alexis got a vibe that he was well aware of how attractive he was. She gave him a quick grin but it disappeared when her eyes caught a glimpse of a golden band around a very important finger.

Yep. Another bastard. Go figure.

"It's going," she stated, keeping her tone flat and aloof.

The man tossed his polished black shoes and briefcase in a plastic bin, ramming it up against hers, causing her bin to buckle forward. "Where you heading?"

"Home," she clipped. It felt strange calling Texas that, but she figured now was as good of time as any to start.

"And where might that be?"

"Texas."

They stepped forward, following their belongings through the line.

"Where in Texas?" the warm, husky tenor of his voice smoldered and oozed with sexual desire, which caused the hairs on the back of her neck to stand on end. She forced herself not to shiver in disgust.

God, this asshole's persistent!

"The DFW area."

The man clapped and rubbed his hands together. The sound was so loud that Alexis jumped. "Talk about my lucky day. That's where I'm heading. Maybe we could meet up for dinner one night. You could show me the sights of the great state."

A very frustrated Alexis turned around and propped her hands on her hips. She gave the man her best smile, batting her eyelashes. "Sure. I'd love to."

A huge smile exploded across the man's face. "Fantastic!"

She tilted her head, her lips twitching. "Only one question. Will your wife be joining us?"

All color drained from the man's face. His smile faltered and Alexis thrilled in the way his throat moved when he swallowed. "I, uh...well, um," he stuttered, rubbing the back of his neck.

"Look, pal. The next time you want to pick a girl up in an airport, take that off." She pointed to the wedding ring on the man's finger. "Better yet, don't try to pick a girl up in the airport or anywhere else for that matter. Go home and be a man. Love the woman who actually committed herself to your sorry ass. How about that?"

An older woman, standing behind the want-to-be heartthrob, snorted in laughter at Alexis' outburst. She covered her mouth with her wrinkled hand, her cheeks turning a light shade of pink. Her silver hair was parted down the middle and pulled into a bun at the back of her neck. She wore reading glasses that sat on the tip of her nose. Her eyes were hazy blue, like glass that bubbled. She wore a faded calico dress with a thin cardigan over it, buttoned at her neck.

Alexis gave the woman a quick wink and turned on her heel to face the front of the line again.

"Boarding pass and identification please," the heavyset female security officer requested as Alexis approached the front of the line. She handed the TSA official her boarding pass and license and waited while they scanned her belongings and verified her identity.

When the agent returned her paperwork to her, she leaned in a little closer, her broad face expanding in a twisted grin. "Thank you for telling that sleazeball off," she hissed. "It's nice to see decency in action."

"My pleasure," Alexis snickered and walked through the metal detector.

"Have a safe and pleasant flight." The agent flicked her fingers for the slimeball to hand over his identification. He still appeared green from his encounter with Alexis, which made the whole encounter worth it to her.

"Thanks." Alexis grabbed her shoes and bag from the end of the conveyor belt. She perched herself on one foot, sliding her shoe back on then proceeded to complete the same process with the other foot. With shoes in place, she flopped her bag over her head, wrapping it across her chest and proceeded to her departure gate where she would wait to travel to her new home.

The echo of his shoes against the tiled floor pounded in Ryan's ears. For a man in such good shape, he felt the complete opposite with the way his lungs strained for air. He was never late. Ever. And today, for the first time in his life, Ryan had overslept. Most of the night he'd tossed and turned, his mind never shutting down, but instead it was filled with memories of Alexis York. When he finally found slumber, he managed to sleep through his alarm and made himself late for work.

After an eleven day stretch, Ryan was on his way home. He always enjoyed his visits to New York City, but he still preferred the warmth of the south.

He hooked his finger in his collar, opening his airways. The muscles in his legs burned. Not only had he overslept but he'd missed his morning workout. Now he was running without stretching. This was going to be a craptastic day. He could feel it.

Why does JFK have to be so massive? he griped to himself.

Ryan weaved in and out of the crowd, growing more and more frustrated. Last night a ghost from his past reappeared. He couldn't count how many times he'd searched for Alexis York online with absolutely no success in finding her. He'd given up locating the girl he once called his best friend, pretty certain the reason he couldn't find her was because she'd married some well-to-do New Yorker and was living the highlife she deserved.

When the Facebook request appeared on his phone, Ryan thought he was dreaming. After all this time, she'd found him. He poured over the few pictures she'd posted of herself. There was one of her in a lab coat and scrubs, captioned, *"Last day of rounds,"* that he fell in love with. Her long, dark, chestnut hair hung in waves around her slender shoulders and her caramel colored eyes glistened with excitement. The girl he once knew had grown up, and Lord help him, she was even more gorgeous than he remembered.

He'd almost messaged her when he realized she still lived in New York. All he could think about was catching up with her, but a post on her wall stopped him. She was moving. Where to, he didn't know. She'd neglected to include that information in her post, but he didn't feel right in bothering her when she was probably busy. Instead, he decided to wait until he got home to contact her. Maybe then they could schedule time to meet up sometime.

The sight of his gate made him slow his pace and relax a little. As he approached the counter, he heard a small voice ring out, "Mommy, look. A pilot." He stopped and turned in search of the small voice. The admiration of children was one of his favorite parts of being a pilot. He loved their little smiles and the way they bubbled with excitement. He was already late, so what did it matter if he took a moment for a child. It wasn't as if the plane could leave without him.

A little girl in a bright yellow sundress and pigtails gleamed up at him. Her mother patted her on the head and smiled at Ryan. He approached the family. "Is it all right if I...?" he trailed off, his eyes silently requesting the mother's approval to engage with the child. She gave him a single nod and he knelt down to make himself eye level with the little girl. "What's your name?" he asked.

"Carin," she stated with pride. "Carin Ross."

Ryan extended his hand to her. She accepted his hand, shaking it hard and abrupt. "Not so hard, Care," her mother scolded.

"Nah, she's got a great handshake." He casted a discrete smile to the little girl's mother, who seemingly relaxed at Ryan's response. "It's nice to meet you, Carin. Where're you flying to today?"

"Virginia. We're going to see my daddy."

"Is that so? Well, you tell your daddy I said hello."

"I can't. Daddy's dead." The girl dropped her eyes. A frown replaced her once bright smile. Her little hands tugged at the waist of her dress as she swayed back and forth.

Ryan's heart sank in his chest. He glanced up at the mother's face, her eyes swimming with tears. "I'm so sorry for your loss," he stated, sorrow and respect coloring his timbre.

"He died fighting for what he believed in," she stated, her voice filled with tears but her words strong and clear.

"Army?"

"Marines."

Ryan gave her a quick nod. During college, he'd joined the Air Guard Reserves to help pay for his tuition. He was never called up for active duty, but he had the utmost respect for those who were. He gave Carin's shoulder a gentle squeeze. "You're daddy was a brave man. You remember that."

Carin met Ryan's gaze. "He's a hero," she heralded.

"Yes, he is. And so are you." Ryan stood up, and saluted Carin and her mother.

Ms. Ross straightened up, tears streamed down her cheeks. No further words were exchanged. They didn't need to be. His salute was an honor in the likes of the Ross family. Ryan reached into his carry-on and pulled out his extra uniform hat he always had with him. He placed it on Carin's head with a smile. With a click of his heels, in a military fashion, he turned from the Ross family and made his way to the departure gate.

At the door of the jet bridge, a young ticket agent swiped a tear from her eye. She gave Ryan a smile and opened the door for him, not saying a single word. Once the door closed behind him, Ryan raced down the bridge to the awaiting aircraft. When he reached the door, Makenna Davis, the chief purser, stood waiting for him with a cup of coffee and a smile. "About time you showed up for work, Fisher." She glanced over her shoulder toward the cockpit and announced, "Captain, our straggler has arrived."

Ryan groaned, shaking his head. "Don't even start."

"Start what?" Makenna teased, gracing him with a wily expression. "I can't remember the last time you were late. Or have you ever been late?"

"Never!" Kix called out from the cockpit.

Ryan sniffed, cutting his eyes to Kix and biting his tongue. He removed his hat and exchanged it and his luggage for the cup for coffee. Makenna giggled, patting him on the back. "Oh, buck up. It happens to the best of us," she noted, picking up his bag and placing it in the captain's luggage compartment.

"Not to me," he groused.

"You're human. Give yourself some slack every once in awhile."

Ryan slipped into the cockpit, taking his seat to the right of the captain. Captain Kix Jones smirked, his eyes cutting to Ryan. "I want details."

"Huh?" Ryan muttered behind the lip of his coffee cup.

Kix dropped the preflight checklist clipboard in his lap and stared at Ryan with the most incredulous look on his face. Ryan knew exactly what Kix believed had caused Ryan's unusual tardiness, because it was something that had happened to Kix more times than Ryan could count. Kix was what one might call the perpetual bachelor. He'd been married once, but being in the air proved to be a bit more challenging for him in the monogamy department.

Many nights, Ryan found himself at the hotel bar watching Kix at work with the ladies. It almost had become a sport to keep score on how many women Kix could pick up. He often wondered what it was that attracted women to the captain. Kix was in his mid-forties; slightly balding, sandy brown hair with gray peppered through it, pale blue eyes, and a small gut that hung over his pants.

Ryan once had the unfortunate circumstance of seeing Kix in the locker room. After that experience, he was sure the captain had stopped developing at the ripe age of fourteen. There was no way it could be the size of his package that attracted women. This left him with only one conclusion: either it was true what they said and size didn't matter, or that man had to have one talented tongue.

"Oh, c'mon, kid. Just one juicy little detail."

"There are no details. I overslept. That's it," Ryan grumbled, swiping the preflight checklist from Kix. He took another swig from his coffee and set it aside.

"Gah!" Kix snarled. "You're too young for there to be no details."

"That's it?" Ryan repeated, this time forming a question.

He gave Ryan a nonchalant shrug and started back to work. "Anyone else, I would've called them a liar. But you...meh. When you say you overslept. You overslept."

Ryan rubbed his jaw and glanced over the checklist. "Am I really that predictable?"

Makenna stuck her head into the cockpit. "Not predictable. Dependable." She gave Ryan a wink and disappeared again.

Kix let out a boisterous laugh. "Thanks, Kenna!"

"Anytime!" she shouted back.

The two men set to work, preparing for the flight. As they worked, Ryan's mind wandered back to Alexis. It was true his only reason for being late was lack of sleep, but he hadn't been completely forthcoming about the nature of his insomnia. While it had been many, many years since he had last seen Alexis York, not a day went by where he didn't think of her. He'd always hated how they lost touch.

They'd promised to call once a week, because long distance calls weren't cheap. And they'd kept that promise for some time. Ryan had even taken on a part-time job as a busboy to pay for their weekly calls. He loved talking to her about her new life in New York and always kept her in the loop about the on goings in Edenton. But slowly the calls moved from once a week to twice a month, then to once a month. Then there were no calls, only the occasional letter or email. And soon, even those disappeared. He blamed no one. Time and distance played its toll on their friendship.

After high school he moved to Florida for college. Between school and the Air Guard, Ryan had little time for much of anything. He'd been to so many places and seen so many sights. London, Paris, and Riyadh, were just a few stops along his journey. Little did anyone know, there was a box of postcards, all made out to Alexis, at the top of his closet at home. It had become a sort of tradition with him. Each new city, each new country, he picked up a postcard for her. It didn't matter if he didn't know where to mail them. This had been his way of keeping her in his heart, always.

Ryan scratched the top of his head, his ink pen dangling from his lips. He glanced over the checklist twice, initialed it and handed it back over to Kix for him to do the same. Ryan was a stickler for detail. Safety was key to him and it was one of the reasons why every captain that flew with him loved him. Nothing got past Ryan.

By this point, passengers had started to board the plane. It was almost time for takeoff and no matter how many times he flew, Ryan always felt a twinge of excitement before the plane lifted into the air. He loved the feel of the controls at his fingertips and couldn't wait for the day he'd become captain.

"Hey, guys," Makenna addressed the two pilots as she entered the cockpit. Her jet black hair draped over her shoulder like a dark veil and her dark blue eyes peered behind her cat-eye glasses. Around her neck dangled a red scarf. It was against airline dress code, but no one said anything to her about it. Makenna was a tenured flight attendant and damn good at her job. Pilots fought to have her on their flights and there was no way any of them would complain about something as insignificant as a scarf.

"Sup?" Ryan quipped.

"Just wanted to let you know all passengers are on board and the manifest is complete. Pre-flight drink service is underway."

"Speaking of which." Kix lifted his coffee cup, dangling it at Makenna. There was some heavy sexual tension between the captain and chief purser, but Ryan knew Makenna would never give Kix the time of day. Everyone knew of his playboy ways and Makenna was better than that. Her restraint made Ryan protective of her. He adored Makenna like a sister and didn't want to see her hurt by the captain, no matter how much he respected Kix.

Makenna cocked her head. "You know what, just for that, you can get your own coffee."

"Kenna," Kix whined, drawing out on every syllable of her name.

"Nope," she smacked. "Get off that lazy ass of yours and get your own coffee."

"Lazy!" he rebuked. "I'm not lazy."

"Whatever. We all know Fisher runs the show while you sit back and jerk off."

Ryan's head fell back in laughter. "She pegged you!"

Kix huffed and stood up. He popped Ryan against the back of the head and followed Makenna from the cockpit. Ryan laughed harder, pulled on his headset, and switched the radio to the control tower frequency.

Just as Ryan received the clearing for departure, Kix reappeared in the cockpit sans a cup of coffee. "Everything set?"

"We just received clearance. I thought I might end up flying this bird by myself." Ryan nodded his head toward Kix's empty hands. "What? No coffee? Or did Makenna finally give you a chance to join the Mile High Club?"

Kix slapped his knee and buckled over in fake laughter. "Ha! Been there, done that. Besides, the purpose of the mile high club is being in the air. If you'd ever pull your dick out and use it, you'd understand." He closed and locked the cockpit door. With a shake of his head, he slid back into his seat.

"I'll take that as a no," Ryan stated.

Kix buckled himself back into his seat. "We both know the answer to that one. But, I did see a passenger that would knock your socks off. She damn near did mine."

"Ah, that explains the missing cup of coffee."

Kix wrapped his headset over his crown, pulling the mouthpiece down to his lips. He settled his hands on the yoke, reviewing the coordinates Ryan had entered in for him. They were all set to take off. He spouted off a few instructions to the control tower and then turned to Ryan. "You should go check her out when we're in the air. You won't be sorry."

Ryan groaned, rolling his head from side to side. "I swear you have the libido of a teenager."

"There's nothing wrong with a healthy sexual appetite," Kix argued. The taxi had pulled away and the cockpit was now in control of the craft. Through Kix's mastery of flying, the plane was set into motion. It picked up speed along the runway. The nose started to rise, lifting the commercial aircraft from the ground.

Ryan loved how the sky looked as they started to ascend. There was no greater rush than gaining speed and taking an object that shouldn't be capable of flying and make it soar to the Heavens.

As soon as the plane was off the ground, Ryan lifted the wheels.

"How about you make the announcement, Fisher."

Ryan jerked his head to Kix. "Are you sure, sir?"

Kix gave Ryan a wink. "Don't question your captain." There was a playfulness to his tone, but also a note of seriousness. Ryan graced him with a smile and switched the frequency in his headset to the main cabin.

"Good morning, ladies and gentlemen, this is your first officer, Ryan Fisher, speaking. I want to welcome you aboard this nonstop flight from New York JFK to Dallas. Our expected flight time is three hours and forty-eight minutes. Your flight is being flown today by Captain Kix Jones. He's assured me we have a smooth flight ahead of us today. So, I will now turn off the seatbelt signs." Ryan flipped off the Fasten Seatbelt sign as promised. "Please feel free to move about the cabin if necessary. However, we, the crew, ask that if you are in your seats, to please keep your seatbelts fastened in case of unexpected turbulence. Otherwise, please sit back, relax, and enjoy the flight. If there is anything we can do to make your flight a more pleasant experience, please let us know."

Once his greeting was complete, he switched his frequency back to the departing tower and listened to their inflight instructions.

"Nicely done, Fisher," Kix noted.

"Thank you, sir."

"So, as I was saying…"

Ryan laughed. "Seriously, Captain, is that all you have on your mind?"

"If you saw this babe, you'd have a raging hard on too."

"I have a bit more self-control than you."

"You wouldn't be able to maintain that haughty smirk of yours if you knew what she looked like."

Ryan dropped his smirk, trying hard not to laugh. "Fine. If it makes you feel better, tell me what she looks like."

"She has these big brown eyes, and long flowing brown hair," Kix described. "And her legs," he let out a guttural groan, "I could imagine those lanky limbs wrapped around my neck. She was toned in all the right places, and had a rack on her that would bounce in your face as she…"

Ryan waved his hands for mercy. "Okay! I think I got the mental image here."

He really did have the perfect mental image. The woman Kix described sounded like the same woman that had invaded Ryan's mind the night before, causing him to oversleep and be late to work. While there was no way it was the same girl, Ryan felt a little flutter in his chest. A smile twitched the corner of his mouth as he recalled the memory of the old ladder he used to climb into her bedroom at night.

When they were eight, their parents thought their sleepovers were adorable. Alexis would sing and dance for Ryan, while he regaled her with details of the last plane model he'd acquired. They would make tents in her bedroom and camp out. When they were fourteen, their parents started to worry that it might be inappropriate for them to sleep in the same bed. There were several arguments about how Ryan and Alexis' bodies were changing to which they ignored. They knew they were only friends and their parents needed to get a clue to that as well.

That argument ceased after Cora's passing.

The day of Cora's funeral, Ryan stuck to Alexis like glue. Even at the tender age of fourteen, he could feel his friend's pain. He loved Cora and thought of her like a sister. He grieved for the young girl, but worried about Alexis. She took the death of her sister hard. All through the funeral, he held her tight. He remembered how his collar was soaked with Alexis' tears, but not once did he complain or attempt to change his shirt.

That night he left her, at the bequest of their parents, only to be awakened by her screams from across the street.

Ryan didn't think twice. He ran to her side. The moment he wrapped his arms around her, she calmed down. Miles and Melanie quickly realized Ryan's importance and the innocence of the arrangement. So, after that, their parents said nothing about them sleeping in the same bed. They knew nothing was going on between Ryan and Alexis besides sleeping.

Not that Ryan wouldn't have minded something more to have happened. For as long as he could remember, he was in love with Alexis York. She was beautiful, popular, and smart. But aside from all that, she had the soul of a poet and the freedom of a pilot. Every night he held her in his arms, close to his body. Many nights he would lay in silence listening to her breathing, while his hands would tenderly caress her.

Her body was created just for him. It had to be. There was no other explanation as to why she fit to him like a perfect puzzle piece. But no matter how much he loved her, he knew she was out of his league. Alexis would never see him as anything more than her best friend. So with a heavy heart, he kept their relationship platonic.

"Why didn't I think of this before?" Kix bellowed.

Ryan jumped, pulled back to reality. "Think of what?"

"I should check the passenger manifest for her name."

Ryan's eyes rolled upward. "Let it go already," he grumbled.

A knock came to the door of the cockpit. Ryan leaned back and unlocked the door. It opened and Makenna stood at the entrance, her face pinched with aggravation. She blew her hair back from her eyes.

"Everything all right?" Ryan asked.

"Not really. I have a passenger who's about to drive me bonkers. Ever since you turned off the fasten seatbelt sign…" she trailed off.

"What's wrong?"

"She wants to speak with you."

Kix started to unbuckle his seatbelt. "What about?"

"Not you, Captain. She wants Fisher." She cast a sideways glance to Ryan.

Ryan pushed back. "Me?" He poked his own chest and wondered why this woman would want to speak with him. Not that he minded, but he was second in command. This wasn't a commonplace occurrence. People usually wanted the captain, not the co-pilot.

The stray hair fell back into Makenna's eyes, only agitating her more. She thrust her hand through her midnight locks, forcing the hair out of her face. "Yep. You."

Kix laughed, smacking Ryan on the back. "Good luck, Buddy. Glad it's you and not me."

Ryan winced at the sting of the slap. "I've never had a passenger ask for me before. They're usually disappointed to get me instead of the captain."

Makenna smiled, her over-exaggerated irritation disappeared. "She wanted me to give this to you." As Makenna opened her hand, Ryan leaned over and glanced at the object lying in her palm. He recognized it immediately. It was an old, faded red toy compass. "She said to tell you *forever and always*."

Ryan took the compass and flipped it over between his fingers, examining it closely. It was worn with age, the plastic soft to the touch. As he held the tiny toy in his hand, a huge smile exploded over his face. This couldn't be. It wasn't possible. But the evidence was real. Alexis was there. On his flight.

"What's that she gave you?" Kix inquired.

"It's a compass," Ryan murmured, his own voice sounding soft and distant to his ears.

"Well, no shit, Sherlock. I mean what's it for?"

Ryan flashed Makenna a cocky smirk and turned to Kix. "A compass," he began, with sarcasm dripping from his tongue, "is a device used to determine geographic location. If you didn't learn that much in flight school, maybe I *should* be the one flying this bird."

Kix's mouth dropped to his chest. "Smart ass."

Ryan laughed as he removed his headset. "Maybe, but I have a passenger to speak with." He unbuckled his seatbelt, without haste, and stood up, moving around Makenna.

"Passenger in D2," she called out.

Ryan straightened his tie and took a deep breath, making his way out to the main cabin. He looked around the curtain separating the gully from the cabin, and his heart skipped a beat.

Sitting in seat D2 was his Alexis. She was looking in a mirror, applying lip gloss. This was the woman he'd seen in the pictures on Facebook. Poised, sophisticated, and beautiful. Her thick brown hair hung straight down her back. Her lips plump and pink, and her big brown eyes were accentuated with the right amount of eye makeup to make them standout. She was everything Ryan remembered her to be.

He took a deep breath, stepped around the curtain, and walked over to the row of seats she was sitting in. Next to her sat an older woman with hair white as snow. He heard the woman say something to Alexis as he approached, but couldn't quite make it out.

"Excuse me, Miss, but I do believe this is yours," he greeted, a playful hint to his tone. He flashed his best smile as she looked up at him from the mirror. His hand shook, just slightly, as he opened his palm to reveal the toy compass.

The moment their eyes met, time stood still.

For a moment Alexis thought she was dreaming. She'd been on edge from the moment she sat down on the plane. Her palms were sweaty and her heart raced in her chest. The anxiety she felt intensified as the force of the plane lifting off the ground pushed her back into her seat. How the older woman she'd seen in line at security, who was now seated beside her on the plane, slept so peacefully was a mystery to her.

Alexis felt everything from the nose of the plane rising off the ground to the tail that followed. Her ears muffled the higher they went until finally they popped. She looked out the window, enamored with how the city began to look smaller from her vantage point, which only added to her terror.

The plane took them over Manhattan and then turned, heading west. She swallowed back her panic long enough to whisper a sweet goodbye to her home and friends. Anxiety mixed with anticipation gripped her as the reality of it all started to sink in. She was really doing this. After all her hard work, dedication, and sacrifices, her dreams were finally coming true.

A pleasant smile settled on her face as she watched New York disappear under a blanket of clouds. And while her fingers dug into the armrest, there was a peace in her soul about the decision she'd made.

That was until *his* voice came over the speaker. Gone was the peace, and in its exchange was a full blown panic attack. After all this time, with no contact and nothing more than a silly friend request on Facebook to give her insight into his life, she'd managed to find herself on the same plane with the boy who was once her everything.

The fasten seatbelt signs went dark, but Alexis couldn't move an inch. She was in a state of shock. Everything inside of her told her that she was hearing things. It had to be her imagination playing tricks on her. She was not hearing his voice. What were the odds of Ryan being the pilot of her plane?

She rubbed her hands over her face, fighting the uneasiness inside her. All she wanted to do was jump up from her seat and rush to the cockpit, but even she knew that would be a fool's mission. Logic be damned, because she had to see him. She had to let him know she was there. Alexis waved at the flight attendant, who held up one finger, signaling for her to hold on.

She growled at the woman's inability to see how important this was for her. Her leg bounced with nervous energy. She waved at the flight attendant again, only to receive another vague demand for time. Impatient, she reached down into her bag and grabbed her wallet, removing the tiny, plastic compass she'd placed in it the night before.

A fortunate circumstance, she mused.

This small token was the one way she knew, without a doubt,

Ryan would believe it was her.

Alexis bounced anxiously in her seat waiting for the flight attendant to assist her. Her aggravation intensified by the second. Patience was never a virtue Alexis displayed and this woman was trying her to the nth degree.

Her irritation bubbled over when the raven-haired woman glanced in her direction then disappeared. She unbuckled her seatbelt, ready to become a lawbreaker, when her attention was pulled by the sweet, elderly woman sitting next to her.

"How do you know the pilot?"

She turned her head to see the woman staring at her through clouded, blue eyes. Her face, wrinkled with age, wore a bright smile. There were age spots on her face and hands, but they didn't deter from what Alexis could've only assumed was a knockout of a woman back in her day.

"I beg your pardon?" she asked politely.

"You came unglued the moment our pilot made his announcement, so I'm only able to assume you know him. Which makes me curious as to how." Her voice shook as most old women's do.

"Oh." A small chuckle rumbled Alexis in her chest. Feeling a little embarrassed, she squeezed the compass in her hand and let out a soft sigh. "We went to high school together."

"There's no more special a bond as that of high school sweethearts," the old woman cooed.

Alexis shook her head. "Oh, no, ma'am. We were only good friends."

The old woman's smile dropped. "But there was love there."

Heat rushed through her cheeks. Alexis shook her head.

The woman's smile returned exposing her bright white teeth. Alexis couldn't determine if they were dentures or dental implants. But she was certain of one thing; her teeth were too perfect to be natural.

"I highly doubt that. It's written all over you. How long has it been?"

Alexis lifted her eyes to the ceiling. A sense of nostalgia engulfed her. "Over fifteen years."

"He must've been something special."

"Even to this day, I'd say he's the greatest man I've ever known. I hate that we lost touch, but things change. People grow up and distance tends to pull friendships apart."

"Sadly, that's true." The older woman stretched, and sat up straighter in her seat. Her back hunched slightly with age, and her cardigan skewed around her waist. "So what is it you do, my dear?"

"I'm a doctor," Alexis boasted. She couldn't help but feel extremely proud of that accomplishment.

"Lovely. What an achievement for one so young."

Her blush deepened when she realized she was bragging. "Thank you, ma'am."

"Please, stop calling me ma'am. You're making me feel old," she chuckled and extended a shaky hand. "My name is Mildred. Mildred McCallum. Most people call me Millie."

Alexis accepted her fragile hand and shook it. "Alexis York. It's a pleasure to meet you."

"The pleasure is all mine, I assure you. You know, Doctor, you remind me a lot of my late husband." The old woman's smile faltered as she released a small sigh. She glanced down at the faded gold wedding band on her finger, circling it with adoration and compassion.

There was a tug at Alexis' heart, seeing the love this woman had for her departed husband. It honored and saddened her to be privy to someone who knew such love. "How so?"

"He was a sweet man, kind to the bone." The woman's eyes sparkled with a memory. "I see that same kindness in your eyes. Not only that, he was a spitfire, as are you."

"Me? A spitfire?" An amused smile tickled her lips.

"You did put that man in his place back at security."

If Alexis hadn't already been blushing, she would've been after that reminder. "Oh, Heavens. I'm so sorry about that. There are times my mouth gets the better of me."

"You have nothing to be sorry about. He deserved much worse."

"Amen to that. So, how long were you and your husband together?"

"Fifty-two years."

"Wow!"

Millie's grin widened. "We were high school sweethearts. That's how I could tell about you and your pilot fellow. There's something in the eyes that shows a pure love like that."

Alexis chewed on her bottom lip, letting her guard slip. "I did love him. It just wasn't meant to be."

Mildred patted her hand, her ghostly eyes filled with sympathy. The compass rattled against her palm when Millie's hand touched hers. The old woman stared down at the faded red compass in bewilderment.

"May I ask, what's that you have in your hand?"

She flipped the circle over to reveal the large green N on the white face of the toy. "It's a compass. Ryan gave it to me before…" she drifted off. The irony of the situation struck her. She was moving then when she left him, only to find him again during another move.

"A compass to lead you home," Mildred whispered.

Alexis was stunned by the woman's words. Her mouth dropped and tears swelled behind her eyes. Suddenly the sound of Ryan's voice echoed those words in her head.

"Excuse me," a sweet but firm voice interrupted them. "I apologize for the wait. How might I help you?"

Alexis looked up to see the woman with raven black hair and deep blue eyes staring back at her, from behind a pair of cat-eye glasses.

"Yes, ma'am. I'm sorry to be a pain, but I really need to speak with the first officer."

"The first officer is currently working to ensure the safety of this flight. Is there maybe something I can help you with?"

Alexis' chest deflated at the finalization in the attendant's expression. Still determined, she knew there was only one other way to reach Ryan, for him to know she was there, even if he couldn't come to her.

"May I ask your name?"

The attendant nodded. "Yes, ma'am. It's Makenna."

"Well, Makenna, I understand the first officer is very busy ensuring the safety of this flight, and I'm more than appreciative of that. All I ask is for you to do me one tiny little favor."

Makenna straightened her back, her head cocked to the side in curiosity. "And that might be?"

"Take this to him and tell him an old friend is waiting for him here," Alexis stated, handing the compass to Makenna. The flight attendant looked bewildered as she accepted the toy from the passenger. Her eyes darted from the compass and then back to Alexis.

Makenna turned the plastic toy over in her hand. "This is very unorthodox and against regulations." She stretched her hand out, ready to return the toy to Alexis, when Millie clasped Makenna's hand, closing the toy in her palm.

"It's nothing more than a tiny toy—"

"Yes, I—"

"There's no harm in taking the pilot a toy from a dear, old friend."

The hard shell of Makenna's exterior melted, and Alexis felt like she could breathe again, if only for a moment. Millie might've just saved her reunion with Ryan. "I'll see what I can do," Makenna stated, tucking the compass in her skirt pocket.

"Thank you so much. Please tell him, 'forever and always.'"

"Forever and always?" Makenna repeated, her brow furrowed, wrinkling her nose.

Alexis nodded. "He'll understand."

Makenna gave Alexis a faint smile and turned away, moving toward the front of the fuselage. Alexis could only hope she was heading to the cockpit.

Once Makenna was out of sight, Alexis squealed in excitement, flailing her arms and legs like a child. Her enthusiasm caused Mildred to laugh.

Alexis ran her fingers through her hair and suddenly realized how she must look. "Oh, God," she breathed in terror.

"Calm down. You look beautiful. You'll blow him away," Mildred encouraged.

"I'm a mess."

In a panic, she stood up to adjust her shirt, wishing she'd worn something more sophisticated than a t-shirt and holey skinny jeans. Alexis dropped back down into her seat, the realization that there was nothing, short of changing, that could enhance her appearance.

Everything seemed so surreal. The fact that she had dreamt about Ryan the night before hadn't slipped her mind. Now here she was, about to see him again after all this time. The butterflies fluttered frantically in the pit of her belly just thinking about it.

Alexis reached for her carry-on and retrieved her makeup bag. She brushed her hair, applied a fresh coat of mascara and brightened her smile with some lip-gloss.

"You look beautiful, doctor," Mildred said again with a soft laugh. She patted Alexis' knee like old women do to their grandchildren, trying to comfort her.

"Thanks," she muttered, tossing her makeup back in her bag. That's when she heard the voice that made her heart skip a beat.

"Excuse me, Miss, but I do believe this is yours."

Ryan held out the compass to Alexis in his large hand. For a moment, Alexis stared at him, unable to believe her eyes. All of those old feelings came rushing back through her. Time hadn't changed a thing.

He looked even better, in her opinion, than he had in high school. The pictures on Facebook didn't do him justice. He was tall with bronzed skin, freshly kissed by the sun. His features looked chiseled and lean muscled, sculpted and hard. His eyes smoldered with hues of green beneath thick black brows. His sharp nose, offset his features, leading her eyes to his smooth, soft lips. His clean-cut jaw was hard and square, completing his perfect face.

Her eyes raked over him from top to bottom. He looked delicious in his uniform. So enticing, in fact, that she mentally chided herself for having inappropriate thoughts regarding stripping him out of said uniform. In short, he was her fantasy made flesh.

"It's doctor," she replied with a wink.

A deep throaty laugh resonated from his chest. "Ah, yes, my mistake. I believe this belongs to you, *doctor*."

Alexis stood up, her smile beaming for all on the plane to see. It didn't matter to her that all eyes were on them. All that mattered was Ryan was there.

"Ryan," she whispered. "Look at you. You look great in that uniform."

"You like?" he asked, as he did a little circle for her with his arms outstretched.

"It suits you well."

"You look amazing, too."

"Thanks," she replied with a soft blush. His crooked smile grew until all of his teeth were exposed. His grin was contagious. She couldn't stop smiling because of him.

"Well, do I get a hug or did you pull me from work just to stare at me?"

Alexis laughed and carefully stepped over Mildred, taking Ryan's outstretched hand. The moment their skin touched, electricity crackled in the air between them.

As soon as Alexis cleared Mildred's legs, she wrapped her arms tight around Ryan's neck. She closed her eyes and breathed him in. He still smelled the same as he always did. The scents of mint, sugar, and cologne filled her lungs. He smelled like home. Ryan rested his closed fists on the small of her back, pulling her flush to his body.

"It's good to see you," she whispered in his ear. Neither of them had expected the swell of emotions they felt. It was as if all the years apart had vanished into thin air.

A single tear trickled down Alexis' cheek as they broke their warm embrace. Ryan gently wiped the tear away with his thumb.

"It's good to see you, too," he softly spoke. His fingers brushing across her cheek.

"It's been too long," she stated.

"It sure has."

"I can't believe you're here. It was crazy enough that you accepted my Facebook request last night but now…" she released a familiar sigh, "you're here."

"I was going to message you," Ryan admitted, "but saw you were moving and I didn't want to bother you. Is Dallas a layover for you?"

"Nah, it's my destination."

Ryan's grin widened again. "No way! You're kidding me?" he exclaimed.

"Not at all. I start my new job on Monday."

Ryan scratched the top of his head, laughing. "Oh, wow. This is wild."

"Why?"

"Because *I* live in Dallas. It's my home base."

Alexis covered her lips with the tips of her fingers, staring at him. Her heart was beating a mile a minute. "Oh, wow," she repeated him.

"Can you meet me after the plane lands? I really want the chance to talk to you, but I have to get back to work."

Alexis patted his rock hard bicep through his white uniform shirt. "Good God, Ryan, what's in there," she exclaimed playfully, squeezing his arm.

His eyelids appeared heavy as his gaze dropped to her hand. Long black lashes shielded his eyes, and his tongue darted out over his luscious lips. "I workout when I can," he murmured.

Alexis recalled the pictures of him on Facebook, and smiled. "It doesn't hurt to be an IronMan survivor, either," she noted.

He cocked his head, eyeing her. "Looks like someone's been

checking out my page," he teased, his voice heady and raspy, melting her to her very core.

She raised her hand, her blush burning through her skin. "Guilty."

Ryan chuckled. "I have to admit, I've tried locating you before but could never find you."

Alexis felt her insides leap at once. He'd looked for her. She'd been on his mind all these years. A smile broke across her face she couldn't nor wouldn't dream of containing.

"I just opened that account about a week ago at my Mom's behest. She figured it was a good way for her to keep up with my on goings and such."

Ryan bowed his head. "How's your mom doing?"

Alexis shifted from one foot to the other. "Good, I think. On our way to the airport, she informed me she's dating a guy named Dan."

"Sounds like we have a lot of catching up to do." He rubbed his hand along his jaw and chuckled.

"That we do," she noted with a smile. "How about your parents? They're well, I hope?"

His eyes fell on her lips. He shifted his weight from one foot to the other and scratched the back of his head. "Mom and Pops are doing great. Pops retired not too long ago and is about to drive Mom up a wall, but other than that, they're good."

Alexis held him with her adoring stare. "That's wonderful to hear."

"So, you'll meet up with me?" he asked, his voice laced with hope.

"Yes, of course, I will."

"Awesome. We'll be landing at terminal B, gate fifty-four. When you get off the plane, take a left and walk a few feet. On your left hand-side, there's a pilot's lounge. Go in and give them my name."

"That's it? Just your name?" she inquired.

"Yeah. They may ask to see your ID, but I'll make sure

everything else is taken care of."

What had previously been a minor skipping in her heart rhythm was now a massive pounding against her chest. The butterflies were no longer just in her stomach, but fluttering around her body as excitement overtook her.

"I guess I'll see you then."

Ryan hugged her again, but pulled away too soon for her liking.

"Until then," he whispered. His smile faltered, nearly breaking her heart to see it fade. It reminded her of the day they said goodbye, and that was a memory best left in the past.

Determined to see his smile return, she stood up straight, mocking a military fashion and flattened her plump lips into a straight line. "Get to work, Fisher," she barked.

Ryan returned her stance and saluted her. "Yes, sir!" he snapped back.

He then grabbed her by the neck and mussed her hair, like he'd always done when they were kids. She screeched and smacked his hands away from her head. "I can't believe you just did that!"

Laughter resounded around the cabin from the viewing passengers, watching as their co-pilot reunited with his old friend. Ryan winked at her, adding to the show for his new audience.

"I'll see you in a couple of hours. Deal?"

"Deal." She tried to flatten the mess he made of her hair.

He placed his hands on both sides of her head and kissed the top, before turning on his heel. He took a single step away, then suddenly stopped. Turning back around on his heel, he extended his hand to her. There laid the compass, awaiting to return to its rightful owner; having managed to keep its promise of guiding her back home to him.

"Here, before I forget."

She closed the small distance between them and retrieved her treasure. The moment their hands touched again, palm to palm, skin to skin, her whole body melted, sensuous heat flooded her veins. Their eyes locked together, and from the look on his face, she couldn't help but wonder if he'd felt it, too.

"You're really a sight for sore eyes," he whispered. He pulled her back into his arms and hugged her so tightly that she could barely breathe. "I've missed you."

She couldn't move. The idea of letting him go seemed impossible to her. It didn't matter that they promised to see each other in a few short hours. So much time had already been wasted. She didn't want to waste any more.

"I've missed you, too." Reluctantly, she released him. "Get back to work. I'll see you soon."

He nodded and opened the curtain that separated the compartment from the galley. He looked over his shoulder at her one last time then disappeared behind the curtains.

Alexis turned around to see Millie smiling at her.

"What?" she asked, as she took a step closer to Millie. Every eye was on her, whispers filled the compartment, but she didn't mind. They all saw her with her Ryan. Of that she was proud of.

"I can't resist," Millie said as she stood up to let her pass.

"Can't resist what?" Alexis sat down, crossing her knees.

"Saying I told you so."

"You did what?" she asked with a laugh.

"I knew he would be smitten with you the moment he saw you. True love reunited."

Alexis gave Millie a placating smile. "If you say so."

"It's very true, Doctor York. It's written all over his face."

Alexis toyed with the compass in her hand. Looking down at it, she wondered if it smelled like him. "He's my oldest friend. I'm sure that's all you saw."

"Believe as you wish, but trust me, doctor, I'm right."

Alexis patted her withering hand. "I would never doubt you, Ms. Millie."

Millie laughed, placing her hand over Alexis'. "Smart girl."

Alexis reached down under her seat and obtained her bag again. She slipped the compass back into her wallet for safekeeping.

For the remainder of the flight, Alexis enjoyed carrying on with Mildred like she had known her all her life. She told Alexis about Mitchell, their children, grandchildren, and even great-grandchildren. Millie inundated her with family photos, regaling her with such sweet memories. Her favorite were the stories Millie told her about her life with Mitchell. She envied the love she had for her husband, and hoped one day a man would love her as much.

Thankfully, time seemed to speed by. Alexis was grateful for having such a wonderful cabin mate. Millie not only kept her mind off her fear of flying, but she also helped keep her mind off of the fact that Ryan was sitting only a few feet away from her, and that she was about to see him again soon.

"Ladies and gentlemen, this is your captain speaking," a husky voice, with a slight northwestern twang rang out over the PA system. "We have begun our descent into Dallas/Fort Worth International Airport. Currently the weather is..."

Alexis' pulse soared. This time it wasn't her fear of flying causing her nerves to race, but the mere fact that landing this plane meant she'd see Ryan again very soon.

The fasten seatbelt sign blinked on and Alexis' whole body became a bundle of nerves. Her knees started to bounce with anticipation as Makenna announced for everyone to put their seats back into their upright positions. Mildred patted her knee, forcing it still.

"It'll be all right. You'll see. Fate has a funny way of working things out," Millie encouraged.

"Thank you, Ms. Millie. I wouldn't have made it through this flight without you."

"It's been my pleasure. Plus, you've given me a great story to tell my son."

Alexis released a loud laugh.

The plane started its final descent. The landing was very smooth, but she still hated the jerking feeling it left her with when the wheels touched the ground. She found herself wondering if Ryan had anything to do with the landing. Her fear somehow appeased by the idea of him at the reigns.

When the fasten seatbelt sign turned off, everyone started standing up, and gathering their belongings. Alexis was just as eager to get off the plane as the rest of the passengers, but her first order of business was sending her father a message to let him know she would be running a little late. After all, she had a date with the first officer. Even if it was just two friends catching up on old times, she was still as nervous as she would have been on a first date.

As she exited the cabin, she glanced up from the text message she'd sent her father to notice the cockpit door was open. She peeked inside to see Ryan and the captain going over their systems. Ryan turned around and caught her eye, giving her a cute wink. Heat burned through her skin, painting her cheeks and neck. She giggled like a little girl with a crush, which made her blush even more.

Alexis wiggled her fingers at him and then moved to exit the plane.

"Fisher wanted me to reassure you that everything's ready at the lounge for when you arrive," Makenna whispered, startling Alexis.

"Thank you again for all your help."

Makenna smiled. "My pleasure. Enjoy your stay in Dallas."

Alexis nodded and departed the plane.

Once they exited the jet bridge, she hugged Millie. "Enjoy your time with your son. I know he'll be so happy to see you."

"Thank you, doctor. And enjoy your time with your pilot friend. I'm sure it'll all work out accordingly."

"I will. Thank you," she whispered. Alexis gave her fragile hand a tender squeeze then released her, bidding her farewell.

With butterflies fluttering in her stomach, she collected her luggage from baggage claim, and followed Ryan's directions to the pilot's lounge.

Alexis stopped in front of the lounge and let out a heavy sigh. This was it. She was about to spend an afternoon with her old friend, catching up. She opened the door and walked inside. "No turning back now," she told herself, as the door shut behind her.

"Holy shit! That's your childhood chum? You can't tell me you didn't tap that. Seriously, Fisher, when did your balls drop?" Kix squawked, almost falling out of his seat, as he watched Alexis exit the craft.

Ryan rubbed his hand over the back of his neck, flustered. "No, I never *tapped* that, as you've so eloquently put it. Alexis was my best friend growing up."

Best friends indeed. Alexis had always been pretty to Ryan, and while the pictures he'd found online revealed she'd turned into a stunning woman, those photographs really didn't do her justice. In real life, she was more beautiful than he could've imagined. Trim, lush, curvy, not at all stick-figure skinny as so many women believe they must be in order to be beautiful. Long, flowing brown hair and sultry brown eyes that could easily melt a man where he stood. She was the vision of a goddess. All woman. The way those jeans hugged her hips and that t-shirt contoured to her supple breasts made the man inside him release a possessive growl.

"If I had friends like that..." Kix trailed off, thrusting his hips.

"I get it," Ryan groaned.

"Yeah, I bet you're going to *get it*." Kix gave one last hard thrust, followed by an insinuating wiggle of his brows.

Ryan's eyes fluttered with a roll and he shook his head, fighting the urge to laugh. Kix was a thirteen year old boy trapped in a forty-plus year old man's body. "Enough. It's not like that. We haven't seen each other in over fifteen years."

"Well, if you're not interested in taking advantage of an *old* friendship, you know I'll gladly take her off your hands," Kix suggested.

"Dream on, Captain," Ryan laughed, but there was a warning, protective vibe to his tone.

"If you say so, but..."

"The plane is clear, Captain," Makenna announced, interrupting Kix. Ryan's shoulders dropped in relief. That meant his shift was almost complete. Anticipation bubbled inside him, a beast gnawing at his chest, aching to get to the girl who waited for him.

"Thanks, Kenna," Kix responded, cutting his eyes up to her and flashing her a winning smile.

"Don't give me that puppy dog look." She glared at him, her hands placed on her hips. "And leave the kid alone." She flailed one hand toward Ryan. "Can't you see he's already a ball of nerves. Geez," she scolded the captain.

Kix sniffed in aggravation and started to mimic her, over exaggerating her movements. Makenna popped Kix upside the head and grinned. Kix flipped her the bird and the two of them had a laugh, which took the attention off of Ryan.

Ryan mouthed a *thank you* to Makenna before pouring himself over the post flight checklist. The seconds seemed to tick by so slow that no matter how many tasks he accomplished or how fast he completed them, they took forever to do.

He glanced down at his wristwatch and released an unintentional guttural groan, realizing that only ten minutes had passed since Makenna gave the all clear. He began checking the gauges, knocking another task off his list when he felt a tap on his shoulder. Ryan glanced over to find Kix smirking at him. "You know, I can finish this up if you have some place you have to be," Kix offered.

"I can't do that to you, Captain," Ryan stated, his sense of responsibility overpowering his need to get to Alexis. "I'll finish my work."

"Are you insane, Ryan?" Makenna exclaimed. Ryan jumped. It was rare for her to call him by his first name, so he took immediate notice and gave her his undivided attention. "For once in his life, this man has offered to do something decent. If you don't take him up on it, I might have to spank you."

"Oh, I'll take you up on that suggestion!" Kix volunteered. Makenna gave him a dirty look that caused both men to sink back into their seats.

"Just because I have a friend waiting on me doesn't mean my responsibilities disappear," Ryan noted.

Without warning, Kix grabbed the clipboard from Ryan. "Go, Fisher. She's waiting. If I was you, my ass would've left you high and dry already."

Makenna ducked out of the cockpit, leaving the two men to duke it out on their own. Ryan opened his mouth to argue his case further, but Kix's face dropped from the all smiles Ryan knew to a serious expression. "Don't make me order you off this craft, Ryan."

Ryan smacked his lips shut and gave his captain a quick nod. Kix started whistling *"Dixie"* off key and set to work. Ryan slowly stood up and gathered his jacket, carry-on, and hat. "I appreciate this," he said and exited the cockpit.

As Ryan passed the galley, he caught sight of Makenna who was taking inventory. "Thanks again," he told her. "He pretty much just ordered me off the plane."

She blew her hair back from her eyes and smiled up at the young pilot. "He's persistent when he wants to be," she claimed with a wink.

"Is that what we're calling it?"

Makenna laughed. "At the moment."

"Well, between you and me, I think he has some twisted fantasy…" he leaned in closer to her and whispered, "…that I'm about to get laid."

Makenna shook her head, rolling her eyes. "That sounds about right for him," she groused.

Ryan draped his jacket over his shoulder and placed his hat on his head with a pop against the brim. He gripped the handle of his luggage with his free hand. "He can keep on dreaming. It was never like that with Lex and me."

Makenna pursed her lips, adjusting the scarf around her neck. "A sick man's fantasy. Now quit stalling. She's waiting."

"Okay! I'm going, I'm going," he chuckled. Ryan kissed Makenna on the temple. "Give him hell."

Her head tilted to the side, bobbing in a tiny nod. "Just for you. Have a good time with your friend."

"Thanks. I plan on it." Ryan slipped out the door of the aircraft. Rather than walking, he trotted down the jet bridge, his luggage bouncing behind him. He had to restrain himself from breaking into a full sprint. Run or walk, it didn't matter. Nothing could get him to Alexis fast enough.

Meanwhile, Alexis stood at the entrance of the pilot's lounge, her body a bundle of nerves.

This room looked like any other airport bar. A wooden bar top with green leather-bound bar stools pressed against it. A handsome, young bartender stood behind the bar wiping down the glass in his hand. Tables and chairs were stationed around the room, some filled, some not. The air smelled fresh and the lighting was bright, unlike dive-type bars or nightclubs she'd visited when Jenna was on the prowl for her next cheating slimeball.

Her cell phone vibrated in her hand. She glanced down, expecting an angry response from her father. Instead she got a message from him freaking out about the fact that he hadn't realized she was coming into town today. He stated he wasn't even in transit to the airport and informed her to get a cab and he'd pay for it, because he was in a meeting that he couldn't get out of to come for her.

Alexis re-read the message. Anger and hurt swelled inside her. For weeks she'd reminded her father of her arrival and while it didn't surprise her that he'd forgotten, it still stung.

"Can I help you, miss?" a husky voice cut through her thoughts.

Alexis looked up into the blue eyes of the bartender. She cleared her throat, shoving her phone into her pocket. "Um, yes. I'm Doctor Alexis York. I'm supposed to meet Ryan Fisher here."

"Ah, yes. I was expecting you. May I see some identification?"

Alexis opened her messenger bag and retrieved her wallet. She flipped it open to her driver's license, and presented it to the bartender. He studied it for a moment, before he glanced between it and her. The picture was kind of old, reflecting a time when she'd chopped her hair off into a short wedge, but in her opinion, it still looked like her.

Ugh. I'm going to have to update that when I change over my license. She mentally added the new chore to her to-do list once she got her new address taken care of.

"Thanks." He waved his hand out toward the open floor. "You can have a seat anywhere. My name's Chad. Can I get you anything?"

"White wine," Alexis replied.

Chad slipped a wine glass down from the rack and pulled a chilled bottle of wine from the cooler. He poured up her drink and handed it to her. Alexis withdrew her credit card from her wallet and slid it over to him as she took her drink. "You want to start a tab?"

Alexis took a sip from her wine glass. "Sure."

Taking her credit card, Chad placed it by the register and started back to cleaning the bar.

Alexis picked up her wine glass, and carted it along with her luggage over to an empty table. She sat down, positioning herself with her back against a wall so she could see the entrance. Her legs bounced with anticipation for Ryan to arrive. Nervous energy coursed through her. The urge to jump up from her seat and start pacing the floor was almost overwhelming. To stop from making a fool out of herself, she dug into her pocket and extracted her cell phone.

She'd promised her mother a text when she arrived. She typed out a message, unable to contain her smile as she relayed the news to her mother.

Touched down in Dallas. You'll never believe who I ran into. Ryan Fisher. Call you later when I'm settled in. Love you.

She decided it was probably best not to inform her mother about her father's abandonment, again. Her mother didn't need to worry about her being alone in a new city without transportation. Only two days. That was all she had to wait before her car would arrive. It was being hauled across the country with the rest of her belongings. When her mother wanted to buy her that car, she thought the woman had lost her mind. She'd never needed a vehicle in New York. Mass transportation had more than taken care of her needs. Now, she understood. It was her ticket to

freedom and independence.

The entrance door opened and Alexis' eyes shot up but her heart sank when she realized the newcomer wasn't Ryan. She lifted the glass to her lips, taking a sip of her wine, which sloshed around with the rhythm of her bouncing knees.

"Is this seat taken?"

Alexis' eyes darted up to find Ryan standing in front of her with his hat tucked under his arm and his uniform jacket hanging by the hook of his finger, draped over his shoulder. She forced down the mouthful of alcohol, trying not to choke. The liquid felt like it expanded in her throat, causing her to almost gasp for air. It landed hard in her stomach, rattling the butterflies that resided there.

"Well," she rasped, placing her glass on the flat surface. "I was waiting for someone."

Ryan tossed his hat on the table and hung his jacket on the back of the chair. A cocky smile plastered across his face. "Lucky for me, I beat him here." He opened his arms to her, his brows lifted in expectation. "You going to leave a guy hanging here?"

Alexis bounced from her seat and met his embrace. She closed her eyes, breathing in the scent of his cologne. It was new, yet familiar. She'd caught the scent during their hug on the plane, but here, now, it engulfed her. Sandalwood, musky, with a hint of citrus. She'd determined in herself to find out what the name of his cologne was, because it just became her favorite scent in the world.

Her fingers gripped the back of his shirt and they swayed, holding tight to each other. His nose buried in her hair and his hands rested against the small of her back. This felt good. It felt right. "I still can't believe it's you," she whispered. "I dreamt about you last night."

Ryan pulled back, his eyes bouncing. "Really? What kind of dream?"

Alexis wiggled from his grasp, smacking his chest. "You dirty dog, you. Not *that* kind of dream!"

Ryan released a hardy laugh. He stepped around her, and

pulled out her chair, as Chad arrived with a fresh drink for Alexis and a cold beer for Ryan. Alexis seemed surprised by Chad's sudden appearance and disappearance as she accepted her seat. Ryan dropped down in the chair beside her, pulling it up to the table. He leaned forward with his beer placed between both hands. "So, tell me. What did you dream about?"

A light blush painted her cheeks. She took a sip of her fresh wine, searching for the words. "While I was packing, I found our old year book. It made me think back to our last day together," she muttered against the rim.

"It makes sense you'd dream of that. So, I take it that's why you had the compass?"

Alexis bent down, taking the compass back out of her bag. She twisted it around between her fingertips, watching the dial move to continually face north. "It is. I don't know how long it's been packed away with that yearbook, but after I found it, I couldn't put it back in there."

Ryan reached out, taking the compass from her hand. He lifted it in the air, examining it in the light. "I can't believe this thing still works."

"I know, right?"

Ryan handed the compass back to Alexis who slipped it back into her wallet. He took a swig from his beer, and leaned back in his chair, dangling one arm over the backrest. Alexis crossed her legs and tried to poise herself. The mere fact they were in the same room together was better than any silly dream she could ever have.

"So…"

"So," she echoed back.

"What have you been doing with yourself for the last fifteen years? I want to know it all. School, work, family, friends…boyfriends" —he tilted his head, his eyes narrowing— "*girlfriends?*"

A smile lifted the corners of her lips, and the chime of her laughter filled the air. He'd changed. Shy, boyish Ryan now had a wicked sense of humor that matched her own. She liked this side of him and it made her wonder what else had changed about him.

She circled her finger around the rim of her glass. "No boyfriends, and I tried the girl thing but it never amounted to more than a college fling." She peered up at him through her eyelashes.

He slumped forward with his mouth gaped open. "You must tell me everything."

And she laughed again. This felt good. The conversation between them flowed with ease. She told him about her life, her friends, her patients, and her new job. She couldn't remember the last time she'd talked that much about herself. Not that she ever minded, but Jenna was typically the center of conversation when they were together. It felt nice to have someone hanging on her every word that wasn't a patient waiting for her to drop the bad news.

"What hospital will you be working at?"

Alexis folded her napkin in triangles. "Agape Medical Center in Grapevine."

"I take it this job's a great opportunity for you then?" he inquired, draining the remainder of his beer.

"It really is. The money alone is amazing and rare. Most fellowships are shitty pay."

"That's why I can't wait to make captain. Don't get me wrong, I make decent money, but captain pay is a substantial increase."

"I bet. At least you don't have hundreds of thousands of dollars in school debt hanging over your head."

Ryan picked at the label on the bottle. "You got me there. I got a scholarship to college and what that didn't cover was taken care of through my Air Guard Reserve pay. I had flight school paid off in no time."

"Smarty pants," Alexis teased, tossing a napkin at him.

He caught it, laughing. "As if you have room to talk. Nerd."

"Geek."

Ryan tossed the napkin aside and reached for her hand. "I'm so glad you're here. I've missed you."

Their smiles disappeared and the atmosphere around them

changed. She placed her hand over his, the feel of his skin on hers was mesmerizing. His green eyes pierced hers, touching her very soul. Never in her life had she felt this with anyone but him. To have him still illicit this kind of reaction stunned her. "I've missed you, too," she breathed.

They moved in closer to one another. The warmth of his breath mingled with hers, washing over her skin. Her eyes started to drift close, anticipation coursing through her veins. She had no idea why she was allowing this to happen, but she didn't want to stop it. All of the feelings she had as a girl rushed back, setting her whole body aflame. She knew him, even if fifteen years had passed, she still knew him. And he knew her.

"Fisher!" Ryan jerked back. Alexis tried to catch her breath, her eyes opening to meet his. He smiled at her, giving her a coy wink before he sat back and looked over his shoulder at their intruder.

"What do you want, Hart?" he demanded, throwing an arm in the air.

A tall man with brown hair and deep green eyes moved toward them. His stride was smooth, straight, and he carried himself with authority. He flashed a confident and debonair smile that highlighted his full lips. Dressed in a pilot's uniform, she noticed the bars on his shoulders. He was a first officer like Ryan. The white uniform shirt formed to his shapely chest, and accented his golden skin.

He placed a glass on the table, and turned the empty chair beside her around, straddling it as if he had been invited to sit down. "I want to know who we have here." He lifted up from the seat to lean over the back of the chair and across the table. "First Officer Declan Hart," he introduced himself, offering her his hand.

She cut a glance at Ryan who was glaring at their newcomer. He wasn't anymore happy about this guy interrupting them as she was. She figured she had every right to toy with this man. "First Officer. Oh, my. That must mean you're a pilot." She fanned her face with her hands.

Ryan covered his mouth with his fist, hiding his smirk.

Declan grinned. "Right you are, sugar. And from where you sit, I take it you like pilots."

"What do you mean?" she wondered, acting innocent.

"Well, you're sitting here with my boy Fisher in a pilot's lounge. It seems befitting you like pilots."

Alexis chewed her bottom lip then turned to Ryan. "You didn't tell me you were a pilot, too. And here I thought when you fucked me in the bathroom during our flight you were just another passenger. I've hit the jackpot."

Ryan choked on his laugh as Declan exclaimed, "You inducted her in the Mile High Club?"

Alexis and Ryan couldn't hold back any longer. They fell against each other laughing, exactly as they had done when they were young. This wasn't the first time they'd put the play on a dumb jock. Declan's brow furrowed and his lips flattened. "Damn, I fell right into that one."

Alexis shrugged. "I'm not an idiot, pal. First of all, he's in uniform, too." She nudged Ryan with his elbow, giving him a quick wink. "And second of all, as you pointed out, I am in the pilot's lounge."

Declan brushed his thumb across his nose. "Point taken. Do you have a name?" It was impossible to deny that she liked this guy. He had an air about him that oozed charisma, but even with his amazing green eyes and tight, hard body, in her mind, he couldn't begin to compare to Ryan.

"Doctor Alexis York," she noted, offering the hand she'd purposely not given earlier. Declan stood up and leaned over the table giving her a good shake.

"Where ya coming from, Doc?" he questioned.

"You know I was scheduled to fly in from New York today," Ryan inserted.

Declan grinned, shrugging one shoulder. "I didn't ask where you came from, did I?"

"Guys! Do I need to step outside and give you two lover boys some space?" Alexis joked.

Declan laughed and Ryan slumped back into his seat, letting his smile slowly curl the corners of his lips. Alexis kicked out her leg, hitting Ryan in the shin. That did it. His smile returned in full force.

"Sorry, Lex," he mewled. "Declan, here, is my roommate and a major pain in my ass."

"Likewise," Declan announced.

Ryan punched him in the arm and Declan returned the favor. They both laughed. Soon Alexis joined in, not sure what she was laughing at. Before she realized it, Declan had made himself a part of the party.

Declan Hart was funny. He was also smart, but his demeanor eluded to the notion that he didn't like people knowing that. He used his charm as a means to get what he wanted. Much like she and Ryan, he came from a small town in Utah. Alexis was intrigued to learn he'd been a physics major before attending flight school.

A couple of hours had passed and the friendly banter never let up. Alexis hadn't even noticed the time until her father texted her wanting to know if she'd made it home safe. She ignored his message, feeling he didn't deserve an immediate response. Not that she had a problem hailing a cab, she'd done it a million times in New York, but he'd abandoned her again, and well, he'd have to wait until she was actually home to get a reply from her.

"How long are you going to be in Dallas?" Declan asked. He downed the remaining contents of his drink in one gulp.

"Indefinitely," Alexis admitted, her smile widening as she glanced over to Ryan. Ryan reached out, capturing her knee. She hadn't even noticed that she was bouncing her legs again. The heat of his touch penetrated her jeans, which calmed her leg instantly, but also sent tingles up her limb.

"And now we can make up for lost time," he claimed. She placed her hand on top of his, giving it a squeeze.

"Fifteen years is a long time to make up for," Declan mentioned, "Mhm. Have you told her about Reagan, yet?" He clapped his hands, a flare of excitement in his tone as a mischievous grin lighted his cheeks. "I bet she'll be so excited to meet you."

Alexis' eyes cut to Declan. She slipped her hand away from Ryan's, her body stiffened with confusion. "Reagan? Who's that?" Her heart lodged in her throat, praying that Reagan was Ryan's cat. Or maybe his dog. Possibly a fish.

Ryan reached for her hand, linking his fingers with hers. He felt calm and steady, no matter how many darts he shot in Declan's directions. "She's my—"

"*Girlfriend,*" Declan announced. "She's his girlfriend."

Ryan shot Declan an unamused look. "Jesus, Declan! She's not my girlfriend."

Declan laughed, slapping his hands against the table. "She's a girl and she's a friend. Get it?" He pretended to tap a cymbal and pointed at Ryan with a clownish grin. *"Girlfriend."*

Ryan dropped back into his seat, rubbing his index finger and thumb across his forehead. Yes, he and Reagan had slept together, *once.* A mistake he regretted to this day.

Alexis once again pulled away from him. Tense and rigid, her face contorted as confusion crossed her features. All of their shared smiles and laughter were gone. A sort of invisible barrier seemed to appear around her. A wall that created a strange awkwardness between them. She sipped her wine, finishing off another glass.

Damn Declan and his stupid sense of humor.

"Lex," Ryan straightened up, and reached for her hand. "Ray's a friend. Nothing more. I swear." When Alexis said nothing, he continued, "Really, Lex. It's not like that. We've been friends for years."

Alexis patted Ryan's hand, and let out a strained laugh. "It's no big deal."

Ryan smacked his hand over his face. "Seriously, it's not like that," he stressed.

Her laughter became lighter with his lingering discomfort. "No, really. It's not a big deal. I get it. Friends with benefits and all that," she chuckled.

"Great benefits," Declan insinuated, rubbing his hands together.

Her eyes narrowed, honing in on Declan and a single brow raised in a sarcastic expression "You sharing in Ryan's sloppy seconds?" she popped back, giving Ryan a little wink.

The weirdness started to subside when Ryan realized she believed him. Declan snorted, "Excuse me, Doc, but who's to say I didn't have her first?"

Alexis' mouth curved into a witty grin. "Because Ryan's charming and witty, and he does have a way with women."

"Yeah he does. It's sickening," Declan complained.

"Stop it, you two," Ryan rebuffed them, his face burning red. He still had the urge to beat Declan within an inch of his life for the stunt he tried to pull. But he would wait. Alexis had taken the situation in stride, which subdued his vindictive tendencies. However, that didn't stop him from formulating a plan to rip Declan a new one when they got home.

"Tell me, was he like that as a kid?" Declan asked. He clicked his tongue against the roof of his mouth as he crossed his arms over the back of his chair, and dropped his chin on top of them.

"He's always been the purest of hearts," Alexis admitted.

"When I was at my lowest, Ryan knew how to make me feel better."

Ryan felt his heart constrict in his chest. He thought back to many, many years ago when he held this wonderful girl in his arms as she mourned the loss of her baby sister. She told him then that he was the only person who could fill the void left inside her. That he alone knew how to make her feel better. Those words echoed loud in his mind. He swallowed hard. "You were my world."

"Like Reagan is now?" she asked, her voice squeaking.

"Meh. Reagan and I became friends due to sports." He bit the inside of his mouth and tore his gaze from hers. It pained him to think that she felt she was so easily replaceable. Reagan was a wonderful person, although a little outspoken at times, and a great friend, but there was no comparison between the memory he had of Alexis and the friendship he'd developed with Reagan.

"Sports!" Alexis let out a gasp, covering her mouth. "Really?"

"Why the shock?" Declan questioned. "Our boy here is a three time IronMan survivor."

Alexis gripped Ryan's bicep. "Oh, I know, but there was a day when his only functioning muscle was his brain."

"No way!" Declan laughed, clapping his hands together.

"Yeah. He was so scrawny."

"And yet you adored me," Ryan snarked.

Alexis dropped her hand from his arm, which left a warmth that seeped deep under his skin. "That's an understatement." Their eyes met and a beautiful smile exploded across her face, thrilling him to his very soul.

"What about you?" Declan wondered.

"What about me?" Alexis asked. Her leg seemed to have a mind of its own. Much like she had when they were younger, she had a twitch that included her leg bouncing uncontrollably. Out of the old habit resurfacing, Ryan placed his hand on her knee stopping her.

"Do you have a boyfriend?"

She released a boisterous laugh, and while Ryan already knew the answer to this question through their previous conversation, his heart still jumped at what his roommate might be hedging toward. "Nah. School and work have been my sole focus for far too long."

"That's not good," Declan claimed. "All work and no play makes Lexi a dull gal."

She raised her eyebrows, meeting Declan's gaze. "Dude! You don't even know me and you just called me dull!"

Declan scooted his chair forward, pressing the backrest against the lip of the table. He lifted up, moving closer to Alexis. "No, I didn't. And did you just call me dude?"

"Damn, right I did, *Dude!*" she repeated. Ryan had to fight the urge to laugh. Alexis was back in full force. In high school, he'd seen many guys try to take her on and fall short every time.

"Look, all I'm saying is you work hard. You should reward yourself with a little fun in your life," Declan clarified.

"And you're the guy to make that happen?" Ryan volunteered, sarcasm dripping from his lips.

Cutting his eyes to Ryan, Declan smirked and rubbed his chin. "It's a thought."

Ryan clenched his fists under the table. Declan hitting on Alexis bothered him. The feeling startled him, reminding him of all the times he watched guys back home attempt to get in her pants. Not that many of them succeeded, but he certainly didn't want Declan to fall into that limited few category.

"Thanks, but no thanks," Alexis stated.

Mentally, Ryan pumped his fists in triumph.

"All I'm suggesting is we get to know one another better," Declan persisted. "Go out for drinks. Maybe a little dinner. Some dancing afterward."

Alexis ran her fingers through her hair, pushing it away from her neck. She leaned forward, her lips curled upward. Declan wore an expression of triumph. "Look," Alexis started.

Ryan bounded up from his seat. "Declan, a word," he growled, interrupting Alexis.

Declan pursed his lips and gave Alexis a wink. "I'm being

summoned." Alexis chuckled, a look of relief flashed across her face as the two men walked away.

"Dude, what the hell do you think you're doing?" Ryan demanded when he was certain Alexis could no longer hear them.

"What does it look like I'm doing?" Declan cut a glance back at the table, smirking.

"Back off," Ryan hissed.

"Whoa! Is there something I need to know about this girl? Did she pop your cherry or some bullshit like that?"

Ryan dropped his chin to his chest, shaking his head. His irritation was almost blinding. "She's my friend. I'm not going to have you screwing with her head."

Declan arched a brow at him, resting his hand on Ryan's shoulder. "So, does that mean you want her?"

"No! I told you, she's my friend, and I don't want her to get hurt. I know how you are."

"And how might that be?" he snorted, almost defiant.

"You're a dick!" Ryan yelled.

Declan gave Ryan a quick squeeze, and barked out in laughter. "Guilty as charged, but you forget, I know you're not a saint. I've seen the chicks you bring home."

"This isn't about me. It's about her."

"And she's a big girl who can handle herself."

Ryan glanced over to Alexis. She pretended not to watch them talk, by keeping her eyes on her cell phone. She looked up and caught Ryan's eye, a blush painted her cheeks. She slipped her bottom lip between her teeth and Ryan had the urge to pull it out with his own. He shook the fog of that idea from his mind, and returned his focus to his conversation with Declan. "Seriously, man, back off."

Declan patted Ryan on the cheek, but said nothing. He pushed Ryan's head, chuckling, and darted back toward the table where Alexis sat. Ryan stood there, unable to move. Declan leaned over and wrote something on one of the napkins Alexis had, then folded and handed it to her. No doubt, he'd just given her his number.

Ryan tucked his hand into his pockets and started toward them when Declan grabbed the handle of his luggage. "It was a pleasure meeting you, Doc. Call me sometime."

He threw Ryan an unabashed grin and marched out the door, calling back, "See you back at the apartment."

Asshole.

"He sure does think highly of himself, doesn't he?" Alexis prompted as Ryan dropped back down in his chair, crossing his arms over his chest.

"I'm so sorry about that. Declan is a great guy and a good friend, but he can be a bit..." Ryan snapped his fingers, his tongue darted out over his lips as he searched for the words most appropriate to describe his best friend.

"Arrogant, cocky, self-assured," Alexis offered.

He nodded, his lips curling toward his nose. "Yeah. I'd say those are very astute evaluations."

"We could also include, handsome, alluring, and sexy."

Ryan covered his face. "Lex!"

"What? I can't help it that you have good looking friends."

Ryan's eyes opened wide. Heat boiled inside him at the sound of those words falling from her lips in regard to Declan. He chewed the inside of his mouth, jealousy swelled inside him. "Sure, if you like that tall, dark, and handsome type. But you know how they say men can only think with one brain at a time?" He glanced back toward the door. "Well, that's true of Declan, except he only ever thinks with *that* brain."

Alexis' head fell forward in laughter. Ryan's aggravation subsided at the sweet sound. He watched her, enamored by this person who'd been gone for so long, yet in less than a few hours had completely wrapped herself back into his heart. Her cheeks reddened and her smile brightened, and he couldn't help but join in her laughter. When their laughter died down, Ryan patted his stomach. "I'm hungry. You want to go get something to eat?"

Her smile faltered. "I'd love to, but I should go." She grabbed the bag at her feet.

"What? No. Don't let my asshole of a roommate ruin our fun."

"It's not Declan. I have to go sign my lease or I won't have a place to sleep tonight." She stood up and wrapped her messenger bag across her chest. "This has been amazing, Ryan."

His shoulders slumped just a little. "It really has been. We need to get together soon."

"Absolutely." She leaned down and kissed his cheek. The warmth of her lips against his skin sent molten lava burning through his veins.

As she started to sail away, he stood up and grabbed her by the wrist. She stopped, looking down at his hand. The sweetness of her perfume engulfed him, awaking some primitive piece of himself that had laid dormant in her absence for far too long. He rubbed his thumb along her wrist, keeping her locked in place.

"Where ya heading? I can drive you."

"You don't need to do that. I'll grab a cab."

"Nonsense. Cabs are expensive. We'll take you to sign your lease and then go get dinner. Now, tell me where's your new place? I won't take no for an answer."

Alexis opened her mouth but nothing came out. She snapped it closed then opened it again. He got the impression she was trying to work out a way to let him down easy, but she didn't realize that refusing him wasn't an option. Before long that precious smile of hers caressed her lips. With that, his heart started to beat again.

Ryan pulled her to him, and ensnared her in his embrace. Her arms wrapped around his neck, her face suddenly buried in the crook of his neck. She took in a deep breath and he closed his eyes, savoring the feel of her against him. "Is that a yes?"

Alexis looked up to meet his eyes. "As if I could turn you down."

With a deep sigh, they stepped apart. Ryan stacked their bags together, refusing to let Alexis handle any luggage other than her messenger bag. He slipped his jacket on, and placed his hat on his head. With the luggage in one hand, he wrapped his free arm around her shoulders. Alexis leaned into him just like she always had in high school as he guided her out of the lounge and through the airport to his awaiting vehicle.

Once the luggage was secure in his car, Ryan hopped in, where Alexis waited, and started the engine. "So again I ask, where's your new place?"

Alexis snapped her fingers. "Yeah. That might help." They laughed as she fumbled through her bag for her cell phone. "I know it's on Inca." She found the evasive object and withdrew it from her bag. "Ah-ha. Here it is." She thumbed through her contact list and found her new address. She lifted the phone for Ryan to see. "2690 Inca Street," she recited.

"Talk about ironic," he noted, as he wrapped his arm over the back of her seat and turned around so he could see to back out of the parking space.

"What is?" They exited the parking garage and started through the spaghetti junction that is DFW International Airport.

"The fact that you'll be living only two streets away from me. We're practically neighbors again."

"Are you serious?" she squeaked. A hint of excitement lifted her voice.

Ryan smirked and grabbed her by the back of the neck. "I get to harass you daily now. It'll be like old times."

Alexis smacked his hand away. "Just like old times?" she mocked.

Ryan's lips turned into a roguish grin. "Are you suggesting that I should crawl into your bedroom window every night?"

"Um, aren't you a little *old* to be climbing into a girl's bedroom? It's kind of stalkerish if you ask me."

"Old?" Ryan gasped. "You're calling me old? And stalkerish?"

She shrugged, her brown eyes dancing in amusement. "It wouldn't be the first time I've called you a stalker. And while it was sweet when you were a teenager, sneaking into my room now when you're what...forty-five? That's just creepy."

"Oh my God! I'm thirty-one just like you."

"That's practically ancient for a man. Your best years are behind you."

"Are you kidding me? For a man, age equals distinguished. A woman – well, you're just decrepit."

Alexis' head fell back in laughter. "Decrepit? Really? Look at me? I'm in my prime. You, on the other hand, have wrinkles around your eyes. And I bet you have loads of gray hair already." She reached up and popped his hat, knocking it off his head.

He tried to stop it, but it fell into the backseat. "Didn't anyone ever tell you not to distract the driver?" He rubbed his hair to make it spike a little having been flattened by the hat.

"This coming from a guy who flies planes for a living."

Their banter flew fast and easy between them as they drove through the city of Grapevine. Traffic wasn't nearly as bad as she'd expected. She'd seen much worse in New York, even though she was certain these Texans would refute her beliefs.

Ryan turned on to Inca Street and slowed down searching for Alexis' building number. It wasn't difficult to locate the apartment complex. One of the reasons she'd chosen it, aside from it being practically within walking distance from work, was because it reminded her of the brownstones back in New York.

"2690, right?" he asked, pulling into the parking lot in front of the main office. She took in a deep breath and nodded. "This is a great neighborhood. I think you'll really like it here."

He turned off the car and hopped out. She watched as he walked around the front of the vehicle and appeared at her door. He opened it and offered her his hand. "Welcome home, my friend."

"Thank you, Ryan." She took his hand, slipping out of the vehicle.

"Anytime. Now let's get in there and sign that lease before they force me to take you back to my place and hold you hostage."

Alexis stiffened at his suggestion. Her eyes were wide and her cheeks flushed a deep crimson. "Now, we wouldn't want that, would we? Think of what Declan might say."

"The bastard would demand to share his room with you," he growled.

"And you have a problem with that?"

"Damn right I do. He might be my friend, but I know how he is."

Alexis smirked, starting toward the large, double doors of the main office. "And how might that be?"

"A dirty, rotten scoundrel," he declared, resting his hand at the small of her back.

"Really?" she snorted. "You realize you sound like a gangster in a 1950s mafia film. All you needed to add was '*see-see*'." She dropped her voice, adding a terrible fake Chicagoan accent.

They entered the building, arms wrapped around each other, laughing. A tall, heavy set man, wearing suspenders met them at the door. His thick glasses made his wide eyes bigger but his bright, sincere smile softened his features. "Good afternoon, folks. What can we do for you?" he heralded in a loud, booming voice.

Alexis introduced herself and explained she was there to sign a lease. The man returned the introduction, advising her his name was George, the leasing manager. He was quite friendly and more than accommodating, taking her back to his office to complete the paperwork. As she signed here or initialed there, Ryan sat beside her, nudging her, poking her, and tickling her. Anything to touch her but to also make her laugh.

"You two are an adorable couple," George beamed. "How long have you been together?"

A mischievous smile played across Ryan's handsome features. He gave Alexis a quick wink and turned to the man. "Oh, my. About fifteen years," Ryan joked.

"That's amazing. But you're not living together?"

Alexis tried not to laugh. "We'd kill each other," Ryan continued. "Lex is great in the sack but she snores terribly."

"And Ryan," she added, "is packin' it." She wiggled her brows. "But he's borderline OCD. The man color coordinates his sock drawer."

"That's a shame. Love requires compromise. If you two gave each other a chance, I bet you could get past the little things. A love that lasts that long deserves a true chance," George cooed, resting his face in his hands.

Ryan felt a twinge of guilt for leading the poor man on. He glanced at Alexis who was licking the tip of her pen as she read over something in the fine print. "We're really not together. We're just friends," he admitted.

The man's face squished together in disbelief. "I would've sworn…"

"That's what knowing someone all your life will do for you," Alexis noted, her eyes still scanning the page.

"That's amazing. What a beautiful friendship."

Alexis turned the page, scribbling her signature on the dotted line. Ryan had to bite his tongue to keep from commenting on her doctor's scratch.

After all the i's were dotted and t's crossed, George handed Alexis a set of keys. "The gold one's your apartment key and the silver is your mailbox key. Apartment 10A is your unit."

George shook hands with Alexis and Ryan before they left the office. As they walked out, Ryan leaned in and whispered to Alexis, "I can't believe you brought up my OCD tendencies."

"You started it," she hissed back. "You mentioned my snoring." She sidestepped, shoving into him. "Which, by the way, I don't snore."

Bumping her with his hip, he smirked. "You really think I'm packing it?" He lowered his eyes down below.

Alexis linked her arm into his, sidling up next to him. "You forget I've seen you naked and in swim trunks."

"Yeah, when I was like ten!"

She shrugged, smirking. "How do you know I'm awesome in bed?" she chortled.

Ryan glanced down at her, his lips flat but his eyes danced. "I know you're awesome at snoring." Alexis growled, shoving Ryan away. She got into the car before he could open her door but he caught it before she closed it. He leaned into the car and grinned. "Ryan one, Lex zip."

She smashed her hand against his face, pushing him back. "Take me home, dork."

He closed the car door, lingering for a moment to see her smile when she thought he wasn't looking. Her dark lashes fanned across her cheeks and the curve of her lips lifted in a heart stopping grin. The longing inside him made his chest ache, but he pushed it down. Way down. Having her there, near him again, reminded him of the past. A past that only haunted him in his dreams. But she wasn't a dream. She was there. Time was giving him a second chance to do whatever it was he was supposed to do.

Resting his hand over his heart to cure the ache, Ryan walked around the car, getting into the driver's seat where he drove her to their next destination—her new apartment.

The sun had started to disappear in the western sky, setting the heavens on fire. Nightfall approached as Ryan and Alexis drove around the complex to find her new apartment. When they located the correct building, Ryan parked in her assigned spot. Alexis was out of the vehicle and heading toward her apartment before Ryan could get out of the car. He chuckled at her enthusiasm, sliding out of the car and retrieving her luggage from the trunk.

"Apartment 10A, that's me," Alexis sang. She fumbled with the key, struggling for a moment to get it into the lock. Between Ryan hovering over her and her excitement, she was a ball of nerves.

"You need me to do that for you?" Ryan asked, a hint of

facetiousness colored his tone.

"Would you like an elbow in the nuts?" she challenged.

"That's not fair. I've got luggage in my hands. I have no way of protecting the family jewels."

"Then you might want to hush it."

Alexis bit her bottom lip and inhaled through her nose. Back at the bar, she hated the urge she had to cry and scream and curse at Declan's proclamation over Ryan having a girlfriend. Not that she could've expected less. Ryan was handsome, funny, and successful. Plus the smell of his cologne left her weak in the knees. It was childish and foolish to feel jealous of a woman she'd never met, but she did.

She slid the key into the lock, then tilted her head upward to blow a raspberry at Ryan. The corner of his mouth lifted, but he said nothing. He nodded toward the door as a silent request for her to complete the process.

With a quick flick of her wrist, the lock unhinged and she opened the door. Darkness shrouded the apartment as they stepped inside. What neither of them expected was for the door to spring forward, closing itself behind them. Unable to see, Alexis scrambled for a light switch.

"Ow," she screeched, almost toppling over Ryan. He dropped the luggage in order to catch her, but was met with air. Alexis had managed to keep herself stable. Ryan stepped forward and his ankle found the discarded luggage.

"Son of a bit…" his words slurred. "Where's the damn light switch?"

Alexis stifled a laugh, hearing him mutter a slew of curses under his breath. "Someone has a potty mouth," she teased, feeling along the wall.

"That's nothing," he groused, his teeth gritted tight while he rubbed his now bruised ankle.

"Found it," she hollered. The lights came on, blinding them both. Alexis blinked several times, while colorful orbs danced before her face. Slowly her eyes focused to see Ryan leaning forward rubbing his leg. He looked flustered and one step backward would send him flying over the offending luggage.

"What an odd place to put a light switch," he stated, noticing her hand on the hinge side of the door.

"Is Texas always backward like this?" she teased, moving into the living area.

"Not typically, but they do believe bigger is always better," he deadpanned, retrieving her bags from the floor before someone fell over them again.

Alexis knew her place would be furnished, but this was more than she'd expected. It was a gorgeous loft apartment with a high, wood beamed ceiling and white brick walls. A wall of glass sectioned off the loft area, designed perfect for a master bedroom. A little bar area separated her living room from the kitchen. Everything was stainless steel, from the kitchen appliances to the bar. Hardwood floors and stainless steel light fixtures completed the modern yet antique styled abode.

She turned around to find Ryan standing at the door, her luggage in hand, with his eyes on her. His smile was content and his posture comfortable. He seemed pleased to be where he was. Her mind drifted back to a time when that content smile was positioned across the bed from her. He fit here with her now just as much as he had then. It was strange to think that she'd been without him for so long, but now it felt like no time had passed.

"You can set those right there, Ryan." She pointed toward a stainless steel sofa table pressed against the back of a cozy, white sofa. "Thank you for bringing them in."

Instead of dropping them this time, Ryan placed the suitcases on the floor. He settled one hand on the headrest of the couch and rubbed his jaw with the other. "Do you have to keep all this furniture or can you use your own stuff?"

"That's the beauty of my agreement. I don't have to keep any of this, but I hated my ratty stuff from home and figured anything was better than that crap."

"If that's the case, what on Earth could be in a moving

truck?" he inquired, scratching his head.

Alexis meandered to the kitchen, opening up cabinets and drawers, looking inside. "A television, books, knick knacks, all my kitchenware, clothes," she shrugged, "you know, all the stuff that accumulates over the years and fills every box you can find."

Ryan bobbed his head. "That makes sense. So, how'd you find this place? It's pretty amazing." He extended his arm toward the stairs, making a show of the space.

Alexis ambled toward the staircase. "It was kind of luck, really. I found it online and did a virtual tour. Mom insisted on having Dad check it out, which I did."

Together, they started up the stairs. The closeness of Ryan sent her heart racing. His hand hovered over the small of her back, never quite touching her. "Where does he live now?"

Alexis stopped and turned to face him. Ryan looked up at her, tilting his head to the side, a curious smile curling his lips. "Dad lives in Plano," she replied.

Her gaze moved out over her apartment. It wasn't as big as she'd expected, but it was still much larger than her little hole-in-the-wall back in New York. And it was more beautiful than she'd dreamed. It was the perfect place for her to make a new home. "Oh, I need to take pictures and post them to Facebook. Mom and Jenna will go nuts over this place." She bounced with joy, yanking her phone from her pocket.

Ryan popped his neck, backing down a step to give her room to snap pictures. Alexis pressed her body against the glass banister aiming her phone toward the living room. From the corner of her eye, Alexis caught a glimpse of Ryan watching her. His eyes danced and his smile never wavered.

"You need some of the bedroom, too," he goaded, taking a step toward Alexis. She laughed, letting him direct her up the final steps into her master suite. The loft was as large as the lower level, with a bathroom at one end and a little nook on the other that would be perfect for a makeshift office. "Wow," he breathed, as he reached the top step.

Alexis skipped to the bathroom, her mouth dropped at the marble countertop and huge shower. She took a quick picture and sauntered into the bedroom closet that was almost as big as her kitchen back in New York. She couldn't even begin to imagine filling it up. Of course that meant another picture.

Back in the bedroom, Ryan called out to her, "You're not going to believe this, but you can see my building from here." Alexis shoved her phone in her pocket and rushed out of the closet to find him poised by the window, holding up one of the wooden slats. He waved her over to take a gander.

She slid up beside him, the heat of his body pulsed around her, driving her insane. "You see that black building?" She hummed, trying not to show him how he affected her. "That's me."

"You weren't kidding when you said we're practically neighbors again."

They backed away from the window, turning to face the bedroom. In the center of the room was a large, undressed bed. Nervous tingles fluttered in her stomach. The memory of a young man, no more than sixteen, sitting on her bed with a book in his hand flashed through her mind. His wild, unkempt hair was shoved under a backward ball cap, but his smile burned bright. That same smile reflected back at her now. The face was older, wiser, and more defined, but that smile was the same.

"You thinking what I'm thinking?" he wondered. He jerked his head toward the bed, waggling his eyebrows.

Oh she was. Her bed had always been a special place for them. They'd spent countless nights talking, laughing, dreaming, and crying there. Those memories were a part of her, sculpting her into the person that stood before him now. She recalled how he held her tight; almost to the point she couldn't breathe, soothing her pain. His touch was exactly what she needed. Cora dying had left a huge, gaping hole in her chest, and only Ryan could fill it.

"Why would he do this, Ryan? How could he hurt Mom like that?" She sobbed into his chest.

They lay together, covered under her sheets, sheltered from the cool air the open window let in. "I wish I knew."

She looked up into those eyes she trusted. "Because of him I've lost everything."

Ryan brushed stray hairs from her face. "Not everything. You still have me."

"He left us...alone. To go off with that woman," she spat.

"I'll never leave you," Ryan whispered to her.

"But because of him, I have to leave you," she cried.

"Never. You're always here." He pressed her hand to his chest. "Always."

"Lex?"

She shook her head and smiled to fight the heartbreak of the memory. "Were you thinking this?" She stepped toward him, shoving him back. He landed on the pillow-top mattress with a bounce. Alexis covered her mouth, giggling.

"Oh, you're gonna get it now," he warned, his eyes wild with mischief. She tried to escape, but Ryan was too quick. He caught her hand, pulled her down to him, and started to tickle her ribcage. She bucked and laughed, fighting his advances, but he was relentless. He reached behind her kneecap, and pressed his fingers into the one spot that no one but him knew about. It sent her into a fit of laughter so high pitched it almost had no sound at all.

"Ry...Ryan!" she gasped for air. "Stop. Can't...breathe...stop!"

She tried to push him off but instead found herself ensnared, his hand holding both of her wrists captive. He pushed them up, holding her arms over her head as his free hand slipped back along her side. She squeaked and squirmed, their bodies touching everywhere. As their eyes met, his tickling slowed to a stop. Heat filled the room, sizzling around them. The air grew dense, and their laughter died into breathless panting. She could feel each beat of his heart against her chest, matching the expedited rhythm of her own.

"I can't believe you're here," he rasped, as he brushed her hair back from her face. "You don't know how many times I've dreamt of you."

Alexis licked her lips, drawing her bottom lip between her teeth. She could see the truth in his eyes. This whole day, being with him again, her own dream, it all seemed so surreal.

Closer they moved into each other, to the point she could feel his warm breath sweep over her face. She closed her eyes, waiting for the sweet press of his lips against hers, when something started to vibrate between them.

"What the...?" Ryan jumped back.

Her eyes fluttered opened. The loss of Ryan left her feeling cold and alone. She dropped her hands to her hips, shoved her hand in her pocket, and extracted her phone. Miles had text messaged her, almost frantic since she'd yet to reply to his last message. Aggravated, she rolled her eyes and typed out a quick response to her father. After she pressed send, she scooted to the end of the bed where Ryan sat with his head in his hands. A state of chagrin marred his expression.

"I'm sorry about that. It's my dad."

Ryan turned his head, his smile faint, but still present. "No worries. Your father just saved you from being tickled within an inch of your life. That's all."

The moment was gone. In its place was the return of Ryan and Lex, best friends forever. Alexis shoved her feelings back down into the pit of her stomach, a feat she'd perfected over the years and nudged him in the shoulder. "In your dreams, buddy boy. You've never been a match for me. You remember that time I had you pinned down in the backyard and Dad thought..." she trailed off.

When Ryan and Alexis were fourteen, their parents became concerned about them sharing the same bed. They kept their worries to themselves for the most part, but on that day, Alexis and Ryan had gotten into one of their usual tickle wars. Alexis had Ryan pinned to the ground, straddling his hips and holding his wrists above his head, much like he'd just done to her. Ryan had an apprehension for people blowing on his neck and so she took advantage of the opportunity to make him squirm. Her father walked outside and lost his mind at what he'd mistaken as two teenagers making out. He locked up the ladder Ryan had used to climb into her bedroom at night, claiming they were too old to sleep in the same room. It stayed locked up until after Cora's death.

Ryan let out a little laugh. "I do. Miles was furious. I remember thinking he was going to have a stroke. That vein in his forehead pounded like a jackhammer."

"If he'd only listened."

"He's a father. If I saw my little girl in that situation, I can't say I wouldn't react the same way."

"You want kids?"

"Someday."

Alexis reached over and took his hand. After all their years apart, this still felt right. Their friendship hadn't died. It had simply been put on hiatus. "You'll make a great dad one day."

"How do you know? I could've become a serial killer in the last fifteen years."

Alexis turned her body, her knees pressed against his, slightly shaking. He placed their linked hands over his knee, keeping hers still. "Nah. You never could stand the sight of blood and if you were going to kill anyone, it would've been me for the lifetime of wedgies I gave you."

"True," he snickered and bounced off the bed. "You know what, let me help you make this bed real quick and then we'll grab some food. I'm famished."

Alexis stood up. "Sounds like a good plan to me." She strolled into the bathroom and opened the linen closet. It was empty. She rushed to the bedroom closet. It too was empty. "Shit!"

"Now who's got the potty mouth?" he hollered back.

Alexis dragged her feet back into the bedroom. "You're not going to believe this, but there are no sheets or towels here."

"And you didn't pack any in your bags?"

Alexis shook her head. "I didn't think about it. They're all on the moving truck." She plucked at her eyebrow, irritated. "I've never rented furnished. I guess I expected," she pushed an exasperated breath through her gritted teeth, "I don't know what I expected."

"Well, shit," he laughed. Alexis turned red in the face. "Not to worry. We can hit Target on our way to dinner and pick up a few essentials."

"You don't mind? I mean, I can call Dad." She hated the thought, but it was her idiotic mistake. Ryan didn't deserve to be stuck shopping due to her error.

"Stop it. There's a Target just up the street. I'm happy to help. C'mon." He motioned for her to follow him down the stairs.

With his back turned to her, she released a sigh. It was a stupid mistake but one that had won her some extra time with Ryan. At the top of the stairs, she took a final picture of her bedroom. Ryan stood in the center of her living room, watching her. She turned around and snapped a shot of him. "Welcome to my Facebook page, Ryan Fisher," she chortled.

"You better have gotten my good side."

All sides of you are good.

"If you think scratching your ass is a good side, then yep. I succeeded."

Ryan gave her two thumbs up then pretended to pick his nose and flick it. Alexis snarled but laughed. She rushed down the stairs, grabbed her wallet from her messenger bag, and followed him out the door.

All the way to Target, Ryan reeled over what almost happened in her bedroom. He couldn't believe he'd allowed himself to get lost in the moment like that. It wasn't like him. He'd had his fair share of women, but he'd never let himself lose control like that. Had her phone not buzzed, he wasn't sure what might've happened, but he was certain he would've kissed her.

He wanted to kiss her.

He needed to kiss her.

All of the emotions he had dammed up inside him for the last fifteen years broke free at the sight of her flushed cheeks and sweet lips. The sound of her laughter did things to him that had his stomach tied in knots. For the life of him, he couldn't recall the last time he'd felt this way about a woman, but about a girl, the memories were clear and present. Alexis York was the only person to ever make his soul feel alive.

"Hell," she said, getting out of the car, "I could've walked here."

Ryan closed her door and cleared his throat. "Don't you dare walk here. I'll take you anywhere you need to go." He wrapped his arm around her shoulders, drawing her into his side. Just like when they were kids, she fit him curve to curve.

"Thank you, but my car'll be here Sunday. I'll be good until then."

The automatic doors slid open, allowing them to pass through into the store. "Still stubborn as ever."

"You know me," she chortled.

Ryan grabbed a shopping cart. "I'd like to think I do." He gave her a little wink and began surveying the store. "Now, where to start. You need towels, bedding, and Cracker Jack."

"Cracker Jack? Still? Do they even make that stuff anymore?"

Ryan released the buggy and clasped his hands over his heart. "A boy never forgets his first love." That glorious blush he adored so much returned to her cheeks. He wondered if she understood the double meaning to his comment. He shrugged off his overthinking mind and gave her a quick wink. "And of course they still make it, silly woman. So you better always have it in stock when I come over."

She placed her hands on her hips, glaring at him. "Is that a threat?"

"Nope. Just a fact."

They bounced aisle to aisle checking out the merchandise. Ryan suggested she buy Spongebob Squarepants bedding. When she turned her nose to it, he picked up a Hello Kitty sheet set.

Once again she snubbed his idea, so he searched the aisle and found the perfect bedding. A burgundy set with soft cotton sheets and a matching comforter. She squealed and tossed it in the buggy. Next came navy terrycloth towels and washcloths, followed by two, fluffy pillows.

"Two?" she questioned.

"Well, I need something to sleep on," he teased.

"In your dreams."

If she only knew.

After she'd picked up a few wall prints, a new full-length mirror, and some little odds and ends, he led her to the grocery section where they tossed a few snacks into the basket. Ryan memorized each item she placed in the cart, noting how she didn't count calories but seemed cognizant of what she ate. He respected that. Food was a major part of his IronMan training, so he paid close attention to everything that went into his body. But when it came to sugar, he permitted himself the occasional cheat — especially for Cracker Jack.

As they approached the front of the building, there was a long aisle, clear of customers. Ryan cut a glance at Alexis and started pushing the cart like he was riding a skateboard. He began to pick up speed, leaving Alexis behind.

"What are you doing?" she called out.

He jumped on the back of the cart, throwing his arms out wide, yelling, "I'm king of the world!"

Alexis buckled over, laughing. A little old lady appeared out of nowhere, forcing Ryan to jump off the back. He halted the cart to a stop but not before falling flat on his ass. This turned Alexis' laughter into hysterics. The old woman didn't stop to look at what the commotion was. She simply kept moving.

"You should've seen your face," Alexis cackled, rushing up to him. She took his hand and helped him from the floor. Warmth poured from her skin, setting his veins on fire. It was the very reason he'd touched her as often as he could. She was addicting. The daring look in her deep brown eyes and the way her mouth twitched when she fought the urge to smile caused his gut to ache.

He brushed his knuckles along her jaw. She wrinkled her nose in a cute expression. "Yeah, but I flew, didn't I?"

Alexis nodded. "That you did."

Ryan pulled her into his side, directing the buggy to the checkout counter. As they started to unload her items on the conveyor, Ryan felt his phone vibrate. He pulled it out of his pocket to find Reagan's picture blinking at him.

"You need to take that?" Alexis lifted the large plastic bag with her new bedding onto the counter, but her eyes were honed on the invading device in his hand.

Ryan gave her a quick nod, lifting the phone to his ear. "Hello," his voice shook as he answered.

He looked over at Alexis and shrugged his shoulders. She waved him off with a vague smile.

"Well, hello to you, too." Reagan chipped, a hint of playful sarcasm in her cadence. "Where the hell are you? I thought you were coming over tonight?"

His chest dropped. "Dammit, I forgot."

"Well, unforget and get over here. I got Freebirds waiting on ya," she sang.

His mouth salivated at the thought of his favorite burrito and his stomach growled. "While that sounds amazing, I can't make it. I'm out with a friend."

"What kind of friend? Someone I should be jealous of?" she teased. Ryan looked up at Alexis who tried to pretend she wasn't listening, but it was obvious she hung on his every word. He gave her a wink and watched as her blush crept up her neck.

"An old friend," he answered.

"That doesn't sound appealing at all," she feigned indifference. "Fine. Go have fun with your *old* friend and call me later."

"Will do."

"Later, Flyboy."

The line went dead and Ryan slipped his phone back into his

pocket. Alexis was handing the cashier her credit card, and he wanted to kick himself. He'd had full intentions of paying for everything, sort of as a housewarming gift, but thanks to Reagan, he'd lost his chance to spoil Alexis.

Instead of falling back into their little bubble, Alexis pushed the cart to the car, her head hanging slightly. Her beautiful smile had been replaced with a weary frown and a lined brow. Ryan popped the trunk when they reached the car and they began placing her purchases in the back. He closed the trunk when the last bag was stored and moved to open her car door. When she was secured inside, he strode to the driver's side and got in.

The silence was killing him, to the point he could no longer take it. "Everything okay?" he asked, turning to her.

He could tell by the look in her eyes that the smile she was wearing was forced. "Yeah. I take it that was Reagan on the phone?"

His hands balled into fists. How could he be so blind? After Declan had mouthed off back at the airport, of course Alexis would question his relationship with Reagan. "It was. I was supposed to meet up with her tonight to watch the game and it slipped my mind."

Even her fake smile started to falter. "Because of me."

Ryan slipped his tie off and tossed it in the backseat. Alexis was stiff, her demeanor cautious, a complete opposite of how she'd been before the call. He reached for her hand, and while she let him take it, she didn't clasp his in return. Her trust in him had wavered. His heart sank in his chest. "Lex, it's not what you think. It's kind of our ritual. She and I both travel a lot, so when we're in town at the same time, we tend to get together. Ray is just like another one of the guys."

"Tell me about her," Alexis inquired.

"Um, well," he started. Nervousness clouded his tone. "There's not much to tell. Her name's Reagan Summers, and she's a sports writer for The Dallas Morning News."

Alexis scrunched up her face. "C'mon, Ryan. You can do

better than that."

"I don't hear you telling me about Jenna," he snapped.

She pressed her lips together. "Jenna and I have been best friends since our freshmen year of college. She was in my Ethics class and we bonded over a mutual crush on the professor. She's a pediatrician and has terrible taste in men. Now, tell me about Reagan."

Ryan let out a hesitant sigh. "We met several years ago at an IronMan event. She was writing an article on a local guy who was participating. When she couldn't find him, she interviewed me instead. We sort of hit it off."

"And you started dating?"

"No. Ray and I have never dated."

"But you *have* slept together?"

His jaw went slack. "Um…"

"I figured as much," Alexis chuckled. "I've been there before."

Ryan felt a twinge of jealousy prickle under his skin. He hated the idea of someone having something so casual with Alexis. She deserved to be cherished. "No. It only happened once," he admitted, "and I knew then it wasn't right. I care for Ray. She's one of my best friends, but that's where it ends - friendship. I've never felt anything for her beyond that." Ryan rushed his fingers through his hair. "Yes, we crossed a line we shouldn't have in a moment of weakness. But it's a line I won't cross again."

"A moment of weakness?"

He took in a deep breath. "She'd broken up with her asshole of a boyfriend that night. We had one too many drinks. One thing led to another and well…" He dropped his eyes.

Alexis linked her fingers in his, her true smile returning. "Always the gentleman."

"I wasn't that night."

She gave his hand a squeeze. "I'm sure you were. She's lucky to have you."

"Thanks," he mumbled, a hint of disappointment shook his

timber.

"Now, take me home and go spend time with her. I've stolen enough of your time tonight."

Ryan jerked his head up, his heart sinking in his chest. "No. We're going to eat."

Alexis shook her head. "Nah. I'll order a pizza and you're going to your friend's place."

His shoulders sagged. "Really. I want to spend time with you. I haven't seen you in fifteen years."

She patted the tops of their linked fingers. "We can hang out later. Go." A tremulous note hung in her voice, but her stubbornness was ever present.

With regret in his heart, he did as she asked. But instead of going to see Reagan, he headed home. There was no way he'd enjoy a burrito and a baseball game now. Not when he felt so terrible. Not when he wanted nothing more than to find a ladder and crawl into Alexis' bedroom window and make the ache in his chest go away.

Once he had a shower and unpacked, he flopped down on his bed. Declan wasn't home, so he figured he'd headed over to Reagan's to watch the game. Ryan reached for his phone on the nightstand and checked out his Facebook page. Alexis had posted the pictures of her new place. He chuckled at the candid photo she'd taken of him in her living room. His tie was skewed and his grin was wide, but that silly picture was now his favorite of himself all because she'd taken it.

Exhausted, he made his own post, making sure to tag her in it, then shut off his phone. He closed his eyes and allowed the memory of finding Alexis on the plane consume him. In no time, sleep took him, and in his dreams he was back in that room with her, where he felt he should be.

Where the sun had once shimmered, casting its heated glow on the city, now hung a heavy moon, hazed by drifting puffs of clouds. Headlights brightened the road as Ryan pulled away. Alexis slinked down to the floor, resting her chin on the windowsill. Her eyes followed his vehicle until it was out of sight. A loud thud shook the walls as her head made contact with the sturdy plaster.

She pulled her knees to her chest, willing him to come back, even though she knew he wouldn't. She'd sent him away. Deep down, she knew she'd done the right thing in doing so. He had plans, and had the tables been reversed she knew he would've done the same thing. The fact that he was back in her life was enough, more than she could've hoped or asked for.

The weight of her heart thumped in slow motion reverberating off the walls in her chest, echoing in her ears. In the dimly lit room, her mind played tricks on her; casting a glow of Ryan before her. He wore the same pained expression on his face he had when she forced him to leave. She wanted to erase that look, to bring back his smile. She hoped spending time with Reagan would do just that.

Bright headlights reflected in her window. She rolled back to her knees, checking through the slats of the blinds. A sliver of hope beckoned her, praying he'd turned back around, but the car kept on. It wasn't him. In a huff of frustration, she pulled herself off of the cold floor and flipped on the lights. The bags she'd wrangled into her apartment, refusing Ryan's assistance, scattered around her. She kicked the bedding bag, watching it slide toward the staircase, stopping short of the bottom step.

She grabbed the remaining bags, balanced them on both arms, and wobbled to her kitchen. She thrust the bags onto the counter. She began to unpack them and put everything away in the pantry. A tender smirk lit her face when she pulled a package of Cracker Jack from one of the bags. Her fingers brushed along the white lettering, as her mind drifted back to Ryan.

Wonder what he's doing right now.

She let out a little sigh, shoving her hand in her pocket for her phone. With a slide of her finger, the phone came to life. It took her no time to open the pictures she'd taken of her apartment. She'd meant to post them to Facebook before leaving with Ryan but the thought had slipped her mind. A small bubble of laughter filled her chest at the sight of him in her living room. He looked as if he belonged. Moments later, she posted the pictures with a quick note to the world that she was at her new home. Once the pictures were uploaded, she finished filling her pantry and called for a pizza.

While she enjoyed her dinner, she received a text message from Jenna.

Who's the hottie?

Alexis wasn't surprised that Jenna noticed nothing more than the pilot lingering in her living room.

He came with the place.

Almost instantly, Alexis' phone chirped with a new message.

I'm on the next plane to Texas if they're giving those away!

Alexis barked in laughter.
She typed out,

All you have to do is pick the age, weight, and size.

The phone started to ring. Alexis accepted the call to find Jenna's pretty face staring back at her. She had bright green eyes offset by a long, slender nose, and her skin was covered in freckles. Her blonde hair was pulled up and a huge, devious grin lighted her lips. "Penis size?" Jenna greeted.

Alexis grinned, making her way to the sofa, plopping down. She drew her knees to her chest and rested her chin on top, holding her phone out in front of her.

She'd known Jenna for over a decade. Their friendship budded over their mutual hate/crush on their professor. While he was hot, he was also a massive asshole with an arrogant chip on his shoulder. Most of their time was spent making fun of his quirks or analyzing his dashing good looks. From there, they became inseparable.

"Pretty sizable," Alexis joked, recalling a teenage Ryan in swim trunks and how she'd often wondered what he looked like without them.

Jenna pursed her lips. "Tease. What time is it there?"

"I'm only an hour behind you, woman. You act like I moved

overseas."

A flicker of sadness crossed Jenna's face. "It feels that way. I know I told you to go, but I need you here. It sucks not having a wingman or in your case, wing woman."

Alexis snorted at the irony behind her best friend's choice of words.

"What's so funny about that?"

"Nothing. Nothing. So, who's the lucky guy this week?"

Where Alexis was cautious of men, after all she'd seen first hand what they could do to a woman, Jenna jumped right in, not caring what happened to her heart. To Jenna, each guy was trustworthy until he proved himself otherwise, which they always did. It was one of the many endearing qualities Alexis loved about her friend, even if she had to be the one to pick up the pieces after a guy shattered Jenna's heart.

"You remember Allen down in the lab?"

"No!" Alexis gasped.

"Yep."

Alexis covered her face, shaking her head.

"You know I can see your reaction," Jenna smacked.

Alexis dropped her hand, her face stone cold. "And you know he's got a girlfriend, right?"

"He did. They broke up."

Alexis bounded off the couch. She held the phone out in front of her, as she walked toward the stairs. On her way up, she grabbed the two pillows off the floor that Ryan had insisted on her buying and the bedding bag. "When? Because the last I heard he had full intentions of proposing."

Jenna waved her hand in front of her face. "That was a rumor, but he told me he dumped her. Now, I have a date with him tomorrow night, and I need you here to keep me in line."

Alexis tossed the bag and pillows on her new mattress, and her phone beside it. She unzipped the bag and poured its contents out on the bed. "Like I could help you. With or without me, you'll be wrapped around his dick before the night's over."

"Yeah, you're right." Jenna covered her mouth, hiding her snicker. "So, really, who's the guy in your apartment? I noticed he was in uniform, so I assumed you went back to your old ways."

A light blush crept across Alexis' face. "My old ways?" she squeaked.

"Yeah. We both know how you had a thing for pilots in college. Remember that one in Vegas. Although my favorite will always be the Cancun guy. Damn he was sexy."

Alexis glared down at her phone. "I wasn't that bad!"

Jenna inspected her nails. "I'm not the one who's been in Texas all of what, eight hours, and already had a hot, sexy pilot in her apartment. So, spill the beans, sister."

Alexis released a soft, nervous laugh. "Fine. If you must know, I did hang out with a few pilots today." Alexis figured she'd throw Declan in the mix to give Jenna a thrill. At the thought of Declan, she reached into her jeans and pulled out the napkin he'd written his number on. She held it up for Jenna to see. "One even gave me his number."

"Fuck me. I'm jealous."

She dropped the napkin on the bed beside the phone. "Oh, stop it. You're about to get your groove on with Allen."

"So. You have two pilots. Wait." Jenna shook her head. "There was only one guy in the picture. Which one was he and why did you only get one of their numbers?" Jenna rambled.

Alexis smacked her hand over her eyes. "Shit. I meant to get the other one's number. It totally slipped my mind. And he's the important one."

"The important one?" Jenna quirked a brow. "There's one that's already important? Who are you and what did you do with Alexis York?"

Here came the moment of truth for Alexis. She nervously cleared her throat. "You, um, remember that guy I told you about from Edenton?"

"Ryan Fisher," Jenna intoned, her head bouncing from side to side. "How could I forget? You talked about him incessantly the first year of school. He was the only other guy you talked about aside from Doctor Fuckable."

Both women sighed at the same time. "Ah, the Fuckable," Alexis mused. They sighed again.

"Okay. Enough about the Fuckable. What about Ryan?"

"I sort of ran into him today," Alexis beamed.

"No way!"

"He was the pilot of my plane, and is practically my neighbor again. He lives a few blocks from me. I can actually see his apartment building from my bedroom window. Oh, and the guy who gave me his number is his roommate."

"No way!" Jenna repeated, almost a shrill squeal.

"Yes way!"

"I'm a little confused. Why did you get the one guy's number but not Ryan's? Not that I'm complaining. I'm pretty fucking proud of you right now, but that seems kind of awkward, even to me."

Alexis grabbed her phone off the bed and landed on the unmade mattress. She propped one of the pillows she'd bought under her head and held the phone up in the air over her face. The words spilled from her, explaining every detail from the moment she found Ryan on the plane to his call from Reagan. When she was done Jenna smirked, twirling her long, silky lock of hair around her finger. "Damn, girl."

"I know. Who would've thunked it?" Alexis bent her legs, crossing one knee over the other. Her leg dangled in the air, bouncing in its usual, uncontrollable fashion.

"Not me. Two pilots, one night. You're my new hero."

"Stop it. Ryan left for Reagan without giving me his number. That kind of says something, don't you think?"

"Because you told him to. Had you not forced him out, he'd still be there with you. As for the number, of course, he wasn't too concerned. He knows where you live and he has you on Facebook now. You're at his fingertips. Easily."

"I didn't think of that."

"Yeah, and had you not forced the man to leave," Jenna drummed her fingers together in front of her face, "he might've been in that comfy bed with you."

Alexis jumped up, pushing herself up against the headboard, the pillow contoured to her back. "Not even. Ryan and I were never like that."

"But you did say you shared a bed together until you moved. I'm sure he'd be *more* than happy to share a bed with you again."

"You're one twisted bitch, you know that?"

"Yep. That's why you love me."

"Damn right it is."

"Lexi," Jenna dropped her voice, her face moving in closer to the screen.

"Yeah?"

"I have a feeling about this, and you know how I am about my feelings."

Alexis nodded, planting her feet on the mattress.

"Try to remember that you and Ryan aren't sixteen years old anymore."

Alexis curled her toes around the soft sheet at her feet. She could feel the heat rise in her face. "I know that. Believe me, I do."

Jenna scratched her eyebrow. "I don't think you understand. My point is, you're grown up. Ryan is a man. A man who seemed a bit threatened by his roommate. Not that I blame him."

"Okay, now you're reading too much into things."

"I don't think so." Jenna fiddled with her earring. "His warning you off from Declan is a clear 'hands off' in man-speak. He claimed you."

"He wasn't claiming anything. He's protective of me. Old habits die hard, I guess."

"Protective! Alexis, he all but whipped out his dick to club you with it." Jenna began grunting like a caveman, pounding on her chest. "Me Ryan. You Alexis."

Deep, rumbling laughter exploded from Alexis' chest. Underneath the laughter she felt a surge of intrigue at the idea of

Ryan exposing himself to her. Tingles trickled down her spine at the thought. She rubbed her hand over her face. That was the second time Jenna led her to thinking about Ryan and his nether regions. "Oh my god! Stop that! We're just two old friends, all grown up, as you so eloquently put it, getting reacquainted."

"Reacquainted? The man almost kissed you."

"I didn't say that!" Alexis screeched. "I said it got awkward for a moment."

Jenna shrugged. "And I read between the lines. Had your dad not messaged you, that man would've kissed you."

"Look, Jenna, it's not what you think. We were never like that."

"Whatever, girl. Think what you want. So, tell me more about the illustrious Declan. He sounds like a treat."

Alexis tried to envision Declan's face in her mind. The way his lips curled in a seductive smile, and his gem-like, smoldering eyes, shadowed by his thick brow, but no matter how hard she tried, her mind returned to Ryan. His soft bronze skin stretched over his taut, defined muscles. The way his smile brightened her mood. His illustrious green eyes, almost pale in comparison to Declan's but more beautiful than the most precious of stones.

"He sounds dreamy," Jenna mused. "So does Declan."

Alexis chuckled. "They're both very good looking men. Now, about this date with Allen," she deflected.

Sometime later, the two women had everything plotted out for Jenna's impending date. When the last detail was finalized, Jenna whispered, "I miss you already, Lexi."

"I miss you, too. It isn't going to be the same without you."

The pain of losing her friend ripped another hole into Alexis' heart. In her mind, she was losing one to regain a former. Give or take was the name of the game.

"Get some rest. We'll chat again tomorrow," Jenna said. "And, Lexi?"

"Yeah?"

"Keep your mind and heart open. I know what you think of

men, not that I blame you, but something good's coming your way. I feel it."

"I'll try. Later, girly."

"Goodnight."

Alexis pressed the button to end the call. She was once again surrounded by silence, save the sound of a cricket singing outside her window. She lay back down on the bed, and listened to the cricket's siren song. Her mind started to drift off to Ryan, wondering what he was doing and if he was enjoying his time with Reagan. She imagined them cuddled up on the couch, munching on snacks while watching some sports thing. They'd laugh and touch, and the image chilled her. She had to know more. There was no harm in her finding out more about his life.

She glanced down at the crumpled napkin baring Declan's number. She grabbed it and entered it into her phone, shooting him a quick message. If anyone could tell her about the person Ryan had become, it would be him. Besides, he was a nice guy and it didn't hurt making new friends.

His reply came back almost instantaneously. He made her chuckle and a conversation ensued between them.

Chatting a bit with him, she found herself tired. She balled her fist in front of her mouth, stifling a yawn, surprised how only an hour time difference could affect her. She slipped off the bed, and proceeded to dress it with the bedding Ryan had picked for her.

Another chirp added to the sound of the cricket's song outside. She glanced at her phone, now lying on the nightstand. The flash of a green light blinked back at her. She finished making the bed and fell back onto the mattress. Alexis switched on her phone to find a Facebook notification pending. She opened the app and tapped the little world icon where she found a picture of Ryan staring back at her.

Alexis raked her teeth over her bottom lip and clicked the message board.

Flew back in from NYC today. Lo and behold a blast

from the past hitched a ride on my jet. She followed a certain compass, and did as it directed, leading her back into my life. <u>Dr. Alexis York</u>, would you care to share a box of Cracker Jack with me?

She quickly commented to his post.

Thanks to a certain pilot, I have some in my pantry. I'll share, but only if I get to keep the prize. I found they come in handy.

Several minutes passed and Ryan didn't comment back. She figured he got caught up in his game with Reagan.

Another message came through from Declan, but she couldn't will herself to look at it. Entirely spent from all the emotions she had endured throughout the day, Alexis decided getting undressed before she passed out wasn't an option. She pulled her phone cord from her messenger bag, plugged it into the wall, hooked up her cell, and slipped under the covers.

There she waited, until slumber finally took her into the dream world where she, once again, dreamt of Ryan, but this time she found the man instead of the boy waiting for her. The compass in his hand and a smile on his face.

"Dad, it's not necessary." Alexis attempted to argue with her father. The man was stubborn, and was never willing to take no for an answer when his mind was set.

"Nonsense. Kellie and Henry are dying to see you. Besides, it's not good for you to be cooped up in your apartment all day. We're coming to get you."

Alexis sat on the kitchen counter, her toes dangling toward the floor, her legs swinging back and forth. A cold slice of pizza sat on a plate beside her. She hadn't eaten cold pizza for breakfast since grad school, and the slice of pepperoni had her name on it.

"Yesterday was a long day and tomorrow will be even longer. All I want to do today is relax. How about we get together next weekend?" she countered, trying to mask the frustration in her voice. She knew moving to the area would lead to her seeing more of her father and his family, but she wanted to prolong the inevitable for as long as possible.

"You can relax here. I'm sure you have nothing there to eat and Kellie makes a mean pot roast," he pushed.

A knock at the door diverted her attention. She hopped down from the counter, her bare feet planting against the cool, porcelain tiles, and moseyed to the door. A quick glance out the peephole revealed Ryan standing on the other side with a drink carrier, holding four cups and a white paper sack squeezed between his fingers underneath. She gasped at the sight of him. His dark hair played peekaboo under a backward ball cap. From her vantage point, she could see his sculpted chest fitted under a green Dri-Fit pullover, which brought out the jade speckles in his eyes.

She stepped back, glancing down at herself. After her shower, she'd slipped into yoga pants and a t-shirt. Not expecting company, she was ready for a cozy day at home, lost in a book. Between her father and now Ryan, that wasn't going to be an option. "Dad, hold on. Someone's at the door," she explained to her father. She pulled her hair out of its messy ponytail and shook it loose. With a deep breath, she held the phone at her side and opened the door.

A flicker of something, Alexis wasn't sure what, passed over Ryan's face the moment their eyes met. She narrowed her brow, scrutinizing his expression, but the look was gone as quick as it appeared. In its place, his brilliant smile appeared. "Hey you."

Alexis waved him into the apartment. "Hey back," she mouthed, lifting the phone back to her ear. "Dad, can I call you back?"

"I'm coming by to get you later, Lexi. There's no backing out of it."

Defeated, she sighed. "Okay. We'll talk about it when I call you back."

As she said goodbye to her father, Ryan migrated to the kitchen. He set his treasures on the counter, removing breakfast pastries from the bag. "What's that?" She flitted into the kitchen, sniffing the sweet, bready goodness he had buffeted before her.

"I didn't know what you'd want. So, I got a coffee, black," he lifted one cup out of the carrier, "a vanilla latte," he indicated to another cup, "a mocha, and a caramel macchiato. And before I forget, I need your number, because this would've been a whole lot easier if I could've called to ask."

Laughter bubbled in her throat. "You know you could've Facebooked me."

Ryan let out a groan. "I didn't even think of that."

"Give me your phone." He did as he was told. Alexis entered her phone number in his contact list. Before returning his phone to him, she quickly made a call to herself so she'd have his number as well. "Better?"

He stood there, his eyes fixated on the phone in his hand. A sudden smile appeared on his lips that spread warmth throughout her body. "Much. Now, how do you take your coffee?"

She hopped up on the counter and snapped up the caramel macchiato. He nodded once. "Noted."

"Upside down, extra caramel and an extra shot, if you're taking notes for the future."

He curled his lips in concentration, his eyes squinted, before a smile formed and he gave her a thumbs up. "I'll never forget. Now," he picked up the plate with the cold pizza, "breakfast for frat guys, really?"

She lifted a shoulder in a half shrug. "A girl's gotta eat."

He dropped the plate back on the counter, shoving it aside. "Yeah. No." He waved his hand over the baked goods. "Help yourself. We have cinnamon rolls, croissants, bagels…"

"You got a cheese danish in that mess?" she asked, cutting him off.

He slipped the requested pastry from the bag, handing it to her. "Some things never change."

A soft moan rumbled in her chest as she took a bite. "All depends." She covered her mouth with the back of her hand, swallowing down her food. "Do you have an apple fritter in that bag?" Her head nodded toward the sack with a cocky smirk.

Shifting his eyes, Ryan reached into the bag, extracting a large doughnut. She pointed her index finger at him, howling. "I knew it!"

Ryan dug his teeth into the fritter, ripping into its doughy flesh. "So good," came his muffled retort.

She popped the splash stick from the mouth of her coffee cup, and took a sip. "Thank you for this. I didn't expect you to come back this morning."

"I was in the neighborhood," he teased.

"You're a nut."

"I know it. Sorry for interrupting your call with your dad, though. I would've called…" he tapped his phone and shrugged.

"No big deal. He's determined I come over today."

"And you don't want to go?"

"Not particularly." She finished off her danish and washed it down with a large gulp of her coffee. She made a mental note that Ryan went for the latte, although something told her he would've preferred the caramel coated coffee if given the chance. "But it doesn't matter, because Dad'll come get me whether or not I want to go."

Ryan stuffed another bite in his mouth. Alexis caught herself watching the way his jaw moved as he chewed—slow, steady, savoring every single bite. Her breath hitched, mesmerized by his lips. "What if I take you?" The corner of his mouth lifted, leaving her almost speechless.

"Um," she rubbed the back of her neck, kicking her feet. "Thanks, but you wouldn't want to spend the day with my Dad and his family." Her heart sank as the words tumbled from her mouth. How she would love to spend the day with Ryan. Damn her father for ruining yet another moment in her life. To make it worse, Ryan scowled, his jaw jutting out. She sucked her bottom lip between her teeth, her eyes dropping from the whirlwind of emotions that twisted over his face.

He let out a heavy breath, taking a deep swig of his coffee. "It'd give you a reason to leave whenever you want. And besides, it's been years since I've seen Miles." A feeble smile graced his lips. "And Kellie. It is Kellie, right?"

"Yeah," she muttered, a sneer to her pitch.

"How's she doing?" Ryan dared to ask.

Alexis slumped her shoulders, resting her hands on the countertop. "Good, I guess. I don't talk to her much. When I call, I talk to Dad or Henry."

Ryan tilted his head, his brows drawing together. "Henry?"

Her mouth twitched. "He's my brother." Her almost smile turned into a frown. "Well, half-brother."

Ryan licked his fingers clean. She was captivated, once again, by his mouth. The intensity building inside her grew worse when he placed his hand on her knee. "I know that has to hurt. Cora was such an important part of your life. Our lives. She can't be replaced."

Alexis hesitated for a moment before placing her hand on top of his. His warmth penetrated her nylon pants, burning through to her skin, igniting a need deep in her belly. The urge was unexpected and intense. She blinked her eyes trying to wipe away the feeling that ripped through her.

It's Ryan, she reminded herself. *You remember. Boy next door. Childhood best friend.*

But none of that mattered. The need she had for him liquidated her from the inside. She wanted him and that thought alone scared her. Men were dangerous. Even the good ones could rip a heart to shreds.

But it's Ryan!

Cursing herself, she hopped down from the counter, forcing him to release her. "Henry's a good kid. I think you'd like him."

Even putting distance between them didn't stop the memory of his touch from plaguing her. She craved to feel his strength, the warmth of his body pressed against hers. And that endearing look on his sweet face didn't help. Desire mounted in her.

"Then it's settled. I'll run home, change, and escort you to your father's house."

Alexis thrust her fingers through her tresses. "Gah. All the men in my life are so damn pushy."

Ryan puffed out his chest. A magical laugh flowed from his lips. "I'm a man in your life, huh?"

She shoved her hair back from her face, ready to pop off some snarky remark, but Ryan caught her hand. He pulled their tangled fingers to his chest, his free hand wrapping a lock of her hair around his finger. "I'm happy to be a man in your life." The seriousness that coated his tone ripped to her core. She gazed into those deep green eyes, relishing the feel of his fingers slipping through her long locks. "No arguments. Go get dressed and I'll be back soon."

She nodded, breathless. "Okay." Without thinking, she moved to clean up their breakfast remains.

His fingers gripped her shoulders. The heat of his skin started to sizzle through the thin material of her shirt. "Don't worry about this. Go get ready. I'll clean it up and let myself out. Call Miles and tell him *we're* coming."

Ryan pressed a kiss to her forehead, his lips lingered against her skin long enough to make her shiver with burning fervor. A soft sigh whispered from her lips as his mouth brushed across her brow. Her mind was mush, a jumble of incoherent thoughts. "Okay," she repeated, stepping back from him.

Dangerous. So dangerous.

She forced air from her lungs. Her heart hammered in her chest. It didn't matter that it was Ryan, the boy who once knew her better than she did herself, because he wasn't that boy anymore. He was a man, with a life, experience, and that meant he could hurt her. Turning away from him, she bit the inside of her mouth, fighting the ache in her chest.

Friends. We're friends, she chanted.

Upstairs, she shot her father a message letting him know she was coming and bringing a friend. She wasn't sure how she felt about Ryan meeting her extended family, but it didn't matter now, because it was about to happen. A little nervous, she sifted through her limited wardrobe to find something appropriate that didn't include sweat pants or a pair of scrubs.

Damn me and my last minute moving. She tossed a shirt over her shoulder. *I hate when my mother's right.*

Moments later, she heard the front door close. Only then did her body relax. Out of options, she grabbed a pair of jeans and the only blouse she'd brought with her, putting them on. She tucked the front of her purple button-down into her denims and slid on the only pair of heels she'd shoved into her bag. Once her makeup and hair were done, she gave herself a once over in the mirror. Palms sweating, heart pounding, her throat tight; she thought she might lose it. She shook out her hands, bouncing on the balls of her feet.

It's just dinner. Family. A Friend. Nothing to worry about.

She scrubbed her hands over her face. *Yeah right.*

The whole ride to her father's home had been intense. Ryan reappeared at her apartment, not only looking like he belonged on a runway but also smelling of that woodsy cologne she couldn't get out of her head. His black oxford shirt and gray slacks left her feeling completely underdressed, but she knew her father would approve of Ryan's appearance.

They arrived at the home of Miles and Kellie York, laughing and smiling, but there was an intense buzz that hummed between them. Every time he touched her, she felt as though her whole body would ignite into flames. And he seemed to touch her quite often. Things got awkward for a moment when she mentioned his prior evening with Reagan. He admitted to having gone home instead of to his friend's place. She'd never felt so relieved before, but then mentally kicked herself for having such a reaction. She and Ryan were only friends. He could spend time with anyone he wanted to.

As per usual, Ryan was determined to be the gentleman. He opened the car door for her and led her to the porch with her arm tucked in the crook of his. "This place is amazing," Ryan whispered in awe. "How long have they lived here?"

She rang the doorbell, her brow scrunched. "They moved in a few months after Henry was born. So, going on twelve years, I'd say." The house was magnificent. Another reason why she struggled spending time with her father's family. She'd loved her little home back in Edenton, but it was nothing like the castle style house her father lived in now, and definitely nothing like the small two-bedroom apartment she and her mother lived in after moving to New York. Four bedrooms, one of which she knew was still made up for her, made this house the perfect family home. A family she hardly felt apart of.

"I got it, Dad!" they heard a young, male voice coming from behind the door as it flung open.

A young boy beamed at them. His dark hair was combed to the side, almost too perfect. His smile was covered in metal braces and freckles speckled his face. Piercing blue eyes shone behind wire-framed glasses. Henry had grown a good foot since the last time Alexis had seen him, making him almost as tall as she was. She chided herself for not visiting more often. Henry was a good kid, smart, energetic, and most of all, her little brother.

He shouldn't have to pay for the sins of our father. In that moment, she made a promise to herself to be more involved with Henry's life now that she lived closer. It's what she would've done for her sister.

"Lexi!" he exclaimed, throwing his arms around Alexis' neck. She rocked him back and forth, hugging him just as tight. "Hey, Henry. How's my favorite brother?"

He stepped back, glancing at Ryan, but didn't skip a beat. "I made first chair. Did Dad tell you?" Henry played the cello. He was almost as obsessed with music as Ryan had been with planes when they were kids. His passion for music reminded her much of herself when she was his age. Singing was everything to her back then. She had a journal full of songs she'd written over the years, but once she started medical school that journal was put aside for her new passion — oncology.

"That's fantastic! You'll have to play something for us while we're here."

Alexis and Ryan stepped inside the house. Henry closed the door and clasped his sister's hand. "Anything you want. I can even play a few rock songs now. I've been practicing. I'm not as good as 2Cellos, but I will be. Just watch me."

She ruffled his hair, laughing. "You'll be better."

"Lexi," Miles' gruff voice reverberated against the elaborate decor of the home. His blue eyes sparkled. Wrinkles cut into the skin around his eyes, mouth, and forehead. His light blond hair, peppered with gray, was combed almost exactly like his son's. Tucked to his side was Kellie. Her jet black curls were tied at the back of her neck, and her slender frame was sheathed in a designer dress that would fool anyone into believing this woman was a lady. *Almost anyone.*

I don't know of any hospice nurse who could afford Marc Jacobs. Lucky she found herself a goldmine.

Alexis often resented the fact her mother never forced her father to help them after they moved to New York. He owed them, but her mother was too proud. Now, she understood why her mother didn't want his help, and respected her all the more for her strength and courage.

"Dad. Kellie," she greeted them. "You remember Ryan…"

"Fisher," Miles finished for her. "I wondered who Alexis might've already befriended here." He reached out and shook hands with Ryan. "It's been too long."

"Far too long, sir."

"Come, c'mon in. Welcome to our home," Miles urged them. They followed Miles and Kellie to the sitting room. Alexis couldn't stop the smile that flattered her lips as Henry slipped his hand in hers. She felt content and slightly confused, because on her other side was Ryan, holding her in the same manner her father held Kellie. Like a prized possession. A treasure of sorts.

Seated, Miles slung his arm over the headrest of the loveseat, pressed in close to Kellie. Ryan and Henry sandwiched Alexis on the couch. She crossed her legs, hating that she was underdressed. Even Henry wore khakis and a collared shirt.

Poor kid. I bet he doesn't own a single t-shirt thanks to his pretentious mother. I'm going to have to rectify that.

The thought of defiance brought a soft chuckle to her throat. Ryan leaned in. "What's so funny?"

The way his lips ghosted over her ear sent her body into overdrive. Intense heat boiled under her skin. She shifted, hoping a little distance might alleviate the issue, but if she scooted over any further she'd be sitting on Henry. That left limited room for adjustment. "I'll tell you later," she rasped.

"You better."

She gulped hard.

"So, Ryan, what've you been doing with yourself?" Miles unknowingly interrupted the moment between Alexis and Ryan.

"I'm a pilot, sir."

Miles clapped his hands together, a look of pride exploded over his face. "You did it! I'm so proud of you. It's a wonderful thing to accomplish one's dream."

"Thank you. That's actually how I found your daughter." Ryan cut his eyes to Alexis, his lips quirking into a grin. "She caused trouble on my flight yesterday."

"Did not!" she exclaimed, smacking him on the knee. "But that flight attendant of yours needs to be schooled in good customer service."

Ryan dropped his chin to his chest, laughing. "I'll make sure the captain addresses that the next time we fly together."

Kellie stroked Miles' leg. "What a wonderful reunion. And so befitting of you two. I remember when you two were kids and all you talked about were planes."

Alexis jerked her head in Kellie's direction, daggers shot from her eyes. *How dare she talk about our lives before she destroyed them!*

Miles stiffened, perched forward, as Henry shrank back. Ryan reached out, taking her hand. Her murderous impulses calmed, but the fluttering of her heart ensued. This man was going to be the death of her. "It was a reunion meant for storybooks," Ryan stated, his voice smooth and comforting.

Miles pressed a kiss to Kellie's temple. "If you'll excuse me for a second. I need to check on dinner." He stood and flicked two fingers to his daughter. "Alexis, how 'bout you help me."

She knew he meant business. The only time her father ever called her Alexis was when she was in trouble. She gave Henry's hand a quick squeeze and Ryan a wink, before she lifted herself from the couch. With her head held high, she followed Miles down the hall.

Miles turned on her the instant they entered the kitchen. "What the hell was that?"

Alexis skirted around her father, moving to check the pots on the stove. "I have no idea what you're talking about."

"I saw your reaction to Kellie. Had Ryan not stopped you…" He balled his fists at his side, gritting his teeth. "You have no right to treat her like that. She's my wife, and your stepmother. You'll treat her with respect."

"Trust me, I know she's *your* wife," Alexis sneered.

"Lexi, I get it. You blame me for whatever," he waved his hand flippantly, "but…"

Alexis pivoted on her heel, facing her father. "Whatever? *Whatever?* You have no idea what I feel for you, Dad. You never cared to know."

Miles rubbed his hands over his face, letting out a huff of frustration. "Do you really think I'm that blind? I know you blame me for every bad thing that's happened in your life, down to your sister's death."

"Don't you dare talk about Cora!" Tears burned behind her eyes.

"She's my daughter, Lexi. I still ache everyday over her loss."

"Bullshit! You don't miss her. You were too busy playing fuck-a-nurse with the woman who was supposed to help her."

"I fell in love. That's not a sin."

"It is when you're already married to someone else. It is when you tear a family apart for that *love*," she snarled. She sucked in air, forcing back hot tears. He didn't deserve them.

"Grow up, Alexis. You're thirty-one years old. That happened fifteen years ago. Get over it and move on."

Alexis threw her hands in the air. "Where do you get off telling me to grow up?"

Miles rushed his fingers through his hair, disheveling its perfect part. "The day will come, young lady, that a man will sweep you off your feet, and then you'll understand how I feel for Kellie. I loved your mother, but what we had was a wonderful friendship. My soul didn't burn for her like it should've. Your mother understood that, and so should you."

Alexis growled, turning her back on her father. If he only knew the yearning inside her, but thanks to him, the fear that overpowered it was stifling. She couldn't allow herself to ever feel the misery she watched her mother endure. She'd never give into the temptation to openly love someone. Not for them to shove that love back in her face. Love was fragile, always teetering on the edge of destruction. She couldn't trust anyone, ever.

A silence ensued between them. Neither willing to back down from their opinion. Stubborn to the core—a trait they shared, according to everyone who knew them. It wasn't until a small voice interrupted them that the tension in the room broke. "Dad? Lexi? Everything okay?"

Alexis turned to her not-so-little brother and pulled him into her arms. "Of course. Dad and I were just talking about my move."

"That's not what it sounded like. Do you hate Mom?"

She cupped his face in her hands, shaking her head. "No. I don't hate your mom."

"She loves you, you know." His innocent eyes spoke a truth that ripped deep into Alexis' chest.

"I know she does."

"And you love her?" he questioned, his eyes filled with hope.

Alexis licked her lips, glancing over her shoulder at Miles. He propped his elbow on the counter, his brow lifted as if to say she was on her own with this one. "Yes, Hen." One little fib wouldn't hurt the boy.

The answer seemed to appease the young man. "Good. I really like your friend. He's cool. Did you know he used to play the flute?"

Alexis let out a laugh. "Sweetie, trust me, he didn't play the flute. He murdered the thing."

A loud laugh burst from Miles. "I remember that. Oh the nights I wanted to break that damn thing in two. Isaiah and I once plotted to melt it down and discard the pieces."

"It was awful!" Alexis cringed, laughing. The thought of Isaiah Fisher, Ryan's father, suggesting such a thing made it even funnier to her. She used to envy Ryan for the way his parents doted on him. Not that her parents didn't cater to her, but she often felt left in the background while Cora took center stage. Most people would think that bothered her, but it didn't. She had Ryan and he was all she needed.

"Like two cats fighting."

Henry joined in the merriment, happy to see his sister and father not arguing.

Breathless, Miles opened his arms to Alexis. She stopped laughing and moved into her father's embrace. It didn't mean she'd forgiven him, but for Henry, she'd at least give the impression of forgiveness.

He kissed the top of his daughter's head then turned to his son. "Hen, go get Mom and Ryan. Tell 'em dinner's ready."

The whole house heard the sounds of Alexis and Miles having it out. Ryan tried to keep things lighthearted with Kellie and Henry, inquiring about anything and everything he could think of to keep a conversation flowing, but it was no use. When Henry jumped out of his seat, there was no stopping him. Ryan released a heavy sigh, seeing the pain in Kellie's eyes.

"It's been fifteen years and she still won't let me in." She covered her face with her hands. Her whole body slumped in defeat.

Things started to make more sense now. Earlier that morning, Declan had woken him to let the cat out of the bag that Alexis had indeed used the dreaded napkin. But he was friend enough to share the text messages with Ryan, only after torturing him relentlessly. Ryan read her words, her questions regarding Reagan. There was a lack of trust weaved into every sentence, and now he understood why. The betrayal of her father left scars that no one could see, and if he wanted to earn her trust, he'd have to prove himself.

"Kellie," he started, as he slipped onto the loveseat beside her, and pulled her hands from her face. "I know we don't really know each other, but I'm going to ask something of you. Give me a chance to reach her."

A somber chuckle was muted by Kellie's dainty sniffle. "You think you can? Because not even her own father can get through to her."

"I'm not saying I can, but at least give me a chance," he beseeched.

Kellie looked into Ryan's eyes. Her hazel gaze narrowed, eyeing him in askance. She tilted her head and her face relaxed. One little nod and she gave Ryan's hand a squeeze. "Okay. What've I got to lose? She can't hate me anymore than she already does, can she?"

Henry reappeared at the door, beaming ear-to-ear and slightly breathless. "Dad says dinner's ready, and he and Lexi are laughing."

Kellie turned a weary grin to Ryan. "Looks like you're already making changes in her."

"I'm not that good," he chortled.

"You underestimate yourself."

Ryan stood up, offering Kellie his hand. "That's not in my nature."

Kellie accepted his chivalrous gesture. "I believe that as well."

Together, they made their way to the dining room to enjoy a home cooked meal. Conversation flowed, not always as fluidly as it could be, but easier than anyone anticipated. A walk down memory lane, followed by a cello concert performed by Henry made up the rest of the night.

Throughout the evening, Ryan tried to ignore the constant vibration of his phone in his pocket. Reagan had learned about Alexis through Declan and she was now pestering him for details. He eventually had to respond with a message that he'd call her later, which only created a new flood of text messages from Reagan. Several times he caught Alexis glancing in his direction. He attempted to act nonchalant, but he could see the undercurrent of distrust in her eyes.

Trust me. Please.

By the end of the evening, Ryan dropped Alexis off at her apartment. She didn't invite him inside and he didn't suggest it. He could tell that she was emotionally spent, and it pleased him enough that she'd opened up that part of her life to him. Their friendship had once been the only thing that mattered to them, and if he had his way, she'd remember what life was like when she allowed him in.

All the way home, he relived the evening—the ups and downs. In those few hours with Alexis and her family, he learned more about her as a woman than he could've in days alone with her. Fifteen years was really a long time, and his heart ached over how much he'd missed. He carried those thoughts to bed with him, pondering over every detail until sleep eventually took him to a place where he was once again climbing up a ladder into the bedroom window of the girl next door.

Where ya at?

Ryan shot Alexis a quick text message while marching down the jet bridge.

It had been over a week since he'd seen her and while they'd conversed every chance they had during that timeframe, Ryan still had a distinct feeling of loneliness. It ate at him every night after they'd bid their goodnights. Alone in his hotel room, he'd lay in the bed and stare at the dark ceiling, wondering what she was doing until sleep would finally take him.

Just about to head to the cafeteria for some food. Working late tonight. You home?

Came back her reply.

Face after face whizzed by him as he rushed through the terminal to the parking garage. He didn't care that it was nine o'clock at night or that he was still in uniform. Under normal circumstance, his first destination would've been to go home, change, and then grab food, but now, he cared only about getting to Alexis.

Texting with only one's thumb while walking was no easy feat, but Ryan couldn't stop himself.

Yep. Heading to the car now. Want to meet me at The Kitchen Door? It's a little diner about a block from the hospital. Best coffee ever.

At his car, he tossed his luggage in the back, along with his hat and jacket, then slammed the trunk closed. He popped the top button of his collar and loosened his tie around his neck. By the time he was in the vehicle and the engine on, a text came back to him.

Absolutely! Welcome home. Missed your scrawny ass.

Ryan was about to back out when the reply came. If there was one thing he hated, it was people who couldn't put their cell phones down long enough to drive. He put the car back into park and grabbed his phone. A huge smile ignited his face as he sent her a reply:

Perfect! On my way now. And thanks, good to be home. As for my ass, we've discussed this. It's not scrawny anymore. And I do think you have a slight obsession with my postiere. Would you like me to send you a picture?

He dropped his phone into the cup holder once the message was sent and backed out of the parking space. His fingers gripped the steering wheel tight, fighting the compulsion to read her next message as he merged onto the freeway. DFW airport was a cluster in itself without giving into the temptation to look at his phone. He had to remind himself it was only a fifteen-minute drive from the airport to the diner. He could wait.

Upon arriving at the diner, he parked his car and noticed hers was already there. He snatched up his phone and read her message. Ryan curled his lips inward, holding back his laughter. All week long their messages were filled with innuendos. Toeing the line but never crossing it.

No need. I have the one of you in a Speedo saved to my phone. As a matter of fact, I think I'll make that my new wallpaper...well, part of it at least.

Ryan raised an eyebrow, rereading the message as he got out of the car. He rubbed his fingers over his stubble-dusted jaw. "Must not read too much into that," he muttered to himself, but that was difficult to do. He knew the picture she was referencing. It was him at his latest IronMan Triathlon. He was linked, arm in arm, with a few of his buddies, including Declan, in a straight line. While everyone else was shirtless and wearing riding shorts, he was wearing nothing but a black Speedo, a pair of sunglasses, and a goofy grin; and his butt was nowhere to be seen in that photograph.

When he reached the door, he slipped his phone into his pocket and stepped into the diner. The smell of grease and cheese sent his stomach into a tyrannical rumble. The Goth girl at the counter glanced up from her phone and jerked her head toward the dining area. "Sit wherever you want," she droned.

Ryan barely heard her speak, for in that moment, he found what he was looking for. Alexis sat in a booth, her hair piled on top of her head in a messy bun, dressed in dark blue scrubs. She glanced up from the menu, almost as if she felt him enter the building. He was drawn to her, pulled by an invisible line that was attached directly to his heart.

Alexis dropped the menu and waved him over, her smile as bright as the sun. Ryan strolled to the booth, his hands in his pockets, to keep from running to her. When he reached her, his whole body felt like a livewire ready to spark.

She slipped from the booth and wrapped her arms around his neck. The piece of him that had been missing for the last week was restored in that one simple hug. His arms encompassed her and he buried his nose into her hair, breathing her in. She smelled like raindrops after a fresh spring rain. "Hey, you," he breathed, placing a kiss on the top of her head.

"Hey, you," she murmured against his neck.

For the longest time they stood there, holding one another. There was no urgency between them, only the quiet need to be together. A tall, heavyset, woman with jet-black hair peppered with gray approached them. "I see he made it, doll."

Alexis stepped out of their embrace and smiled. Her arm wrapped around his back, and his over her shoulders. It felt good to be holding her. Almost natural. He hated that he'd had to leave her alone to unpack by herself, but duty called. If it hurt this bad to leave her now, he hated to think what it would feel like after they spent more time together.

"He did. Safe and sound." She patted his chest. Ryan smiled at her, brushing his thumb over her cheek. Her eyes fluttered at his touch.

They slid into the booth, sitting opposite of each other, but their hands remained linked together. "Can I get you some coffee?" the waitress asked him.

Ryan glanced up at the woman, catching sight of her name tag, "Please, Judy. That'd be wonderful."

The waitress grinned at his use of her name and teetered off toward the kitchen.

Ryan leaned back, his thumb rubbing the top of Alexis' hand.

"So, how many other pictures have you saved of me on your phone?"

A tinge of pink blushed her cheeks. She batted her eyelashes and pushed her phone toward him. "You tell me."

Ryan turned his head, giving her a sideways glance. "This is a trick. I can feel it. No girl gives up her phone freely. At least none I've ever known."

Alexis released his hand, crossing her arms over her chest. Ryan felt his ribcage pinch at the loss of their skin touching, but being close to her and seeing her brilliant smile prevented the wide open chasm that had been apart of his anatomy for the past week. "Well, I'm not like any other girl you've known then."

Hesitant, Ryan reached for the phone. He looked around the diner, wondering what the other patrons might think of him holding a phone with a pink cover. "Chicken," she muttered in a low tone.

His head shot up and he met her gaze. Her lips pursed and she wiggled her brows, teasing him. "Fine." He swiped his finger over the warm, flat surface of the phone, bringing it to life. Instead of being greeted with a picture of his package, which was what he feared was the whole purpose of this experiment, he found a picture of her with Cora. The little girl he'd known, all knees and grins, held her younger sister in her arms. Cora had no hair, having undergone chemo, but she was still very pretty for a little girl, her eyes shining with love.

He glanced up at Alexis whose smile had faded. "She keeps me grounded," she told him. "Whenever I question what I'm doing, all I have to do is look at my phone and I'm reminded of my purpose in life."

"She'd be proud of you," he noted.

Alexis smiled, but it didn't reach her eyes. "She had a crush on you. Did you know that?"

Ryan glanced back down at the cute little girl and chuckled. "I had no clue."

"She did," came her response in a soft, nostalgic cadence.

"Scrawny ass and all."

This time her smile brightened her eyes, burning deep into his chest. "There you go again with my ass." He lifted his hip, glancing over his shoulder at his backside. "Are you sure you don't need a picture."

Alexis reached over to her phone, her chest pressing against the table, forcing her breasts to push up. Ryan diverted his eyes. She was fully covered by her scrubs, but the image of those sweet mounds in his hands caused his pants to tighten. She didn't appear to notice his discomfort as she tapped on an icon. A gallery of pictures exploded before him, including the one she'd mentioned. "Jesus, woman, how many pics *did* you save of me?"

The table began to move with the vibration of her legs bouncing beneath it. Ryan reached under the table, placing his hand over her kneecaps. She stopped the instant he touched her. Ryan caught sight of her chest rising with an intake of breath. She sat back, crossing her arms back over her chest. "All of them."

He sat up straight, his back pressed into the seat, hoping he concealed the surprise he felt was pretty evident. He'd done the same thing, not that there were many pictures on her page with it only being a couple of weeks old, but he couldn't help himself. He liked having that piece of her with him without the confines of a social network getting in the way.

"Which reminds me..." She grabbed the phone from him and slid her finger over the glass rapidly. When she found what she was looking for, she thrust the phone back at him. Ryan took the phone, but didn't have a chance to see what she was showing him, because Judy reappeared with his coffee.

"Here ya go," she said, resting the cup on the table. A few drops of the hot liquid sloshed over the top of the cup. "Y'all ready to order?"

Ryan picked up the menu, having forgotten about his hunger.

"I'll have a double bacon cheeseburger and fries," Alexis requested, giving Judy her menu.

He handed his menu to Judy. "I'll have what she's having."

"Got it." Judy wobbled back off.

Ryan dressed his coffee with as much sugar as he could manage, the sweeter the better in his opinion; he then picked the phone up from the table where he'd laid it. The picture she'd chosen was of him, wearing a peach colored Polo shirt and a straw fedora. To the left of him was Declan and to the right was Reagan. On the other side of Declan stood a pilot friend of theirs, Shane Devereaux.

His chest felt tight in anticipation. This picture was taken the night he and Reagan had slept together. They were very cozy looking together, with his arm draped over her shoulder. He braced himself for what he expected to be an assault of questions.

Alexis tapped on the picture, glancing up at him. "So, you remember me telling you about the other fellow I work with?"

Ryan, a little confused, nodded.

She pointed to Shane. "She's married to this guy."

Ryan covered his mouth with his hand. "Holy crap. I didn't even think...wait...I thought she was in pediatrics?"

"Pediatric oncology. Same as me. She's ahead of me by a year."

Ryan let out a small laugh. He was certain she would go on the defensive about Reagan. This came as a surprise, a very good surprise. Shane was a great pilot and a good friend. To know that Shane and Mary would be able to keep watch over Alexis when he was away made him feel relieved. "That's amazing. They're good people."

"I agree. Mary's hilarious. A little scatterbrained at times, but I like her. She knows her stuff."

Her phone buzzed in his hand. He glanced down, out of habit, and recognized a text message coming in. It was from Declan. His head shot back up. "You just got a text from Declan."

"Okay." She reached for her phone but he pulled back. Her brow scrunched together. "Ryan, what's wrong?"

"Why is Declan texting you?" His words came out a little more callus than he'd planned, but he couldn't hide his aggravation.

He had no claim on her, he knew that, but not Declan. Anyone but Declan. He was certain he couldn't handle watching his roommate parade her around if they hooked up. It would kill him. And when Declan dumped her, because he would, Ryan would have to kill the bastard for hurting her.

"I don't know. We were just talking," she replied, ripping the phone from his hand.

Ryan rubbed his forehead, his teeth scraping over his upper lip. "I see."

"Ryan, it's no different than your *girlfriend* texting you while at my Dad's house last weekend," she snapped. "I bet you anything she's texted you a dozen times since you landed."

"Reagan isn't my girlfriend! I don't know how many times I have to tell you that. We're only friends. And no, she hasn't." His chest rose and fell in rapid breaths. His pulse was so loud in his ears. He wondered if she could hear it.

"Just like Declan and I are friends. And we were talking about you. I told him you were home. That's it." She slid her phone into her pocket without having read the text. That mere fact alone made him breathe a little easier. Romantic attachments usually enforced the instant reply rule. "Besides, I thought you'd be happy I get along with your roommate."

Ryan leaned forward, clasping his hands around the coffee cup. "I am, it's just…"

Alexis dropped her shoulders, the flicker of defense washed away from her eyes. She reached out and took his hand from the mug, "You want to protect me. I get it."

Their eyes met and his mouth twitched. "Yes."

"Ryan, I knew the moment I met Declan that he was a player. A hot player, but a player all the same."

"You think Declan's sexy?"

"I didn't say sexy." Her eyes bounced as she wrapped her mouth around the rim of her own coffee mug. Ryan caught the mischievous gleam in her eye.

"But you like him?"

"Well, yeah. Sure. What's not to like?" She lifted her shoulder in a nonchalant shrug.

Something inside Ryan howled to keep her away from his roommate. He knew he had no right to be jealous, but it burned through him like wildfire. He chewed on the inside of his cheek, determined to hold his tongue. He could tell her about Declan and the revolving door on his bedroom, but as she'd already stated, she knew Declan liked the ladies. His confession wouldn't tell her anything new.

In a swift motion, Ryan lifted the necktie dangling around his neck up in the air, treating it like a hangman's noose. He sputtered and gagged, making awful choking noises. His eyes lulled into the recesses of his skull, as he imitated being strangled. Alexis stood up, smacking his hand. Her eyes darted around the room to see if anyone was looking.

"Dramatic much?"

He gave one last good tug on his tie, lifting himself up out of his seat, as if he were swinging from the ceiling. His head fell forward and his tongue flopped over his straight, white teeth. She reached over and pushed him hard, forcing him into his seat.

Ryan's laughter mixed harmoniously with hers. "So, what is it that you see in him anyway?" he asked.

"I don't see anything in him, but I do like his eyes." She blew a few stray hairs away from her face. "I've always had a thing for a guy's eyes."

"Eyes? Hmm," he swallowed, pushing his nerves down in order to squelch his curiosity. "And what about my eyes? Do they appeal to you?"

She straightened up, drawing her mug to her lips. The gold flecks in her caramel orbs sparkled as her eyes widened. Ryan enjoyed watching her apparent discomfort. He started tapping his fingers against his cooling coffee cup, saying nothing as he waited for her to reply.

"Well, urm, you see…" she stammered.

His lips twitched into a faint smile. "What's wrong, Lex?

Don't you like my eyes?" He fluttered his lashes at her.

She took another sip of her coffee, swishing the liquid in her mouth, causing her cheeks to puff with the movement of the fluid. He raised a brow, his head bowing a little to meet her eyes. "Lex?"

Her eyes dropped from his gaze. She ran a fingernail under the loose rubber band of her messy bun, seeming to search for the words to answer his innocent but revealing question. He wasn't about to back down. Because of her reaction, he had to know what she really thought about his eyes.

She gulped down her java before spouting off something in a low, deep breath.

He squinted, trying to make heads or tails of what he thought he heard was really what she said. His heart leapt for joy at the idea that she might've actually said, "No one's eyes compare to yours."

"I didn't catch that," he finally said.

Alexis peered up at him from underneath her eyelashes. Confusion was written all over his handsome face. She rubbed her forehead and closed her eyes. "What I said was…"

Two plates landed in front of them with a smiling Judy staring at the young couple. "Two bacon cheeseburgers with fries. You need anything else? Ketchup? Refills?"

Alexis looked down at her cup. "A refill would be lovely when you get the chance."

With a quick wink and a smile, Judy waddled off in search of a coffee carafe. She returned before either of them could say anything, topped off their cups, then disappeared back into the kitchen.

Ryan lifted the top bun and pulled the tomatoes off his burger.

"You know you can order it without tomatoes," Alexis stated, sinking her teeth into her sandwich. A small moan trickled from her lips along with the juicy goodness of the burger. She chuckled and fumbled with her napkin as she wiped her mouth. Ryan had to adjust his pants, as discretely as possible, to compensate for the lack of room that now existed in them thanks to that one little groan. He forced his mind to refocus, which helped to minimize the rising problem in his pants.

"But then I'd missed the flavor of the tomato on my burger." He popped two fries into his mouth, savoring the taste of the salt mixture on the potatoes.

"Um, okay. That makes no sense."

He picked up the floppy tomato between his fingertips. "Look at this thing. I like my tomatoes crisp or in a sauce. Since a burger wilts it, I won't eat it, but I still like the taste of the tomato on my burger, hence me not ordering it without a tomato."

Alexis shook her head, taking a bite of her burger. "Whatever you say," she chortled through a mouthful.

As they ate their meal, they laughed and talked about his trip and her first week as a fellow. Ryan reveled in her descriptions of people. He already knew he didn't like her boss. Doctor Dale Phillips sounded like a real tool, in his opinion. "Mary and I about died when he started ogling Karen's rack. I told you about Karen, didn't I?"

Ryan tossed his last fry into his mouth, patting his belly. "She's the one with the silver spoon up her butt, right?"

Alexis leaned back in her seat, snapping her fingers. "That's her. She called him out, threatening to contact HR. I've never seen anyone backpedal so fast. It was hilarious."

"It sounds like you had an amazing first week."

A quaint smile blossomed over her lips as she reached across the table, taking his hand. "It was a good week, but having you here, now, makes it amazing." She gave his hand a quick squeeze. "Unfortunately, I have to head back. I get off at midnight, but I'm off for the next two days if you want to get together tomorrow."

Ryan linked his fingers through hers. "I'm home for a few days, so that sounds perfect."

His chest ached as she slipped her hand from his, reaching for her wallet. He grabbed her arm. "I don't think so. I've got this."

Alexis shook her head. "You don't need to pay for me."

Judy walked over with the check in hand. Ryan took it before

Alexis could see it, handing cash to Judy. "No change," he told the waitress.

"Ryan," Alexis protested.

"Too late." He beamed with pride.

She shook her head, her chest bouncing with silent laughter. "Fine. I'll get it next time."

As if I'd ever allow that!

They scooted out of the bench seating and walked outside where the night air had started to cool. The sound of planes rumbled overhead, taking off and landing at the airport. No stars could be seen against the dark blanket of the sky. Only the moon hung in the balance of the heavens.

"I guess I'll see you tomorrow," Alexis said, fumbling for her car keys.

"Maybe I can sneak into your bedroom window, tonight, instead." He wiggled his brows.

"Stalker," she chuckled.

"You're the one who downloaded all my pics. I think that's more stalkerish than my wanting to share a bed with you."

Even in the dark he could see the blush creep up her neck. He reached out to feel the heat under her skin, trailing his fingers along her cheek. She closed her eyes, tilting her head into his touch. Leaning in, his lips brushed along the shell of her ear, "I like knowing I'm this close to you at all times." He patted her hip where her phone rested in its safe haven.

"I like having you there," she panted. She looked into his eyes, brown meeting green, vibrant even under the florescent lighting. "I really did miss you."

He cupped both sides of her face. Unable to resist the urge to taste them, just once, he pressed his lips to hers, soft and gentle. The kiss was over before it began, but the power behind it left him breathless. He rested his forehead to hers. "I missed you, too. Text me when you get home."

Caught in his embrace, she placed her palms on his hard chest. The warmth of her hands against his body sent delicious tingles up his spine. "It'll be after midnight, Ryan. I don't want to wake you. I'll call you tomorrow."

"Tonight," he pronounced. "Please."

Pushing up on the tips of her toes, she placed a kiss on his cheek. "Okay. As soon as I get home."

"Thank you." He hated when she released him to leave. All he wanted to do was hold on to her for dear life and never let her go. He craved to feel her lips on his again. The urge was so strong and deep in his gut that it consumed him. Left was a memory that would burn through him for days to come.

Moments later, he stood in the middle of the parking lot watching as she drove away. The ache in his chest was different, stronger after having kissed her. It was a friendly kiss, but the power of it affected him in such a way that he knew he'd never be the same.

When her taillights disappeared around the corner, he climbed into his own vehicle to head home. His cell phone vibrating in his pocket greeted him

You made my night. Thank you for dinner. Goodnight.

The message ended with a heart emoticon. He couldn't contain his smile, but the ache in his chest throbbed, reminding him that she wasn't his. He chanted the word "friends" over and over in his mind.

He sent her a quick reply:

This doesn't get you out of texting me later. LOL. You're welcome. Talk soon. xx

He pressed send and drove home where he unpacked and waited for her goodnight text.

"You're still here? I thought you left over an hour ago."

Alexis glanced up from her computer screen to catch sight of the curvy doctor wearing pink Minnie Mouse scrubs as she entered their shared office space slash conference room. Mary's blonde hair was pulled back into a high ponytail, and she held an electronic tablet against her chest.

With the last notation complete, Alexis closed her laptop. A sigh of relief escaped her lips. "I had a few last minute things to do before I left." She stretched her arms over her head, her joints popping.

"Seriously, woman. I think we can handle things while you're gone."

Alexis waved her off. "I know, but Alana Burk has chemo tomorrow, and I want to make sure Karen doesn't fuck it up. I swear if her Dad wasn't…"

Mary sauntered to the conference table and dropped down into the chair across the makeshift desk from Alexis. She propped her feet on the table, laying her tablet in her lap. "Big, bad surgeon with a small prick and a God complex," she chuckled, "yeah, I get it."

Alexis laughed. "I want to slap her so hard at times…"

"Slap who?" Dale exited his office, taking his usual seat at the head of the table. His silver hair was combed back, and he was dressed as if he were about to head to the gym. His long nose offset the narrow shape of his face making him handsome in an unconventional way.

"Karen," Alexis admitted.

Dale snarled and stood up, barely having gotten comfortable in his seat. Ever since Karen turned him into HR, for staring at her breasts, he kept his distance from her. Even the sound of her name caused the man to cringe. "My money's on you, Lexi, but make sure you knock her out, because that woman's got claws." He curled his fingers, scratching at the air.

"And you know this from experience?" Mary quipped.

The ghostly expression on Dale's face sent both women into a fit of laughter. "I think that's my cue to leave."

"So soon, Doc?" Mary teased. "We're curious how many claw marks she left on your back."

With a roll of his eyes, Dale raised his hand in a huff. "You gals are trouble."

"That's why you keep us around," Alexis interjected.

He shook his head, winking at her. "Stop playing with fire and go home. Doesn't your man come in tonight?"

No matter how many times she told Dale that she and Ryan were nothing more than friends, he refused to believe it. Deep down, she didn't want to believe it either. Since that first night at the diner when Ryan kissed her, everything had changed. The power in that one, sweet, innocent kiss consumed her very soul. It'd been months since that kiss, and while it hadn't happened again, she longed for it. There was an invisible barrier that prevented them from overstepping the friendship line. Many times she told herself it was for the best. She'd hate to lose Ryan again if things didn't work out between them, but her heart disagreed.

Oh, but when they were together, there were times Alexis felt like her whole body would combust at his stolen touches and misplaced kisses. Her skin hummed with want and need, aching for the fire that sizzled through her veins.

"Yes," Mary answered for her. "He's on the red-eye, right?"

Alexis shook her head, having not realized she'd zoned out. "Um, yeah. Red-eye."

"Y'all have any plans for your two days off?" Dale inquired, his hand on the door handle.

"Other than meeting at the diner when he comes in, no."

"Well, sometimes no plans make for the best weekends. Have fun while the rest of us slave away. See ya tomorrow, Mary." He pulled the handle and walked out, waving at them from the glass.

"Goodnight," the two women spoke in unison.

Mary rubbed her shoulder, rolling her neck as she did. "Well, I guess that means you wouldn't want to get a bite to eat with me? Shane's gone for two more days."

Mary and Alexis had developed a bond beyond work. They both had men in their lives that flew the friendly skies. It meant many lonely nights, but together they were able to look past Shane and Ryan's absence. Mary never asked about Ryan and Alexis' relationship beyond day to day details, and Alexis was grateful for her lack of intrusion.

Over their few months together, Alexis had learned a lot about Mary. Mary had grown up in Green River, Wyoming. Not much could be found in Green River, besides coal mines. To say she hated her hometown would have been an understatement. All her life she knew she was meant for something more than being a coal miner's wife, and felt she had the right to reach for her dreams. She had ambitions and aspirations the rest of her peers seemed to lack. Most seemed happy with what they considered to be their lot in life, but not Mary; and for that she became an outsider.

When she graduated high school, she made sure to get into a college that would get her out of town. School led her to Arizona and it was there she met Shane, a cocky pilot in flight school. Now, they were happily based in Texas, and trying to start a family of their own.

"Thanks, but I think I'm going to head home." Alexis stood up, grabbing her windbreaker from the back of her chair. Fall in Texas was nothing like fall in New York. The trees were only starting to change colors and lose their foliage. The temperatures were much warmer than she was used to, but it was October and it felt wrong not to carry a jacket this late in the year. She'd never spent time with her Dad in Texas during the fall season, so this was all new to her. She tucked the unnecessary jacket across her bag and slipped the leather strap over her head. "Rain check?"

"Absolutely. Tell Ryan I said hi."

Alexis stepped around the conference table, and gave Mary a pat on her shoulder. "Will do. See ya later." She walked out the door, a weight lifted from her shoulders. All she wanted was to see Ryan and that would happen very soon.

On her way home, Alexis started to feel drained. She pulled into her local coffee shop, deciding a cup of coffee might not be a bad idea. Due to a long line in the drive-thru, she parked her car and ventured into the cafe.

The moment the doors opened, her senses were flooded with the rich, savory aroma of coffee and sweet milk. She wandered over to the barista counter and waited in line behind two teenagers who were giggling and pointing toward the corner of the store.

"I bet he's gay," one girl noted, as she leaned into her friend.

"Oh, no. He's straight and my future husband," the other sighed in that girlish sort of way.

Alexis followed the girls' glances and noticed a good-looking man, hunched over a book, in the corner of the coffee shop. His short brown hair brushed over his forehead and his green eyes traveled over the pages of the novel without any care of his surroundings. A smile pulled at Alexis' lips upon recognizing the man the girls had been admiring. Declan was dressed in a blue V-neck t-shirt and faded jeans. She couldn't deny, he did look handsome.

Much like her relationship with Ryan had developed, so had her friendship with Declan. Many nights he'd message her while he was away, wanting her opinion on some woman he was about to pick up in a bar. Most times she'd tell him the woman wasn't good enough for him, but he'd better get in there before some other smarmy guy beat him to the punch. Had they met under different circumstances, she suspected that she might've been interested in Declan. He was a no strings attached kind of guy, which appealed to her, and he was very handsome. But no matter how often they talked, she never felt a spark with him like she did Ryan. She simply enjoyed his company, as a friend should.

As she waited her turn in line, Alexis watched the young pilot. It was rare to see him outside his usual boisterous self. Finding him in this setting, with his long legs crossed in front of him, and his nose stuck in a book, presented a whole new light on the man. Alexis was intrigued, never having taken him for a reader.

Obtaining her coffee, Alexis made her way to Declan. "In all the coffee shops, in all the cities..." Alexis quoted.

Declan's eyes darted up from the book, a cool smile formed over his lips. "In all the world. She had to walk into mine," Declan finished. "I love that movie, and what on Earth are you doing here?" he asked, a shy smile dimpling the corners of his mouth.

"I was on my way home and wanted some coffee. What's your excuse?"

Earmarking his page, Declan laid the book down on the table next to his coffee cup. He waved his hand toward the chair in front of him, offering it to her, as he sat up straight in his seat, resting his ankle over his knee. "I just got back in town and wasn't ready to head home yet."

Alexis accepted his invitation. "I feel you there. This whole week has dragged for me." Alexis sipped her coffee. She leaned forward, resting her elbows on the table, tilting her cup back and forth on its axis.

"So, I take it you had a rough day?"

"Not rough. Just long." Her toes pushed up on their own accord and her feet started to bounce.

His brow furrowed as he took a sip of his coffee. "Doesn't Ryan come back on the redeye?"

Alexis bobbed her head, bringing the mouth of her cup to her lips. "Yep. And the only saving grace to my week."

"I guess that means things are good between the two of you?" Declan followed suit, taking a sip from his own cup.

Her face screwed into deep lines, her legs halting. "Yeah...why?"

Declan glanced up at the ceiling. "It seems odd to me that you never spend the night. Unless you do it while I'm out of town, but with Ryan's schedule...I mean, the guy's never home. He'll make captain before he knows what hit him," he rambled.

Alexis' head jerked, her brows drawn together. "Wait? What? Why would I stay the night?"

Declan smirked, biting his knuckle. "Um, Doc, do I really need to explain *that* to you?"

"Oh my god!" Alexis exclaimed, a bright blush flooding her cheeks.

Declan laughed, loud and hard. "I get the whole saving things 'til marriage, but damn, the boy needs to get laid and soon."

"We're not together," she blurted out.

Declan's mouth dropped. "I thought..."

Alexis shook her head. "You thought wrong. He doesn't see me like that."

His brows narrowed and confusion outlined his face. "Are you sure about that?"

Alexis scratched the back of her neck. "Positive."

He inclined his head, a deep sigh pouring from his lips. "If you say so, but I think you're wrong. The man glows when you're around."

Her tongue darted out over her lips, a coy smile playing over them. "You make him sound pregnant."

Declan cocked his head. "Is he?"

Alexis' eyes widened with amusement. "If he is, it's not mine."

"There are tests to prove that, you know?"

Alexis was stumped. She laughed, but had no retort. An awkward lull developed between them. Declan shifted in his seat, the tip of his finger circling the rim of his cup. Alexis glanced down at hers, unsure why being together with Declan, alone, felt so weird. Declan chuckled breaking the silence.

"What's so funny?" she inquired.

"I was just thinking..."

"I knew I smelt smoke."

A cocky, half grin twisted Declan's mouth. He crossed his arms over his chest and raised his eyebrows. "You think you're so funny. Just for that, I'm not going to tell you about what happened on my plane tonight."

Alexis let go of her coffee cup, her hands reached across the table to Declan. One of her favorite pastimes was listening to Ryan tell stories about things that happened on his planes. She had to hear Declan's. "Tell me."

Declan glanced down at her fingers wrapped around his wrist. She caught the look in his eyes and released him, inching her hands back. A strange expression passed over his face, but he pushed it aside, bringing back his cocky grin. Alexis raised her hands, her eyes widened and her lips pursed. "Don't leave me hanging here."

His shoulders lifted with a silent laugh as he retold the story of a young couple's misadventure into the mile-high club. By the time he had completed his tale, Alexis was buckled over in laughter.

"You've got to be kidding me!" she quipped, panting from her bout of laughter.

"I swear on the moon. It sounded like someone was dying in the lavatory. When we finally got the door open, his pants were around his ankles and her foot was lodged so deep in the toilet it took two attendants and the husband to get her out." Declan scratched his head. "Come to think of it, it didn't sound like someone dying so much as a pig squealing."

Declan imitated the sound the woman had made.

Mid-sip of her coffee, Alexis sputtered her drink, spraying it everywhere. "Damn it," she grumbled, still laughing at the mental image Declan's story had created for her. She picked up a napkin and started cleaning up her spewage from herself and the table. "I swear you can't take me anywhere."

Declan passed her another napkin, his face bright red from laughing. "I don't mind at all." Alexis took the napkin and wiped it over her chin. "At least I got you to laugh."

Making sure her face was clean, Alexis slurped the last of her coffee. She always hated when that last dropped disappeared. She sighed. "I really needed that. Thank you."

"Want to talk about it?"

Alexis shrugged her shoulders. "Nothing to talk about. Really." She wadded up the spent napkins, and rested them beside her cup.

Declan reached across the table and patted the top of Alexis' hand. It didn't produce the electrical spark that she always felt with Ryan, but Declan's touch was still comforting.

"I'm sorry you had such a shitty day, but I'm glad you bumped into me tonight. Seeing you smile made my day," Declan stated with a wink.

"I'm glad I bumped into you, too," she agreed, glancing at Declan's hand still over top of hers.

The vibration of her cellphone in her pocket caused her to jump. She pulled her hand back from Declan, slipping her phone out. Right on time, Ryan's nightly message arrived. Her weary smile exploded into a genuine one as she swiped her finger over the bar to read the message.

Hope you had a wonderful day. Miss you loads.

"Secret admirer?" Declan questioned. His intention was to sound playful, but it came out more as an accusation.

"Just Ryan," she responded, ignoring Declan's invasive tone.

"I figured."

Alexis' head shot up, her eyes fixed on him. "How so?" Her voice rose an octave, as her shoulders rounded as she took in Declan's accusing tone.

"Just a hunch." Declan rubbed the back of his neck, looking down at the table that held his book, their empty coffee cups, and the massive pile of used napkins. "Look, I'm sorry. I didn't mean that to come out as it did. It's just...your relationship...it seems..." he let out a frustrated sigh. "Can we start over?" A somber smile eclipsed his apologetic tone.

"Of course, but first, explain to me what you mean."

Declan pressed his thumb into his eyebrow, chuckling. "I'd rather not."

Alexis kicked his shin under the table. Declan let out a small yelp and grabbed his leg. "You better tell me," she demanded, "or I won't be so gentle the next time."

"That was gentle?" He rubbed his shin. "Are you always so abusive?"

Alexis crossed her arms, smirking. "Do you really want to find out?"

Declan waved his hands in front of his face. "Fine! You win. Have you ever wondered why I never asked you out?"

Tucking her bottom lip between her teeth, she pondered the question. "You know, now that you mention it..." she chortled.

He tapped his finger against the blackened screen of her cell phone that laid on the table. "Your boy, Ryan."

A small gasp escaped her. "Whatever."

"I'm serious. He damn near has a conniption when I let it slip that we talk. That's why I thought you were together."

Alexis let out a heavy sigh, her smile disappeared. Since Ryan's reaction to their texting several months back, she'd done her best to keep things discreet between her and Declan. It wasn't as if she wanted to pursue him as anything more than a friend, but hearing Declan's description of Ryan's reaction frustrated her. "I told you, he doesn't see me like that."

"I call bullshit. Now, tell me, what's the real story?" Declan inquired.

Her shoulders dropped and her head fell, but for the first time since Jenna, Alexis opened up to someone. The memories of the past flowed out of her like a river of regrets and fears. The death of her sister, the loss of her family, the mere fact that she never wanted to suffer over love the way her mother did, everything she was certain Ryan knew, but never pressed her to explain was all out on the table. When she was done, Declan reached over and grabbed her hands.

"I get it. You've convinced yourself he doesn't see you as more than a friend because you're worried about Reagan, aren't you?"

She took in several deep breaths, before she released them through her nose. "Tell me about her. Ryan's so vague. I know they still hang out, and I can't tell him not to. He owes me nothing, but I feel like he keeps us separated and we each have a different part of him."

Declan scooted back in his chair, his arms crossed over his chest. "You couldn't be more wrong, I can tell you that."

"I know they slept together," she blurted out.

"He told you that?" Declan appeared shocked and a little confused.

She shrugged, picking at her cuticle.

He scratched the top of his head, his face scrunched tight. "I don't know how I can expand any further than that."

"It was silly of me to ask."

Declan reached out to touch her only to pull back. "No, it wasn't. Look, all I know is they slept together once. I know I pull

Ryan's chain a lot about her, but I don't mean it. I only do it to rile him up because I know how he feels for you."

"How he feels about me?"

"I'm not touching that one with a ten foot pole." He chucked her chin. "Just trust me when I say, don't worry about Reagan. She's not what I would call the committing kind of girl, if you know what I mean." He clicked his tongue as he gave her a suggestive wink.

"Fine." Alexis waved a hand in dismissal. She should've known Declan would've defended Ryan. And while he only meant to make her feel better, in turn he made her worry more. From what she'd seen on Ryan's Facebook page, Reagan was gorgeous. She could easily understand why Ryan might be attracted to her. Determined to not let it bother her anymore for the night, she rolled her shoulders and released a cleansing breath.

She returned her gaze to her phone, knowing Ryan was probably wondering why she hadn't replied yet. She rested her fingers against the flat surface. "You know, we should bump into each other more often," she suggested. "I've enjoyed chatting with you tonight."

"Remember what I said about Ryan having my balls on a platter? Try more like a skewer."

Alexis blew raspberries, rolling her eyes. "If he can hang with Reagan, I can hang with you."

Declan shook his head. "You're asking for trouble, girly, but I'm game." His laughter filled the cafe. "What do you say to us getting a bite to eat?" he offered.

"I'm not dressed to go out." She pointed to her favorite black scrubs with hot pink trim. Her hair was pulled back, much like Mary's had been, and she knew her makeup was far from flawless. She wasn't the type to reapply even a smidgen of lipstick throughout the day, unlike how many of the other doctors and nurses did. "Plus, I really should be heading home. I told Ryan I'd meet him at the diner when he arrived. I don't want to ruin my appetite."

"I promise we won't ruin your appetite. And you look amazing," he complimented. "Besides, it's not like this is a date or anything."

Alexis laughed and nodded. "True. You have a fond attachment to your testicles from what I understand."

Declan reached down between his legs. "A very fond attachment." He squeezed and shook his package. Alexis gasped, pretending to cover her eyes.

"Point taken, although I have to say, I might need a microscope to find those things."

"Oh, you didn't just insult my thunder down under."

Alexis' mouth dropped open. "And you seriously didn't just call your junk the thunder down under."

It was at that moment Alexis' stomach decided to join in the conversation and grumble with its need for sustenance. "Well, I guess that settles it," Declan announced. "Your stomach just gave you away. Let's get some grub."

Embarrassed, Alexis flattened her hands over her stomach. "Fine. You win that round by default."

Standing up, Declan picked up his book. "Believe what you want, Doc. We both know you were looking."

Alexis smiled with rapt amusement. "True, but not for the reasons you think."

He clicked his tongue, smirking. "Whatever helps you sleep at night, sweetheart." He patted her head, grabbing their trash from the table. While he discarded of their garbage, Alexis snapped up her phone and replied back to Ryan.

It'll be better when you get home. Miss you, too. Be safe and see you soon.

She ended the message with her standard heart emoticon and pressed send. Glancing up, she caught a glimpse of Declan perched by the door watching her. His book was tucked under his arm and his eyes narrowed as she slipped her phone back into her pocket.

He graced her with a flattering smile, bowed his head, and opened the door for her. She stood up and walked over to him, patting his shoulder as she exited the shop. The night air was brisk, making her grateful she'd brought her windbreaker after all. There wasn't a moon in the sky and the stars had no luster, even though it was a cloudless night. She inhaled the cool night air, feeling her phone pulse in her pocket.

"I'll follow you," she noted, pointing toward her car.

"Sounds good."

They parted, each heading toward their respective vehicles. Once inside, she turned on the heat, pulling her phone back from her pocket as she waited for Declan. Ryan had responded to her message with nothing more than a heart, producing a smile to her face. Declan honked at her, bringing her back into the moment. She dropped her phone in the cup holder and followed him out of the parking lot. What she didn't expect was for him to direct her back to his and Ryan's apartment, where they shared in Declan's exquisite cooking abilities, work horror stories, laughs, and one too many bottles of wine.

Home!

Before Alexis returned to his life, long trips had always been Ryan's favorite. He never had any issues working week long stretches. More often than not, he even asked for more flight time. The more hours he accumulated the closer he came to making captain. But now, those trips almost killed him. He stopped asking for hours as often, because spending time with Alexis was his top priority. Anytime they were together his whole world felt complete. He savored their long talks, the sound of her laughter, the way she felt pressed against his body, but more than anything, he loved that she was starting to open up to him.

As soon as the plane landed, he messaged her, but no

response came. He brushed it off thinking she was probably doing her last minute rounds. She'd told him she had a few days off from work, which excited him, as he was off work, too.

When he got to his car, he texted her again. A little reminder that he'd made it home, but he got nothing in response, which was unlike Alexis.

There was a twinge of panic in his gut. Maybe something was wrong.

He shoved it aside as him overreacting and tried calling her. It was possible she'd fallen asleep at the hospital. It wouldn't be the first time that'd happened. When it came to her patients, Alexis was a machine, one of the many qualities Ryan admired about her. "Lex, it's me. I'm sure you're okay, but I haven't heard from you. I'm home. Call me and let me know if we're still meeting at the diner."

But still no response.

He stopped off at the diner, thinking maybe she'd gone straight there, or maybe her phone had died. But when he arrived, there was no Alexis.

Again, he called, "Okay, Lex, you're starting to worry me. Call me, please."

His mind whirled with an infinite number of possibilities of what could hold her up. The swirl of panic in his gut began to trickle up his spine. He headed to the hospital, only to find Mary, who'd informed him that Alexis had left work hours before. This worried him even more. Something had to be terribly wrong.

"Lex," he called her again, "I'm on my way to your place. Please be there."

But she wasn't. Her car was gone and her apartment was dark. That didn't stop him from banging on her door, hoping that maybe she was there but asleep. Who cared if the world was asleep? His girl was missing and it scared him to death.

On his way back to his car, he called her again, "Alexis, where are you? Please, if nothing more, let me know you're safe."

It was only a few blocks to his apartment, and in that time he contemplated contacting the police.

Maybe she's at Miles' place.

The instant that thought came into his head, it left. He knew better. Things between Miles and Alexis had become a little more cordial as time passed, but not by much. He couldn't imagine her staying the night with them. Not if it meant her missing their time together.

All the way home, his heart raced. He imagined the worst. Car accident, leaving her helpless and alone. A store robbery and at that moment some crazed lunatic was holding a gun to her head. So many scenarios filled his head, but never in his wildest imagination would he have expected to find her at his place.

What the hell?

There, parked in his spot, was her car, and next to it was Declan's. Here he was, ready to call the cops and she was there. Relief flooded him at the thought she was safe. A little confused at what she'd be doing at his place, he unloaded his luggage from the car and made his way into the apartment building.

He tried not to think, letting his mind and body go blank as he took the elevator up to his floor. It was quiet, no one around, as he'd expect at that time of the morning. Out of the elevator, he walked down the hall, trepidation mounting in him with each step.

The door opened with a creaking sound, but instead of finding Alexis sitting in his living room, as he'd hoped, he was welcomed by complete darkness. The lights were off and the place was silent. Ryan left his luggage at the door and walked toward the kitchen. He flipped on the light to find dishes in the sink and two wine glasses sitting on the counter. Next to the empty glasses were Alexis' messenger bag and cell phone.

But still no one was around.

He couldn't wrap his mind around what he was seeing. Not Alexis. Not with Declan. That was impossible. The room started to spin. Air wouldn't fill his lungs. Every inch of his body prickled and the walls around him felt as if they'd cave in on him at any moment. He felt crushed. Hurt. Defeated.

Placing his hands on the counter, he steadied himself, and forced air into his lungs. The click of a door caught his attention. He glanced down the hall and his heart stopped. There stood Alexis, sneaking out of Declan's bedroom. Her hair was tousled and she still wore her scrubs, suggesting she came there straight from work.

Blood boiled under his skin. He stood up straight and balled his fists at his side, his teeth clenched together. She stopped the instant she noticed him.

"I was just about to text you. I'm so sorry," came her hushed whisper.

"Save it. I get it. You were a little busy." His body shook with the sting of his anger. Betrayal. All this time he thought things were progressing between them. He longed for her, and he hated how seeing her leave Declan's room made him feel. He wanted to rush into his roommate's room and beat him within an inch of his life.

"Excuse me?" she hissed, as she moved down the hall, glancing over her shoulder one last time.

He extended his hand out toward the vacated door. "You. Were. Busy." He enunciated each word as if speaking to a child. He squared his shoulders, taking in a deep breath. "And I'm sorry if I interrupted y'all. I can leave if you need me to."

"Ryan, it's not what you think. I ran into Declan at…"

He sniffed hard, waving his hand. "It's cool." He played it off. He wouldn't allow her to see how crushed he was on the inside. The nerdy little teenage boy buried deep inside him raised his head, pointing out that, once again, she'd chosen someone else over him. Maybe it would've been better if she'd never come back into his life.

"No, you don't get it." She moved toward him, her hands extended out.

Ryan took a step back. "I do, and it's all good. It's really none of my business."

She hunched her shoulders, her brow furrowed and her face scrunched up. "You don't care?"

"Why should I? It's not like we're together or anything."

Those words almost choked him. He felt his mouth go dry and his stomach lurch. The expression on her face made it even worse.

"You're right. We're not together." Her voice sounded weak, defeated.

She brushed past him to collect her belongings. Everything about that one, little touch set his soul afire and that only added fuel to his anger. He didn't want her to make him feel alive. He hated that all he wanted to do was kiss her and force her to forget Declan ever existed. He backed away, putting distance between them.

"I guess I'll see you later," she rasped.

"Sure. Call me. Maybe we can do something this weekend."

"I thought…" She closed her eyes and shook her head. "You know what, don't bother."

"Huh?"

The hurt that had been so evident in her disappeared. Fury now radiated from her; she was on the verge of explosion. "Don't bother wasting your time on me this weekend. I'm sure you've got better things to do. Or maybe better people."

"What the hell's that supposed to mean?"

"It means, I've lived here for almost four months now and you still haven't introduced me to Reagan. You get your cake and eat it, too. You look down on me for being here tonight, but I'm not supposed to think anything of *her*."

"Are you fucking kidding me?" He threw his hands in the air. "We're back on Reagan again? If you want to meet her, fine!"

"What the hell is going on out here?" Declan stumbled from his bedroom, shirtless. His eyes drooped with sleep and his hair was a mess.

"Nothing," Ryan seethed.

"I'm leaving," Alexis announced. "And thanks for the best sex I've ever had, Deck. We'll have to do it again soon."

Declan's eyes were suddenly wide and awake. "Wha—"

148

Alexis didn't give either of them time to say anything. She walked out the door, and slammed it behind her. The whole apartment rattled at the sheer force behind her escape.

Declan scratched the apple of his ass, plopping down on the kitchen chair. "What the hell just happened?"

Ryan shoved his shoulder. Declan sprang up in defense. "I thought I told you she was off limits," Ryan yelled. He jabbed his index finger into Declan's chest.

The corner of Declan's mouth lifted. "You did."

"Then what the hell was that!" Ryan flung his hand toward the door.

Declan pushed around Ryan, and returned to his seat. "We bumped into each other last night. One thing led to another and we ended up back here."

Ryan slammed his hand on the counter. "What happened?"

"Well, you know, I'm not the kind of guy to kiss and tell, but Lexi, man..." he moaned.

The sound of Declan's voice grated Ryan's nerves. Anger surged through him to the point that a vein in his neck popped out.

Declan broke into a fit of laughter. He buckled over, holding his stomach. "You should see your face right now."

"What the fuck is wrong with you?"

"*Fuck?* Oh, man. You really *are* mad. I wish I had my phone to record this. No one will ever believe that Ryan Fisher has a breaking point."

Ryan shoved Declan's shoulder again, his rage controlled him. Declan stood up, his fists balled at his sides and his laughter disappearing. "Don't think I won't hit you."

"Do it," Ryan sneered. "It'll give me a reason to kick your ass."

Declan crossed his arms over his chest. "God, you have it bad."

Ryan pushed his shoulder again, a little harder. "Don't give me that shit, fucker. I swear to God if you hurt her..."

Declan stepped back, his arms tightened over his chest. "I'm not the one who hurt her, you idiot! You did!"

Dismay and confusion swirled around inside Ryan's head. His mouth dropped and he turned an incredulous look on Declan. "What are you talking about?"

Declan walked around to the sink. He grabbed a glass from the cabinet and filled it with water. Ryan watched and waited. Never in his life had he wanted to beat someone so badly. This supposable friend of his not only banged the one person he'd specifically asked him not to, but was torturing Ryan on purpose.

"Declan," he growled.

On that note, his roommate turned around, taking a hard gulp of water. He released a gasp of satisfaction and placed the cup on the counter. "You're a fucking idiot. That's what I'm talking about," he started, scratching along his stubbled jaw. "Nothing happened between Lexi and me."

"Say what?"

Declan rolled his eyes, and leaned back against the counter, crossing his legs out in front of him. "Listen to the words I am saying. I did not sleep with Alexis York tonight."

Ryan's face contorted. "But I saw her…"

"Coming from my room, yes." He nodded. "We ran into each other at the coffee house last night and I asked her over for dinner. She initially turned me down, because she didn't want to ruin her appetite for your little, whatever the hell it is y'all do, thing. But I convinced her to come anyway. She had a few too many drinks and was in no shape to drive, so I put her to bed. I fully intended on staying awake until you came home, but the next thing I knew, you two were going head to head in here."

"You could've called or texted me. I was worried sick about her."

Declan shrugged. "I fell asleep, and texting you was the last thing on my mind."

"So you two really didn't…?" He bobbed his head back and forth.

Declan laughed. "Nope. Not even a kiss."

Plopping down into a chair, Ryan dropped his head into his hands. She'd tried to tell him that and he refused to listen. "I'm such an ass."

"Yeah, you are." Declan walked back to the table and plopped down into the chair across from Ryan. He nudged Ryan's knee with his knuckles. "But I'll tell you this, you need to man up with her. Either shit or get off the pot."

Ryan tugged at his collar, giving Declan his most disapproving expression. "That's a crude way of putting it."

Declan leaned back, cupping the nape of his neck in his hands. "I'm just calling it like I see it." He hooked his feet around the legs of the chair. "This isn't high school, buddy. You're not that guy anymore and she's not that girl. If she'd been any other woman, you would've already made your move. Stop being a pussy and do it already, before somebody else does."

"It's not that easy. There are things in our past..."

"Bullshit. You're making this so much more difficult than it should be. That woman thinks you hung the moon, but she also thinks you don't care for her in that way."

Ryan rested his elbows on the table. "It really is more complicated than that. Things with her dad..."

"Stop making excuses. You need to man the fuck up. What you're doing is mind games, and that's not your style. It's mine. I mean, I get you wanting to be like me and all, I'm pretty awesome, but don't. It doesn't suit you."

Ryan let out a good hard laugh. "Trust me, you're the last person I'd want to be like. I happen to enjoy the use of my dick and Lord only knows how many diseases you carry. Some probably haven't even been discovered yet."

Declan reached for his water, taking a drink. "Donate me to medical science when I'm gone, but for now, my disease infested body is having a hell of a lot of fun."

Even though Ryan laughed at his friend's crassness, he couldn't push aside the agony eating him from the inside. He reached into his pocket and pulled out his phone. "What the hell am I going to say to her?"

"That you're a sorry dick," Declan stated, matter of factly.

A somber laugh slipped from his throat. "Understatement of the year."

He tried calling Alexis but it went straight to voicemail. His shoulders slumped as he listened to her voice reminding him to leave a message. "Lex, I'm sorry I jumped to conclusions," he spoke to the machine. Declan smirked, giving him a wink. "I should've listened to you. Please call me back."

When Ryan disconnected, Declan stood up and patted his shoulder. "The sun's almost up, so I'm going back to bed."

"I thought vampires didn't sleep," Ryan quipped.

Declan twisted his mouth, his head tilted to the side. "I'm what you might call a traditional vampire. Sleep all day, play all night."

Ryan tried not to laugh but failed. "Yeah, well, rest in peace, my friend. I'm going to Lex's place. I have to apologize."

"You do what you think's best, but I think you should wait. Let her cool off for a bit."

Ryan rubbed his hands over his face. "What if she doesn't?"

"She will. Just give her time." Ryan lifted his eyes at the sound of Declan's chuckle. "Still can't believe I missed getting that on film. You should've seen yourself. I don't think I've ever seen you that pissed."

"Shut up!"

"No! Really! Now I know why they call jealousy the green-eyed monster, because you were one scary green-eyed monster."

"You don't know how to shut up, do you?" Ryan propped his elbow on the table, shaking his head.

Declan grabbed his glass of water, laughing. As Declan stepped around the table to head back to his room, a knock came at the door. Ryan's head shot up. They both turned to look at the door. "Ah, see. All's good in the world. Go kiss, makeup, and then fuck like rabbits. Have lots of babies and be happy."

Ryan's grin dropped, shaking his head. "Only you'd go there."

He stood up and rushed to the door. Taking a deep breath, he turned the knob and opened it. A woman stood on the other side, but it wasn't Alexis. Reagan, tall and slim, with dark hair and big brown eyes, that were almost black, grinned back at him. She raised a white paper sack in her hand, dangling it in front of him like a bone.

"On second thought," Declan proclaimed, "hold off on the sex and babies part."

Ryan slapped his hand over his face. *It's official. I'm screwed.*

Mad as hell, Alexis slammed her foot down on the gas pedal, peeling out of Ryan's parking lot. She was beyond furious with him. Tears streamed down her cheeks, making it hard to see the road, but she couldn't slow down. She had to get away from there and fast.

How dare he treat her as if she were a commonplace whore? So what if she'd stayed the night with Declan. It wasn't as if she was bound to Ryan by anything beyond friendship. His overprotective nature was endearing for awhile but when it led to him treating her this way, it was nothing more than a nuisance.

Rage boiled inside her, pushing her harder and harder over the edge. Conflicted rage and sadness blended inside her. She ached to hit something...or someone.

By the time she reached her apartment, parked her car, and unlocked the door, her cell phone was vibrating. She glanced down to find Ryan's name blinking up at her. Without hesitation, she declined the call and let it go straight to voicemail.

She stumbled into the dark edifice fighting mad and hurt to her very core. "He wouldn't even listen to me," she yelled at the walls, as she shook her fists. "Asshole!"

Her bag landed on the couch with a thud as she flipped on the lights, brightening her home. After all these months, this place had become hers. There were hints of Ryan throughout her apartment, which only angered her more.

She clenched her fingers around her cell, catching the notification that she had a new voicemail. Out of habit, and a little apprehension that work might be one of the awaiting voice messages, she decided it was best to listen. Her anger once again surged while she listened to the fear in Ryan's voice with each new message he'd left her before finding her in his apartment. Anxiety pierced her ears as he made each new plea for her to call him. By the time she reached the last message, she wanted nothing more than to punch Ryan.

"Sure, he believes Declan," she growled, certain Declan had divulged the truth to Ryan.

Making her way into the kitchen, she tossed her phone on the counter. Parched, she fixed herself a glass of water and opened the pantry. Not that she was hungry, but the knot in her stomach needed to be settled. There, on the second shelf, sat Ryan's usual bag of Cracker Jack. How many times had they sat in her living room, cuddled close, eating caramel corn while watching a movie? Too many for her to count.

At the sight of the treat, she slammed the door closed. She chugged the water down, fighting a fresh new wave of tears. He trusted his roommate to be honest with him but not her. The pang of that thought weighed heavy in her chest. She hopped up on the counter beside her phone, her head hung low, her legs swinging.

Jeanne McDonald

This was the reason she didn't let men in. They were stupid. They never listened. And they were self-centered. Everything in the world was always about them. Ryan had proved to be no different, just as she feared.

She slammed her fist down on the hard surface, causing her phone to bounce. "Dammit!" she screeched. Her phone buzzed again. The notification appeared on the locked screen.

I'm sorry. I'm a jerk. Please forgive me. I need to see you.

She closed her eyes seeing Ryan in her mind. Anger, hurt, and betrayal played over his handsome face during their heated argument. In her mind, she could see him now, distraught, worried, and frantic. That didn't take the sting of her own feelings away. He hadn't trusted her and the reality of the situation was he had no right to rip into her like he did.

She pushed her phone away, trying to force herself to ignore him. He needed to know how it felt to be disregarded. He needed to understand he couldn't treat her that way. But the phone buzzed again, reminding her she had an unread message waiting.

Her palms itched, inching closer to the device. No matter how much she wanted to ignore him, she couldn't.

I'm going to bed. Come by later. We'll talk then.

She made certain not to include her usual heart emoticon. He'd told her many times that he loved that little addition to her messages and this was her way of making him aware that she wasn't happy. He needed to understand the hurt he'd caused her, even if through something as juvenile as a missing heart.

Stripping down to her underwear, Alexis climbed the stairs to the loft. She slipped into her usual sleep gear and crashed into bed. This wasn't the start of the weekend she had planned, but there was nothing she could do about it now. Her face in her pillow, she

156

let the anger and hurt pour from her, praying sleep would eventually take her.

"See. Everything's going to be okay," Reagan claimed around a mouthful of breakfast burrito. Never in his life had he seen a woman that could eat like Reagan could. She inhaled food like it was air and still managed to keep a trim body. Of course, he knew that was because of her daily ten-mile runs. The woman was a machine, and when he needed it, she was a great workout partner.

"No," Ryan sighed. "She's pretty pissed and she should be." Ryan bit into his egg, bacon, and cheese burrito, thinking about how he should've been at The Kitchen Door with Alexis enjoying waffles or a cheeseburger at that moment.

"She'll get over it, Fisher," Declan noted, chowing down on a tater tot. "I told you. She needs time. You practically called her a slut, after all."

Reagan choked on her coffee, swallowing hard. "No. He didn't."

"Fuck, yeah, he did." Declan almost sounded proud. "So she threw it back in his face by claiming to have had sex with me."

"Ohhh, she went below the belt," Reagan chortled.

"Literally," Declan added.

"Figuratively," Ryan corrected in a mumble. It wasn't like Alexis had actually slept with Declan.

Thank God! I would've ripped his dick off and sliced it up for sandwich meat.

"I really need to meet this woman." Reagan turned to Ryan. "Which, by the way, when is that going to happen? If it wasn't for Deck, I'd think she was a figment of your imagination." She stuffed her mouth full of burrito, grinning around the overstuffed tortilla.

"Oh my God! Not you, too," Ryan groaned, as he dropped his food on the foil paper it'd been wrapped in.

"Not me, too?" she questioned. "You mean she wants to meet

me?" A smile dangled at the corner of her lips.

"She knows Ryan fucked you," came Declan's muffled response through his mouthful of food.

Reagan jerked her head in Ryan's direction. Her mouth went slack. "Are you kidding me? She knows about that?" She blew a strand of golden brown hair from her eyes, glaring at Ryan. "Why would you tell her something like that? Geez, Flyboy. Did you go stupid or something?" She touched her fingers to her temple before flinging out her hand in a disbelieving salute.

Ryan slumped in his seat. "She figured it out on her own," he admitted.

Reagan smacked her hand over her face. "No wonder she's pissed at you. You go around accusing her of sleeping with Declan but she knows you've slept with me. I thought you were smarter than that."

"That's what I told him," Declan inserted.

"Is that why you haven't made a move on her?" Reagan inquired, slathering picante sauce on her next bite. She tore into the burrito, smacking her lips.

"It's complicated." Ryan pushed his food away, not feeling all that hungry.

"Complicated? Is that code that you're being some kind of pussy?" She tore open another package of salsa with her teeth. "It's easy. You simply ask her out," Reagan supplied.

Declan let out a laugh, not bothering to cover his mouthful of food. "That's what I said. I told him to shit or get off the pot."

Reagan pointed over at Declan. "I hate to admit it, because let's face it, this man isn't all *that* bright—"

"Hey!" Declan objected.

"—But he's right," she continued. "You obviously have feelings for her. You should ask her out." She pursed her lips, raising her brows. "Unless our time together was so magical that I ruined you for every other woman in the world. 'Cause if that's the case, I'm pretty horny right now and could use a romp in the sack." She blew kisses and waggled her brows at him.

Ryan's already plastered scowl dropped even further. "You know better, Ray."

She shrugged, grabbing her burrito, using it as a visual aid. "Oh, c'mon. You have to remember me doing this."

Declan's mouth fell open and his eyes widened. "Holy shit," he hissed.

"I remember all too well what happened between us." Ryan grabbed her by the hand, stopping her. "And the answer's still no."

Reagan pulled away from him, tilting her head in a half-hearted shrug. "Your loss." She poured sauce over her burrito and took another bite.

"What about Declan? He seems interested," Ryan quipped, nodding toward Declan.

"Oh fuck no!" Reagan and Declan shouted in unison.

They both looked at each other and laughed. "I don't care to dip my dick in acid," Declan stated.

"And I have a little more respect for myself than to fuck the walking lab culture." Reagan leaned across the table, grabbing Ryan by the hand. "But really, Flyboy, all joking aside, you need to step up to the plate."

Ryan pulled away, placing his hands on his knees. He thought of Alexis and how that always calmed her nerves. A small smile spread over his face. "It's really not like that between us. My relationship with Lex is much like ours, Ray. We're just friends. Always have been. Always will be."

"That's bullshit and you know it. What you feel for her is nothing like what you feel for me. You light up at the sound of her name. I noticed that much the first time you told me about her." Reagan finished the last bite of her breakfast and washed it down with a swig of coffee.

"Lexi tried to feed me that same line," Declan stated, grabbing his and Reagan's trash from the table, and disposed of it. "I called bullshit on her, too."

"Really?" Ryan perked up.

Reagan and Declan cut their eyes to one another. Ryan cocked his head, glancing between them. "What?"

"You really don't realize it, do you?" Reagan teased. "You've fallen hard for this woman. Very hard."

Ryan waved her off, while he rolled his half-eaten burrito back up in its foil package. "You're delusional." He stood up and marched over to the fridge, depositing his food into the cooler for later.

"Right. Okay." Reagan leaned back, balancing on the back legs of her chair.

Ryan grabbed his keys and wallet. "I'm heading over to Lex's. I'll be back later," he told Declan.

"I thought she said to come by later?" an almost whiny sound flourished from Reagan.

"It is later," Ryan stated. He tossed his keys in the air and caught them in an underhanded swoop.

"Fine. Whatever," she huffed. "Before you go, I wanted to tell you I have tickets to the State Fair tomorrow for the Red River Showdown. I'm covering the game, but I thought you might be interested in joining me back in the locker room before the game."

Ryan reached for his ball cap, slapping it on his head. He pushed it back for a brief moment, tucked his hair under it, and shoved it back down over his forehead. "Maybe. I don't know. I have to make things right with Lex before I make any decisions."

"I'll go if he doesn't," Declan chirped.

"You're in luck, Flyboy," Reagan noted, ignoring Declan's claim. "I have four tickets to the fair, but only one spare locker room pass. Ask Lexi to join us." She threaded her fingers through her hair, letting out a little sigh. "And you can come too, Deck. As long as you don't try to hump my leg again."

Declan let out a howl while he winked at Reagan. "Deal."

She dropped her chair to the floor, planting her hands on her thighs. "We can all hang out at the fair before the game and then you can join me in the locker room. Declan can keep Lexi company while we're away. Easy peasy." She clapped her hands, dusting them off. "Besides, you did say she wants to meet me. This is the perfect situation. Unintrusive."

"Fine," Ryan waned. "I'll let you know what she says."

"Good. Now go kiss and makeup." Reagan bounced out of her chair and met Ryan in a hug. "Trust me," she whispered in his ear so only he could hear. "Come to grips with what you feel for her and fast, because if you don't, someone else will steal her right out from under your nose. And that's a pain I don't ever want to see you endure."

The tone of her voice and the way she squeezed him tight struck Ryan deep in his chest. This was the plea of someone who knew what she was talking about in the most intimate of ways. Ryan pressed a kiss to her cheek. "I will. I promise."

She smacked Ryan across the backside. "Go get her, tiger!"

Declan whooped, hollered, and threw his fist in the air. Ryan tucked his phone and wallet into his pockets and walked out the door. It was only a few blocks to Alexis' apartment, and the sun was now in full bloom, a reminder that a new day was upon him. He'd had no sleep, but he knew he couldn't rest until he saw her. Not after what he'd done.

In his car, he allowed the memories to wash over him like bad reruns. The look in her eyes, the sound of her voice, and even the slam of the door when she left echoed through his memory. He screwed up and he had to fix it. Someway. Somehow.

No matter how hard she tried, she couldn't sleep. Every time she closed her eyes the look on Ryan's face when she left resurfaced. She wanted to call him, to tell him it was okay, but it wasn't. He hurt her and that pissed her off. Ryan was supposed to be different.

She hugged her pillow and let the tears continue to fall. The thought occurred to her that other than her father, Ryan was the only man she'd ever cried over. She'd cried the day she left him for New York and she cried again over him now. He was the only man she'd ever allowed close enough to her heart to hurt her, and it left her feeling confused and even more infuriated.

A knock at the door pulled her from her tear-soaked pillow. She stumbled down the stairs, not caring how swollen her face might look or that her hair was a tattered mess. Whoever was at the door was interrupting her pity party, so what they saw was their own fault.

At the door, she neglected to even peek through the peephole. She didn't care who was there. They'd run like hell the moment they saw her, anyway, which was fine by her. All she wanted was for them to go away so she could return to bed and wallow. She flung the door open and there stood Ryan. Still in his uniform, he had a ball cap on his head, but even the shadow from the hat didn't cover his red, puffy eyes. He raked his teeth over his bottom lip before whispering, "I'm sorry."

All of the anger inside of her evaporated at the sound of those two simple little words. She flung herself into his arms. He held her tight, tears flowed down both of their faces. No words were said, but their grip on one another and the rapid beats of their hearts spoke volumes.

Ryan pulled back, only slightly, and pushed her hair from her face. She found solace in his eyes, forgetting the anger she felt or the pain he'd inflicted. Her walls were starting to crumble, even if she didn't want them to. It scared her to let him in, to let him see all of her, but it was Ryan. He was here when he didn't have to be.

Allowing him to pick her up bridal style, he carried her inside. The door slammed closed behind him of its own accord rattling the walls. He turned just enough to lock the door and started through the apartment, carrying her upstairs to the bedroom. There he laid her on the bed. He kicked off his shoes, tossed his hat aside, and stripped his uniform shirt off, leaving him in his slacks and undershirt. Climbing in behind her, he pulled her back to his chest.

Alexis closed her eyes, relief and warmth flooding her veins as his arms circled around her, holding her tight. His lips, so close to her ear, brushed over her skin when he whispered, "Let's not fight again. I can't handle it."

"Me either," she murmured, snuggling into him.

"I was a jerk. I shouldn't have jumped to conclusions." His chin rested on her shoulder, his nose nuzzled into the curve of her neck. "I should've listened to you. Seeing you come out of his room..." he sucked in a deep breath.

"I know. I'm sorry."

Ryan pressed a tender kiss to her jaw. Her chest rose and fell, lost in the scent of him. She knew she should be mad, and she was, but her need to be with him superseded such emotions. She couldn't bring herself to let him go. His nose buried in her hair, she linked her fingers with his, pushing herself further into the bow of his waist. Ryan let out a tiny moan sending waves of pleasure through her. He slipped their hands down to her hip, resting their joined hands on her thigh.

"I'm the one who screwed up. Please tell me you forgive me," his soft, sincere plea lingered in her ear.

Tilting her face, she glanced up at him. "Shh," she whispered. She pressed her free hand to his stubbled jaw. "It's okay now. We're going to be okay."

The strain in his shoulders relaxed, his whole body melted around hers. Those simple little words soothed their souls, allowing them to find comfort in one another.

Held in each other's arms, they found sleep. Deep, peaceful slumber that neither had experienced since their last sleepover in Edenton as teenagers. But things had changed. They knew it, but how much, only time would tell. For now, they only cared that they were together. The rest would figure itself out. Eventually.

"Boots or wedges?" Alexis lifted the two options to her chest, checking them against her chosen outfit of a denim miniskirt and a red empire waist tunic. "I really should get a cat," she mused. "At least then I'd stop talking to myself." She tossed both pairs of shoes aside, grabbing her black flats instead. "Practical and cute."

She pulled at the tunic while stepping into her shoes. "Maybe a t-shirt and jeans would be better?" Her brow furrowed as she contemplated her chosen wardrobe. Her hair was down, makeup polished, but her level of discomfort and uncertainty was verging at the corner of panicked and terrified. She took in two deep breaths, allowing the memory of waking in Ryan's arms to comfort her.

"Good morning, Lex," *his sweet voice resonated in her ear.* *Warm tingles*

rushed up her spine, and left their impressions on her skin. She sighed in contentment, all of the previous night's events nothing more than a memory.

Grinning, she turned her face to meet his. "Don't you mean good afternoon?"

"It's good whatever it is." His lips pressed to hers, light, gentle, and so brisk that had her whole body not exploded with want and need she wouldn't have realized the kiss even occurred.

She pressed her fingertips to her lips, smiling. It only happened once. Afterward, he spent the day lavishing her in his usual innocent, friendly kisses — the tip of her nose, her forehead, her temple — all just as sweet, but not intimate like the stolen kiss in bed.

The ringing of the doorbell pulled her from her musings. Alexis had been excited when Ryan suggested they accompany Reagan and Declan to the Texas State Fair. Not only would she have the chance to finally meet the illustrious Reagan, but she was curious about this event her father and little brother had told her so much about. She still couldn't wrap her head around some of the food items they'd claimed were amazing. It seemed as if everything in Texas, from chicken to beer, could be fried.

She gave herself one last glance in the mirror, fluffing out her hair. Being used to wearing scrubs, she reveled in the fact she could wear something that wasn't shapeless. She flattened the tunic over her stomach. Her heart rattled against her chest, the panic back in full force.

Here goes nothing.

She skipped downstairs, excited to see him. They'd only been separated for twelve hours, most of which was while she slept, but it felt like an eternity to her. She pulled in a ragged breath as she reached for the knob. Throwing the door open, she came face to face with the boyish grin of Ryan Fisher. His toned, sculpted chest was sheathed in a fitted black t-shirt with the caption "If I was flying, Goose would still be alive", paired with faded jeans and sneakers.

At the sight of him, her heart skipped a beat. The corner of his shirt was tucked in revealing the wonderful way his jeans hugged his hips. Her mind reeled with the way his hard body had wrapped around her, cocooning her in his strong arms. His dark hair was disheveled and his jaw was darkened by two days worth of stubble. A pair of aviator sunglasses covered those green eyes that she knew were bouncing behind the darks shades. His lips twitched into a grin sending her heart into full arrest.

"Wow! You look amazing," he complimented, rubbing his chin.

"And apparently overdressed." Her head bobbed up and down, noting the casual nature of his attire.

Ryan glanced down at his watch. "We have time if you want to change into something different."

The initial plan was for Ryan to drive Reagan and Declan to come pick up Alexis, but after mulling over it the entire day, Ryan gave up his chance at locker room access. Alexis tried to convince him that she was okay with the idea, but Ryan wouldn't hear it. She stopped arguing with him after she saw the determination in his eyes. The line had been crossed in the sand and she wasn't to be alone with Declan again. Not that it mattered to her. While she considered Declan a handsome man, her feelings for him were nothing more than platonic.

"So I *am* overdressed." She stepped back, letting him in her apartment.

"Not at all!" his voice rose as he ripped his shades off his face.

"I'll go change," she stated with a chuckle.

Ryan grabbed her by the arm, pulling her to his chest. The musky scent of his cologne filled her nostrils, making her wobbly at the knees. She wrapped her arms around his back, holding herself steady against him. "You look amazing. Don't change."

"Oh, stop it." She smacked her hand on his back. "Declan and Reagan will be dressed like you so, I'm going to change."

Ryan tweaked her nose. "Always stubborn."

"You know me."

"That I do." He pressed a kiss to her forehead. As she

stepped out of his embrace, an overwhelming sense of attraction engulfed her. She licked her lips, blinking a few times to wipe away the image of her ripping that shirt over his head to reveal his hard body beneath. Ryan tilted his head, his brow raising. "What?" he asked, a mischievousness to his tone.

"Nothing." She backed away, shaking her head. "Nothing at all."

"That wasn't nothing!" he called after her as she dashed up the stairs and dressed in her favorite blue t-shirt matched with a pair of comfy jeans. She glanced in the mirror, giving herself an approving nod before bounding back downstairs.

Ryan had sat down on the couch and was playing a game on his phone. He looked up at her and his face lit up. "Oh, yes. Much better." She dropped down on the sofa beside him. He twirled a lock of her hair around his finger, letting it spring back down to her shoulder. "Not that what you were wearing wasn't amazing, but I'm afraid I might've spent the day beating up every man who looked at you instead of enjoying your company."

Words hung in her throat. She tried to look away, but the magnification of his gaze melted her in place. She cleared her throat and swallowed, forcing herself to speak. "Thanks," she rasped.

He turned off his game and shoved his phone in his pocket. Smooth and graceful, Ryan lifted from the couch and turned to Alexis, offering her his hand. "Now, let's get out of here. I'm ready for a fried Twinkie."

Alexis wrinkled her nose, but accepted his hand. "That sounds like a heart attack waiting to happen."

Ryan tugged her from the sofa; the force of his pull landed her hard against his chest. He smirked, taking her hand and placing it over his firm stomach. Alexis could barely breathe. The closeness of their bodies, her palm resting over his tight abs, had turned her mind into mush. She blinked, trying to clear her head, but then his stomach rumbled against her palm, tickling her. She twisted her hand away, taking a step back, her eyes wide with laughter. The distance between them allowed her to think, but also left an ache in her chest she couldn't define.

"I'm not worried about a heart attack today, Gorgeous," he stated, holding his hand out to her. "All I care about is getting some food in my belly." He patted his stomach with his free hand. "And maybe checking out some new cars."

Hesitant, she extended her hand to him. "Well, all right then." She forced a soft giggle, her mind whirling with a million and one thoughts, but all carrying the same connotation — don't get hurt. Ryan linked their fingers together, drawing her to his side. She exhaled at his touch. "Lead the way."

"Doc!" Declan caterwauled as Ryan and Alexis approached him and Reagan. He rushed up to Alexis, pulling her into a hug. His eyes cut to Ryan at the same time, a facetious smirk pulled the corners of his mouth. "I thought you'd never arrive."

The sun was beating down on them, but there was already a nip to the early fall air. Mid-morning crowds, clad in burnt orange and crimson, were standing in line for the biggest day of the year at the Texas State Fair.

Reagan sauntered over to them, her full lips pursing into a devilish grin. Since she was slated to cover the game, she had to choose her attire wisely. No orange or red for her, but instead a light green V-neck shirt and jeans, and her press pass dangling around her neck. Her hair was pulled up and her sunshades on. She really was a beautiful woman, but Ryan had never felt *that* spark, that unquenchable desire for her, like he did for Alexis.

"Hey there, Flyboy."

Ryan greeted her with a one armed hug, but his eyes remained honed in on the idiot lavishing his girl with attention. "Hey, Ray."

"Go, Sooners!" a random person from the crowd yelled out!

"Go back home. Texas rules!" another shouted in return.

"You missed the fun in the locker room. Declan made an

idiot out of himself."

"And that's supposed to surprise me?" Ryan chuckled.

Declan tucked Alexis' hair behind her ear as he leaned in to whisper something to her. She took a step, shaking her head.

Reagan leaned into Ryan. "Nope," she chortled. "So, that's Alexis?" She nudged him in the side. He pulled his eyes away from Declan long enough to catch a glimpse of Reagan's expression. Her lips were flat, her nose wrinkled and flared on one side, and her eyes burned in Alexis' direction. Ryan blinked, and the look on her face was gone. He shook his head, figuring Declan's antics were messing with his head.

"That's her," he replied.

"Are you kidding me?" Alexis exclaimed, shoving him away.

Ryan felt a surge of anger swell up inside him. His breath was shallow and ragged, his fists balled at his sides, ready to smash Declan's face into the pavement.

"Ah, that's not what you said the other night. 'Best sex you ever had,' if I recall correctly," he announced, proud and sardonic.

Alexis crossed her arms over her chest, her eyes wide and a twisted grin lighting her face. "I'm afraid you're mistaken. That's *not* what I said."

"Bullshit!" Declan protested. "You said…"

"I said you're the worst I ever had." Her hands bounced up and down in an apologetic manner. "I realize a man with your ego size could never understand, but it's not like you could help it. After all, you do have a penis the size of a twelve-year-old."

"Ohhh!" Reagan yelled, laughing and clapping. "She so busted your ass!" She turned to Ryan whose jaw was locked, seething at the man he called a friend and roommate. Reagan rammed her elbow into Ryan's bicep. "I like her. She's got spunk."

A sense of pride swelled up inside him. Alexis looked back at him with her eyes bouncing and her beautiful smile that melted him right to the very core. Drawn to her, his feet started to move. Before he knew what he was doing, he was at her side, pulling her close to him.

Reagan smacked her hand on her jutted hipbone. "Well, do you plan on introducing us or what?"

Ryan tilted his head to Alexis, the feel of her against him caused his chest to ache and his body to tingle. The heat of her skin against his electrified him, her softness tantalized him. He wanted her. No, needed her.

Ryan lowered his hand to Alexis', linking their fingers together. He cocked his head to Reagan and smiled. "Reagan Summers, this is Doctor Alexis York." He extended his hand out to Reagan. "Alexis, this is Reagan."

Alexis smiled, stepping away from Ryan. She extended her hand to Reagan. "It's nice to meet you."

Reagan took her hand but instead of shaking it, she pulled Alexis into a hug. "It's great to finally meet you, too. Fishmouth, over there, has told me so much about you."

Ryan snapped his mouth shut and hung back to give the two women space. All this time he'd kept them apart, not for them, he realized, but for himself. They each represented a different side of him, both equally as important. It scared him to have them together, but now that they were, he couldn't understand what had frightened him in the first place.

Declan slipped in beside Ryan, draping his arm over his shoulder. "Lighten up, man." He jerked Ryan back and forth. "The woman you fucked and the one you want to fuck seem to be hitting it off. It can't get any better than that, unless they agree to a threesome."

Ryan shrugged out of Declan's embrace giving him an evil eye. "You're a dick. You know that?"

Declan lifted his shoulder in a half shrug. "That's all you got?" He leaned into Ryan, both men watching the women as they chatted. "Because I'm telling you now, if you don't get your shit together, I'm going to take her off your hands." Ryan stiffened, his fists balled tight at his sides. "I don't hear any objections. I guess that means free game." He patted Ryan on the shoulder and started to step away.

Ryan grabbed him by the back of his burnt orange Longhorns t-shirt, a curse rumbling from his chest. Declan laughed, not taking his eyes off the two women as Ryan held him steady. "Listen here, Buddy," Ryan growled, "You lay one finger on her, and I swear to God, I'll skewer your nuts and give them to a vendor to fry up as a new Texas delicacy. You got it?" He released Declan's shirt with a swift downward tug, forcing the collar to tighten around Declan's throat.

"Now there's my best friend," he wheezed, trying not to choke. "'Bout time you decided to fight for her." Declan fixed his shirt and walked away, joining Reagan and Alexis.

Declan clapped his hands together, rubbing them together. "You ladies ready to go in? I'm starved. I need me some Fletchers," Declan stated, wrapping his arms over each woman's shoulders.

Reagan and Alexis wiggled free from his grip. "You've already had two corndogs," Reagan whined in protest.

"Then I need to make it an uneven three," he countered. He cut a glance over his shoulder to Ryan, nodding his head. Ryan returned the nod, an unspoken acknowledgement between the two men. Alexis was his. One way or another, she was his, and Declan would keep his bear-mitts off her.

"Everything okay?" Alexis purred so low that the sound rumbled deep in his belly. He wrapped his arm around her waist, pulling her to his side. "I didn't do anything to upset you, did I?"

Ryan leaned in, pressing a kiss to her temple. "Not at all. You're amazing." A light blush colored her cheeks. He reached out and tenderly stroked her heated skin. "Something tells me today's going to be a great day."

She peered up at him through her eyelashes. "Me too. I like Reagan. She's a bit…"

"Mouthy, obnoxious, endearing," Ryan rattled off.

"Yes," Alexis chuckled. They lapsed into a comfortable silence, coming up behind Reagan and Declan. Reagan handed the ticket agent her press pass along with another card. "Are you okay with us getting along?" Alexis whispered.

Ryan tilted his head down to meet her gaze. He cupped the side of her face, brushing his thumb along the edge of her lower lip. "Why wouldn't I?"

Alexis closed her eyes, her breathing heavy. "I don't know…"

His lips came down, meeting the tip of her nose. "I couldn't be happier."

She opened her eyelids, to reveal her eyes filled with worry and confusion. Ryan couldn't resist the urge within him. Declan was right. It was now or never, and he wanted her now. He leaned down, pressing his lips to hers. A kiss so powerful, so strong, that his whole body ignited into flames. Soft, smooth, sweet lips captured by his, craving, longing, aching to be kissed. Her hand slipped into his hair, fusing them together in deep passion unlike anything he'd ever felt before. He wanted to breathe but feared losing the intensity. His body craved to have everything she was willing to give him. When they finally pulled apart, she gasped but the confusion was gone. All that remained was desire. She moved her hands to his chest, and left him to wonder if her heart was pounding as fast as his.

A tiny smile pulled her lips. She was so beautiful with freshly kissed lips that he wanted to do it again and again. Ryan opened his mouth to speak, but was interrupted by the sounds of Declan wolf whistling.

They turned to see Reagan and Declan staring at them. Declan was all smiles, clapping as if he'd just witnessed the greatest performance of his life. Reagan, on the other hand, smiled, but it was cold, fake, and almost pained. She nodded to Ryan and turned her back to them. Ryan struggled to understand her expression. Just the other morning, she was encouraging him to take the next step with Alexis. It didn't make sense for her to seem upset now that he did.

"Let's go, you two love birds. I'm starving," Declan called out, waving for them to enter the park.

Alexis buried her face in Ryan's chest as he led her through the gates. This was the lightest he'd felt in ages. He couldn't explain it, but kissing her, actually kissing her, made things clear in his head. He knew what he wanted and by the end of the night, Alexis York would be more than a friend. She would be his — always and forever.

"Oh my God!" Alexis bellowed.

Ryan covered his face with his hand, wheezing in laughter.

Reagan stood there, mouth gaped open, as Declan shoved an entire Fletcher's corn dog in his mouth. The man seemed to be a bottomless pit, having attacked three more corn dogs since they entered the Fair.

"Are you sure you're not gay?" Alexis snickered.

Ryan tugged Alexis closer to his side, pressing his face into the curve between her neck and shoulder. "He sure can deep throat like a porn star," Ryan added.

Alexis wrapped her arm around his waist, loving the way he felt next to her. This was easy, right, perfect, but most of all, scary as hell. That kiss outside the park had left her breathless and wanton. Her heart raced at the mere thought of him kissing her like that again, and she ached for it, which frightened her. With Ryan, things were different than they'd been with any other man she'd ever been with. He knew her thoughts and innermost secrets. She trusted him, which scared her more than anything. Trusting someone with her heart was her greatest fear.

Ryan pressed a kiss to her neck, sending sweet tremors over her skin.

"I got skills!" Declan bolstered, his mouth so full his words came out muffled. He punched the air, holding the clean skewer in his hand like a trophy.

"Oh, hell," Reagan balked. "Those aren't skills." She wiggled her brows. "You haven't seen skills until you've seen me in action. Right, Flyboy?" She nudged Ryan in the arm, laughing.

Ryan's head shot up, his eyes narrowed, glowering at Reagan. In the last few hours, Reagan had made comments—some obvious, some subjective—in reference to hers and Ryan's relationship. Alexis almost felt sorry for Reagan. Much like her, Reagan came into this situation thinking they were on even footing—both friends of Ryan's. But Ryan changed the rules of the game the instant he kissed Alexis. They all felt the shift. For the most part, Alexis had been able to overlook some of the things Reagan had said, understanding her and Ryan shared a past. What she struggled with was when Reagan insinuated to their extended relationship.

"I don't know," Ryan popped back. "I'm sure we'd have to ask Gabe about that. As if any of us really care about your extracurricular skills."

"Gabe?" Alexis questioned.

"My worst mistake," Reagan retorted.

"Her ex," Ryan clarified.

Declan managed to swallow everything in his mouth. "Yeah, that guy was a douche." He tossed the stick in the trash, dusting his hands off. "Okay, I'm bored. What do we do next?"

"We've yet to do anything fun —" Declan raised his hand,

about to interrupt Alexis, but she forged on, "—aside from watching Deck stuff his face." Declan took a bow. Alexis laughed, shaking her head at him.

"Looking at cars wasn't fun?" Ryan teased.

Alexis patted his arm, chuckling. "I'm not even going to warrant that question with a response."

"You just did," Reagan muttered.

"What do you all say to us checking out the Midway?" Alexis suggested, ignoring Reagan's little comment. "I really want to see that chicken game you were telling me about." She kissed Ryan on the edge of his jaw, savoring the taste of his skin on her lips and the scent of his musky cologne in her nostrils. "I mean, what girl can turn down a game that includes a flying rubber chicken?"

Declan gave her two thumbs up, grinning. "Sounds like a plan."

As they made their way through the crowds toward the Midway, Alexis snuggled into the crook of Ryan's side, his hand flattened against the small of her back. His pinkie brushed along the waist of her jeans, barely dipping down beneath the fabric, setting her skin aflame.

Declan led the way, occasionally glancing over his shoulder to the others, but content to be the lone man, checking out every woman he could find along the way. Reagan traveled along beside them. Every so often, she'd reach out to touch Ryan's arm, or grab him to look at something, pulling him away from Alexis. But Ryan always returned back to Alexis, drawing her in closer than she had been.

Alexis glanced around his chest, meeting the other woman's gaze. "So, you excited about the game today?"

Reagan shrugged. "I've covered this game every year for the last three years. I always enjoy it." She pulled at Ryan's elbow. "Last year, Ryan joined me in the press box. Remember that night, Flyboy? We got so wasted afterward."

"Yeah. I remember," he intoned.

"We can do that again tonight, if you want," she suggested.

"Tonight?" he queried, his brow furrowed.

Reagan lifted an eyebrow, taken aback by his forgetfulness. "Um, yeah. I thought you were going to the game with me?"

Ryan scratched his jaw. He rolled his head, popping his neck. "I'm sorry, Ray, but I can't." He glanced down at Alexis, smiling. "I have plans for later."

"Make sure to take that shit back to her apartment." Declan turned around and started to walk backward. "I don't want to be listening to 'Oh, Ryan. Oh, Ryan. OH, RYAN!' all night." He squirmed and wiggled, making the world's worst mid-climatic faces imaginable, as he insinuated what she and Ryan would be doing later. With a wink, he turned back around, continuing his strut down the Midway.

The thought burned deep inside her. Their bare skin touching, hands caressing, tongues tasting, limbs tangled. Alexis blinked back the mental images that flooded her mind.

"Oh, I just thought..." Reagan trailed off, her mouth turned down. She pushed a few stray hairs back from her face, turning away from them. "You know what, never mind what I thought."

Ryan took in a heavy breath that only Alexis had noticed, but gave no other reaction. Tense silence surrounded them for a moment. Alexis struggled with what to say to fix things between Ryan and his friend. She felt as if she'd intruded on something sacred between them, causing a riff.

"Oh, Lexi, look!" Declan grabbed her hand, pulling her away from Ryan. "There it is." They rushed up to the vendor stand where a row of rubber mallets attached to small catapults faced a rotating vat of water with six cooking pots bobbing inside. Hanging at the back of the stand were hundreds of stuffed animals waiting to be won. Ryan stepped up behind her, wrapping his hands around her waist. "See something you want?"

She looked up into his sweet, twinkling eyes, reliving the moment he kissed her. "Yeah, I do," she breathed.

Ryan leaned in, pressing his lips to hers. Fireworks sparked between them. Her heart thundered against her chest as she reached up and cupped the side of his face. His fingers tightened around her hips, pulling her back against him. Her soft moan was muffled by his passionate kiss. The desire between them was so strong there was no concealing it.

"Ah, young love," the middle-aged carny said. "How 'bout you win this young lady a prize?"

Ryan kissed the tip of her nose, stepping beside her. He handed the man a few bucks, glancing at Declan. "You want in?"

"Hell, yeah, I do."

Ryan handed over a few more bills. "Hook my friend up, too."

The carny nodded, giving each man three rubber chickens. "What you need to do is place the critter on the end of the catapult and use the mallet to make it land in one of the pots. One in, wins from the first shelf, two from the second and so on."

Ryan nodded to Declan, who grinned, while slapping his chicken on the catapult. Ryan did the same. He tapped his cheek with his index finger, waggling his brows at Alexis. "For luck."

She planted a kiss on his cheek, grinning. Reagan stepped up to the other side of him, patting him on the back. "You got this, Flyboy."

Ryan tilted his head, giving her a wink. "You bet I got this." He tucked in the arms and legs of the rubber doll, maneuvered his catapult to where it was angled a little to his left, then watched and waited. First try he got it in. Declan wasn't so lucky.

The carny yelled out they had a winner. Ryan smiled and shook his head. "Two more tries."

"Going for a bigger prize," the man yelled for everyone to hear.

Second try and Ryan managed to get the chicken in the pot again. "Winner, winner!"

Alexis bounced, clapping and cheering. "I can't believe you did that!"

"I can," Reagan stated, confident and proud. "He did this exact same thing last year. Remember that huge bear you won for me? I still have it."

Declan shouted, pumping his fists in the air. His second chicken landed in a pot, barely, but it was in there.

Ryan jerked his head, cutting his eyes to Reagan. Alexis tried hard to ignore the moment of anger that passed between the two of them. She wasn't sure what was going on, but whatever it was, it had knocked Ryan off his game, because he blundered the third shot. The water made a loud plunking noise as the rubber chicken missed its mark.

Ryan slammed his fists down. "Son of a..." he stopped himself from finishing the curse.

Alexis rested her hand on his back. "Hey, two out of three is amazing."

"I'll say," Declan mumbled, watching his third chicken land on the ground. It didn't even make it to the water.

"Sure is," the carny agreed. "You can choose a prize from the second level, little lady."

Alexis pursed her lips together, feeling Reagan's stare on her as she made her choice. "The purple monkey."

The man hooked the monkey, pulling it down from the rack and handed it to Alexis. She hugged it to her chest and then hugged Ryan. "Thank you."

Ryan tugged a lock of her hair, curling it down around his finger. His smile waned but sincere. "You're welcome."

"What about mine?" Declan asked. He pointed out a little blue M&M toy on the first shelf. The man grabbed it and handed it over to Declan, who in turn handed it to Reagan. "It's no stuffed bear, but technically Ryan did pay for it, so it works for you either way."

"Thanks," Reagan snapped with a roll of her eyes, accepting the gift.

"Hey, if you don't want it..." Declan reached out ready to reclaim this unappreciated present.

Reagan shook her head. Sadness and frustration clouded her features. She thrust the plush toy back at Declan and stormed off.

"What the hell is wrong with her today?" Ryan groused.

Alexis grasped Ryan's wrist, directing his attention to her. "Go to her. She needs you."

"What she needs is a good spanking," he sneered.

"Oh, I'm willing to give it to her!" Declan exclaimed with glee. "I saw a vendor stand over there," he pointed over his shoulder, "with riding crops that would work perfectly."

"Hush, you two," Alexis scolded. "She needs her friend, not a spanking."

"Damn," Declan hissed, snapping his fingers.

Alexis cupped Ryan's face, drawing his lips to hers. She noticed how his pulse jumped when their mouths touched. Before the kiss could become heated, she pulled back. "She feels left behind right now. Go talk to her."

Ryan touched his fingertips to her lips, slightly trembling. His eyes burned with desire, sending waves of heat through her body. "I should've kissed you a long time ago." He brushed his lips back over hers, lightly tracing his tongue along her bottom lip. She wanted so much to open up to him, but knew if she did, there'd be no stopping the wildfire that was sure to follow.

"Ryan," she whispered, "you have all the time in the world to kiss me, but right now, Reagan needs you."

Ryan tapped the tip of her nose and smiled. "Fine. You win. I'll meet you over at the Texas Star." He looked over at Declan, his mouth set in a hard line. "Take care of my girl, but keep your damn hands off."

Declan snapped a salute. "Aye aye, Captain."

With a final gentle caress to her cheek, Ryan slipped off into the crowd to seek out Reagan.

When he was out of sight, Declan took Alexis by the hand, slipping it into the crook of his arm. "That wasn't easy for you, was it?"

"Nope," she muttered, her throat tight making it hard to swallow.

Declan maneuvered them along the Midway. He patted the

top of her hand. "You're a good person for doing that, just so you know."

"Yeah." Her eyes dropped to the ground. The burning of unshed tears forced her to blink.

"You worried?" his tone teasing. She lifted her eyes, meeting the hard green of Declan's. He stopped walking, turning her to face him with a gentle tug, his expression suddenly serious. "Are you?"

She exhaled a harsh breath. "Is he going to hurt me?" A tear escaped down her cheek leaving its mark on her skin.

Declan met her gaze, his eyes full of truth and determination. "He'd rather die than hurt you."

"Reagan!" Ryan called out, finally having caught up with his runaway friend. His irritation with her mounted to an exponential limit. All of her little comments, no matter how innocent they might've seemed, hadn't fallen on deaf ears. Ryan had taken account of each one as if she were shoving a knife deep into his gut. Reagan was more than a friend to him. More like a sister, and her behavior had left him feeling confused and a bit angry.

"Lee," Reagan spoke into her phone, holding a finger up to Ryan. He came to a stop, his brow lifted at her silent command. Ryan crossed his arms over his chest, meeting her intense gaze as she continued her phone conversation. "I'll be over there in an hour or so." There was a long pause, her hand propped on her hip. "I've already done my locker room interview." She rolled her eyes, and tapped her foot. "Are you serious? You want me to interview the OU team?" Another long pause, followed by a deep exhale. "Fine." She disconnected the call and slipped her phone into her pocket.

"Everything okay?" Ryan asked.

Her face twitched, her lips rolled up toward her nose. "My boss wants me to go interview OU before the game. No biggy."

Ryan shoved his hands into his pants. "That's not what I'm

talking about. What's going on with you today? You're not acting like yourself."

Reagan lifted her chin, her fists balled at her sides. "I don't know what you're talking about. There's nothing wrong."

Ryan pulled his hands free, wrapping his fingers around her shoulders. "Ray, this is me you're talking to. What's eating at you?"

A flash of frustration clouded her face, as she pulled away from him. "Nothing, Ryan. Just go back to your *friend*."

Taken aback, Ryan cocked a brow, his head tilted to the side. "Is it Lex?" he questioned. "Do you not like her?"

Reagan let out a guarded chuckle and started to walk away. "Men are so obtuse," she muttered.

"Then what?" he barked, grabbing her by the wrist, turning her to face him. "What the hell have I done to piss you off today? You can't tell me that it's nothing, because I know you better than that."

She ripped her hand back from him. "Of course it's Alexis, you idiot!"

A little shocked, Ryan took a step back. "So you don't like her, then?"

Reagan groaned, throwing her hands in the air. "You really don't get it, do you?" She attempted to retreat again, only for Ryan to thwart her attempt. She faced him, her shoulders squared and her head held high. Ryan could see the aggravation burning in her eyes.

He ripped at his hair, his own irritation boiling over. "Get what, because I'm not a freaking mind reader, Ray! What am I supposed to get?"

"You kissed her!" she screeched.

Confusion swirled around in his head. He struggled to string words together for a moment. "Um, yeah. I did." He narrowed his eyes, gauging her reaction. "You and Declan told me I needed to take a chance with her, remember? You said you didn't want me to lose her and I would if I didn't take action." Panic nipped at the recesses of his mind.

"I know what I said!" she bellowed, throwing her hands in the air.

A mass of conflicting emotions pressed against his chest. He bowed his head, a deep sigh pouring from his lips as he cupped his forehead in his hands. "I'm so lost here."

"You are? How do you think I feel?"

Ryan lifted his eyes, meeting hers. Deep in her eyes a storm brewed of epic proportions. Out of his mouth fell the first thought that came to his mind. "Are you in love with me?"

Inappropriate laughter burst from Reagan's chest. Passerbyers either jumped at the sound or stopped to look at her for a moment before continuing through the park. "Heavens no. But I can't deny I'm jealous of her. I mean, think about it, Flyboy. It used to be only you and me, but now it's all about the great doctor. She's all you talk about. You have your own little ritual diner thing with her when you come home, and I'm an afterthought. We used to have our thing when you came home. Now, we never hang out anymore. I couldn't even get you to come today without inviting her. It became way too real when you kissed her." Her mouth turned down into a frown and her voice lowered to a mere whisper, "and worst of all, you never kissed *me* like that."

Realization came crashing down on him. He wasn't sure if she was lying about her feelings, but one thing he knew for sure, she was telling the truth about how he'd neglected her, and focused all of his attention on Alexis. He raised his hand, stroking her cheek. "Ray, you're an amazing woman, but what we shared—"

She jerked her face away. "Was a drunken mistake, I know."

Taking her by the chin, Ryan forced Reagan to look into his eyes. "No. It was special to me. We were there for each other when we needed to be. But that wasn't love. We both know that."

She closed her eyes, a single tear slid down her cheek. "I know it wasn't. But I do care about you, deeply."

Ryan brushed the tear from her face. "And I care for you, too. I'm sorry I've been such a jackass lately. I never realized how this was affecting you."

"It shouldn't have affected me the way it did."

"I think it should've. If the tables were turned, I can't say I wouldn't feel the same."

Reagan blinked away the tears, taking in a deep breath. "Thank you. And I'm sorry I've been a shit to Lexi today. It's not her fault that I'm a twit."

"You're not a twit." Ryan chuckled, wrapping his arm around Reagan's shoulder. "And it's because of her I came to find you."

Reagan slipped her arm around his waist, glancing up at him in surprise. "Really?"

"Yeah. She told me you needed me." Ryan kissed the top of Reagan's head.

"You've got yourself a good one there, Flyboy. It takes some major lady-balls to let your man run off after another woman."

Ryan laughed, lifting his leg behind him to kick Reagan on the backside. She squeaked and shoved him away. Her mouth twisted into a half grin, as he pulled her back to his side. "I think you'll really like her if you give her a chance."

"Well, she does have a thing for my best friend, so that proves her to at least be smart." She snapped her fingers, a wild-eyed grin donning her face. "Oh, and she can bust it out on Declan, which is a major plus in my book."

"See. I told you if you give her a chance." He laughed. "Now let's get over to the Ferris wheel before I have to beat Declan off her." He tightened his grip around Reagan's shoulders and lumbered toward the eye of Texas.

"Anything for you," Reagan whispered, skipping along beside him. "But if she hurts you, I call dibs on kicking her perky, little ass," she added with a wink.

Ryan curled his leg up behind him to kick her again, but Reagan dodged him. His laughter filled the air as he pulled her back. "It's a deal, my friend." He squeezed her shoulder. "It's a deal."

"A Ferris wheel?" Alexis shrilled. "You never said anything about a Ferris wheel!"

Panic swirled up inside her. Her palms were sweating, knees shaking, skin blanching, the very thought of getting into one of those gondolas made her sick to her stomach. She backed away from the metal tower of death. There was no way anyone would get her into that rickety old thing. A plane was bad enough, but there were no harnesses in a Ferris wheel and everything was wide open. Not to mention the fact it stopped throughout its cycle around or that she could plummet to her death if some teenage lackey didn't do his job right.

No, sir. Not happening!

Declan scratched his head, staring up at the two hundred plus foot ride. "What did you think we meant by the *Texas Star*?" he questioned.

"This is Texas. Everything is named Something Star. For all I knew you were taking me somewhere else to eat."

An amused chuckle bubbled from his chest. "Okay. You got me there, but you can't come to the fair and *not* ride the Ferris wheel."

She licked her dry lips, cupping her hand over her eyes as she peered up at the top of the monster. "Oh, yes I can."

"You're not scared, are you?" Declan inched toward her, his face lit up with mischievousness.

"No," she drawled. "And you keep away from me, Deck." She swatted at him.

"Excuse me?" Ryan's voice rumbled behind her. Alexis turned to find him tearing his arm off of Reagan's shoulder, ready to rip into Declan. "I thought I told you to keep your damn hands off."

Declan laughed, lifting his arms in the air. "I didn't touch her. She's freaking out over the Ferris wheel."

Alexis gasped, her gaze shifted back and forth between Ryan and Declan. "I wasn't freaking…"

"Oh, yes you were. You were in full on panic mode," he observed, as he dropped his arms, and crossed them over his chest, daring her to disagree.

Ryan cocked his head, his brows bunched together. "Really?" He reached for Alexis, pulling her to his chest. She wanted to shove away, humiliated by Declan's truthful claims. She didn't want anyone to see her as weak, especially not Ryan. But the instant his lips pressed to hers, so light, so caring, all of her inhibitions disappeared. "Don't you like Ferris wheels?" he murmured against her lips. "The one ride where we can be cuddled together, doing this." His lips met hers again.

She was almost ready to give in to him, when she heard a child scream in terror from the heavens. She looked up, and stiffened, her panic back in full force.

Reagan, who'd hung back when Ryan released her, must have sensed Alexis' discomfort. She came marching up, tapping Ryan on the shoulder. "You know, guys, maybe we should forgo the Ferris wheel this year. I really need to head over to the Cotton Bowl anyway." Reagan's tone was sincere, which made Alexis feel all the more guilty and childish for fearing something as silly as a Ferris wheel. This was obviously a tradition of theirs and she was ruining it.

She took in a deep breath, forcing a smile. "Thanks, Reagan, but I'm okay. We can go up."

"If you don't want to—" Ryan started.

"We don't have to," Reagan finished. "I really *do* need to get to work."

"Yeah," Ryan noted, thrusting his thumb in Reagan's direction. "She has an interview to complete before the game."

"Another one?" Declan inquired.

"Yeah, Lee wants me to interview the coach from OU and a few team members, if possible."

Alexis glanced between Ryan and Reagan. There was a calm between them, which led her to believe that they'd made things right. And him having his arm around her shoulders when they marched up sealed her assumption.

Alexis reached for Ryan's hand, pulling it to her lips. He stretched his fingers, splaying them along her cheek, his thumb slid over her bottom lip. He leaned in, kissing her with such tenderness she wanted to melt into him. "Next time," he breathed against her lips. Ryan rested his forehead against hers

"Are you sure?" she whispered, peering into his eyes.

A slow smile stretched across his lips. "I have something better in mind."

"Bow-chicka-wow-wow," Declan sang, thrusting his hips.

Without taking his eyes off Alexis, Ryan flipped Declan the bird, which caused Reagan to snort. "Holy shit! Declan was right. She does bring the beast out of you." Reagan bumped her hip into Ryan pushing him aside. She took Alexis by both hands. "Before he jets you off to whatever romantic setting he has in mind, I want to apologize. I've been a bitch today."

Alexis grinned, pulling Reagan into a hug. "You weren't a bitch. Ryan was being an insensitive prick."

Ryan gasped as Declan and Reagan burst into laughter. Declan hugged Alexis up tight in his arms, rocking back and forth. "You give him the ride of his life. Lord knows he needs it."

Alexis smacked his chest. "You're a sick bastard, you know that?"

A wicked grin pulled at the corner of Declan's mouth. "And proud of it."

Ryan stepped up behind her, pulling her hips to his. The heat of his body against hers sent Alexis' heart racing. His nose grazed along her earlobe and her stomach constricted with want. "Ready to get out of here?"

Alexis closed her eyes, her senses heightened. She could feel the way his hands pressed into her pelvis, suggestive and full of longing. Her ears honed in on the unsteady rhythm of his breathing. She could almost taste him on her tongue, aching to feel his kiss — deep and wanton. Ryan pulled her hair back from her shoulder, trailing his nose up her neck.

"Yes," she breathed.

He pressed a light kiss to her jaw, just below her ear, before moving around her. He took Reagan in his arms, giving her a hug. "Knock 'em dead."

Reagan laughed, patting his back before shoving him away. "Thanks. Now get out of here."

Ryan and Declan shook hands and pulled into a quick man hug. Alexis heard Ryan whisper to his friend, "Take care of her for me."

Declan gave a swift nod. "She's safe with me, Fisher."

Moments later, Alexis found herself exiting the Texas State Fair. The sun was starting to set and the heat of the day was giving way to the chill of the night. It'd been an interesting day, but the night held promises she'd only ever dreamed off. They reached

Ryan's vehicle and before he opened the passenger door for her, he pulled her into his arms, kissing her with such fervor, he left her breathless.

"My place?" she asked, forcing air into her lungs.

His mouth quirked into a grin. "You read my mind."

Her apartment was dark as they entered, except the light that constantly remained on above her stove. Only the sound of her own heart beating could be heard. Or was that his heart? She had no clue, but she knew it was strong and consistent. The whole drive to her apartment had been a sort of innocent yet sensual game. Foreplay. He trailed his fingers along her leg, never reaching where she ached for him to go. His intermittent glances and coy smiles rattled her, teasing her with promises of what was to come.

The click of the deadbolt echoed through the room. Ryan approached her, his green eyes smoldering in the dim light, but still there was no rush in him. No pushing, no gnashing of teeth, no ripping each other's clothes off in a mad haste as two people attempted to ravage one another. Instead, he was calm as he extended his hand to her. She accepted, lacing her fingers through his, as she followed him up the stairs.

In her room, Ryan turned to her. His outstretched hand cupped her cheek. Heat burned through her skin. Her heart clenched in her chest at the look of love on his face. Fear, want, need, acceptance, these things haunted her. Her mind waged in war at what the light, sensitive touch of his fingers trailing down her cheek to her neck meant. She hungered for his love, which frightened her. Giving herself to him could only lead to hurt.

Oh, but it's so worth the pain for the pleasure.

Ryan tilted his head, his gaze deep and wanton, as he pulled her close to him. "If you only knew," he breathed, brushing his lips over hers, slow, steady, and with purpose.

Alexis slipped her hands around his neck, savoring the feel of his firm mouth to hers. "Knew what?" she rasped.

"All those nights in bed with you, growing up, how I ached to hold you just like this. I dreamt of it." He trailed his hands down her back, digging his fingers into her backside. "To feel you." His lips traveled along the column of her throat, his nose brushed along her jaw. "To taste you." She whimpered at the feel of his tongue darting out against her hypersensitive skin. "To inhale you." His mouth reached the collar of her shirt. Pushing the neckband aside, he placed small, feather light kisses on her exposed collarbone. Her head fell back and her eyes clamped shut. "To call you mine."

She toyed with the hairs at the back of his neck, lost in his words and sweet touches. Her chest tightened when he stepped back just enough to meet her eyes. The lump in her throat made it hard to speak. She remembered clearly how much she wanted this as a teenager, to have him want her, and here she was, after all these years, discovering he'd felt the same way. "Am I yours?" she whispered.

"Oh, yes. You're mine."

He stepped backward, his knees hit the side of the bed. Alexis watched, frozen in place. She liked the way his nose wrinkled when he claimed her and the glimmer in his eyes while he gauged her. He wiggled his finger, beckoning her to him. "Don't make me wait any longer." He licked his lips, his teeth grazing his bottom one.

Alexis stepped toward him, her heart fluttering as fast as a hummingbird's wings. Ryan gripped her hips, pulling her to him. His mouth captured hers, coaxing his tongue between her lips. A tiny moan escaped her as his fingers moved under her shirt, sliding along the waist of her jeans.

She trailed her hands up his spine, wrapping them around his shoulders. His tongue moved against hers, caressing, tangling, rolling, and tasting, without haste. Ryan took what he wanted from her. He commanded her, possessed her with ease. The intensity of his touch was exhilarating. Everything about him called to her. His smile, his laugh, his body, his hopes, his dreams. She wanted it all.

Needing him badly, Alexis took another step forward, pushing Ryan down on the bed. He bounced, propping himself on his elbows, but didn't move further. Her knees hit the mattress between his, bending slightly. She rested her hands on his shoulders, dragging her nose along his jaw, planting sweet kisses just below his ear. It amazed her how his scent swirled around her. Musky, manly, and all Ryan.

Swift and steady, she pulled back, ripping her shirt over her head. She moved to straddle his hips, pressing her center against him. Ryan dug his fingers into her hips, thrusting up into her. She had to steady him, for the friction was exquisite, but she refused to rush anymore than he had. This was their time. Their moment. She couldn't imagine it being any more perfect. There was time for rough, aggressive sex with him later. Just the thought of taking him with force made her insides quiver. But right now, she wanted more. She needed more. She needed him.

Ryan sat up, pulling her to his chest. His hands moved up her back, tracing the ridges of her spine. Their mouths met in a kiss that could ignite the heavens. A shiver rose through her as he moved his hands to her stomach, slipping them up over her chest. Cupping her breasts in his hands, he hooked his thumbs under the fabric of her bra, and pushed the satin material aside, exposing her nipples. Gentle at first, he pinched her hardened peaks. When she moaned, he increased the pressure, rolling them between his fingertips.

"I want you so bad," she panted in his ear, taking his earlobe between her teeth and sucking it. Ryan let out a moan that resonated through them both.

Reaching behind her back, Ryan snapped the hooks of her bra, pulling the barrier away from her skin. He tossed it aside, taking her pebbled mound between his lips. She hissed at the contact, her fingers threading through his hair. The warmth of his mouth against her teased her senses. Goose bumps broke out over her skin.

She gasped and swallowed, her head fell back, giving him a

191

clear passage. Ryan lavished each breast with attention, careful to tantalize her, but stopping before she reached the point of no return. When Alexis couldn't take the torture anymore, she dipped her hands down, dragging the hem of his shirt up his torso. Ryan lifted his arms in the air for her. She tugged it over his head and discarded the fabric without care.

Seeing him, really seeing him for the first time as a man, not a boy, did things to her mind and body that she'd never anticipated. It was almost as if he were made by the gods for her alone. His sculpted, bronze chest led her on a journey down his firm, tight abs. The passion that had developed between them seemed unquenchable as clothing began to disappear from their bodies. Her hands longed to touch him everywhere, to learn everything about his body. Strength exuded from his hot, smooth skin. His muscles flexed, rigged and tight with each enticing touch. Whatever she'd been expecting, he was more. The boy in her mind was gone. In his place was a strong, confident man, who understood how to make her body feel alive.

Both naked, Ryan flipped them so he was hovering over her. He reached between them, coaxing her legs open for him. Cool air whispered against her overheated skin. She squirmed in anticipation, not knowing what he would do next, but aching for whatever he had to offer. He smirked, lowering himself down, kissing her stomach. "I told you, I want to taste you."

Her head shot up, eyes widened at the sight of Ryan slinking between her thighs. She trembled at the thought of his mouth on her most intimate of places. Her heart began to race, as she felt his mouth against her pelvis. That's when he licked her.

Reflexes took over, her hips jerked in response, aching to feel him more. And he gave her more. Slow at first, his tongue moved, intense but gentle, but as her moans grew louder, his tongue became more forceful. Magic. That's what this man was. Pure magic.

Relentless, Ryan slipped his tongue into her depths.

"Ryan." His name slipped from her tongue. She gripped his

hair in her hands, her body tense with need. "Please," she begged.

No one had ever touched her like this. It was as if Heaven had been transferred to Earth and she was being given the privilege to glimpse it, just once. Each flick of his tongue, graze of his teeth, built pressure inside her. When her climax ripped through her, every muscle of her body constricted, quivering with pure satisfaction.

Ryan raised his head, his smile full of pride and his eyes burning with hunger. He licked his lips, moving up the length of her body, before positioning himself at her center. "You're so beautiful," he whispered, pushing her hair back from her face. "And you're all mine."

Yours! She knew she should be scared of his proclamation, but instead, it thrilled her.

Ryan rubbed himself against her, testing her, teasing her. She reached between them, wrapping her fingers around his sizeable erection, pushing him to go further. He pulled his hips away from her, shaking his head. "Condoms?"

"I'm clean," she admitted, hating to ruin the moment, but she knew he needed to know. "We have to be tested for work."

He grinned pressing his lips to hers. "I've never been with a woman without a condom. I'm clean, too."

Something about him saying he'd never felt a woman without a condom thrilled her. She may not have been the lucky one to take his innocence, but she wanted to be the first woman he truly felt. "Then don't use one."

"I...uh..." He seemed confused, almost frightened.

"I'm on the pill. I have been since I was sixteen. Please. Feel me. I need you to *really* feel me."

Whatever battle waged inside of him disintegrated at her plea. He didn't hesitate. He pushed inside her, slow, inch-by-inch, until he was fully submerged in her depths. His breathing shallow and beads of sweat speckled his brow. "Are you okay?" he grunted.

She cupped his face, kissing him hard and deep. "Better than okay."

Their mouths locked together, and hands roamed as he thrust in and out, steady yet ragged. Aching desire pulsed between them as their bodies moved together in perfect harmony. The sweet taste of his kiss coated her tongue, and when she couldn't resist any longer, she erupted around him, but that wasn't enough for him. He pushed harder, still slow and steady, until she climaxed again. When she thought she couldn't take any more, he proved her wrong, taking everything she had to give. Finally, he let himself go, granting her wish of being his true first. Skin to skin, soul to soul, this moment bonded them together.

The night played on, each second spent together giving and taking, until both were completely sated. Well past midnight, Ryan and Alexis lay in the bed, only a sliver of the moonlight slipping in through the window. He held her in his arms, caressing her silky skin. Never had a woman made him feel this way. The very thought of letting her go caused his chest to ache. Alexis fit with him, in every way. She was tight, supple, and the sound of her orgasm was a song he could listen to on repeat and never get bored of it.

"Lex?" He pressed a kiss to her temple.

Alexis hummed.

"Tell me something."

She shifted her position, resting her elbow on his chest, as she met his gaze. He touched her kiss-swollen mouth, images of biting those seductive lips running rampant through his mind. "Why didn't you want to get on the Ferris wheel earlier?"

Ryan noticed the way her pulse jumped. He couldn't quite make out her expression, but something told him it mimicked her reaction from earlier in the day.

She started to draw small patterns over his chest. "It's complicated."

"So, you're afraid of heights." It was more of a statement than a question. He'd suspected it earlier, but a little surprised, because he didn't recall such a fear from when they were kids.

Her fingers trailed down his stomach and back to his chest. "Not really heights, per se. It's more like a fear of falling."

"How long have you had this fear?"

A slight tremor shook her. Ryan twirled a strand of her hair around his finger, not pushing her, simply waiting for her response. She took in a deep breath. "All my life," she answered, pressing her lips to his chest.

"So does that mean you're afraid of flying, too?"

"Yes." Her voice sounded so small.

"All those plans we had of travelling together, flying the world, and you were scared to death?" He couldn't believe it. Never in his life had he felt so guilty. Had he known she felt that way, he never would've subjected her to all those years of planning adventures. "Why would you...?" his question trailed off. He wasn't even sure what he was asking.

Alexis lifted her hand, resting it against his neck. "I would've done anything for you, and I figured if I had to fly, at least I'd have you with me."

"Would have?"

Her lips met his, light and gentle, but there was a sort of sadness in her tone as she stated, "Still would."

Ryan grinned against her lips. "Let's get out of here," he promoted, moving out from underneath her.

Her face scrunched up. "It's nearly one in the morning. Wouldn't you prefer to...you know?"

"Damn, woman. I'm not a machine," he teased. In reality, his body automatically reacted to her suggestion, but he had different plans, for now. "I need sustenance. Now, let's get dressed." He stood up from the bed, unabashed by his nakedness, offering her his hand. "Let's go for a ride."

Alexis twisted her lips. "I thought I already did," she said, waggling her brows.

Ryan's hand dropped along with his mouth, a little tongue-tied. A burst of laughter ripped from his chest. "Get that cute ass of yours out of the bed before I have to spank you." He opened his palm to her.

"Oh, really?" She smacked her lips. "You and whose army?"

Ryan's face turned stone cold as he stalked toward her. "I believe I don't need an army to take you down. As you so eloquently put it, I've already done that."

"Proud of ourselves, are we?"

Ryan grinned, liking this game. "No need to be proud when I speak the truth. And you really should consider just doing as I say, because I don't lose, sweetheart. Ever."

"Oh, hell no!" She started to back away, but he was quick. Where she moved, he maneuvered to block her. Ryan relied on his training, both as a pilot and a triathlete to wrangle her in. It tickled him that she was so unsuspecting of his moves.

"I thought you said you wanted to go somewhere," she squealed, shrinking away from him, laughing.

"Too late. Your ass is mine, York." Ryan crouched down ready to pounce his prey.

"Don't you dare!" She scrambled, moving to the side of the bed, ready to jump for it. Ryan made a dive for her but missed. "Ryan, no!" she squeaked.

Arching his back, Ryan winked at her. "Yes! I told you, you're mine, and I meant it." Ryan smirked at the expression on her face. Those words rang true in more than one aspect. He dodged to the side of the bed for a tactical advantage, but she diverted from him again.

"Give it up! You couldn't catch me when we were kids and you can't do it now," she jibbed.

"Oh, that's it!" It was time to show her who he was now. He made a rush toward her, catching her in one fell swoop. His arms locked around her like a cage, pulling her close to his body. She wiggled and squirmed against him as he tickled her, relentlessly. They laughed and played, as if they were two kids again, but their bodies knew otherwise. Any reasoning he had for leaving disappeared. Gone was his hunger for food or the need to get her away from the thoughts of their past. No, he wanted her. Again and again. And he'd have her.

Ryan stopped tickling her, his gaze rushed down to her heaving chest. In the glow of the moonlight, he'd never seen anything more perfect than the woman trapped beneath him. His already pounding heart was viciously trying to escape through his throat. She already owned him, fully and completely.

He leaned in and kissed her, the taste of her on his tongue was something meant only for him. That one kiss exploded into a wave of passion and lust. The sweetness of their previous lovemaking was absent, leaving only the raw need. He entered her body in one swift, sweet push. Each thrust of his hips grew harder and filled her with more force than he thought was possible.

A little worried he might be hurting her, he slowed his movements, but Alexis wouldn't have it. She gripped his hips, digging her nails into his flesh and pushed him to keep going. That was all he needed to lose control.

The bed rocked against the wall; Alexis held on to the headboard for support. Harder. Deeper. Faster. He slammed into her over and over, never relenting until they reached their climax, together. The world exploded in a string of lights, breathless screams, and delicious quivers. In those wee hours of the morning, Ryan claimed her body as Alexis took ownership of his soul.

"Lex?" Ryan's eyes fluttered open upon finding the spot beside him empty and cold.

"Yeah?"

Alexis sat at the end of the bed, her knees drawn to her chest, as she peered out the window. Darkness still shrouded the world, but the morning glow lightened the sky to hues of blue and green. Ryan shifted in the bed. Alexis remained unmoved, her back turned to him, closing herself off. The distance between them worried Ryan.

"You okay?"

"I'm fine." Her voice sounded lifeless.

"You're lying to me."

He sat up, pushing the covers away from his body and crawled to the end of the bed. He pulled her between his legs, drawing her to his chest. She swiped a tear from her face, her head falling back against his breastbone. Yet even with her this close, she felt a million miles away. Whatever was going on inside her was pulling her away from him. After the night they'd spent together, this behavior confused him. It even aggravated him.

Only hours earlier he'd been awaken by her kissing him. She'd taken him again, made him hers. He'd never spent a night like that with a woman. There'd been times he thought he'd been in love, but none of his past girlfriends ever made him feel the way he did with her. He shared things with her that he'd never even considered doing with another woman. The memory of her touch was forever ingrained into his memory and on his heart. It killed him to see her crying when he felt so happy.

"Talk to me," he pleaded.

"I don't know how." Her torpid tone and sniffles ate at him.

This wasn't the woman he taken to bed with him. No, this was an imposter who'd body snatched his Alexis. It had to be. He'd expected to wake once again to another round of great sex, the best he'd ever had, and then spend a day with her before he had to set back out to work the next day. This couldn't be happening.

"Alexis, please don't shut me out. Just tell me what I did wrong, so I can fix it."

She jerked around, facing him. Her red eyes and swollen nose sent another dagger to his chest. "You didn't do anything wrong. That's the problem. You're perfect. Too perfect." Her hands flung around as she spoke. "I've never known anyone to be so sweet, kind, funny, and possessive. Do you know how sexy that shit is?" She scrubbed her hands over her face. "And handsome. You were cute when we were kids, but Jesus, look at you." Her hands waved up and down his bare chest. "And oh my god, I can't begin to tell you how you made me feel last night, but Ryan, I'm not the right girl for you. I'm not the right girl for any man." A new swell of tears left tracks down her cheeks.

Ryan reached up, drying her eyes with the pads of his thumbs. "What makes you think that?"

"Because it's the truth. If we keep this up, one of two things is going to happen. Either you'll hurt me or I'll hurt you. It's inevitable. Nothing lasts. Look at my parents. They loved each other once and we see how well that turned out."

"Yeah, but then look at mine. They've been married for thirty-eight years and are still happy. You can't compare us to anyone else." He brushed her hair back from her face, cupping her cheeks in his hands. "You can only take us one day at a time."

She sucked in her bottom lip. "But what if this doesn't work? Then not only do I lose you as a lover but as a friend. I don't think I can handle that. I already lost you once. I can't lose you again."

"And you won't. You're not going to lose me. Ever."

Alexis jumped back, her feet landing on the floor. She started to pace, ripping at her hair. "Don't make promises you can't keep. You don't know what tomorrow holds."

Ryan moved from the bed, gripping her by the shoulders. "And neither do you. That doesn't mean we should stop living today because we don't have a promise for tomorrow."

"But what if I can't give you what you want?" she screeched.

"What I want is you!" he yelled back, shaking her slightly. "I want you. Nothing more."

"What about love? A family? You said you want kids."

Ryan released her, rushing his fingers through his own hair. "I do want those things. And I'd love them with you, but that doesn't mean I want them right at this very moment. I want to get to know you again. I want to learn why your brows pinch together when you're focusing on something really hard, or why you hum that tune all the time, or why you're always bouncing your knees." He placed his hand over her chest, feeling her heartbeat against his palm. "I remember the girl, but I want to know what makes the woman tick."

Alexis looked up at him, her eyelashes soaked with tears. "Why do you want to know those things? Why do you want me?"

He raised his hand, stroking her cheek. "Because you're the most amazing person I've ever met. You listed all the qualities you see in me. Well, let me do the same for you." Ryan led her back to the end of the bed where he sat down.

"In you, I see a beautiful, smart, fiery woman who's made me feel things I've never felt before." He gripped her by the hips, pulling her between his knees. Her hands landed on his shoulders and his body instantly reacted to the warmth of her skin. "Do you feel that? You do that to me. I'm possessive only with you. I've never—and you can ask anyone—been that way with any other woman. You bring it out of me. I want to rip Declan's head off, and any man for that matter, for even looking at you. You're mine. From the moment Makenna brought me that silly little compass on the plane, I felt whole again. You make my heart feel whole again."

"Always and forever," she whispered.

"Always and forever," he repeated.

Ryan slipped his arms around her waist, pulling her into his lap. "I'm so sorry," she cried. "I've ruined everything."

"Not at all. I'm glad you opened up to me, though. You mean everything to me, Lex."

She lifted her face and wiped the tears from her eyes. "That's what scares me, because it's exactly how I feel about you. You're my world."

Ryan felt a staggering wave of relief. He smiled, kissing the tip of her nose. "Give us a chance, Lex. That's all I ask."

She nodded her head, her eyes screwed shut. "Okay." Silence engulfed them. Ryan rocked her in his arms, kissing her smooth skin. She was still gloriously naked and more beautiful than any woman should ever dare to be. Her dark hair was wild and carefree and her skin flushed and pink from their romps throughout the night. Ryan reached behind him and pulled a blanket around them.

The longer they sat there, the more she relaxed in his arms. The silence was comforting, almost a promise between them. He pressed a kiss to her temple. He dared to break the silence as he asked, "You hungry?"

"A little."

"What do you say we get dressed and go get some breakfast?" Her lips brushed against his. "Okay."

She slipped off his lap, taking the blanket with her. Ryan caught her eyes shifting down to his hips. His body had reacted to her sweet kiss in delicious ways. He leaned back, placing his weight on his hands. "I told you, you do things to me."

She groaned. "This is not the way to get me out of here."

Ryan stood up, pulling her into his arms. "Go get dressed, woman." He swatted her behind. She glared at him, stomping her feet. Ryan laughed. He flicked on the lights to find his own discarded clothes. "We have the whole day to play," he teased. "But first, I need food."

Alexis dropped the blanket. "Fine." It was Ryan's turn to groan, as she bent forward, giving him the most glorious view of her body.

"Oh, you're good," he grumbled, slipping on his pants.

"Just playing your game," she teased, as she pulled her pants on without her panties.

"Too good," he growled, forcing himself to get dressed.

In no time, they were both dressed and in the car.

The drive was a quiet but cozy one. The sun was more than a shadow over the horizon, bringing to life the dawn of a new day. There was a chill in the October air, so Ryan turned on the heater to keep her warm. When they reached their destination, he parked the car.

Alexis' brow furrowed in confusion. Ryan had brought her to the airport, of all places. They parked in a field, close enough to the runway to feel the planes rumble as they made their descent or landing, but far enough away to be safe.

"Um, what happened to us getting food?" she questioned.

He reached behind them and pulled a blanket from the backseat. "I thought we could watch the sunrise first." He jumped out of the vehicle. Within a few strides, he was at her door and helped her out of the car. "I love coming up here," he mused.

"Especially in the mornings."

Leaves crunched under their shoes and the soft grass rumpled with each step they took. "It's beautiful."

Ryan wrapped his arm around her waist, drawing her into his side. "I know you fear falling, in more ways than one."

"Ryan," she whispered.

"No. Hear me out." He kissed her temple and released her. He withdrew the blanket from under his arm and spread it out over the grass. "You're the first and only woman I've ever brought here. Not even Reagan has been to this spot with me. I come here to think. This is peace to me. To watch the planes coming and going. Each one holds a new adventure for its passengers." Ryan walked around to the driver's side of the car and reached through the window. He turned the headlights off and turned the stereo up.

Alexis sat down on the blanket, pulling her legs beneath her. Ryan plopped down beside her, crossing his legs out in front of him. "This is a new adventure for us. There maybe disturbances along the way, but that's what makes life fun."

The chill of the morning air licked their skin. They should've felt cold, but neither of them seemed to care. Ryan moved in closer to her, stroking his thumb over the top of her hand. The clouds slowly passed across the sky, coloring the sliver of sun with a haze.

A plane made its descent to the earth. From where they sat, they could smell the rubber meeting the pavement and the ground rumble as the wheels made contact. "But what if we crash and burn?" she wondered.

"We won't." Ryan turned to her, taking her hands in his.

"What makes you so certain?"

His face blossomed with hope. "Do you trust me?"

She smiled, kissing him tenderly. "That's a silly question."

He shrugged. "Then trust me to protect you. Trust me to never let you fall."

Alexis chuckled. "That makes no sense, Ryan. I thought people were supposed to fall in love."

Ryan tapped the tip of her nose. "Falling hurts. Love's not

supposed to hurt. It's supposed to free you, to lift you higher. To make you fly."

"But I'm afraid of flying."

Ryan shook his head, confident in himself. "No. You said you're afraid of falling. I'm not going to let you fall. I'm going to make you soar."

Engulfed in a peaceful silence, Ryan and Alexis sat gazing at the taxi that pulled up to the airplane. A soft wind blew past them, ruffling Alexis' hair around her face. Ryan brushed back the straying strands from her eyes and tenderly kissed the top of her head.

"This one goes out to all the lovers tonight," the radio DJ announced. The sweet melody of a ballad from their high school years filled the air around them.

Ryan bounded to his feet, his hand extended toward her, and requested, "Dance with me?"

"What?" Alexis chirped in shock.

"Pretend it's prom night and I've just made sweet love to you for the first time." He winked at her. "Now, we're back in the auditorium and it's the last dance of the night. So, like I said, dance with me," he coerced.

She laughed, taking his outstretched hand. Ryan pulled her flush against his chest and began swaying to the beat of the music. With her pressed against him, he couldn't help but feel every emotion well up inside him. Alexis was his center. His rock. Without her, his life seemed meaningless.

"Who did you take to prom?" she teased.

Ryan dipped her down, kissing the hollow of her throat. "Stephanie Jargowsky."

"Are you serious?"

Ryan pulled her back to him, leading her to the rhythm of the music. "Yeah, well, my best friend left me all alone. I had to take someone."

"But Stephanie?" she whined. "That bitch always hated me."

Ryan laughed. "She was jealous of you. But have no fear,

nothing more than a kiss happened between us."

Alexis shot him an amused look. "Oh, really?"

"She was a terrible kisser," he snarled. "All tongue. I think she even licked my nose."

Alexis dropped her head back in laughter. "Now that's funny."

"Not to the eighteen year old version of me who still cringes at the thought of her." He shivered and gagged.

"So," she purred, "I'm a good kisser?"

Ryan rubbed his nose to hers. "The best I've ever had."

He stopped swaying and tilted her face to his. Under the expanding sunlight and the glow of the runway lights, her brown eyes popped with an expression that he knew only as love. Slowly, he let down his guard and moved his lips toward hers.

"Ryan," she breathed, her chest rising in anticipation.

"Alexis." Her name fell from his lips like a beautiful love sonnet.

There he kissed her. Not to take from her, but to give to her. In his kiss, held his soul. He wanted her and nothing more. Just as he started to drop her down to the blanket, ready to make her his again, right there in that field, the song changed, halting his movements.

A deep voice echoed from the radio, interrupting them with childish lyrics.

Alexis and Ryan stared at one another, laughing. "This is like the worst song ever," Alexis screeched.

"What the hell is wrong with that DJ?"

"You tell me! You're the one who picked this station." They laughed, but started to sing, unable to contain their childish exuberance. Before long, Ryan and Alexis were both bouncing and singing about a life in plastic being fantastic.

Later, they made a trip to their favorite diner before returning to her apartment where they shared a day of making love and getting to know one another all over again.

Alexis sat on the counter in Ryan's kitchen. Her legs dangled back and forth as she watched him create his culinary masterpiece. It was Christmas Eve and everyone they loved had gathered together at Ryan and Declan's apartment for an unusual holiday feast. While Ryan and Alexis were holed up in the kitchen, the rest of their guests were gathered in the living room, chatting, drinking, and watching a Christmas film.

"Lex, Baby, taste this. Tell me what you think." Ryan lifted his index finger to her lips, which was covered in spicy mayonnaise. He wore a hachimaki wrapped around his head, making him look silly but adorable. His handsome face was lit up with his bright smile; his eyes gleamed with Christmas spirit.

Alexis leaned forward, taking his finger between her lips, sucking the creamy garlic concoction from his skin. She watched as his eyes dilated, widening at the sound of her moan and the swirl of her tongue around his forefinger. She released his appendage with a pop, licking her lips. "Perfect."

A crooked sort of grin twisted Ryan's mouth. He leaned into her, pressing a sweet but tantalizing kiss to her lips. "You know you can't do that to me right now," he whispered.

"Do what?" she teased. "This, perhaps?" Alexis cupped the side of his face, her tongue sweeping over his lips. He accepted her invitation without haste, their mouths meeting in a sensual kiss.

"If only we didn't have everyone here," he panted when she'd freed him.

Grinning in confidence, she patted his cheek. "True, but just wait 'til we're alone tonight. The things I'm going to do to you..."

Ryan let out a moan, shaking his head. "Such a tease."

"Yes, well, had you not insisted on making a meal like this tonight," she waved her hand out, indicating the massive spread of sticky rice, nori, seafood, and fresh vegetables Ryan had set up along the counter, "we might've had some alone time." She tossed a carrot in her mouth, thrusting her legs out, then slamming them back against the counter.

Ryan reached over, placing his hands on her knees, stopping her legs from moving. "Yes, but you love sushi," he spoke with conviction.

Alexis swallowed down her bite. Those green eyes of his burned deep into her soul. No matter how hard she tried to fight the feelings that ached inside her, they always seemed to win out. Neither of them had said the dreaded L-word, but at moments like this, she wanted to. Love still frightened her, but the longer they were together, the more comfortable she became with the thought of giving herself to one person. And Ryan was worth it.

"True, but I would've been happy with a turkey that bakes all day, leaving time for the fun stuff before company arrives. Besides, who eats sushi for Christmas dinner, anyway?"

Alexis recalled Ryan's love for the holidays from when they were children. She remembered sitting up with him on Christmas Eve the year they discovered that Santa Claus wasn't real. Unlike most children, Ryan wasn't upset to discover the myth. Instead, he took it as a challenge to make Christmas all the more special each year. Now, as an adult, he maintained that tradition by decorating his apartment with the most festive of decorations. Alexis swore he must've followed every DIY site available, because the man could put Martha Stewart to shame with his holiday flare.

Ryan tweaked her cheek before grabbing his chef's knife to dice up cucumbers. "I wanted to make this a special night. I'm wearing my hachimaki and everything." With a steady hand, Ryan sliced through the vegetable with swift, smooth precision.

Alexis reached over, nabbing some crabmeat. "And you look adorable, but this isn't holiday food."

"It's holiday food in Japan," he huffed, scrapping the veggies aside with his knife. He reached for his bamboo-rolling mat, laying it flat on the counter.

"Is that where you learned to make sushi?"

Ryan placed a slice of seaweed on the mat, smoothing sticky rice over the nori. "I've been to China, but not Japan. I'd love to go, though."

"Me, too. All that culture and history," she mused.

Ryan piled his favorite toppings onto what would soon be a sushi roll. "That would mean you'd have to fly."

Alexis tenderly touched his jaw. "True, but then again, I'll have my sexy pilot who promised to never let me fall."

She locked her arm around his neck, pulling him in between her legs. Their mouths met in a kiss that ignited the room in passion. Gone was the need of her stomach. In its place was a longing, a deep desire for the man who'd held her captive, both in heart and soul.

Ryan dug his messy fingers into her hips. Alexis threaded her hands in his hair, attacking his mouth with vigor and insatiable need. Their tongues twisted and twirled, hungry for nothing more than the taste of each other.

Melanie, Alexis' mother, entered the kitchen smacking Alexis on the knee. "Get a room, you two," she chortled. Melanie snatched a cucumber from the cutting board, popping it into her mouth. She leaned against the opposite side of the counter as Ryan pulled himself from Alexis' grasp and returned to rolling sushi. A tinge of red colored Ryan's face, highlighted by the cocky grin drawn upon his lips.

"Mom!" Alexis screeched, her eyes bugging.

"Oh, stop it. I'm glad to see you so happy."

"Ain't that the truth," chimed in Shannon, Ryan's mother. She sauntered into the kitchen, wearing her traditional holiday sweater over her long, slender torso. "I always knew there was something between the two of you, even as kids."

Declan entered the room behind Shannon. "Oh, yeah!" he exclaimed. "Now this is what I'm talking about. I want all the dirt you have on them as kids. They're both very hush, hush about their childhood." He grabbed a California roll that Ryan had just set on the serving plate. Alexis snickered at the irritated look on Ryan's face. Declan shoved the whole roll in his mouth, his cheeks puffed out from being overfilled. He gave Ryan two thumbs up as he forced the food down his throat.

Melanie rubbed her nose, laughing. "Dirt." She raked her teeth over her bottom lip. "What kind of dirt do we have on them, Shannon?"

Shannon rubbed her hands together; a sadistic gleam twinkled in her eyes. "Hmm. That's a good question." She turned to Declan. "What do you want to know?"

Declan leaned against the wall, crossing his arms over his chest. "Anything. I'm sure you've got the skinny on all the good shit."

Laughter bubbled from Melanie. "Well, let's see. I bet you anything that Ryan has a box of Cracker Jack in the pantry right now."

Alexis and Ryan cut eyes to each other, both grinning. Declan shoved off the wall, and opened the pantry, producing a bag of the delectable treat. "This is a given." He shook the bag a time or two then threw it back in the pantry, slamming the door shut. "I want the good stuff. Stuff no one knows about but them."

Melanie rubbed her hand along her chin. "Did either of them ever tell you they shared a bed almost every night until they were what..." she paused, her eyes shifted to the heavens as she pondered their age.

"At least sixteen," Shannon inserted.

Mouth gaped open, Declan's head jerked back and forth between Ryan and Alexis. "No!"

Ryan chuckled, starting his next roll. "Yeah. For awhile I had to sneak into her room."

"For a while?" Shannon inserted. "Try forever. I remember the first night it happened, though. Ryan was five. Scared the bejesus out of Isaiah and me. I sent Isaiah over to your place," Shannon nodded toward Melanie, "to ask Miles for his help in searching for Ryan. They decided to go upstairs to ask Alexis if she might have a clue where Ryan was, only to discover that he was in bed with little Lexi."

Declan snorted in laughter. "Aw! How precious."

"Yes, but at one point," Ryan added, ignoring Declan's remark, "I had my ladder to climb."

"Until Mom and Dad took it away," Alexis complained. "That's when he had to start sneaking in."

Melanie fanned her hand out in dismissal. "We always knew you were there, Ryan," she noted, her tone teasing.

Alexis tilted her head, "That's kind of cruel, Mom. The poor guy had to climb a tree to get into my room."

Melanie shrugged her shoulders, the corners of her mouth turned up. "At least we didn't put bars on your window like your dad had suggested."

"Wait? Hold on?" Declan gesticulated. "You're telling me you were in her room every night, and you didn't even cop a feel? Not even once. What kind of an idiot are you?"

Alexis grabbed a carrot from Ryan's cutting board, throwing it at Declan. "He's a good guy, thank you very much. He took care of me."

"Oh, so you did cop a feel?" Declan teased, a mischievous expression brightened his face.

"Maybe once," Ryan muttered.

Alexis jerked her head in Ryan's direction, astonished. She didn't recall that ever occurring. Melanie, Shannon, and Declan burst into laughter.

"I think I accidently stumbled onto something here," Declan jeered.

"Stumbled onto what?" Isaiah questioned. The much older version of Ryan, ambled over to his wife, bumping her in the hip with his. He gave her a little wink and turned to the crowd, crossing his arms over his chest.

"Oh, geez!" Ryan muttered, his eyes locked on Alexis.

"Only the fact that your son was feeling up my daughter when they were kids," Melanie recounted, fighting to keep a straight face.

"As if that's any kind of news. I would've been disappointed otherwise." Isaiah gave Alexis and Ryan a playful wink.

Jenna stumbled into the kitchen, followed by Melanie's boyfriend, Dan, along with Mary and her husband, Shane.

Alexis could easily understand her mother's appeal to Dan. He was tall, towering Ryan and Declan, with thick bands of muscles outlining his body. For a man in his fifties, he was built like a rock and still quite handsome. His blue eyes brightened whenever her mother was near. For the most part, Dan was the complete polar opposite of her metrosexual father, dressed in his pressed jeans and fitted t-shirt that highlighted every ripple on his body.

Dan slipped around to Melanie, wrapping his arms around her. Alexis felt her stomach drop. It was nice to see her mother happy, but the nagging distrust of men left her unsettled. She wanted to like Dan, and she felt a semblance of fondness for the kind man, but she worried that Dan would hurt her mother just as her father had done. The thought sickened her.

"Sounds like the party's in here," Jenna announced.

Declan waved the rest of the dinner party into the kitchen. He reached into the fridge, grabbing bottles of beer and handing them out to everyone. Alexis popped the top off of two, giving one to Ryan. "Join us. We're getting the skinny on these two." He poked his thumb toward Alexis and Ryan.

Alexis took a long pull from her beer, feeling the heat rise in her cheeks. She glanced around the room to those she held dear to her. Jenna, saucy, sweet, and once again single, kept making eyes at Declan. It came as no surprise that Declan returned the favor, bestowing cute little winks and sly touches on her best friend from New York. In Alexis' opinion, Declan was a wise man for noticing the curvy blonde with a heart of gold. But as always, she had the urge to warn her friend that messing with Declan was like playing with fire. He would burn her.

"Oh, you mean," Jenna cleared her throat, "I wonder what Ryan's doing right now. Do you think he misses me?" she attempted an impersonation of Alexis.

"I didn't sound like that!" Alexis screeched.

Ryan set his knife down, cocking his head. "When was that?"

"Freshman year of college. If we weren't talking about you, we were talking about Doctor Fuckable," Jenna announced.

"Oh, yeah. Doctor Fuckable. I remember him," Melanie included.

"Do tell us about Doctor Fuckable," Mary hedged, slightly intrigued. Shane held her close to his side. Mary wore a red and green sweater matched with black jeans and boots. Alexis envied how she always looked so well put together. Even in scrubs, Mary managed to maintain a stylish flare. Shane stood an inch taller than his wife. He kept his head shaved to compensate for the balding pattern that had arranged itself over his skull. Most people might look at them as a mismatched couple, but in a strange way, they fit perfectly together.

Alexis covered her face with her hand, shaking her head. The conversation exploded and before long, laughter echoed through the room as Alexis' life unfolded for all their friends.

It felt nice to be surrounded by those she loved, new and old. Ryan finished preparing dinner—a beautiful cascade of sushi and sashimi that was tantalizing to the eyes and enticing to the taste buds. As they ate, they broke off into a menagerie of conversation. Occasionally, it would all turn back into one, especially when Declan stabbed his chopsticks into his sashimi rather than grabbing it properly. Eventually he gave up and obtained a fork to finish his meal.

Empty plates and drained bottles of beer and plum wine mosaicked the table. Ryan rested his arm on the back of Alexis' chair, leaning back as he discussed a book he'd recently finished with her mother and Dan. "If you like historically accurate Victorian fiction, I would highly recommend it."

"I've never even heard of it," Melanie admitted. "But it sounds amazing."

"You're welcome to borrow it. I have it in my room," Ryan offered.

"Are you sure? I can download it later."

"It'll give you something to read while you're in town. Let me go get it for you."

As Ryan scooted his chair back to leave the table, there were three rapid knocks at the front door. He glanced down the table at Declan who was putting the moves on Jenna. "Were you expecting anyone else?"

Declan shook his head. "Not that I know of."

Ryan lifted his hachimaki, scratching his forehead. He tilted his head to Alexis, smiling. "Would you mind grabbing that book for your mom while I get the door?"

"Sure. Where is it?"

"It's either on my bookshelf or in the crate in my closet." Ryan pressed a kiss to her cheek and bounced up from his seat.

Alexis watched as he made his way to the door before getting up. "I'll be right back," she announced to their guests.

She trotted down the hall to Ryan's bedroom. The echoes of

conversation faded into the background as she closed the door behind her. Her first stop was to the huge bookshelf that spread along the wall next to his closet.

She loved the way his room felt. It reminded her of a more grownup version of the one they'd spent so much time in when they were kids. Model planes worked as bookends on the shelves where books were stacked tall and wide.

It took some time, but after careful evaluation, she couldn't find the title of the book he'd requested. She entered his closet, looking for the aforementioned crate. Her eyes darted around the small walk-in closet. Nothing was out of place, everything neat and tidy. His uniforms were hung with care, all lined up and evenly spaced. She slid her fingers down the arm of his jacket, bringing the cuff to her nose. Eyes closed, she breathed in deep. It smelled of him.

She opened her eyes, catching sight of the crate at the top of the closet. It was too high up for her to reach, so she grabbed a chair from his bedroom and hoisted herself up. She tugged on the heavy, orange crate full of books, and as she did, something flew over her head, landing on the floor in a strewed mess. Startled by the flying object, she let out a little yelp then laughed at herself. For all she knew, Ryan was hiding bats in his closet.

"I'm Batman," she growled, again laughing at herself. Alexis glanced down at the floor to see the flying object was a box filled with papers.

She finished pulling the heavy crate down, careful not to fall backward in the process. Grunting at the object in her arms, she dropped the box of books on the floor and pounced down beside it. She knelt to the ground and began to clean up the mess she'd created. Scattered over the closet floor were postcards indicating various regions of the world. Alexis smiled at the realization that these were places Ryan must have visited.

She collected the cards from the ground, one by one, reliving his traveling experience through each picture. On the back of one, she noticed he'd written something. Much to her surprise, it was her name. One after another, she turned the postcards over to find they had all been made out to her. However, it eluded her as to why he never sent them to her.

So much confusion plagued her. Each little card was a secret that Ryan had kept from her. They'd been so open about their past with each other. She knew of his previous relationships, just as he knew of hers. All of their experiences were out on the table, or so she thought. Yet, in her hands she held proof of a piece of Ryan he'd refrained from sharing with her. To make things worse, the piece he held back was *her*.

"Lex, Baby, you in here?" Ryan's voice reverberated from within his bedroom. Alexis sat still, her heart pounded in her chest. These cards were physical representation that he'd never forgotten about her. That he'd thought of her, just as she had him, all those years they were apart. Tears started to burn her eyes.

"Lex?" Ryan poked his head into the closet.

The smile on his face dropped at the sight of her crouched on the ground, clutching the postcards. "All these years?" she whispered, holding the postcards up to him. She pinched her brow, and her head slightly shook in a continuous motion.

Ryan dropped to his knees and focused on her. "I'm so sorry."

"Sorry? You hid these from me," she gulped.

"You don't understand."

"Make me understand, because I thought we promised no secrets."

"We did!" Ryan implored. He rushed his fingers through his hair. "After we lost touch, I tried so hard to forget about you. To forget our plans to travel the world. But, no matter how hard I tried, you were always there in the back of my mind. It became a habit, almost an obsession, for me to collect a postcard every place I went for you."

Alexis raised the cards in front of her face, fanning them out and waving them. "But why didn't you send them to me?" she whimpered, brushing away her tears.

"I no longer had your address. I tried to find you online, but couldn't," he replied, taking the stack of cards from her, placing them on the floor. "And while it might sound crazy, I could never forget about you. Ever." His eyes met hers, warm and caring. He reached for her hands, linking their fingers together. "Every place I went, you were there with me."

The irony of it all wasn't lost on her. She looked down at their clasped hands. "Answer me something. It's been bugging me all night," she inquired.

His brow pinched and his head cocked to the side. "Anything."

"Tonight, when Declan asked if you ever touched me, were you joking when you said yes?" She sucked in air, her mind reeling.

A hint of pink colored his cheeks. His mouth twitched. "No, I wasn't joking. Please don't hate me for that."

"Hate you!" she exclaimed. "All those years I thought you preferred girls like Stephanie Jargowsky. She was smart and pretty." She dared to look at him. His green eyes were wide and brimming with tears.

"So are you, Lex. You always were. I thought you'd never want a scrawny guy like me." He moved in closer to her, cupping her face. "If I'd only known how you felt."

She rested her hands over his. The desperation in his eyes evident. "Ryan?" her cadence low, barely a whisper.

"Yeah?" His thumb traced the line of her bottom lip.

"How long have you loved me?" She met his eyes, searching for the truth. Ryan dropped his hands, running his tongue over his lips. He sucked in a deep breath, his hands clenching into balls in his lap. He tried to look down, but she refused to let him. She pushed up on her knees, tugging his chin upward to meet her gaze. "Please tell me."

His jaw stiffened and his shoulders straightened. He looked at her, determination in his eyes. "For as long as I can remember, I've loved you."

"Always and forever," she breathed.

Ryan nodded. "Always and forever," he repeated.

Tears burned down her cheeks as her wall of distrust disintegrated. All this time he'd loved her. That kind of love was impossible, only written in fairy tales, yet here it was. Right in front of her.

Unable to speak, she pressed her lips to his. She wanted so badly to tell him she felt the same way, but words weren't enough. They would never be enough.

She wrapped herself around him, drawing him in. Her heart pounded in her chest. Her need for him burned hot. Ryan enveloped her in his arms, gripping her shoulders. Their mouths fused together, barely allowing for air. She didn't need to breathe as long as he held her.

Pulling back, she cupped his face in her hands. "I've never told anyone this, but I blamed myself for my parents separating. After Cora died, I shut down. You remember how I was. Had I been a better daughter to them," her brow furrowed, "I know this is childish to believe, but maybe Dad never would've cheated. Since then, I've allowed that experience to mold and shape me. I've let the fear of being hurt consume me. It's prevented me from saying the very thing that's in my heart." She swallowed hard and those three little words fell from her lips. "I love you."

Ryan inclined his head; his mouth twitching and his fingers brushing her hair back from her face. "You love me?"

"More than life itself," she croaked. "You really love me?" Hope filled her timbre.

He released a heavy sigh. "With all that I am."

She reached up and removed the hachimaki from his forehead, tossing it to the side. Sliding her fingers through his soft, dark tresses, she pulled his face to meet her lips. Soft but firm, their mouths bonded them together. In a single, graceful move, Ryan flipped her on to her back. He hovered over her, the look of pure love in his eyes. A gasp escaped Alexis' chest as she wound her arms around his neck forcing him to press down on her. His body encompassed her, cradling her, protecting her heart as he promised he'd do.

Everything about this was right. The feel of his body, the way their lips danced together in perfect harmony, the intoxicating way his tongue slid over hers. His very taste, his scent, his heat, and his passion, they were all enhanced by the simple declaration of love.

Passion burned like a wildfire between them to the point that Alexis wanted to lose herself in the moment. Ryan caressed her side, his hand moving steadily along the curve of her hip, until he reached the back of her knee. He lifted her leg around his waist, pressing into her.

The atmosphere sizzled with desire, but most of all they were consumed by the love they felt. She slipped her hands between them, needing to feel him. Ryan pulled back, a tender smile on his lips, as he stopped her from unbuttoning his jeans. "You have no idea how bad I want you right now, but we can't."

"Why not?" she whined.

Ryan lifted his head and graced her with the sexiest of grins. "Because we have company and I can't promise when I make love to you that either of us will remain quiet."

Alexis dropped her head back to the floor, laughing. "Fair enough."

With reluctance, Ryan lifted himself from the floor. He took her by the hands and pulled her up with him. "Merry Christmas, my love." He pressed a sweet kiss to her lips.

"Merry Christmas, my heart."

Moments later, they were back with their friends and family, joined by Reagan and her boss, Lee. The night wore into the morning and Alexis couldn't recall the last time she'd felt such happiness. On Christmas Day, she was awakened by sweet kisses from the man she loved. It was a day of memories, that she'd cherish...always.

The bright red duvet brought a sense of color to the otherwise stark white room. The only other color in the space was from the blonde wood furniture. From the vantage point of his hotel room, Ryan could see the dancing fountains of the Bellagio just down the strip. Every time he flew into Vegas, he stayed at the Mirage, even though the airline would never pay for the expenditure due to cost.

Ryan enjoyed the sights of the strip and the Mirage was a prime location. Not overly expensive, which was good on his wallet, but lavish enough to make the experience memorable. The only thing missing on this trip was Alexis.

It'd been a few weeks since Christmas and things couldn't have been better between them. Every time Alexis uttered those precious words of love, the Earth moved for him. They'd spent nights chatting about their past and how they'd both misread the signals between them. It was something to laugh about now. And laugh they did, because none of it mattered. They were together and the universe had managed to correct itself. Or maybe it was fate simply giving them a second chance to correct past mistakes. Either way, Ryan wasn't about to let the opportunity pass him by. Alexis was his everything and he was determined that she'd never feel that kind of rejection from him again.

Not caring where his clothes landed, Ryan stripped out of his uniform. In nothing but his boxers, he leaned against the window. With his head pressed against his forearm, he watched as the water swayed back and forth, glistening in the bright lights of the sunlight. A heaviness weighed on his heart. It had been over a week since he'd been with Alexis. His body missed her. He ached to touch her. To hold her. He loved the way she purred when she was about to climax and how her body formed to his when they made love.

He glanced at the watch she'd given him for Christmas, counting down the seconds to when he could call her. He was two hours behind her in time at the moment, which was torture. The time zones often killed their nightly chats.

He closed his eyes, orbs of light flickered against his eyelids, as his mind swept back in time. The sound of her laughter, the warmth of her touch, the smell of her skin, the feel of her lips pressed to his, the sound of her moans when they made love, and the look in her eyes afterward. That look that told him no one in the world could ever love him the way she did.

Rubbing his palms into his eyes, Ryan blinked several times to bring the fountains back into focus. He inhaled deeply, willing the ache away. A reprieve came when the sound of his cell phone filled the air around him. Ryan lunged across the king-sized bed, grabbing the phone from the charger on the nightstand. A picture of him and Alexis flashed in front of him.

He swiped his finger across the screen, answering her, "Hello,

Gorgeous."

"Hey, you," her sweet voice echoed over the phone.

"What ya up to?"

"I just got home from Henry's recital."

"How was it?"

"You know Henry. The kid nailed it," she bragged.

Ryan loved the sound of pride in her voice for her little brother. The two had grown closer over the last few months. She'd even brought Henry along on a few of their dates. Ryan never minded. He enjoyed listening to the kid. There was an energy about Henry that reminded Ryan of when Alexis was a girl. She didn't even realize how much she and Henry were alike in so many ways. The only sorrow he felt was when Henry would say or do something that reminded him of Cora. Those were the times he'd see sadness in Alexis' eyes, because every time it happened, she'd notice it, too.

"I'm not surprised. He is your brother, after all."

Alexis let out a little chuckle. "I made sure to video it for you. I'll post it on Facebook in a bit. He's obsessed with you getting to see it."

Ryan flopped over on his back, propping his head up with a pillow. "He's a good kid."

"That he is."

Over the phone, Ryan could hear her rustling around. "What on Earth are you doing?"

"Sorry. I was getting undressed."

Oh, God! Slay me now!

"Really?" he coaxed. "Are you naked?"

"Ryan!" she shrieked.

"What? I can't help that I've been thinking about your naked body all day and the many things I intend to do to you when I get home."

Alexis moaned, that guttural sound reverberated through Ryan. Being near her caused his whole body to tingle with desire, but the sound of her voice amplified the reaction with them so many miles away from each other.

"What are you thinking?" he whispered, his voice dripping with seduction.

There was a pause. Ryan listened to her swallow. He smirked, adjusting the reaction his body was having in his boxers. "I'm trying not to think about what you intend on doing to me when you get home."

"Why would you want to do that?" Ryan reached down into his boxers, stroking his erection. "There's nothing wrong with me wanting to touch you...to taste you."

She whimpered. "Ryan, please."

"Please is right. Do something for me." When he was answered with heavy breathing, he pressed his lips to the phone and murmured, "Touch yourself for me."

"Do what?" she hissed.

Ryan twisted his lips in a smirk, his hand applying pressure where he needed it the most. "You heard me, Gorgeous. Let me hear you pleasure yourself." His heart rate started to rise as his strokes became longer, harder. The mental image of Alexis touching herself had heightened his senses.

"I can't do that," she whispered, apprehensive. The arousal in her voice suggested she was interested, but needed a little persuading.

"Sure you can," he coerced. "I'm touching myself right now." He heard her gasp. "I'm imagining I'm buried deep inside you. So warm. So tight. And oh so mine." His moan rumbled in his chest. "Please, Lex, touch yourself for me."

"Oh, God, Ryan," she whimpered.

Triumphant, Ryan listened close to the sounds of her breathing as it increased and her sheets rustling. He closed his eyes and allowed his hand to work. "Tell me what you're doing," he urged.

Holy hell! Not in the plans, but definitely hot!

Ryan could hear her adjust the phone. "Um," she paused. "I've slipped my hand into my panties and I'm touching myself."

"How wet are you?" A long silence. "Lex, tell me. I want to know you're dripping wet for me. Think about me touching you. My fingers, my mouth. I need to know."

A single word passed her lips. "Very."

Ryan jerked his hips at that simple, little word, unable to stop the husky growl that escaped him. "Oh, fuck me."

"I wish," she simpered.

Emboldened, Ryan stroked harder, applying ample pressure where she would've been wrapped tight around him. "I'm thinking about you right now. How tight you are when I'm inside you. So perfect. So soft. So wet. The sound of your moans. Your cute little laugh. Tell me what you're thinking about. Do you see me?" he coaxed.

Alexis swallowed hard, her breathing erratic. "I feel your lips on my neck," she rasped. "The way your long fingers work me, light and gentle but always strong and tempting."

"Mhm. Push your fingers in, Gorgeous, just as I would."

"Oh, God, Ryan!"

"Tell me how it feels," he goaded. Ryan increased his speed, needing the friction. The sound of his palm against his skin was soft but vibrant. His stomach tightened, fluttering with his imminent release. He wanted to last as long as she did, but hearing her in this manner made it rather difficult for him to keep his focus.

"It feels wonderful," she gasped. "I feel your tongue slipping inside me. Deeper, deeper…" her voice trailed off in a hushed whisper.

His hand moved faster. He needed her to reach her release or he was going to explode. "Slip another finger in. Think of me filling you up. Pounding you hard and fast, just like I know you like it." His body began to arch toward his hand. There was no controlling it. He closed his eyes, ready for that flash of light, that sweet sensation of his climax ripping through his body.

"Fuck." That single little word slipping past her lips drove him crazy.

223

"What's happening?" he begged.

"I can feel...I can..."

Every nerve in his body was ready to explode in agony. "Let go," he demanded, his voice dripping with desire.

The sweetest sound in the world filled his ears as Alexis found her release. She whimpered his name, breathless and mumbling, her sweet whispers drove him over the edge. His whole body shook hard from his own climax. Warmth flooded from him, pouring out of him. He was in complete overload from the sound of Alexis pleasuring herself for him as well as his own ministrations. He couldn't remember ever experiencing something so erotic.

"Ryan?"

"Hmm?"

"Tell me what you feel right now? Did you..."

Ryan looked down at his stomach. "Oh, yes. I certainly did."

"What did you see when you...did?"

Ryan smirked, reaching for some tissues to clean up. His girl was such a little minx. He loved it. "I imagined you riding me, so I could watch that gorgeous body of yours take me in."

"So you like it when I'm on top?"

"Very much so. I get to see all of you that way."

"I'll have to remember that," she purred.

Ryan let out a laugh, discarding the tissues. "See that you do." There was an easy silence between them, the same silence that always engulfed them after having sex. It was peace, happiness, and pure ecstasy.

"You okay over there?" he dared to break the silence, worried since he couldn't feel her in his arms or see her face.

"Oh, yes. I do, however, wish it'd been your tongue on me, so I wouldn't have to change my panties, like I am right now."

Ryan held back his laugh, slipping his fresh boxers over his legs. "Sweetheart, had it been my tongue on you, you're fine ass wouldn't have been wearing panties and I'd probably still be going."

Alexis released a sweet exhale. "Are you trying to kill me?"

Ryan held the phone against his shoulder as he washed his hands, drying them off with a towel. "Absolutely not. I'm simply stating a fact. I never get enough of you."

"You'll be the death of me, Ryan Fisher."

Ryan tossed the towel aside, making his way back to the bed. He plopped down, resting his arm behind his head, propped up against the pillow. "Anything for you."

"You're too good to me, you realize that, right?"

"Nothing's too good for my girl."

He heard her stifle a yawn, and realized how much later it was for her than him. It pained him that he wasn't there in bed with her, to cover her up, letting her fall asleep in his arms.

"You sound exhausted. I'll let you get some sleep." His chest ached the moment he realized he wouldn't hear her voice again until he got home the next day.

"It's been a long day. You come home tomorrow, right?"

"Yeah. I'll be in around eight tomorrow night." Ryan reached over, rummaging through his paperwork for his flight information. "The flight number is six-thirteen. Wanna meet at the diner?"

"You know I do."

Ryan tossed his paperwork back on the nightstand. "I'll see you tomorrow."

"Tomorrow," she whispered.

"I love you. Sleep well."

"I love you, too. Sweet dreams." Her soft whisper disappeared with the dead silence of the phone. For a moment, he sat there with the phone to his ear. The ache in his chest was back in full force. It pained him to be away from her, but he was up for captain soon. Once he made captain, then he could slow down and spend more time at home.

He tossed his phone aside, and laid his head back on the pillow, lost in his thoughts. He could imagine how she looked at that exact moment, curled up in the bed, on the cusp of dreamland.

So beautiful.

Time passed slowly, and sleep wasn't his friend. That was the plus side to being in Vegas. The city never slept. He jumped out of bed and slipped into a pair of jeans and a t-shirt. Tonight he'd blow off steam by hitting the poker table and tomorrow he'd be back in the arms of the girl who ruled his world.

"Seriously?" Mary dropped her jaw. "You've never had phone sex before?"

Alexis lifted her wine glass in front of her face, her humiliation burned through her skin. "Jesus! No! I've never been with a man long enough to even consider such a thing."

Mary reached across the table, pushing the glass down from Alexis' face. "There's nothing to be ashamed of. Shane and I do it all the time." Mary shrugged, sitting back in her seat, taking a sip of her wine. "It's the only way to keep the spice alive. Try sexting, too. Send him a picture of you wearing nothing but your stethoscope. He'll love it."

"You can't be serious," Alexis replied, downing the remainder of her glass. She set the glass on the coffee table, and leaned forward, resting her elbows on her knees. She and Mary had suffered through a long, hard day at work. Nothing seemed to go right. Computer failure. Disgruntled nurses. Overly sensitive patients. All in all, it was what people would call the day from hell. After it was all over, they agreed to enjoy a drink at Alexis' place before Ryan returned home.

"Absolutely. I sent Shane a boob shot just a bit ago. He loves when I do stuff like that."

Alexis chewed on her thumbnail, her knees were bouncing so hard her elbows slipped. "I don't think I could do something like that."

Mary swirled the red liquid around in her glass, glancing at Alexis from over the rim. "Ryan's been gone, what, a week?"

"Ten days," Alexis muttered, cutting through her thumbnail with her teeth.

"See. And it gets lonely for you both." She placed her feet on the coffee table, crossing her ankles.

Alexis buffed her jagged nail over her jeans. "Yeah."

"But he loves you and wants only you," Mary rattled.

A smile presented itself across Alexis' lips. It still felt weird to her that love was even in the equation of her relationship with Ryan. She'd fought against it for so long. But being with him, loving him, was easier than breathing. "True, but," she gave a timid shrug, "I don't know. I just don't think I could do it."

"Sure you could." Mary snapped her fingers. "You know, Valentine's Day is right around the corner. You could have boudoir pictures done for him."

Alexis leaned back in her chair giving Mary an incredulous look. "You're crazy. You know that? Certifiable even."

Mary rolled her eyes, her eyelashes fluttering for dramatic flare. "Just wait. Now that you've crossed the sexy time threshold, you'll do it more often. You'll get bolder each time, too."

A flush crept up Alexis' cheeks. She pressed her hands down on her knees to keep them from bouncing any harder. "It was hot."

"I bet it was," Mary quipped, her brows wiggling.

Alexis glanced at her watch. Her heart leapt in her chest. Ryan would be landing soon. After his little game from the night before, all she could think about was getting him home and having her way with him. She'd grown accustomed to how her body ached for him until he returned home. But, oh, the reunion was worth the ache.

"You know, I should probably head out of here. Ryan should be home—" Mary was cut off by the sound of Alexis' phone vibrating on the table. "Just as I thought," she tittered.

Alexis smiled and glanced down at her phone. Her smile faded as she looked back up at Mary. "It's Dale," she noted, a little concerned that her boss was calling her. There was an instant sinking feeling in her gut. He'd only call her when she was off duty if one of her patients had passed away.

At the same time, Mary's phone started to chirp. She placed her glass on the table and pulled her phone from her pocket. Her face scrunched as she scrutinized the screen. "It's Karen."

"Okay, this is weird." Alexis grabbed the phone and swiped her finger across the screen. "Hello?" she answered at the same time Mary did hers.

"Alexis," Dale responded, breathless and frantic. "I'm so glad you answered. I'll skip the formalities and get straight to the point of my call. A plane went down in one of the fields near the airport. All hospitals have been placed on alert, but since we're one of the closest to the wreckage site, we're receiving the majority of the casualties. I need all available hands in the ER immediately."

Her hand flew to her mouth. Her mind instantly turned to Ryan. "A plane accident?" Alexis gasped. "Where was it coming from?"

"I'm not sure."

A calm, sickening stillness washed over Alexis. Goose bumps formed over her skin. Her stomach dropped and her throat tightened. "Flight number?"

"I have no idea, all I know is our orders," Dale stated.

Alexis glanced up at Mary who was blanched white. Her eyes wide and brimming with tears.

"Doctor York, are you still there?"

She bit her lip, fighting back her own tears. This couldn't be happening. She shook her head, choking back the sickening feeling that swept over her. Maybe it wasn't Ryan. There were hundreds of flights entering the airport every hour. She sucked in a ragged breath.

"Alexis?"

Alexis swallowed hard, dislodging the large lump in her throat.

Stay positive. It's not Ryan, she told herself. *I'd feel if something was wrong with him. Wouldn't I?*

"Alexis!"

"Yes," she managed to whisper.

"I need you up here, STAT," Dale barked.

"I'm on my way," she replied, her voice dead and disjointed.

Mary hung up at the same time Alexis did, but neither said a word. Instead, they started to dial numbers. Alexis called Ryan, but immediately got his voicemail. She tried again with the same result.

Again.

And Again.

No answer.

"Oh, thank God!" Mary cried out, tears poured down her cheeks. "Shane. Are you okay?"

Alexis dialed Ryan again, her legs bouncing at their highest speed. She had one ear turned to Mary, waiting to hear any news.

"Oh, Jesus," she breathed, covering her mouth, as she made eye contact with Alexis. There was his voicemail again. "Are they sure?" A long pause ensued and Mary nodded her head. "Yeah, I'm with her right now." Another pause, the expression on Mary's face had darkened. "I'll tell her."

"Tell me what?" Alexis demanded.

Mary whispered a sweet goodbye to Shane and disconnected her call. "Lexi." Her bottom lip quivered. "I'm sorry." She rubbed her hand across her chin, her head shaking in slow motion.

Alexis slid out of her seat, falling to her knees. "No! Oh, God! No!" Pure terror ripped through her. The world stopped. Her whole body shook with fear. She couldn't breathe. This couldn't be happening. Not when they were so happy.

Mary tossed her phone aside, tumbling out of her chair to reach Alexis. She pulled Alexis into her arms, cradling her. "Shane says he spoke with the airline. They're not sure what happened yet, but rescuers are on sight."

A deep sob ripped out of Alexis' chest. Mary pulled her up from the floor, back onto the couch. She held Alexis tight, allowing her a moment to collect herself. "The hos...hospital needs us," Alexis stammered.

"Are you able—?"

Alexis stood up, rubbing her hands down her thighs. "I c-can," she exhaled, "I have to..." Alexis shook her head as if to fight off some sort of mental disorientation. "If he's there, I have to find him."

Mary bounced off the sofa. "Go change. I'll drive."

Alexis pulled her into a quick hug, then ran up to her bedroom, where she changed into her scrubs. She didn't care what she looked like. There was only one thing on her mind—Ryan. She had to get to him, no matter the cost.

In Mary's coupe, the engine revved as they sped down the freeway. Alexis forced herself to breathe, as she took in deep, slow breaths before she exhaled just as slow. Her body felt cool and clammy, yet sweaty at the same time. Off in the distance, she could see the billows of smoke filling the sky.

In her pocket, she felt her phone vibrate. She ripped it out, a smidge of hope bubbling inside her that it was Ryan calling her to tell her he was safe. That bubble was crushed when she discovered it was Declan calling her.

"I'm already on my way to the hospital," he parried.

"Deck, please, tell me this is a dream." Mary reached across the center console, squeezing Alexis by the knee. Alexis took her friend's hand, clutching it just as tight.

"I wish I could, but I got confirmation. Ryan was on that flight."

"I know. I'm with Mary. Shane already told us. What the hell happened?" she cried.

"All we know from the tower is that they lost altitude. They believe it was engine trouble."

"This can't be happening."

"Are you okay?" Declan asked; his timbre soft but concerned.

The whirl of the engine screamed as Mary weaved in and out of traffic. The closer they got to the hospital, the clearer the fire and smoke became. People pulled over to the side of the road, staring at the clouds of gray smoke and the steady stream of flames licking the mid-evening skyline. "No, I'm not. I won't be okay until I know Ryan's all right. I can't lose him again. Not like this..."

"I know, Doc. I know. It's going to be okay. Ryan's the best pilot I know. He's going to be all right. He has to be," his voice came out in a desperate whisper. Alexis wasn't sure if he was trying to convince her or himself. His words should have been encouraging, but to Alexis they felt empty and meaningless.

"Thanks, Deck." A jolt of emotion stabbed her in the chest. She screwed her eyes shut, fighting her heart with everything she had.

"Alexis, we're here," Mary stated, releasing her hand.

Alexis' eyes flew open to see flames licking the night sky, brightening it with hues of orange and blue. Chaos already filled the hospital parking lot with people trying to find their missing loved ones. "Hey, I've got to go. I'm here and this place is a madhouse."

"I'll be there shortly," Declan stated. "Oh, and Alexis?" There was a softness to his timbre that tugged at her chest.

"Yeah?"

"Ryan never gave up on you, so don't you dare give up on

him."

Amongst all the commotion, Alexis couldn't help but smile at the tender thought. "I'll find him. I promise I will."

"I know you will. Be safe, Doc."

Alexis said a quick goodbye and slipped her phone away. She glanced over to Mary who was in a mad haste to park the car. Every spot, including the assigned parking was taken. They had to park out on the street, but once stopped, they grabbed their stuff, jumped out of the car, and dashed into the hospital.

The hideous stench of blood, smoke, and burnt flesh siphoned all of the fresh air from the lower half of the hospital. Gurneys were being pushed in by the droves. The halls were lined with injured and mangled bodies perched on bleached cotton linens screaming in agony and despair. The pale stains of tears mixed with blood splattered the usually white walls of the facility.

Total chaos erupted in the emergency room. Orders were shouted from every direction but they were mere noise in a sea of panic.

In the corner, Alexis and Mary watched as triage nurses tried to calm family members, begging for information regarding their loved ones.

Mary grabbed a passing doctor, demanding some instructions. The doctor directed them to the triage counter where everyone was discarding their belongings. In haste, the two women did as they were told. Before tucking her bag under the desk, Alexis pulled two things from her wallet— a photo of Ryan and the tiny red compass she'd grabbed before leaving her apartment. Having those two items gave her hope and renewed her faith that she would find him alive.

Together, Alexis and Mary rushed into the corridors of the ER on a mission to locate Ryan. Fear gripped Alexis as she observed the carnage from the wreckage. She covered her face with a surgical mask in hopes to alleviate the putrid odor, but even the cloth covering was of no assistance.

Doctors and nurses rushed by, each one working diligently to tend to patients as fast as they could. Orders were yelled out at random. No one could seem to make heads or tails of what was going on. The only thing they were all certain of was the large amount of bodies flooding in.

Down the hall, Alexis caught sight of Dale. His light green scrubs were covered in blood, and sweat poured down his brow as he tended to an injured passenger. "There's Dale," Alexis yelled to Mary. Mary nodded and they moved toward their boss, hoping to get orders as to where they were needed. Alexis clung to a shred of hope that Dale might even have some information regarding Ryan.

As they approached their boss, a hand reached out from one of the blood soaked sheets, grabbing Alexis by the wrist. Alexis was startled by the touch and turned to see the hand belonged to a man wearing what was once an airline uniform. She searched his eyes hoping to find that hint of green through the blood stained orbs.

"Is it you?" she rasped, observing the man's mangled face. His skin was black and red; burned from the fire. The man only groaned, indicating the severity of his pain.

"Ryan?"

The man garbled something that Alexis couldn't make out. Something about him was familiar, she knew him, but couldn't place him. What she did know was this man wasn't Ryan.

"I'm Doctor York," she offered. "We're going to help you."

"Kix?" Mary moved around Alexis. "Buddy, is that you?"

The man groaned, attempting to nod.

"Holy shit!" Mary hissed. "It's the captain."

Alexis gasped, realizing whom it was. All she wanted to do was grill him about Ryan's whereabouts, but he was in too much pain to talk. She flagged down a doctor in the distance. He darted toward her, while she continued to hold the injured man's hand. "Morphine. This man needs morphine," she instructed.

Mary leaned into Kix. "Are you allergic to anything we should know about?" she asked, her voice raised.

Kix merely moaned in pain.

The doctor produced a syringe from his pocket. "There's

more in supplies. You'll want to stock up," he advised, rushing off before either woman could advise him of their discovery.

Alexis administered the narcotic to Kix. "This'll help. I promise." She patted his hand.

"Fisher," he said, tightening his grasp on her wrist. Alexis jumped, stunned at the amount of strength he displayed in his current state.

"Say that again?" Alexis beseeched him.

"Fisher," his voice wavered as the drugs began to take their effect. "Find him?"

"Not yet. I will though."

Kix squeezed her hand tighter, trying to lift himself from the gurney. "You...have to find him," he struggled, "saved my life."

He coughed hard from talking, causing him to spit up blood. Mary grabbed a bedpan from the foot of his gurney, holding it up to his mouth.

"Kix, you have to calm down," Mary warned. "We're going to find Ryan. Don't you worry."

"Please. He's..." Kix's eyes rolled into the back of his head. His mouth flopped open. The grip he had on Alexis faltered.

"Kix?" Mary called. "Kix. Wake up." She shook him, but got no response.

Alexis checked his pulse. It was there but fading. She yelled out, "I have the Captain here. I repeat, I have the Captain!"

A young doctor rushed over, pushing Alexis and Mary aside. Alexis gave the doctor a rundown of what she'd observed and the medication provided. Mary explained how they knew the man. Alexis glanced down at the doctor's chest, catching a glimpse of the name on his ID badge, Doctor Michael Rucker.

As the two women talked, Doctor Rucker examined Kix. He waved over two orderlies. "We need to get him into the OR, now." He rushed his fingers through his already disheveled blond hair, his brown eyes turned to Alexis and Mary. He produced a faint smile.

"Thank you. We've got it from here," Doctor Rucker advised.

Alexis grabbed the doctor by the arm, not letting him walk

away so easily. "Do you know if we've located the First Officer?"

The young doctor's face contorted. "Not that I'm aware of."

Alexis released the doctor, her heart sinking in her chest. The very thought of Ryan still being among the missing left her feeling cold and numb. She looked around the open space of the hospital. These were people, broken, injured, and in need of her care. It was her job, her responsibility to aid them and while she wanted nothing more in the world than to find Ryan, she had a duty to perform.

She heard Mary say something to the doctor, but didn't pay attention. Everything inside her shut down except the need to assist.

Mary grabbed Alexis by the shoulders. "We'll keep looking," she whispered to Alexis.

Alexis stepped out of Mary's grasp. Her natural instinct kicked in. Push down the pain. Don't acknowledge it. All she had to do was throw herself into her work. It was what she was good at and all she could rely on. "Agreed, but I think we need to separate."

"Um, are you sure?" Mary examined Alexis. "I don't like the idea of…"

Alexis lifted her hand, determination in her stance. "I'm fine, Mary. I get your concern. I really do, but now that we're here, I know what I need to do. Ryan is out there, waiting on us to find him, but we have to help all of them." She pointed toward the rows of beds. "We're obligated to help."

Lines appeared between Mary's brows. To Alexis, it was obvious that Mary didn't agree with the decision, but Alexis knew if they remained together, she wouldn't be able to continue with the job she needed to do. Mary was a reminder that Ryan was missing, and right now, she needed to focus on the task at hand.

Mary pulled Alexis to her chest, hugging her tight. "We're going to find Ryan, okay? We're going to find him."

Alexis clung to Mary; her hands fisted the back of Mary's top. "Agreed."

The two women parted, each going separate ways with a

promise to meet each other, in that exact spot, in two hours. Once Mary was out of sight, Alexis dove into helping the flow of patients entering the facility.

The quarters were cramped with bodies making the rooms hotter than normal. The stench of death surrounded her. Each person she came across, she helped to the best of her ability. Alexis was focused, and driven, which allowed her to block out the constant ache in her chest. That steady thrum of fear that tried to creep into her mind whenever she assisted someone who turned out not to be Ryan, telling her that the man she loved was forever lost.

Work was easy. She could get lost in issuing a prognosis. This was what she was trained for. While lost inside the job, she didn't have to feel. She didn't have to think beyond issuing her next command, and Alexis had no qualms in shouting orders when necessary. The vile smell of blood and singed flesh was sickening. It turned her stomach, yet still she trudged on.

"Tell me what we have?" Alexis asked a nurse as she approached her next patient.

"Female, approximately thirty years old, possible broken pelvis on the right side, left leg broken, and possible concussion."

The woman grabbed for Alexis, crying hysterically. "My son. Where's my son?"

"Calm down, ma'am," Alexis tried to console the woman.

"No! Where's my son? He was in the bathroom on the plane when it went down. You have to help me find him. He's only six," she pleaded. "I never should've let him go alone. Please, help me!"

Alexis turned to the nurse, her brow raised in a silent question. The nurse shook her head slightly, providing Alexis a confirmation that the whereabouts of the child were unknown.

"Kyle!" the woman screamed in agony. "Where's my son? Kyle!"

"I need you to calm down," Alexis commanded, her tone strong and powerful. She looked to the nurse. "Have we verified allergies?"

"I, um," the nurse stammered, looking through the paperwork provided by the medics.

Alexis let out a huff of impatience. "Any day now," she snapped.

The nurse glanced up, a snarl flaring her nose. "Yes. All clear, Doctor," she smarted back.

Alexis pulled a syringe from her pocket and inserted the needle into the woman's vein. "This should help calm her," she instructed the nurse. The drugs did the trick and the woman settled, her eyelids closed. Alexis took the opportunity to examine her patient. "She needs to be sent down for x-rays for her pelvis and then Ortho will need to come put a cast on her leg."

"Yes, Doctor," the nurse replied.

Alexis started to walk away, and the nurse grabbed her by the arm. "Doctor, can I make an evaluation?"

"Are you disputing my prognosis?" Alexis questioned.

"Not at all. You're a good doctor. There's no disputing that, but I think you need to take a step back, though. You almost snapped that woman's head off, not to mention mine."

Alexis met the blue-grey of the nurse's eyes. The woman meant well, but her accusations only brought forth the ache that Alexis was trying to bury down. "I beg your pardon?" she sneered.

"See! Right there. Doctor, step outside. No one will look down on you for taking a break. You need a break." The nurse crossed her arms over her chest in defiance.

"Fine," Alexis barked. She ripped her mask from her face and the gloves from her hands, as she headed toward the exit. It bugged her, because she knew the nurse was right. Not that she'd ever give her the satisfaction of telling her so.

Alexis reached the fresh air of the outside. One glance at the smog drifting in from the wreckage and all of the emotions she'd pushed down spilled forth. She slid down the side of the wall, crying to the point of convulsions. He'd promised her that she'd never have to fall. And she did. She fell hard for him, and now he was going to leave her—alone.

She rocked on the balls of her feet. Tears poured down her cheeks and neck. "Ryan, where are you?" she whispered to the emptiness around her.

"Alexis?"

At the sound of the man's voice, Alexis jumped to her feet, wiping the tears from her face. In the dark corner, she caught the sight of a cigarette being put out against the wall. Declan stepped out of the darkness, a weary expression on his face.

"Declan!" Alexis exclaimed, throwing herself into his arms. Declan encompassed her in his warm embrace. He silently rocked her, letting her cry into his shoulder.

"It's okay, Lex," he whispered, taking on Ryan's nickname for her. "It's okay. Ryan's going to be okay."

"I can't...I can't..."

Declan shushed her, petting her matted hair. "You can."

"No! I can't. I try to shut it all out, to do my job, but I can't."

"You're cutting yourself short, Lex. You're strong, or he wouldn't have fallen in love with you. You forget, I've known Ryan along time. I've watched him with other women." Declan cupped both sides of her face in his hands. His green eyes pierced hers, dark and handsome, but lacking the luster of Ryan's eyes. "Never once did I see him light up as he does with you. Lex, you're his world. No other woman had a chance because you've always held his heart. Now," he pressed his hand over her chest. "Follow your heart. It'll guide you to him."

"My compass." Her voice was tight and thick with grief. She reached into her pocket and withdrew the simple toy. In the palm of her hand, the dim light cast a dark shadow over the compass. Even though she couldn't see the dial, she felt secure simply having it.

Declan glanced down, taking the compass between two fingers. He smiled, refraining from asking her about the significance of the toy. Instead, he held it up in the light to examine the face.

"Ryan gave it to me," she admitted.

"Fitting," Declan hummed. "After all, he's your one true north."

He placed the compass back in her hand. Alexis clasped her fingers around the toy, her eyes clenched closed. She dropped her hand to slip the compass back into her pocket, but managed to miss the opening. The toy fell to the ground, clanking against the concrete. Panic swirled up inside her. She and Declan both dived to retrieve the compass, almost hitting heads. They chuckled and Declan held up his hand, to request she allow him. She nodded her understanding.

Declan reached down, retrieving the tiny toy. He blew across the face, dusting it off. "Not a scratch on it," he chuckled, "well, at least not a new one." He slipped the compass into her pocket for her this time. "Be careful with this. It's the guide to your heart."

Alexis wrapped her arms around him, holding on to the only anchor she had in that chaotic world. "Thank you so much."

"I'm your friend, Alexis," he stated with a smile. "That's what friends are for."

"So, you're finally accepting that we're only friends?" she teased.

"A guy has to accept defeat at some point." He quirked her a grin. "Beside, I'll still tell the world you claimed I was the best sex you ever had."

Alexis smacked his chest, laughing. It felt good to laugh. A release of energy that opened the door for hope. "Yes, but no one would ever believe you."

Declan tapped the side of his nose. "But I can still brag." A moment of silence hung between them. He pushed her hair back from her face. "I hear you're the one who found Kix."

Alexis nodded. "More like he found us."

"Then that means Ryan wasn't too far away. Okay?"

Again she nodded, wiping tears that seeped down her face.

"I'll be right here. Go back inside and find our boy."

Alexis patted her pocket, feeling the compass against her hip. "I won't stop 'til I find him."

Alexis pushed up on the tips of her toes, kissing Declan on the cheek. He smelled of cigarette smoke, after shave, and the fresh night air. With a quick hug and a promise to keep him informed, she returned to the building, where she'd set out to search for her one true love, determined to find him at all costs.

Returning to the ER, Alexis glanced down at her watch. Two hours had already come and gone since she and Mary parted ways.

Was it possible Mary had found him?

Alexis rushed to the location where she was supposed to meet her friend. She skidded to a stop. Her heart sank at the sight before her. Rows and rows of beds lined the walls where she and Mary had last seen one another. Doctors and nurses gathered around gurneys, tending to patients. Alexis bounced up and down in an attempt to see over their heads with little success.

She growled in aggravation, stomping her feet. Pushing through people, she searched for a familiar face.

About ready to give up and get back to work, she heard her

name being shouted above the noise. The sound of her name being called renewed her hope. She shoved through the sea of people, yelling back and waving her arms in the air for Mary to see her.

The masses parted. Like a beacon in a storm, there stood a tired and worn Mary. Her blonde hair was covered with a surgical cap and her facemask dangled around her neck. A timid smile turned up her lips and her eyes watered at the sight of her companion. Alexis sprinted forward, unable to get to Mary fast enough. The two women collided into one another, breathless and in tears. They embraced each other, swaying back and forth.

"Have you found him?" Alexis cried. Her tears mixed with the blood on Mary's scrubs.

"No. There's too many of them."

Alexis pulled from Mary's embrace. She wiped her knuckles under her nose, bobbing her head. "Maybe he's at another hospital. Dale did say all hospitals in this area are on alert."

Mary scratched her head, misaligning the cap on her scalp. "I don't know. I guess anything's possible."

A fresh swarm of paramedics rushed into the hospital, bringing more injured patients. The body count appeared to be never ending. "Jesus Christ!" she swore, pressing her palms to her skull. "This is crazy!" The mass amount of people entering the emergency room didn't stop her from stepping into action. She'd taken a professional oath to serve and do no harm, but also a personal one to find Ryan. They both mattered.

"Alexis?"

"Hmm?" Alexis responded, staring at the new gurneys being rushed in. She blinked, refocusing her attention on what was being said to her.

"I asked if you need me to call his parents?"

Alexis looked into Mary's eyes, a little confused by her suggestion.

"Why would we do that?" she asked, dazed.

"I'm sure they've been contacted by the airline," Mary noted. "But, it might be nice if one of us calls them. You know, to let them know what's happening here."

Alexis scratched the back of her neck, still watching the throngs of gurneys being rolled in. "But there's no news of his whereabouts as of yet," she stated, wringing her hands together. "We can't call them until we find him."

"I just thought they might like to hear your voice, Lexi. This has to be scaring the shit out of them. I know it is me. And I can't begin to imagine what you're feeling."

A wave of misery washed over Alexis. "I don't want to think right now," she choked. "And I can't call them. Not until I know for certain he's okay." Dismay and terror swirled inside her head. She pushed it down, deep into her gut, forcing the pain to cease. It was the only way she could get herself back on track. She lifted her eyes to meet Mary's gaze. "We can't stop." She pointed around the room. "These people need us." In a little whisper, she added, "He needs us."

Mary gripped Alexis by her shoulders. "Okay." She forced a smile on her face. "Let's get back to work."

Alexis pulled Mary into a hug. "Thank you."

Mary patted her back. "Of course."

"Oh, and Declan's here. I ran into him outside smoking. Did you know he smokes?"

A somber chuckle cut through Mary's lips. "I knew he used to. Guess the stress is getting to him. Not that I blame him."

"Neither do I." Alexis pulled a fresh pair of gloves over her hands, ready to get back to finding Ryan.

"There you two are," Dale called out. "I've been looking everywhere for you. I expected you to check in hours ago."

Alexis and Mary whipped around to find Dale stalking toward them. He appeared as exhausted as they felt. "We couldn't find you," Mary fibbed.

"So we went straight to work," Alexis added.

Dale nodded, accepting their answer without consideration. "Fine, fine," he mumbled. "Alexis, can we talk?"

From the look in Dale's eyes, Alexis had a sneaking suspicion she knew what he wanted. Ryan must've been found. Feeling Mary's eyes on her, Alexis pulled her gloves off her hands and tossed them in the trash. "Of course," she replied, "Is it about Ryan? Has he been found?"

Dale took a deep breath, glancing between the two women. His eyes swam with tears. "There's no easy way to put this, so I'm going to be frank," he started. "A new load has arrived, all fatalities. Among them were a couple of crew members." He licked his lips and blinked back the tears. "I'm so sorry, Lexi, but one is believed to be Ryan. I need you to accompany me to the morgue to identify the body."

Alexis wrapped her arms over her stomach, her chest heaved as tears exploded from her. She clenched her teeth together, trying desperately to breathe, but all of the air in the building seemed to have been sucked out the instant Dale suggested Ryan was dead.

Frozen in place, Alexis tried to think. She tried to move, but couldn't.

It wasn't possible. It couldn't be. This had to be a cruel joke. Images of Ryan flashed through her mind. His smile. The sound of his laughter. That insatiable sweet tooth of his. Even the way his eyes would roll back when he reached his climax. All of these little things, things she'd never noticed with anyone else, but with him seemed great and noteworthy.

Mary wrapped her arms around Alexis. "I'm so sorry, Lexi," she whispered, her voice filled with tears.

A jagged breath couldn't drown out the sound of her heart breaking in her chest. This had to be some cruel cosmic joke. After all those years of being separated, to find one another in one of the oddest places, to falling in love, only to have him taken away from her, there was no doubt about it. This simply had to be a joke.

Breathe, Alexis coached herself. *Just breathe.* She swallowed back the lump that was forming in her throat.

"I've contacted Ryan's family. They gave permission for you to identify him," Dale explained further.

"We were just talking about contacting them," Mary

confirmed. She squeezed Alexis tight, but Alexis felt so numb that even the pressure of Mary's hug was empty.

Alexis rolled her shoulders, popping her neck. Nothing could break through the numbness in her soul. Helplessness boiled beneath her skin.

"Alexis are you all right? You look awfully pale. Would you like to sit down?" Mary asked.

"No," Alexis croaked. "I'm fine. I need to see him."

Dale shook his head. "We can wait 'til his family gets here," he offered. "I really think you might need to—"

"I'm fine," Alexis interrupted, her tone obstinate. She straightened her back, forcing her chin out in a stubborn angle. "Please, take me to him."

The room started to spin. She felt nothing but the pounding of her blood pulsing through her veins. Reaching into her pocket, Alexis withdrew the tiny red compass. She glanced down at the toy and for the first time since Ryan had given it to her, it didn't point north. It was as if, in that moment, the compass knew that her one true north was gone. The compass could never point her back to Ryan because her heart was gone.

Tears burned her eyes, as she squeezed the plastic figure tight in her hand. "Mary, will you come with me?" she wept.

"Absolutely, Sweetheart."

"Follow me," Dale instructed the two women, turning around on his heel.

As they walked, Alexis found her mind wandering back to when they were children. How much he had changed over the years, yet after all that time, he was still the same sweet boy from across the street that had stolen her heart during their youth. The same boy who always had something sugary in his hand. The boy who would light up whenever they were together. He was the boy who loved books and enjoyed music. The same boy who could make her laugh when she wanted to cry. He was the boy who held her hand at her sister's funeral. The boy who stood beside her when she faced moving to New York. However, Ryan was more than a boy, now. He was a man. The man who made her realize that love wasn't a weakness. It was her strength. Ryan was the man she fell in love with. The boy was only a memory.

Not a word was spoken between the three of them as they travelled through the halls of the hospital, taking the elevator down to the basement, to the morgue. When they arrived at the morgue door, they were greeted by the medical examiner.

"Alexis, you'll have to go in alone," Dale advised.

Unable to speak, Alexis simply nodded her head. She swallowed hard, staring at the cold, metal doors that led into the morgue.

"I'll be right here," Mary said, squeezing Alexis' hand.

Giving it a return squeeze, Alexis released her friend's grasp, letting her hand fall limp at her side. The coroner opened one of the double doors, holding it for Alexis to follow him. "This way, Doctor," his deep voice instructed.

She trudged into the room; each step feeling weighted, as if she were facing her own execution. Her mind now void of anything but her surroundings, she walked just beyond the door and glanced over her shoulder. Mary and Dale were holding one another, watching her. Their eyes filled with tears and their lips trembled.

The morgue door closed with a thud. The very sound made her jump. She turned her head and settled her focus on the room. The walls of the morgue were tiled from the ceiling to the floor in pure, glossy white. Sterile chemicals filled her nostrils, burning her nose with each breath she took. Lined in perfect rows were trays of bodies covered in white sheets. It occurred to her that each tray held the body of someone's loved one.

Step by step, Alexis followed the coroner down the aisle. With each metal tray they passed, a sense of desperation swelled inside her. Any one of these people could be Ryan. Horror struck her that his body, his beautiful face could be lying on one of these slabs. He deserved more than a cold metal table to lie on. It made her sick inside to think he was in this dreary place.

Could it be possible that I'll never see his smiling face again?

She chewed her bottom lip, her fingers clenched shut. Her shoulders dropped. All of the pent up emotions, everything she'd tried not to allow to interfere with her job, was ever present.

How could she survive knowing he would never be there to rescue her again? How could she live with herself, knowing that she would never touch him or smell his cologne on her skin again? Did she tell him enough that she loved him? Was it ever possible to tell him enough?

Her heart screamed out her love for him, aching to feel his breath on her skin or to see his warm eyes staring into her face once more. He was gentle. Kind. Possessive. And hers. The years may have separated them, but time could never take away the love she held for him.

The room started to spin with each wave of emotion that poured over her. He couldn't be gone. He had to be alive. He'd promised her he'd never let her fall and she was falling now more than ever.

Pull yourself together, York. You're a professional. You've seen people die thousands of times. Hell, you were there when Cora died. This is no different.

But she was wrong.

This was different.

Cora had been special to her and she still carried the grief of her loss, but Ryan had been there to hold her together when her sister passed. Who would be there for her now? She would be alone.

Ryan was the other half of her soul. That was why she could never fully let him go, why she kept the compass all those years, and why she could never give her heart to another. He was the piece of her heart that was never hers to give. His love was infinite and finite. It was beyond the realms of nature. His love was everything.

The coroner stopped in front of a table near the end of the row. "If you'll please step over here," he instructed, extending his hand to where he wished for her to be.

Squeezing her fists into a tight ball, Alexis realized she'd been holding the compass in her palm the entire time. She looked down at the small plastic object. The dial spun around and around, in constant motion. It felt as lost as she did.

Alexis slipped the compass back into her pocket and walked around to the side of the table. Chills beveled her skin, making her hair stand on end. The heart in her chest had practically stopped beating. The medical examiner stepped in front of her. "I don't think I need to explain to you how this works," he said.

For the first time, Alexis looked at the man that had been her guide. He was rather short for a man, standing only a few inches taller than her. The sterile lighting in the room washed out his caramel colored skin and his brown eyes, while warm, had lost their sense of humanity after working among lifeless bodies for so long. On his scrubs, hung his name badge, Doctor Joseph McCall.

Nodding her head, Alexis' eyes moved over the covered form in front of her. It was obviously a male figure about Ryan's height. The facial profile was defined, much like his, but it was hard to tell with the sheet over it. Her mouth pooled with metallic liquid. She tried to swallow but her throat felt tight and closed.

Prepared for the worst, at least she thought she was, Alexis watched as Doctor McCall gripped the corners of the sheet between his fingers. The cover lifted from the man's face, revealing the person underneath.

For a moment she stared at the body, cold and emotionless. Her mind didn't register what she was looking at. She couldn't move. The world had physically ceased to exist for her.

Then all at once, every emotion that had been void and vacant swelled forth. Alexis buckled forward in a flood of tears. She thought she had prepared herself, but the truth was, nothing could have prepared her for this.

She cupped her hands over her mouth and stared at the lifeless form. "Please," she cried, waving her hands. Alexis stepped back, incapable of breathing. With her back pressed against the wall behind her, she could feel the cold tiles through her scrubs.

"Please!" she screeched again, waving for Doctor McCall to drop the sheet.

Slowly, Joseph placed the cover back over the body. Alexis watched as the lifeless form disappeared from sight. She slid down the wall, covered her face in her hands, and sobbed.

The metal doors of the morgue creaked open and Alexis stepped into the corridor. Both of her hands were balled at her mouth. Every inch of her body trembled. Evidence of her despair had cut lines along her face. All color was washed from her skin. Her hair was flat and lifeless. The sag in her shoulders revealed the heavy burden of heartache she bore.

Her tear-swollen eyes honed in on Mary, who was sandwiched between Dale and Declan. Alexis thought nothing of Declan being there. He was family. They were all family.

On bated breath, everyone waited for her to confirm their fears. She glanced from Dale to Mary then to Declan. Concern, grief, and fear masked each one of their expressions. She shook her head, her face twitching with emotion. Her hands dropped to her stomach as a fresh swell of tears overpowered her.

"Oh, God!" Mary gasped.

Alexis waved one hand, the other flattened firmly at her belly. Her voice caught in her throat, trapped by the sobs, which cut through her. Finally, she forced sound to come from her mouth. "It's not him," she blurted out in almost a harsh scream. All the energy she had left drained from her and she fell to the floor in a puddle of tears.

Declan released Mary and rushed toward Alexis. He skidded to his knees, scooping Alexis into his arms. "It's not him," she repeated, her voice a mere whisper now. Thick tendrils of hair had fallen over her face. Declan smoothed her hair back, kissing her temple. His touch was soothing, but it didn't calm her.

"It's all right," Declan said, his nose buried in her hair. "Everything's going to be okay." He rocked her, holding her tight to him. The pressure was exactly what she needed to close the chasm in her chest, but his scent and the shape of his arms weren't right. He wasn't Ryan.

Mary dropped to her knees and crawled to where Declan held Alexis in his arms. She encompassed them both in her embrace. Together, the three friends cried. For the fear of losing Ryan. For the hope of finding him. For the love they all felt for the man who'd brought them together.

Alexis wiped the tears from her eyes. She pushed against Declan's arms, struggling to stand. Declan released her, offering his hand as she wobbled to her feet. Dale rushed to her, taking her other hand to help steady her. From the corner of her eye, she could see Dale give her friends a serious look. She couldn't allow that to persuade her from her mission. Ryan was still out there, waiting for her to find him. "I'm fine." But even to her own ears she could hear the weakness behind her words. It didn't matter. All that mattered was finding Ryan. "I have to get back out there." She willed her body to move.

Dale grabbed her by the arm. "Alexis, stop. You need rest."

"No," her voice was shaky and quiet. She shook free of Dale and stumbled forward. Her whole body felt drained, almost as if it weren't hers anymore. Every ounce of energy she had was gone. Shock was setting in, but while her body was weak, her resolve was strong. "I must find him."

Declan pulled himself up from the floor bringing Mary along with him.

"Alexis, honey," Mary approached her, pulling her into a hug, "Dale's right. You need rest. We'll keep looking, but you just experienced something traumatic. You need to recoup."

Alexis shook her head. "No. You all aren't taking a break, and neither will I. I can't stop. Don't you see that?"

Dale rested a hand on her shoulder. "Yes, but like Mary said, we didn't just endure the trauma you did. A small break doesn't make you weak."

She shrugged away from Mary and Dale. "I've worked forty-eight hours straight with no break. I can handle this!" She threw her hand out toward the elevator. "There are people out there who need us. All of us. Me included." She buckled forward, the air in her lungs dense, her head splitting inside her skull. "Please," she pleaded. "I can't rest until I find him."

"They're both right, Doc." Declan came up behind them, resting his hands on Alexis' shoulders. "You'll be no good to him like this. Ryan would be pissed if I let you continue when I know better."

"Go lay down in my office," Dale instructed. "If we find him—"

"When—" Mary corrected.

Dale nodded. "Yes, *when* we find him, you'll be the first we notify."

"I can't," she cried.

"You must," Declan demanded.

"Don't make us give you a sedative," Dale commanded.

Unable to fight them any longer, her shoulders slumped and she fell back against Declan.

"Deck, take her upstairs to Dale's office. We'll head back to the ER." Mary reached for her hand, giving it a good squeeze. "We'll find him. I swear to you. Please rest."

"I hope you know where you're going, because Dale's office could be the john for all I know," Declan joked.

A faint but forced smile appeared on Alexis' lips, as she released Mary's hand. "Some pilot you are. Can't even find an office."

"I'm a great pilot," Declan boasted, pulling her into the crook of his side. "I follow directions well. So, navigate, woman. We got to get your energy back for when we find our boy."

A strangled chuckle gurgled in her chest, as she leaned into him and allowed him to walk her down the hall. She felt the pull of her emotions tugging inside her. The world was off course, and maybe her friends were right. A quick break could set her back on path to finding her heart and soul.

"Alexis," someone whispered her name, "wakey, wakey."

A little stiff from sleeping on a couch, she shifted her position but kept her eyes closed. The peace and numbness of sleep surrounded her and she didn't want to leave that comfort just yet.

Small hands shook her by the shoulders. "Lex, wake up."

Alexis' eyelashes fluttered, eyelids lifted, and big brown eyes opened to find an outline of someone hovering over her. She could barely make out their form, but there was something all too familiar about this person.

"There you are. I thought I'd lost you. We have so much to catch up on and so little time to do it in." That voice. She recognized it. Like a dream or a memory. But from where?

"Huh?" Alexis croaked. She felt confused, dazed, and disoriented, but strangely calm. Nothing seemed to make sense. Her mind felt heavy and foggy, yet clear and light. Deep in her chest, her heart ached, and her eyes felt like rocks in their sockets, but they were masked by the sweet peace that seemed to wash over her. There was no pain, even though there was. It was the oddest sensation she'd ever experienced.

She squinted her eyes, trying to focus on the person poised over her. Should she be afraid of this person? The odd feeling of serenity that surrounded her told her that she had nothing to be afraid of. Alexis rubbed the ball of her hands into her eyes, causing them to throb even more.

"Careful there. You've had a rough day. I'm sure you're probably feeling like you've been beaten within an inch of your life."

The voice was distinctively female. Almost childish in sound.

Alexis shifted her weight onto her elbows, pushing herself off of the soft surface of the sofa. The faceless figure stepped back, giving her room to move. The soles of her ballet slippers tapped against the linoleum, keeping Alexis aware of her presence. Alexis groaned as she stretched her exhausted body; every joint popping with each move she made. With her eyes closed, she rolled her neck, relieving even more of the tension from her sore body. What happened to make her so tense?

Alexis looked up at the shadow, squinting her eyes. "Who are you?" she asked, a twinge of uncertainty prickling her skin.

The little girl giggled, skipping in place. "Guess."

Eyes narrowed, Alexis tried to focus on the bouncing figure. "Just tell me who you are," Alexis groused.

"Oh, you were never any fun with guessing games," the child complained.

Stepping out of the rays of the fluorescent light stood a little girl wearing a tutu and holding a glittery wand. Her dark tresses were wound tight in perfect ringlets and her big, brown eyes were almost liquid, like molten chocolate. She wore a smile that could only be made by angels.

Alexis covered her mouth, her eyes widening in recognition. "Cora?"

The girl laughed, clapping her hands. Her wand flapped in the wind. "I didn't know if you'd recognize me like this." She twirled around, her tutu fluttering with the air.

"Of course I do!" Alexis squealed, throwing her arms around her baby sister. She smelled of sunlight and fresh cut grass on a summer day, like she always had. "You always wanted to be a dancer. I used to sing and dance for you because..." her voice trailed off. Because of the leukemia, Cora became tired too easily. Her heart was willing, but her body wouldn't allow her to dance. So, Alexis took it upon herself to dance for her sister when she could.

Alexis took a step back, staring at the illusion of her baby sister.

"Don't be sad. I can dance now." Cora pirouetted on her toes, flittering about in perfect form.

Alexis smiled, grabbing Cora by the hand and pulling her to her chest. She rocked her sister in her arms, amazed at how real she felt. "I've missed you so much."

"I've missed you, too," Cora whispered. "It's been lonely without you."

Alexis pulled back, looking into her sister's deep brown eyes. "Wait? If you're here, does that mean I'm..."

A chirp of laughter burst from Cora. "Don't be silly. You're not dead."

"Whew, that's a relief," Alexis mused. Cora withdrew herself from Alexis' hold, dancing about the empty space around them. Alexis furrowed her brows, a little confused by the whole situation. "Okay, if I'm not dead, then what are you doing here?"

Cora stopped dead in her tracks. She approached Alexis and directed her back to the couch she'd been lying on. Cora dropped her gaze to Alexis' now closed fist. Alexis followed Cora's eyes to her hand. Slowly, she flexed her fingers open to find a small red compass in the palm of her hand. Something touched the recesses of her thoughts. The fuzziness felt as if it was fading and her mind conjured up the face she'd been searching for. Then, like a flood, memories of the accident invaded her mind. "Ryan!" she gasped, trying to stand up. "I have to find Ryan."

"Sit down, Alexis," Cora commanded with such authority she had no choice but to obey.

Tears spilled down her cheeks, adding more pressure to her already aching eyes. "It's not Ryan, is it?" she pleaded. "Ryan's not dead, is he?"

Without a word, Cora took the compass from Alexis' hand. She examined the face, flipped it over, and rubbed her thumb over the worn red plastic.

Alexis tilted her head, her face scrunched in confusion. "Cora, please. If you know anything about Ryan…"

"Funny things, compasses," Cora noted, ignoring Alexis' pleas.

"It's just an old, broken toy."

"This," Cora held the compass up in the air, allowing the light to shine around it, "is more than a toy, and it's far from broken."

Alexis lifted her eyes to look at the compass. It was spinning out of control, just as it had been when she entered the morgue. "I dropped it earlier and that must've busted the mechanism in it. See." She pointed to the spinning hand. "It doesn't point north anymore."

"That's because you're lost."

"I don't understand. Aren't compasses supposed to help people find their way? Make the lost, found?"

Cora shook the toy, watching it spin. "This compass is a reflection of you. As long as you knew Ryan was safe, it pointed north. Ryan has always been the other piece of your soul." Cora let out a little sigh. "I was always jealous of the connection you had with him."

Alexis furrowed her brow. "Jealous? Because you had a crush on him?"

"No, silly! Because he's your soulmate."

"Hold on. Are you trying to tell me that soulmates are real? They're not some crap made up by writers to sell some shitty books?"

Cora tsked at her sister. "How can you be so obtuse? Soulmates are a rare but wonderful thing. Even now, don't you feel the pull for him? The connection? You must." She rolled the compass between her fingertips.

Alexis closed her eyes, her heart sinking in her chest. She did feel the pull for him. It was that very need that drove her, pushed her to find him. She couldn't live without him. That much she was certain of.

Cora took Alexis by the hand and placed the compass into her open palm. "This compass only points to your one true north when you believe in him. The moment you lost faith that he was okay was the moment this compass stopped pointing north."

Alexis closed her hand around the compass, her eyes welling with tears. "I don't know what to do. I'm so scared."

Cora pulled Alexis into her warm embrace, holding her tight. "Alexis, you do know what to do."

"I do?" she whispered through her tears.

"Yes. Follow the compass. Follow your heart."

Alexis pulled back, wiping the tears from her eyes. She looked down at the compass; its hand was spinning wildly. It looked how she felt - lost and out of control. Alexis slid her thumb over the scratched and faded plastic.

"My heart is lost," she admitted.

"Just believe," Cora whispered. "And remember, you're not alone."

Alexis lifted her eyes, a smile bright on her face, but instead of finding Cora looking back at her, she was stunned to find Ryan had replaced her sister.

Alexis reached up with her free hand and brushed back the bangs that had fallen against his forehead. She marveled at how handsome he looked in his uniform. The bright glow of the fluorescent lamp highlighted the midnight blue tones of his soft black hair. His piercing green eyes twinkled with love.

She threw herself into his arms and cried. "I've been searching for you everywhere. I thought you were dead."

Ryan pulled her back, cupping her face in his hands. "I'm always right here." He placed a hand over her heart.

"I love you so much. I can't live without you. You have to know that."

Ryan took her hand in his, pressing the compass into their palms. Leaning forward, he placed his forehead to hers and whispered, "In those moments you feel lost, alone, or confused, pull it out and let yourself remember. Let this compass lead you back home. Let it lead you back to me. Forever and always, okay?"

Her lips flattened as the tears began to once again flow. Ryan smiled, so tender and sweet, a beacon of hope and love. Two souls, once lost in the darkest of nights, found in the sunlight of true love and friendship.

"Okay," she breathed.

Ryan placed his hands on her shoulders, and started to shake her. "It's time. You have to wake up now."

"No. Ryan. Don't leave me."

"I'm not. I've always been here. I'm simply waiting on you. Now, Alexis, wake up."

"Ryan," she wept. "No. I want to stay with you."

The harder he shook her, the darker his figure became. The peace she'd felt evaporated like air being sucked through a vacuum. All of the buried emotions came pouring forward. The dam had broken, and everything that was being held back, crashed over her. She was suffocating.

"Alexis!"

"I can't lose you. You can't leave me."

"Wake up, Lex," Ryan demanded.

Her eyes flew open and she jumped straight up into a sitting position. Someone stepped backward, giving her space. "Calm down. It's okay. I'm not going to hurt you." He knelt down in front of her, placing his hands on her knees. "Hey, you," Declan said, a tender smile creasing the corners of his mouth. "You okay?"

"Where am I?"

"You're in Dale's office. Remember, I brought you up here to rest."

Alexis shook her head, recalling the memory. "Sorry. I only meant to rest my eyes. How long have I been asleep?"

"About two hours."

Alexis bounded off the seat, pushing Declan backward. He barely caught himself before hitting the floor. "Two hours. Jesus! Why would you allow me to sleep that long? I have to find Ryan."

Declan leaped up and grabbed her by the shoulders. "That's what we came to tell you." He motioned toward Mary, who was standing next to the door. A bright but exhausted smile lit her face.

"We've found him," Mary announced.

"He's alive?"

"Yes!"

Opening her hand, Alexis glanced down at the compass that had left an imprint in her skin. No longer was it spinning in wild circles. It had stopped and was pointing north. "Let it lead you back to me."

"I'm sorry?" Declan asked; his eyes narrowed on the toy in her hand.

"He's alive!" Alexis squealed.

"Yes! He's alive."

Joy poured from her as she threw her arms around the unsuspecting pilot. Declan picked her up off the floor and twirled her around in circles. They laughed and cried; holding to one another like two siblings would in a time of joy and relief. There was something magical in the air; love found, hearts reunited and hope renewed.

Declan placed her back on her feet, a huge smile on his face. "You want to see him?"

"What kind of a question is that? Of course!" she exclaimed.

Taking his hand, Alexis slipped the compass into her pocket and exited the office. As they walked out the door, she grabbed Mary by the hand, pulling her close. In her heart, she whispered a word of thanks to Cora. Because of her sister, she'd found her heart, and she was going home, to Ryan, where she belonged.

Fear knotted in Ryan's chest. The flashing lights of the ambulance and the high-pitched siren pierced his ears. There was so much pressure on his chest that it was almost impossible for him to breathe. He tried to speak. He wanted to scream, but the mask the medics had over his mouth prevented such a thing.

Alexis! He cried out in his mind. *I have to get back to her!*

All his life he'd loved only one woman. Now, more than ever, he realized that. Alexis York was meant for him. They'd always been connected, even when they were separated.

His eyes fluttered closed. They were heavy and it felt better to close them. He heard someone shout in his ear to open his eyes. He obeyed, but not without some hesitation. Behind those closed eyelids he could see the one person who drove him to survive. Alexis pushed him to not give up. It was the sound of her voice that enabled him to rip out his own seat restraints and pull Kix from the burning cockpit. Without her whispering in his mind, he wouldn't have been able to push forward and help other passengers get out of the wreckage.

Through blurry eyes, Ryan managed to take in his surroundings. Now, somehow, he was being rushed through hospital doors. The gurney bounced, jerking him when they turned a corner. He rasped out in pain, the tightness in his chest muffling his voice.

"We have a male, early thirties, possible broken ribs," a man yelled out.

Who are they talking about? Ryan wondered.

The accident flashed inside his mind. Images of fire, the smell of smoke, the screams of people expanded in his head. It was him who was hurt. But how? He hadn't been hurt before, other than a sharp ache in his leg. Nothing was making sense to him. Everything came in scrambled little pieces.

He pressed his mind to remember. While he could feel it on the edge of his brain, all that came to mind was Alexis. Her tender smile, the sound she made when she giggled, her sweet scent syphoned the smell of smoke and the terror of screams from his mind.

It was no use.

All he could feel was Alexis.

I feel her! he realized.

His body jolted to life. She was here, in this place. He could sense her, almost as if he could hear the very sound of her heart beating.

"I found him!" a familiar voice cried out. He felt a hand on his forehead and someone opened his eyelids, forcing light into them. "We've been searching for you," the voice told him.

Ryan tried to smile, but something covered his mouth. The urge to reach up and pull off whatever it was over his nose and mouth was overwhelming, but his arms couldn't move. He jerked his hands. "Easy there, buddy. It's all okay now. You're safe," came the sweet female voice. "I'll be right back. You hear me? I'm going to get Alexis."

Alexis! his soul cried out. He fought against the restraints, but the pain in his chest grew tighter. Ryan gasped for air; the mask on his face was suffocating him. So much was going on around him that he couldn't tell what was real and what was a dream. Was it possible that he'd dreamt the nice woman telling him that Alexis was there? All he knew for certain was his love for Alexis kept him from fading into the blackness that hovered around him.

"Baby," her soft voice called to him. A force so strong threw him into stillness. "I need you to calm down." He couldn't move even if he wanted to. The sheer force of heat and electrical current running through his veins pinned him to the bed. Ryan forced his eyes to open wide. A tired, heavy haze coated his vision, but the dim outline was recognizable to him. It was Alexis standing over the bed. "Baby, I need you to listen to me. You've been injured. Your left leg appears to be broken, as do your ribs. We're taking you for x-rays now."

Ryan grunted, flexing his fingers. Alexis gripped his hand, settling his speeding heart. "I'm not going to leave your side. You hear me? I'm right here. I love you so much." Her free hand pushed his hair back from his face.

I love you, too.

And with that, everything went black.

Ryan opened his eyes, disturbed by the sudden shift in his bed. He turned his head, disoriented, to find Alexis slipping in beside him. A nagging feeling twitched inside of his chest. His body tingled with the realization that this didn't feel quite right. Alexis never snuck into his bed; it was always the other way around. "Lex?" he sleep whispered, "What's going on? You okay?"

Alexis pulled the covers over them, curling into his side. "I'm scared," she replied, her voice low and breathy.

Ryan flipped over, pressing their bodies close to one another. "Of what?" In the recesses of his mind, he heard something. It sounded like a chirp. He disregarded it as Alexis having left the window open and a bird was singing its nightly song.

"Of losing you." Her honesty pierced his soul.

"That's not going to happen."

Alexis trailed her fingers down his cheeks. The touch was so soft, so smooth, and so intimate that it confused him. She'd never touched him like this before. Or had she? His mind struggled against the feelings. It was natural. It felt right. Yet somehow it felt fresh and new. Strange to the point of being familiar.

"I love you so much. I can't lose you."

The young boy inside him whooped and hollered that the girl of his dreams had admitted to loving him, which confused him all the more. Was he a boy? Alexis was very much a woman. A beautiful, smart, successful woman. That had to mean he was a man. But he didn't feel like a man. Nothing made sense, but it all felt fresh and painless. His first instinct was to distrust the lack of misery, but he stopped himself. He didn't want to disturb the hazy bubble wrapped around his mind.

Ryan peered into her eyes, the dark chocolate gaze of home. A ghost of a smile quirked his lips. "I love you, too," he stated with certainty. "And I promise, you'll never lose me. Ever."

"Always," she started, her lips inching closer to his.

"And forever," he finished, their mouths connecting in a deep kiss that reached his very soul.

When Alexis pulled back, he could see true love in her eyes. "Can I stay here, please?"

Ryan touched his fingertips to her lips, aching to know if this was really happening. "I never want you to leave."

He rolled over onto his back, allowing Alexis to rest her head on his chest. With her in his arms, he closed his eyes, allowing sleep to pull him back under. She was there, with him, and while none of this made sense, he couldn't bring himself to care. All that ever mattered to him, and all that would ever matter to him, was Alexis.

A gentle snore resonated in his ears. Sounds of medical equipment beeped in a nonsensical pattern around him. His body felt stiff, sore, and constricted. His eyes were heavy. There was a slight throb inside his skull. His head felt fuzzy and strange. Nothing made any sense to him.

With a slight flutter, Ryan opened his eyes to the bright light of an unfamiliar room. He was in a rather lumpy bed, in an almost uncomfortable position. He tried to move but something tugged at his hand. Tilting his head, he caught sight of the impeding object. Clear cannulas protruded from his hand. From the corner of his eye he could see bags hanging above him, dripping fluids into the tubes.

Was this all real? He didn't know. Reality seemed elusive to him. Nothing seemed real yet everything felt right.

A subtle shift in the bed caught his attention. He turned his head to find Alexis lying beside him, sound asleep. She'd managed to curl up in a ball on the mattress next to him. Her position appeared terribly uncomfortable, yet she seemed to be sleeping soundly. He lifted his hand to touch her face, but the mangled mass of IV tubes restricted his movement.

"Lex." His dry, weak voice cracked.

"You're awake," a voice he recognized whispered.

Ryan turned his head to find his mother sitting in a chair next to the bed. "Mom?"

Shannon Fisher scooted forward, taking him by the hand. Her blonde hair and dark roots were washed out in the odd light of the room. Her sharp nose rounded at the tip and her blue eyes looked tired and weary. "Hey there, sweetheart. How ya feeling?"

Ryan opened and closed his eyes. His throat burned. "A little thirsty."

Shannon grabbed a cup of water from a bed table and moved to press the straw to his lips. Ryan tried to lift his hand to touch the straw, but there was yet another tube taped to his face. It felt strange and very uncomfortable. "Don't," his mother warned, "you need that."

Ryan dropped his hand and wrapped his lips around the pliable straw. He drank the cool liquid; savoring each drop as if it were the first time he'd ever ingested water. "Thank you," he panted, letting the straw fall from his lips.

Alexis shifted against him, letting out a small, sleep-filled groan. Her hand moved to his chest with her nose nestled against his neck. "How long have I been here?" he asked.

"A couple of days," Shannon noted.

"And Lex?" His eyes moved down the beauty who rested beside him, her legs tangled in a white hospital blanket.

Shannon reached across him, brushing the hair from Alexis' sleeping face. "Just as long. She's only left you when she's had to work and even then she's checked in on you constantly. Like she is now. Actually," she glanced down at her watch, "I'm supposed to wake her soon. She has to get back to her rounds. I never realized how driven she is."

"No," he requested. "Please let her stay a little longer."

With a tender smile and a quick nod, Shannon moved away from his sleeping angel.

Ryan tried to adjust his position, but the pain was more than he could bear. He glanced down at the end of the bed catching sight of a huge lump beneath the sheet. Slowly, he pulled back the cover to reveal a white cast encompassing his leg. "How bad am I?" He released a heavy sigh, which added pressure to his chest, causing him to wince.

"Not as bad as you could've been," Shannon started. "Your left leg is broken in two places and you have three bruised ribs. You're lucky they're not broken. Aside from that, only minor scrapes and bruises."

Ryan licked his lips, pushing himself to remember. Everything still felt strange and fuzzy in his head. None of this made sense. "But how?"

"From what we were able to gather, you assisted Kix out of the cockpit. After that, you went to help others. Mind you, you did all of this on a broken leg, which had to come from some sort of adrenaline rush or something."

Ryan knew better. It was more than adrenaline. The thought of Alexis pushed him. She was a constant presence in his heart, always leading him to where he needed to be.

"Anyway," she continued, "after pulling three other people from the wreckage, you happened across the lavatory where a child was trapped. The structure of the plane wasn't sound, and when you extracted the little boy, it gave way. Medics found you, cocooning him with your body, buried under a pile of debris."

Like a light being turned on, everything about that night came into focus. He remembered the sound of a child crying and the fear in the little boy's face. "Is he okay?"

Shannon lifted from her chair, placing a tender kiss to her son's forehead. "Not a scratch on him. You took the brunt of everything. You saved his life."

A sense of humbleness filled Ryan. He felt grateful for having been able to assist the child. It was worth the discomfort he currently felt.

Ryan flexed his fingers. At the end of his index finger was yet another medical device hooked up to him, shining bright and red.

I must look like a cyborg.

He tried to take in a deep breath, but the beeping sound increased. "You need to stay calm," Shannon advised. "Alexis said breathing will be painful for awhile."

"That's an understatement," he grunted. He further examined the stark white room. There was another chair in the corner, near the window, empty save a briefcase his father always carried. "Is Pops here?" he wondered.

"He's with Melanie and Miles in the cafeteria getting some coffee."

"Alexis' parents are here, too?" he gasped in surprise.

"With their significant others, of course." Her tone sounded almost sarcastic. "Reagan came by yesterday, but I guess she had to fly to Philadelphia for work. Declan's girlfriend, Jenna is also here."

"She's Alexis' friend from New York, Mom." Ryan tried to laugh, but the pain it inflicted was too much. "Declan doesn't do girlfriends," he rasped.

Shannon leaned back in her chair, crossing her arms over her chest. "That may have been true in the past, but my Mommy-senses are tingling."

"Mommy-senses, really?"

She pursed her lips and shrugged one shoulder. "Don't underestimate my mommy-senses, young man. They always knew you and Alexis would end up together."

Ryan shifted his eyes to Alexis and though it hurt, he smiled. "Okay. I'll grant you that one, but I'm still skeptical about Declan."

Shannon cocked a brow. "Doubt all you want, but I'm right."

A peaceful silence filled the room. Alexis stirred and her subtle snoring stopped. Her eyes fluttered open.

"You're awake," Ryan breathed, smiling.

"That's my line," she replied, grinning brightly.

Her precious smile tugged at his heart. The sound of her voice set the universe straight. This moment, this woman was his reality.

"Well, kids, that's my cue to exit stage right." Shannon thumbed toward the door. She stood up and leaned over Ryan, pressing a kiss to his forehead. "I'll be back soon."

"Love ya, Mom."

"I love you, too, son."

Shannon reached out and touched Alexis' cheek. "And you, too, sweetheart." She stepped around the foot of the bed and exited the room, closing the door behind her.

At the sound of the door clicking closed, Alexis lifted her head and pressed her lips to Ryan's. His heart skipped a beat or maybe two. The pain in his chest was nothing in comparison to the hunger and power behind her kiss. He could feel everything she'd harbored inside as it poured into that kiss. The power that burned between them could light the city. He tried to lift his hand again to cup her face, but winced when the catheter under his skin pinched.

She pulled back, her eyes filled with fear, concern, anger, lust, but most of all, love. "Are you okay?"

"Yeah," he grumbled. "The IV is twisted."

Alexis slipped off the bed, moving to the machine. Her body heat left an absence beside him that he hated. She worked the cords, adjusting the bags and even checking the readings until he was untangled. "Better?" she asked after her work was finished.

Ryan lifted his now freed hand, wiggling his fingers. "Much. Thank you."

Alexis leaned over, pressing her lips to his. This time, he had the freedom to touch her, savoring the warmth of her skin against his palm. There were no parents, no doctors, or nurses around. Nothing could hold him back from kissing the woman who'd held him even in his dreams.

Within moments, their kiss turned from sweet and innocent to sizzling and wanton. One hungry kiss turned into another until they were both breathless. Ryan felt the pain, but it was like a nagging hum in the back of his mind. All he cared about was being there, in that moment, with Alexis.

"Well what do we have here?"

Both of them jerked their heads toward the door to find Declan, standing against the frame with his arms crossed over his chest. A haughty smirk tilted his lips. Neither of them had heard him open it, as they were consumed by their reunion. "The guy's barely awake and here you are about to jump his bones. Lucky bastard."

"Jealous much?" Alexis stood up straight and tugged at the hem of her top, resuming a more professional appearance.

"Damn right, I am," he shot back. Declan shoved off the door and strutted into the room. "Ryan has all the luck."

Ryan tried hard not to laugh to avoid the pain. "Not all the luck," he winced when uncontrollable laughter bubbled from his chest.

Alexis twisted around, examining one medical device then another. Her true smile dropped and a manual one replaced it. Ryan had never noticed it before, but she had two different smiles. He liked the true smile better. "On a scale from one to ten, ten being the worst, what's your pain level?" Her voice had turned professional.

Ryan reached up, brushing his thumb along her wrist. "I'm fine, Lex."

Her face twisted and her brow scrunched together as she considered his words. "Okay," she said. "I have to go make my rounds, but I'll be back very soon with your dinner."

"Don't be gone too long."

She leaned over and pressed a sweet kiss to his lips. In the background they could hear Declan grumble and groan like a kid watching its parents kiss.

"I won't be. I promise."

She sidled around the bed, and kicked Declan in the back of the knee as she crossed his path. He hobbled for a second, slinging a slew of curses.

"That's what you get for being a dick," she caterwauled, heading out the door.

"I'm always a dick," he bellowed back, rubbing behind his leg. "Damn, she's got good aim."

"Actually, I think she was aiming for your crotch," Ryan teased, his smile widening.

Declan glanced at the door and back to Ryan. He scratched his head. "Nah," he blurted out and sauntered over to the chair Shannon had vacated earlier. "So, how ya feeling, buddy? Ready to start training for your next IronMan?"

"You know it," Ryan balked. "I bet I'll make my best time yet sporting this cast."

"You'll be back on your feet in no time."

Ryan shifted, trying to find a more comfortable position. It seemed a hopeless feat. "This damn bed is probably the most uncomfortable thing I've ever been in." He squinted his eyes, thinking for a moment. "On second thought, that hostel in Costa Rica might've given this thing a run for its money."

"Yeah, I know what you mean," Declan slipped.

"How might that be?" Ryan quizzed.

A bemused smile appeared on Declan's face. "You know Alexis' friend, Jenna?"

"Yeah," Ryan bleated.

"Well, we got bored waiting on your sorry ass to wake up from your beauty sleep." He wiggled his eyebrows.

It took a moment for Ryan to consciously understand what Declan meant. Then it hit him. "Oh, gross! You had sex in the hospital?"

A smug Declan shrugged. "I had a few hours to kill and Jenna, well..." He released a soft sigh followed by a starry grin.

"Oh, man. Mom was right," Ryan droned.

The enchantment was broken. "About what?" Declan took on the defensive.

Ryan let out a raspy laugh. "You and Jenna are together."

"No!" he rebuked. "It's not like that. She's gorgeous and great in the sack."

Ryan cocked his head to the side. "Really? So this was the first time you slept with her?"

Declan rested his elbows in his lap and leaned forward, picking at his cuticle. "No."

"How long have you been seeing her?"

"I told you it's not like that!" Declan retorted.

"Okay, fine. How long have you two been sleeping together?"

"Um," Declan rolled his eyes toward the ceiling. "Since Christmas, but we're *not* dating. She lives in New York. I live in Dallas. Long distance never works."

"So you do care for her?" A smile rounded Ryan's lips. He'd never seen Declan react to a woman like this. It was nice to see his friend did, indeed, have a heart.

"What's not to care for? She's got an amazing ass."

"Right. Like that's all. Look me in the eyes and tell me she doesn't have you by the balls. Tell me," Ryan urged, his nose wrinkling as he taunted his friend.

Declan jumped up and slung himself to where he stood over Ryan. "She sucked my balls. Does that count?"

Ryan shuddered.

"Knock, knock." Alexis peeked her head around the corner. Declan flopped back down in his chair. "I come bearing gifts," she announced. In her hand was a hospital tray. "We have to take things slow, but I thought you might enjoy a little something to eat." Alexis balanced the tray in one hand and pulled a rolling bed tray away from the wall toward him. She placed the tray on the stand and lifted the lid. "We have some chicken noodle soup, Jell-O, and tea. Does any of this sound appealing?"

Ryan snarled. "Not really. You couldn't have snuck in a cheesecake or maybe a box of Cracker Jack? I need something with sustenance to it."

"Ryan Zane Fisher, you'll eat the soup first to see how it settles on your stomach. After that, we'll discuss other options," she ordered.

"Oh!" Declan whooped. "Now who's got whom by the balls?" He buckled over in laughter, smacking his knees.

"Hush!" Ryan protested.

"Excuse me?" Alexis turned a brutal, almost terrifying expression on Declan.

"Did the temperature just drop in here?" Declan mumbled, shivering.

"How about you go find Jenna," Alexis demanded.

"You don't have to tell me twice." Declan bounced up out of the chair. He smiled down at Ryan. "Good luck with Doctor Lecter. I hear balls are her favorite delicacy."

"Out!" Alexis pointed toward the door.

Declan waved his hands. "I'm going. I'm going. Geez!"

Ryan hissed in laughter. He grimaced at the pain, but it was worth it to watch Alexis put Declan in his place.

When Declan was out of sight, Alexis turned back to Ryan and slipped a box from her pocket. It was Cracker Jack. "I couldn't let him see me sneak this in." She beamed from ear to ear. "All I need is him getting all uppity about me not following protocol."

"Oh, my god. I knew I loved you for a reason. Gimme!" Ryan flinched his fingers at her. She ripped open the top of the box and poured a few pieces in her hand before feeding them to him. "My angel," he purred, chewing the sweet popcorn.

"Anything for you." Alexis leaned in pressing a kiss to his lips.

"You mean that?" he whispered, lifting his hand to her neck.

"Of course I do."

"Then kiss me again."

She flashed him a seductive grin and laid her lips to his. Heat sizzled between them, but she pulled away sooner than he'd wanted. He groaned at the loss of her touch. "You have to rest before we can have fun."

"But I don't want to!" he complained.

Alexis withdrew a syringe from her other pocket. "Yes, you do, because the sooner you get better, the sooner you get out of here. And the sooner you get out of here, the sooner I can..." she leaned in and whispered in his ear, "enjoy Declan's aforementioned delicacy."

Ryan closed his eyes and moaned. "God, you're good."

"I'm the best, Baby. Remember that." She injected the medicine into his IV.

It didn't take long for him to begin to feel drowsy. He struggled against it at first, but the heaviness of his eyelids won out. As they started to close, Alexis leaned in and whispered close to his ear, "I love you."

"...you, too," he mumbled, feeling the darkness overtake him.

Alexis pressed her lips to his. The pressure felt sweet and inviting, almost as good as the darkness that had invaded his bloodstream. "Sleep, my love. I'll be here."

"Where are we?" Alexis questioned, a slight giggle was in her voice. Ryan had promised her an adventure. One that would take her breath away. He'd insisted on the blindfold that had obstructed her vision. She was forced to rely on him to help her from the vehicle.

"Where do you think we are?" he purred against her ear. A glorious shiver rumbled its way down her body. His very closeness and her lack of certain senses left her feeling vulnerable yet wanton.

Alexis squeezed her eyes tight, as if that helped anything, but used the tense pressure to help her focus. Heat encompassed her, not only from the sun, but from Ryan's hand resting on her hip. She swallowed and tried to focus in on the sounds she heard. Birds. The light rustle of trees. Then there was a hum in the distance. It was faint but distinguishable. She could feel the ground vibrate beneath her feet. Her hand reached for the blindfold as fear struck her heart. It had been five months since Ryan's accident. While he'd long since returned to work, she still struggled every time he left her side. "No," she squeaked.

Ryan grabbed her hand, stopping her from pulling it away. "Not yet," he warned.

Anger swelled inside her. He knew her fear of flying had intensified since his accident, yet he had the nerve to bring her to a place like this. "What airport are we at?" she demanded, fury rolling off her. It couldn't be DFW, because their drive had been at least thirty minutes long. On top of that, the sounds were not that of a large airport.

Ryan let out a soft sigh and loosened the knot of the blindfold. It slipped away from her eyes. "McKinney National," he stated, tucking the blindfold in his pocket. In front of her was a small hangar. Off in the distance, she could see another hangar and a plane being taxied onto the runway. "A friend of mine has a DA20-C1. I thought we could take it out for a spin today."

"You thought wrong!" she shrieked.

"Lex, please. I only want to show you there's nothing to be afraid of."

Her eyes flashed to the plane sitting on the runway. To her, it was a metal contraption of death. "Why are you doing this?" she demanded, terrified. Her arm flailed out toward the plane. "Nothing to be afraid of? Are you kidding me? I don't see how you aren't scared to death of that thing after all you went through," she spat.

Her palms were sweaty, her stomach tensed in a massive knot. Simply being this close to a plane made her head swim with fear.

"People have car accidents every day, but that doesn't stop them from getting back into them. Flying is in my blood, Lex, and I only want to share it with the woman I love most in this world."

Alexis rubbed her hands down her jeans. Angry tears swam in her eyes. "Do you not know me at all?" She sucked back air, determined to not let the tears spill over.

Ryan drew her to his chest, his lips dipping close to her ear. "I do know you, Alexis."

The feel of his heart against her back, and the overwhelming scent of his cologne mixed with that musky aroma that was all Ryan stilled her. "But this?" She tried to sound perturbed. She failed. Just being close to him melted away her irritation. The very rhythm of his heartbeat acted as a salve to her fear.

"I know you're a strong, confident woman. One that I love very much. It pains me to see you slip into your shell every time I leave for work. But most of all, I know you can do this," he persuaded.

"But what if I don't want to?" she whined.

His lips closed around her earlobe, sucking gently. He clasped his hands around her waist, tugging her backside flush against him. "For me?"

Her knees were already shaking with fear, but now, they were weak from his very presence. She closed her eyes and released a soft hum. It was no use. He'd played dirty and won.

She cleared her throat. "All right," she agreed, "but I won't promise to like it."

Ryan released her, slipping his hand into hers. She suddenly regretted agreeing to him. "Are you sure that thing is safe?" She hesitated.

Turning to her, Ryan pressed a soft kiss to the tip of her nose. "I promise you, I'll never let *anything* happen to you."

A surge of panic expounded inside her, shaking her, but the simple truth to his words and his soft touch expunged the fear enough to allow her to take a step. Then another step. Until finally they were in front of a hangar. Ryan squeezed her hand as a mechanic exited the building.

"Ryan?" the man called out.

"Brian," Ryan yelled back and waved. Ryan glanced to Alexis, giving her a wink. Alexis tried to pout, but it was difficult when she could see the pure excitement in his eyes. She hadn't flown with him since the day she moved to Texas. However, this was completely different. Now, it was just the two of them.

Brian wiped his hands on a rag and stuffed it in his pocket. He greeted Ryan with a warm handshake. "Glad you could make it. She's all gassed up and ready for ya." Brian pointed to the craft on the tarmac.

"I really appreciate this."

"It's no problem at all. Glad to do it."

Ryan wrapped his arm around Alexis. "This is my girlfriend, Alexis York. Lex," he pointed to his friend, "This is Brian Mead. He used to work at DFW."

"Pleasure to meet you," Alexis stated, extending her hand to him.

Brian lifted his hands, showing her the grease stains on his skin. "The pleasure is all mine." Alexis dropped her hand and smiled with a slight nod of her head.

Ryan kissed Alexis on the temple and moved toward the plane. He walked around it, examining every inch of the craft. "Isn't she a beaut?"

"You realize that thing scares the shit out of me, right?" She eyed the propeller, leery of its ability to lift off the ground, let alone guiding a hull of metal through the friendly blue skies.

"I do, but I hope to change that." Ryan tucked his hands into his pockets, shuffling his feet as he made his way around to the tail of the plane. Despite her fear of the aircraft, Alexis couldn't take her eyes off him. He looked good enough to eat.

"I assure you, she's quite safe," Brian assured her. "She's just had a full tune-up."

"She's perfect," Ryan purred. He stepped beside Alexis and took her by the elbow, leading her to the plane. The closer they got to the monstrosity, the higher the panic level mounted inside her. Her initial instinct was to pull back, and run as far away as possible. Ryan's grip on her tightened, stealing any chance she might have of escape. He helped her into the passenger's side, locking her into the soft, leather seat.

"Relax," he murmured, kissing her lips.

"Easy for you to say," she muttered out of earshot, as he walked around to the captain's side.

Ryan hopped in and closed the glass door down on them. Alexis forced air into her lungs feeling like the lid of her own coffin had just been sealed. She swallowed hard releasing the hold she had on the seat cushion. Her eyes drifted down to see her claw marks imprinted in the leather.

Ryan started the engine. The whole plane rumbled with life. He glanced up, a sweet smile appearing on his handsome face. After a check of the gauges and a few other little things that Alexis had no clue about, Ryan pulled back on the control stick and the plane started down the runway.

She felt her lungs collapse in her chest. Her tongue stuck to the roof of her mouth. This was it. Her imminent death. At least she would go with the man she loved. Although she wasn't sure how much she loved him at that particular moment, putting her through such hell.

His eyes swept back and forth out in front of them. The faster the plane barreled down the pavement, the faster her heart raced in her chest. It took everything she had not to claw her way out of the aircraft. She did the only thing logical to her, aside from closing her eyes and praying for a quick death. She turned her head and focused on Ryan. Awe sparkled in his eyes. Sheer joy emanated from him. If only she could appreciate the beauty of the man sitting beside her instead of dwelling on the panic that flooded her bloodstream.

He reached over, taking her by the hand. Her pulse jumped, not from the flight, but from the fire that always burned through her when he touched her. "Alexis, trust me," Ryan pleaded, his tone calm but heartfelt.

That one little word—*trust*—triggered her memory, pulling her back in time.

The day Ryan returned home from the hospital, everyone had gathered together to celebrate. Her apartment had never felt so cramped, but filled with so much love. Ryan sat in his favorite chair, in the middle of her living room, being catered by everyone. The sounds of laughter reverberated everywhere.

Off in her kitchen, Alexis caught sight of Kellie talking to Dan. The interaction infuriated her. This was the same woman who'd stolen her father from her mother, and now that wasn't enough. Now she wanted her mother's boyfriend. Alexis wouldn't have it.

In a fit of rage, she set off to give Kellie a piece of her mind. She didn't care if everyone heard her, including Henry. It was time this woman was called out for her home wrecker ways.

Just as she was about to approach them, Melanie grabbed Alexis by the arm. "Don't you dare, young lady."

Alexis snapped around to her mother, only to find her father standing beside her. "What the hell? Do neither of you see an issue with that!" She threw her arm in the direction of a laughing Kellie and a smiling Dan. "You can't tell me you don't, Mom. Not after..."

"Enough!" Melanie barked. Alexis stood cold still. Her mother had never taken a tone like that with her before. "You need to grow the fuck up."

Taken aback, Alexis' mouth dropped. "Excuse me?"

"You heard me," Melanie fumed.

Miles stood there, watching his ex-wife and daughter, his arms crossed over his chest and an amused smirk on his face.

"But, Mom," she snapped.

Melanie shook her head. "Alexis, I love you, but this has gone on for way too long."

"I don't understand. After what that woman did to you, to our family...?"

"Now hold on..." Miles started but Melanie lifted her hand, stopping him mid-sentence.

"Let me tell you a little something. It takes two." Melanie's mouth was stern.

"Yeah. I know. Dad had his hand in this." Alexis glared at her father. His chest rose and fell, but he continued to allow Melanie to run the show.

"You're not understanding me, Lexi. I'm talking about your father and me. Not Kellie."

Puzzled, Alexis stepped back, her face drawn. "You're right. I don't understand. You did nothing wrong. They *cheated on you.* They *tore our family apart."*

Melanie shook her head. *"Oh, my darling. How wrong you are."* Melanie took Alexis by the arm and led her to the bottom step of the staircase. She sat down next to her daughter and rested her hands over Alexis'. Miles joined them, leaning against the bannister.

"I don't see how I'm wrong, Mom. They did cheat on you."

Melanie looked up at Miles, a sad sort of expression clouded her face. *"But not before I cheated on your father."*

"What?" Alexis and Miles echoed in unison.

"You never slept around on Dad!" Alexis exclaimed.

Miles cocked his head. *"I agree with her there, Mel. You never did."*

Melanie reached up and took Miles by the hand. *"I may not have physically cheated, but my checking out the way I did while Cora was sick, was cheating. I cheated you of me."* She turned to Alexis. *"You see, I neglected this family, starting with your father. But sadly, I also neglected you. I thought by putting all my energy into Cora, I could save her. My heart was in the right place, but it was also wrong."*

"That doesn't mean you cheated on Dad, though. And he didn't have to sleep with Kellie."

Melanie nodded. *"True, but I didn't have to leave the two of you alone either. Do you even remember how many nights you ate at the Fisher's because I didn't feel like cooking dinner?"*

"Well, yeah, but I was already over there playing with Ryan," Alexis countered.

"I could've called you home to eat, but I didn't. I was selfish." Melanie dropped her hands to her lap. *"I'm not condoning what your father and Kellie did, but I've accepted my part in why it happened."*

Alexis shook her head, furious. *"You act like this was your fault. But it's not. You're a good mother. You were a good wife. He,"* she pointed to her father, *"betrayed us both. He betrayed Cora."*

Miles knelt down in front of Alexis and Melanie. *"I did betray you. I will never deny that, but Alexis, I love you. I love Cora. Not a day goes by where I don't miss her. And this might shock you, but I still love and miss your mother. You're all a part of me. You always will be. I never meant to hurt you. You have to believe me."*

Tears swam in Melanie's eyes. "I believe you."

"I'm so sorry," he whispered, cupping the side of Melanie's face in his hand.

Melanie pressed her palm over the top of his hand. "I'm sorry, too."

"I'm so happy to see you happy again. Dan's a great guy."

Melanie released a soft laugh. "He's amazing."

Alexis rushed her fingers through her hair, confused and perplexed. "Wow! I don't get it. Your significant others are over there flirting and you two are apologizing to each other."

Melanie leaned forward, resting her elbows on her knees, looking out toward the crowd. "Do you trust Ryan?"

"Of course I do!" Alexis squelched.

Melanie pointed toward him. "Yet there he is, talking to Reagan right now. Dare I say, they're even flirting."

"That's different."

"How so? Dan's a good man. I trust him just like you do Ryan," Melanie stated plainly.

"And I trust Kellie," Miles added.

Melanie shifted, pushing her knees against Alexis'. Taking both Alexis and Miles by the hand, she clasped them all together, as a family for the first time in years. "A relationship is built on trust."

"I get that, but Mom aren't you afraid that you'll get hurt again?" Alexis tried to pull her hand from the trifold, but Melanie held her tight.

"You can't let fear steal your chance to love. If you and Ryan part ways, which I don't ever see happening, but if it happens, don't let that deter you from loving again. Love is learning. It's taking chances. It's making mistakes. But most of all, it's allowing yourself to trust and be trusted."

"But how?"

Melanie looked to Miles and back to Alexis. "For starters you forgive your parents for being human."

Alexis chuckled softly.

"And then," Miles included, "you allow yourself to be human. Life is messy. Enjoy it."

"Open your eyes," Ryan's voice broke through her thoughts.

All those years she'd spent hating her father for tearing her family apart, but she never looked past the indiscretions to the man who she'd always loved. Since that night, she had a different relationship with her parents. She had a better understanding of who they were and who she was.

A smile appeared on her lips and her eyelids fluttered open. In front of her was the expansive, pale blue sky filled with white clouds for as far as the eye could see. The sun dominated the heavens, ruling the birds and air. When they'd become airborne, she wasn't sure, but she knew, somehow, her fear was gone. In its place was nothing but love.

Ryan rubbed his thumb over hers. She turned her head to find him staring at her. "You okay?" His voice filled with worry. "I thought this might help you get past your fear, flying with me, but if you need me to land…"

Her eyes scanned the sky, serenity wrapping around her. "This is amazing," she ruminated. "Is this how you always see things from up here?"

The tone of her voice relaxed him. Ryan returned his eyes to his instruments. "Oh, yes. It makes you respect the universe for its immense beauty."

Skylines speckled the ground. People appeared no bigger than ants. From that distance she felt invincible.

"Are you sure you're okay, Lex?"

Alexis leaned over, pressing her lips to his jaw. "Very much so. I trust you."

They were cruising the air, free. Ryan dared a glance at Alexis. Her smile was more magnificent than any sunset he'd ever witnessed. "You trust me," he repeated. His face bloomed with happiness.

"Absolutely. I trust that you'll always be there to catch me if I fall."

His smile broadened. "Then let's go on an adventure."

"Every day's an adventure with you." All of the noise in the plane faded away. The very world was at their feet. Nothing could touch them. Their love was timeless, and their hearts beat as one. Where they were going, she didn't know. And while there may be turbulence ahead, as long as they were together, that was all that mattered. She smiled and relaxed back into her seat, tilting her head to take in his handsome face. "And I wouldn't have it any other way."

Epilogue

It felt strange being back in this place, where it all started. Alexis stood on the porch of the Fisher residence and stared out at the house that held so many childhood memories for her. A bright red "For Sale" sign sat in the front yard. Shannon had told her the family who purchased the home from her parents had recently moved to Charlotte, leaving the house vacated. Sadness weighed her heart at the thought of no one living there.

A light September breeze ruffled her hair. It felt good against her heated skin. Summer was almost gone, but it still clutched the small North Carolina town in its grips. From inside the house, she could hear the joyous laughter of family and friends. Everyone had convened to watch Ryan run his first marathon since the accident. She was so proud of him when he crossed that finish line. He'd completed his therapy, trained hard, and while he still had a ways to go to qualify for an IronMan, he'd done amazing.

Her eyes drifted heavenward. The sun started to set and the

sky filled with stars that couldn't be seen in Dallas or New York City. There was a clarity about small town life that she'd lost living in big cities for so long. Out there she felt different, like a piece of herself she'd lost had been found.

Drawn to her childhood abode, Alexis stepped off the porch. The front door was no longer blue, as it had been when she lived there, but painted white. The trim was still the same, peeling a little, but unchanged. Time was frozen with that little house. It was where she grew up. Where she learned about life and love. It was where her family was still whole. While they were unified now, it was different.

She missed Cora, but loved Henry. He was growing up so fast. Many times she found herself watching him play his cello and thinking about how much Cora would've adored him. They would've been the best of friends. She was certain of that. And her animosity toward Kellie had subsided. The more she thought about what her parents had said, the more she realized how blinded she'd been by her own hurt. Besides, Kellie wasn't all bad. If not for her, Henry wouldn't exist.

The warm asphalt of the street heated her bare feet as she meandered across it. She stepped on the plush grass of the front yard she and Ryan had spent so much time in as children. It wasn't as full and green as she remembered, but that didn't take away from the memories she held dear to her heart. In her mind, she could almost see the lanky boy that was now the man she loved, racing around in the grass, pretending to fly his favorite plane. She would lie in the grass and watch him, while telling him of her own plans. So many hopes and dreams were made in that yard. If the lawn could talk, it would share secrets she'd long forgotten.

Her next steps led her to the concrete drive. A huge grease stain filled the center of the pavement, but next to it were three sets of handprints that were forever embedded in the slab. Ryan and Cora had played along when she wanted to turn the driveway into their own Walk of Fame. Her father had been furious with her for leaving those imprints after he'd spent so much money to repave the driveway. She chuckled at the memory of Ryan trying to convince her dad it was his idea. Even Cora tried to cover for her. Her smile faltered at the sweet memory of her little sister before she got sick.

Alexis let out a tender sigh and walked up the driveway. Above the garage was her old bedroom. Gone was the ladder Ryan had used to sneak in. The tree that had guarded her window was cut down. Now it was a shell of the place where she'd spent her nights dreaming big, talking to Ryan, and growing up.

Alexis sashayed up the steps of the porch. Their old porch swing had long since been taken down, but she could still see the hooks protruding from the gable. The wood flooring was worn and splintered. Age had set in on the little abode.

She brushed her fingertips over the soft wood of the bannister. Just to touch this space ignited something inside her. So much was changing around her and being there, in that moment brought back a feeling of innocence.

It led her to think about the baby bump that was starting to round Mary's stomach. Mary had cried the day she told Alexis she was pregnant. No one knew it, but she and Shane had been trying for years. They'd given up hope and had stopped trying. That's when their little miracle was conceived.

"Lex?" Ryan's voice was decadently smooth as he pierced her thoughts.

She rested her hands on the porch rails and leaned forward. "Hey, you."

A tall, well built man lumbered across the street. That same boyish grin, which won her young girl's heart, beamed back at her. "What you doing?"

Alexis swayed from side to side, allowing the bannister to hold her weight. "Just taking a walk down memory lane."

Ryan stepped up onto the porch. "Can I join you?"

Alexis sidestepped to give him room beside her. Ryan leaned forward and rested his elbows on the wooden rail. "There's no one else I'd want to take this journey with, *Captain*."

"Silly woman," he muttered under his breath.

She loved the expression he got whenever she addressed him by his new title. His promotion wasn't unexpected. He'd more than earned the flight hours he needed, but his humility about the advancement was endearing, and in Alexis' opinion, quite sexy.

"Captain Ryan Fisher. It has a sexy ring to it," she teased.

Ryan rubbed the back of his neck, his eyes drifted down. "Oh, stop. You act like it's some sort of big deal."

"It is a big deal! You deserve it."

Ryan cut his eyes to her and grinned. He leaned over and planted a quick peck to her cheek. "So, tell me. Where's memory lane taking us?" Ryan reached for her hand, linking their fingers together.

"You remember Pinky?" she chuckled.

"That damn gerbil of yours?" he groaned. "I hated that rat."

"It wasn't a rat!" she gasped.

"Lex, it was an oversized rat and I was its favorite snack."

Alexis dropped her chin, laughing. "But you were so sweet when he died. You buried him right there for me. Remember?" She lifted their joined hands and pointed to the specific spot in the yard.

"I do. You kissed my cheek that day because I made him a coffin. I didn't want to wash my face for a week. Mom was ready to kill me," he chortled with a wink.

"I don't remember that, but I'm not surprised. You were the sweetest boy in the world."

Ryan twisted his torso slightly. "And now?"

Alexis turned to meet him. She wrapped her arms around his neck, pressing a tender kiss to his lips. "And now you're the man I love with all my heart."

"Mhm. I like the sound of that." He rested his forehead to hers, staring deep into her eyes. She toyed with the hair at the nape of his neck.

"Maybe we should head back over there," she mewled. She dropped her arms and turned back to view the house across the street. "You did leave Declan alone with your parents, after all. That's a method for disaster."

"Pops, Declan, Louis, and Reagan are all talking sports, and Jenna was trading recipes with Mom. I think everyone's safe for the moment."

Alexis nodded, thinking about Reagan and her new boyfriend, Louis Salazar. Ryan had gone all fan-boyish when he met the professional baseball player, until he realized Louis' relationship with Reagan. That's when the big brother, twenty-question routine went into action. Reagan was ready to beat Ryan to death by the time he was done with his interrogation. She even begged Alexis to call him off, but all Alexis could do was laugh.

Ryan rested his elbows on the bannister, locking his hands in front of him. "You know, it's funny," he said, his brow furrowed in thought, "they say you can't go home again. But I think they're wrong."

"Why's that?" Alexis placed her hands on the rail, crossing her legs at her ankles.

Ryan shrugged. "Because we never really leave home. It's always with us. Everything that happened between these two houses," he motioned his hand back and forth, "is a part of who we are. It's for that very reason why we can take walks down memory lane."

Alexis chuckled. "Yeah, I guess you're right."

Ryan reached behind his back and popped a box of Cracker Jack from his back pocket. "What do you say to a little dessert?"

Her face bloomed with nostalgia. "Absolutely."

Ryan ripped the box open and poured some of its contents into the palm of her open hand. She tossed a piece of caramel corn into her mouth, crunching it between her teeth. "You remember the last time we were on this porch, doing this same thing?" she inquired as Ryan threw several pieces into his mouth.

He quickly chewed his mouthful of popcorn and swallowed. "Yeah. I remember almost kissing you that day."

"I remember that, too," came her sheepish reply. "I wanted

you to so badly."

Ryan held the box out toward her, silently offering more candied popcorn. She reached into the box grabbing a few kernels and peanuts. "If I'd only known then what I know now." He shook the box, rattling the popcorn inside.

"I don't think I would've been able to leave if you had kissed me," she admitted.

"Now, I really wish I would've," he paused and looked into the box, "Then again...maybe...you know what, no I don't." He pulled a peanut from the box and tossed it in the air, catching it in his mouth. He grinned with mischievous pride. "I like where we are," he noted. "I love who we are. And if things had been different, I don't think we'd be here right now."

He dumped more popcorn in his mouth, catching the toy packet between his fingertips. He handed it over to Alexis, who flipped the red and white packet in her hand. "You think we'll find another compass in here?" Her eyes twinkled at the memory.

Ryan chewed through his mouthful and swallowed hard. "We don't need another one. Our love is our compass now. It's what brought us here to this moment."

Alexis leaned over and placed a kiss on his cheek. The heat of his skin still sent her heart into wild palpitations. Would she ever get used to that feeling? She hoped not.

Alexis lifted the packet, her brows raised. "May I?"

Ryan glanced into the box, confirming it was empty. "Go for it."

She ripped the top of the waxy package open and dumped the contents in her hand. At first the object didn't register. The early evening light sparkled against the purest stone she'd ever seen. In her palm was a beautiful platinum band, with a perfect square cut diamond in the center, which was encrusted by smaller diamonds creating a boxed in effect. It twinkled with such magnificence in her hand that it set a prism of light shimmering against the wooden rail.

She blinked rapidly trying to reason out what was going on. It had to be some kind of joke. She'd heard it before, the ring in the Cracker Jack box, but that was an urban myth. Turning her head to get Ryan's opinion, she was surprised to find him down on one knee.

Her free hand flew to her mouth at the sight before her. "Ryan?" she rasped.

He took the ring from her palm and smiled. "In this yard, so many years ago, I shared my dreams of flying with you. Since then, I've spent my life exploring this world, traveling the globe in search of happiness. But the irony is, what made me happy wasn't over an ocean or cruising the heavens. My happiness was and has always been in my own backyard. I love you so very much. You're my very world and I'm asking you now if you will do the honor of becoming my wife?"

Her face scrunched in a tear filled smile.

"Alexis Melody York, will you marry me?"

"Yes," her answer came out as a whisper. "A million times yes." He slipped the ring on her finger and gently kissed it, as if to seal the bond between them. "It's beautiful."

"As are you, my darling. As are you." Ryan lifted to his feet and pulled her into his arms. When their lips met, the world ignited around them. Fireworks exploded. The heavens sang a tune of two hearts beating as one.

From across the street, they heard a loud wolf-whistle. Ryan and Alexis pulled apart to find everyone standing on the Fisher's porch watching them. "You're officially whipped! Find the ball and chain. They're gettin' hitched!" Declan yelled.

Jenna jabbed her elbow into Declan's stomach. "Don't ruin their moment," she chastised him.

"But, but, baby," he whined.

Jenna placed her hands on her hips, giving Declan a stern look.

Ryan burst into laughter. "I think you're the whipped one, my friend!" he yelled out.

Declan grinned, placing a kiss to Jenna's lips.

Reagan gave them two thumbs up. Louis stood behind her, his arms wrapped around her waist in a loving embrace. In the back stood Ryan's parents. Both smiling with pride.

Alexis buried her face into Ryan's chest. Heat burned through her cheeks, but he could only hold her and laugh. "They were in on this, weren't they?" she queried.

"It started out with me visiting your mother and Jenna in New York to buy the ring," he admitted. "Everything else blew up from there."

She cocked her head, catching a glimpse of everyone still watching them.

"You're not upset, are you?"

Alexis tilted her face, lifting her hand to Ryan's cheek. "I couldn't be happier than I am at this very moment."

A crooked smile curved Ryan's lips. He tucked a stray curl behind her ear, allowing his hand to linger on her neck. Then, he pressed his lips to hers, forgetting about the audience watching them. When their kiss broke, Alexis closed her eyes and rested her head on Ryan's firm chest. She listened to the sound of his heart beating, the rustling of the wind in the trees, and the crickets singing their nightly love song. She breathed in the scent that was especially Ryan mixed with the aromas of the summer. A new memory, one she would cherish until her dying breath, forever embedded itself in her heart. "I love you."

"I love you, too." Ryan ran his fingers down the length of her velvety, soft hair. His lips perched next to her ear, he whispered, "Always."

Alexis raised her head to meet his gaze. A smile spread across her face, so blinding it could've lit the night sky. Pure bliss filled her soul as she pledged, "And forever."

About the Author

Jeanne McDonald is an author, a mother, a wife, a student of knowledge and of life, a coffee addict, a philosophy novice, a pop culture connoisseur, inspired by music, encouraged by words, and a believer in true love. When she's not spending time with her family, she can be found reading, writing, enjoying a great film, chatting with friends or diligently working toward her bachelor's degree in literature. A proud Texan, Jeanne currently resides in the Dallas/Fort Worth area with her family.

Also By Jeanne McDonald

A Ray of Hope

The Truth in Lies Saga
The Truth in Lies
The Certainty of Deception
The Truth Be Told

Taking Chances Series
Indulgence